Falling for F:

Love and Flamenco in Seville

By Barry O'Leary

To Liz

Thanks very much for buying my book. Hopefully it will remind you of the good times in Seville and see what it's like to fall in love with someone from another country.

All the best

Barry
xxx

Text copyright © Barry O'Leary 2017

All Rights Reserved

The right of Barry O'Leary to be identified as the author of this work has been asserted by him in accordance with the Copyright, Designs and Patent Act 1988.

This is a work of fiction. Names, characters, and incidents are either the products of the author's imagination or used in a fictitious manner. Any resemblance to actual persons, living or dead, or actual events is purely coincidental.

To my wife,
so we always remember how we became one and to stay strong during difficult moments.

Acknowledgements

I love writing this page as it means the book is done and ready. It would never have been done and ready if it hadn't been for several people, so I'd like to thank them.

Thanks Tony for reading over this while you were out pushing your son in his pram. Your proofreading skills are excellent, maybe you should become a professional proofreader? Better than working for Woolworths. Appreciate your help over the years, see you soon for some beers. SMCB.

I'd like to thank my editor, motivator, general life coach and all round top sport, Denise O'Leary, better known as Auntie Den. Den is an amazing woman, brilliant writer, and even better editor. She constantly told me to edit the typos, but I just couldn't find the damn things, eventually I did (with the help of a proofreader (and no, not Tony, a professional proofreader), and now I hope they are all gone. When you write a book, to begin with you write it for yourself. Then when you write it a second time you try to imagine the reader, and take them on the journey, well, as I wrote this book, Den's face was constantly there, egging me on, making me write: choose the better word, twist the plot further, make the ending more dramatic. She has been a great inspiration in my life, and sure she will continue to do so, she'd better do anyway. Cheers Den. Mucho Amoro.

Auntie Marg has also been a great inspiration to me, in fact it was her who suggested I first started writing when I came back from travelling. Thanks for reading over the book Marg, and also helping me with the book description and cover. Soon we'll be together for some red wine, but in glass bottles (as opposed to plastic ones).

Can't forget my two sisters. Again, living in another country, away from them both, is so hard at times. I think of you both every day, and still hope that one day you'll both come and live with us here…who knows. Thanks for all your support with my writing over the years, hopefully this time it has paid off.

I'd like to thank my parents for believing in me. You can't ask for more than parents who constantly support you in life, are always there when times get hard, and who inspire you to make them proud. I think that's what life is about, making people proud, but people who care to you. Thanks for all your love and support. Not a day goes by that I don't remember how much you have helped us over the years. Deciding to actually stay in Seville and build a life here was a three year decision, it wasn't easy to give up my country and be far from my family, but in the end, love won.

Which brings me on to my biggest inspiration…

My wife is my true number one fan. Let's be honest, I started writing this book for her. She knows which parts relate to us, and which are fictitious. She also knows what it was like to fall in love with someone from another country, to have you life totally turned upside down by another person. That day when she came in my class, with her 'Looking for Paradise' t-shirt on, she might have been looking for paradise, but it was me who found it.

Just like Charlie and Mercedes, we had our fair share of problems. At the start we never knew if we were going to stay together, but in the end it was pure love which kept us together, and still binds us through this thing called life which we are all in, not knowing where we are going, or what is going to happen next. All I know is that we found each other, by some strange miracle, two people from different countries, who met in a classroom, and who ended up married with two wonderful kids. You know you mean the world to me. Now you actually have to read it, Darling, get your dictionary out. I hope you enjoy it.

About the Author

Barry O'Leary is a writer, and English teacher, based in Seville. This is his first novel, but third book. He has also published Teaching English in a Foreign Land, and How to Become an ESL teacher.

When he's not prancing about in front of Spanish students, telling silly anecdotes and sending people out of class, he's writing. Morning, noon, and night, depending on the time of year. He loves reading travel and contemporary fiction books and is often surfing the net looking for new books to read. He also owns a blog A Novel Spain, which is about how he sees life in Spain. You can also subscribe to his email list via his website.

He is married to a lady from Seville, who may have slightly influenced his decision in writing this romance novel. He also has two children, who keep him busy and stressed at lunch time, but he loves them just the way they are (when it's not lunch time).

CONTENTS

Chapter 1 CHARLIKIN'S WORST DAY EVER   8
Chapter 2 SICK OF MUMMY'S BOYS   43
Chapter 3 LOVE AT FIRST FLAMENCO   62
Chapter 4 THE TRUTH OF FLAMENCO   91
Chapter 5 ALL OR NOTHING   127
Chapter 6 SPOTTED AT LAST   154
Chapter 7 A TRUE PERFORMANCE   184
Chapter 8 FIRST DANCE   216
Chapter 9 PROMISES   234
Chapter 10 ESCAPISM   250
Chapter 11 SEMANA SANTA   277
Chapter 12 PRIDE   306
Chapter 13 THE APRIL FAIR   340
Chapter 14 DECISIONS   356
Chapter 15 ADIOS   368

Chapter 1 CHARLIKIN'S WORST DAY EVER

Northwood Hills, on the outskirts of London

"CHARLIKINS…" shouted Marge, Charlie's mother, from outside his bedroom door. "It's time to get up, Charlikins."

Why did she insist on still calling him Charlikins? It was such a poncy name. A sort of name for one of those Care Bears his sister used to have lined up on her dusty windowsill. Why couldn't she just call him Charlie, or young man, or son? "Are you awake, Charlikins?" she said, thumping on the door.

"No, I'm not," he replied, muffled from under his pillow.

"Then how are you speaking to me?"

"Because I talk in my sleep," he said, lifting the pillow to shout.

"Well, maybe you can move your arse in your sleep too; before your father gets back from work. Move it." She added a couple of firm thuds on the door.

She could bang all she wanted, but he refused to get up; not until his alarm went off. He still had two minutes. As he curled up in a ball and pressed his face to his slightly damp pillow case, he felt a familiar pang of doubt, preoccupation, and nasty fear.

Today was the day that would hopefully change his dull and monotonous existence. Three life changing events were about to take place. Three key moments which could set him up forever. He glanced at the post-it on his alarm clock.

Get that bloody deal
Win Bandoff

Ask out Cass

The first challenge of the day—getting that bloody deal—would sort him out with enough cash to move out. It was 96% sure of going through, but in his game, anything could screw up at the last minute.

Charlie had been busting his arse off for a dodgy, cheating IT Recruitment Company—Computer Jobbers—for a year. He'd made 14,459 telephone calls (yes, his bosses kept a record). The majority had been littered with lies, tricks, and ludicrous promises to swindle innocent job seekers out of information.

He'd been trained to blag by the best. He'd call innocent IT professionals looking for a job, offer them a perfect role, in an ideal location, with a stonking wage, reel them in, and then 'rape' them for information. His mission was to find out if they'd had interviews and then trick them into telling him the names of the recruiters. Then he'd pitch them a better candidate, robbing the position from the original job seeker.

It was immoral, nasty, and wrong, which was why he hated his job. As he left the office in Piccadilly each night, guilt would rise up through his body as he retraced all the lies he'd told.

He'd only wanted a job after university to pay back loans and save some money so he could move out, get his independence back, and concentrate on his real dream: becoming a professional guitarist.

He'd tried to fit in with the London wide boys, obsessed with their money, one hundred pound cuff-links, and Armani y-fronts, but he just didn't fit the bill. Charlie was honest and lacked the arrogance, stamina, and cut-throat manner to push the deal through to completion. In the year working at Computer Jobbers, he'd only made one deal, and that had been given to him by his boss. Today was month end, or more like job-end for Charlie if he didn't get that bloody deal.

His alarm clock radio switched on.

"Good morning listeners," said Chris Moyles, "today is the first of July, and it's a beautiful morning across London town. What type of day are you going to have today?"

"A bloody good day," said Charlie as he climbed out of bed, snatching the post-it and sticking it on his forehead. He stopped to look in the mirror. His wispy blond hair was plastered down on one side, making his head look like a strange, deformed pear. He stared deep into his blue eyes and raised his eyebrows. "A bloody excellent day. YEAH!" he shouted as he pulled open his bedroom door and toe-punted the bathroom door.

"AH," shouted his mum, crossing her arms over her knees as she sat on the toilet.

"AH," shouted Charlie. "Lock the door, how many times?" He flinched away, trying not to glimpse his mother desperately trying, and failing, to cover every inch of bare skin.

"Sorry," she said, laughing, which forced out a squeaky fart.

"Perfect," said Charlie as he turned back into his bedroom and slammed the door. "A perfect way to start one of the most important days of my LIFE."

He stuck his head out the window to get some fresh air and saw his Dad slumped in a plastic garden chair resting a cup of tea on his belly.

"All right, Dad?"

"All right, Son?" said Dave as he gazed up. "Mum on the loo again?"

"Yep."

"Always when you wanna go in there."

"Yep. Back already?"

"Sure am. I managed to nip off early. Big day today, isn't it?"

"Sure is," said Charlie, remembering the three life-changing events that were about to take place.

"Getting over one thousand bulbs delivered."

"That's good," said Charlie, sighing. For a moment, he thought his Dad had remembered his massive day. Then he wondered how a thousand new bulbs would fit into his already overflowing garden. His mum banged on his door.

"All done," she shouted.

"'Bout time," he said, darting into the bathroom.

As he did his normal morning routine of back stretches and knuckle clicking to get warmed up for some air guitar, he thought about his second challenge of the day: to win Bandoff.

He was much more confident of seeing this one through, as long as everyone in The Moonraders pulled together. He knew he'd play his part in helping them towards victory. Charlie might not have had the gift of the gab like all those twats in the office, but he was a pure guitar genius.

When he was six, his father had bought him a cheap plastic guitar for a fiver from a dodgy stall down Wembley Market. It had been a joke, just to wind up Marge by buying a noisy present, but they stared in awe once Charlie began copying guitarists on the T.V. He was a natural. He could play Layla by the time he was seven. Dave and Marge soon cottoned on and paid for professional lessons, and by the time he was fourteen, he could play rock, pop, jazz, classical, even country and western. His brain was like a musical sponge and could absorb any tune and play it within a couple of minutes.

As he stood in front of the mirror, practicing his chords with his air guitar, he thought of lovely, sweet Cass singing by his side. Her wavy auburn hair, cute freckly forehead, and soft singing voice. He adored her. His friend, soul mate, and soon to be girlfriend (challenge number three, and the most important). As soon as they won Bandoff, he'd ask her out.

"So, Cass," he said to himself in the mirror as he bopped his head from side to side. "You sang well tonight, as always, don't suppose you fancy going out to celebrate?"

He imagined her smiling as she realised what he was asking. The way she sighed and smiled as the truth finally came out.

"Of course," he said in a higher than normal pitch. "I thought you'd never ask."

"What the hell are you doing in there?" asked his Dad and he banged on the bathroom door.

"Can a guy not get any peace in the house?"

"Apparently not. Have you smuggled in a squeaky voiced circus woman?"

"No, Dad, I bloody well haven't." Charlie switched on the radio.

"Shiny, happy people," sang R.E.M.

"Annoying, flipping parents, more like," muttered Charlie as he got in the shower.

"So, will you be home for tea?" asked Marge as Charlie sat strumming at the dining table with a mouth full of coco pops. He shook his head. "But it's Thursday night, your favourite night: chips, peas, and faggots."

Charlie stopped strumming, swallowed, and turned to his Mum. She seemed to have aged overnight. Her eyes were puffy, her wrinkles deeper, a couple more grey hairs had sprouted out from the forest of orange. He wanted to tell her that he no longer liked faggots. He wanted to be honest. Let her know he'd grown out of eating faggots before he left university. He wanted to admit that he'd given the packets of faggots that she'd sent him to the tramps hanging outside the university campus, but he just didn't have the heart.

"I know Mum, but I'll be at work till late, then we have Bandoff, then I'll probably go out and celebrate."

"Okay, but I'll leave them in the oven, just in case you feel peckish when you get in."

"How do you know I'll be in?"

"Why, going on a date with Cassandra?"

"No," he said, in a sharp tone. How did she always know these things? He began strumming again.

"So, why won't you be in then?"

"I dunno, just might not be; that's all."

"Don't you have a big day at work today too?"

"You could say that."

"Is it month end again?"

"Damn right it is," said Charlie, punching the air. "I'm gonna show those tossers a thing or two."

"Charlikins," said Marge in a falling tone. "Your father and I didn't bring you up so you could call your workmates, tossers."

"But they are; a bunch of money obsessed tossers."

"So why are you there then?"

It was a question that ran through his mind at the end of most hours at the office. Why was he there? He hadn't even wanted to go into sales. Why had he studied Music at Bournemouth University to go into a cruddy sales job? He wanted to be a professional guitarist, but that wasn't something you just jumped into. You had to work at it; like he had been for the last year with The Moonraders.

"Charlikins, are you listening to me?"

"Sorry, Mum. I know you're right, but I'm on the verge of getting a massive deal, one that will finally get my wages over that crappy mark and I can finally start saving some money, maybe move out."

"Move out?" asked Dave, popping his head round the door. "Does that mean I can get a lodger in to pay for my bulb collection?"

"I don't think a lodger would cover the costs," said Charlie. Marge giggled.

"Well, I'm sure we'd save a fortune by not having to buy faggots, anyway," said Dave.

"Whatever," said Charlie, refraining from blurting out that he hated faggots.

"So, what's this Bandoff thingy?" asked Marge.

"It's a band competition. Some big agents are going to be there. The prize is for a contract with them."

"You never mentioned that," said his Dad.

"I did, but you were probably watching Corrie."

"So, it's a big day then, isn't it?" asked his Mum.

"Too bloody right," he said.

"Well, you better get a move on then, unless you want to be late?"

Charlie checked his mobile for the time.

"Shit. I'm gone."

"Wanna lift?" asked his Dad.

"That would be great."

"Don't forget…" said his Mum.

"I know, faggots in the oven."

By the time Charlie stumbled out the packed carriage at

Piccadilly, he was on edge. He hated travelling with so many people brushing against him in the morning, especially when he was trying to build himself up for his important day. He had to call Mr. Pratt; his one and only client and confirm that his candidate Mr. Mamboosa; the best Oracle Database Specialist on the system, was suitable after the interview the previous evening.

If so, Mr. Mamboosa would start the following Monday on a rolling six-month contract, and Charlie would pocket a nifty £1,000 extra a month. He'd then be on enough to save up, move out, and impress Cass.

Once out in the open in London Town, he breathed in the fresh petrol fumes, glanced up at the office looking down on Eros, and smiled. Today was the day: deal, winners, and Cass. He checked his phone.

"All on for tonight, voice is as sweet as ever. Keep your hands in good shape, no sneaking off at lunch for a cheeky wank – Cass xx."

He couldn't wait to see Cass later and confirm their relationship. He just had to remain focused: one step at a time.

His gut wrenched as he walked through the company doors. Even after a year, he still got nervous. Fitting in with an office full of money obsessed dickheads was impossible.

Peter Prick Percy. the most successful, witty, and arrogant salesman at Computer Jobbers was by the lift.

"All right, Charlie Boy?" he said in his 'south of the river' accent. The lift door pinged open. "Got any deals on the cards?" he added as he straightened his tie in the lift mirror and smoothed over his dark eyebrows.

"Might have," said Charlie, following behind.

"Oh, the mystery man of Computer Jobbers strikes

again. How many deals have you made this month again?"

"None yet. Been building up for today, you know, end the month with a bang."

"Yeah, sure. Like you did last month, and the one before, or actually, was that me?" He chuckled to himself.

"Funny," Charlie said, letting out a fake laugh. He thought back to the first time he'd seen Peter Prick Percy at a training session to 'inspire' the new sales team.

"All right fuckers, now listen to me," Peter had said. "A year ago, I was sat where you are; not as shit scared as some of you look, especially you," he said, pointing at Charlie. "Anyway, the boss asked me to say a few words. Well, all I have to say is that last year I made over one hundred grand, and I'm going to do the same this year. So, don't any of you newer fuckers get in my way, or else. Not that you could, of course. I suppose I should say you need to be hungry, be thirsty for money, you need to want this more than your mother wanted her first shag. Keep focused, and be prepared to become obscenely rich. Apart from you," he added, nodding towards Charlie.

Since then Peter had done nothing but put Charlie down, insult his dress sense, and even steal his leads and clients. Every time he'd got close to a client, Peter already had it in his devious bag.

Today would be different though. Charlie had hidden his client's details and withheld them from the system. Completely against company rules, but everyone did it. The deal was his. The lift pinged open.

"Good luck then, Charlie boy. Let's see who's first to ring that bell!"

"Bell-end, more like," muttered Charlie as Percy bowled into the office. Charlie followed behind; keeping his head high as he looked over the sales floor. The ten rows of desks were already half full of men and women standing up, making telephone calls, and telling lies.

He took his seat at the end of the second row and leaned his guitar against his desk.

"All right, Charlie boy?" said Tony- Charlie's boss- as he slapped him on the back. "How's it going? Ready for final day?"

"Too right, Tone. How you doing?"

"Fucking great," he said, running his hand through his greying hair. He leaned closer to Charlie. "Wife woke me up at six to give me a right old <u>noshing</u>; can't beat it first thing in the morning."

"That must have been nice for you," said Charlie, trying to wipe the image from his mind.

"Nice is one way of putting it. I'd say fucking perfect Charlie, just fucking perfect. Now get your arse in the meeting room in the next five."

Charlie wondered just how he'd managed to stick out working with such obscene men for so long. There had to be a less vulgar environment to work in. He'd think about it this weekend as he was sailing down the Thames with Cass by his side, sipping on champagne.

"What's up, Charlie boy?" said Shane; Charlie's only real mate in the office.

"What's up, Geezer?" he replied, slapping him a high-five.

"Ready for the big day?" asked Shane as he switched on his computer, glancing at his perfectly shaved head in the reflection.

"Ready as I'll ever be."

"That's the spirit."

Shane was a decent bloke. He fit in with the wide boys

from London, but he also had a pleasant side, not a deceiving one; like everyone else in the office.

Tony was already in the board room; pacing up and down with his hands deep in his pockets as he rearranged his balls.

"Right, let's get this over. What will everyone close on today? Now, look at the board." As usual Prick Percy was at the top: £50,560 billed so far, then Shane on £41,000, Tyrone on £35,000, Tammy on £20,000, and Charlie on £0,000. Total £146,000. "So, we need another thirty-four thousand to make this month's target, and send us all home with a lovely little bonus before our summer holidays. So, what have you got, Shane?"

"I should have another ten grand today; gone back to one of my old clients."

"Good work, son. Tyrone?"

"I think I'm done."

"No, you fucking ain't. Get out there now and start calling." Tyrone left the room.

"Tammy?"

"About fifteen grand should be signed off this morning."

"Excellent work darling," he said, winking. "Mr. Percy?" Why did everyone call him Mister? Had he been bloody knighted?

"I'm not going to say a figure, but a little birdie has given me a lead worth a cool thirty grand."

"Right, well; let's get out there."

Charlie's heart sank. Had things got that bad that the boss didn't even ask him anymore, to save the embarrassment?

"What about me, Boss?"

"What's up, Charlie boy? You got anything for us this

month?"

"Yeah."

Everyone looked at him.

"How sure is it?"

"Guy had a third interview last night. It's a done deal; thirty grand."

"Well, well Charlie boy, good luck. Now get your arses back to the office and start closing."

That shut them up, Charlie thought as he made his way back to his desk. I'm gonna be the big shot today. He hoped he was, or he'd be out on his ear.

His first call was to Mr. Mamboosa.

"Hello?" said the South African.

"Hey, it's Charlie."

"Ah, hello my friend."

"How did it go?"

"Well, if he doesn't give me the job, then I'll shave my own balls."

"Err, so, is that a good thing?"

"Do you shave your balls?"

"No, no, I don't shave my balls." He caught Shane frowning at him, but he just shrugged. "What did Mr. Pratt say exactly?"

"That I was more experienced than any of the other candidates."

"Okay, so I'm going to call him this morning. Hopefully, you can sign today."

"Great, speak to you soon."

Charlie slammed the phone down and stood up; ready to speak to Mr. Pratt.

"Hello, Pratt's office."

"Hi, is that Stacey?"

"Yes, it is. Who's speaking?"

"Charlie from Computer Jobbers. Is Mr. Pratt there?"

"He's actually on the phone at the moment."

"Okay, I'll hold."

"Sure, one second."

Charlie's leg was shaking. Why was Mr. Pratt on the phone? Maybe it was his wife wishing him a good day, or he had to call his ill mother in the hospital, or it was another agent, trying to get in another candidate. He peered over towards Mr. Prick Percy, and his stomach almost fell out when he saw that he wasn't at his desk. He was never not at his desk unless it was after midnight. Why would he not be at his desk?

"He's still on the phone Charlie, will you wait?"

"I'll call back," said Charlie, hanging up. His bowels were about to fall through, so he went into the men's. As soon as he entered he could hear that wide boy Cockney accent echoing around the room.

"Yeah, you see he's an excellent candidate; just got off a two-year contract as an Oracle database designer."

Charlie darted into a cubicle, pulled down his trousers and boxers, and waited.

"Yeah, so I can send him in the afternoon. How does three o'clock sound? I'll send you his C.V. over soon, right after my next meeting. Great, okay, thanks, Mr. Pratt."

Charlie would have stood up, but he was in the middle of a crap. How had the prick found his one and only client? He hated him. Suddenly he felt sick and dizzy. He drifted into a daze, bending his head down towards the floor as he finished his number two.

When he came around, twenty minutes had passed. His mouth was dry and clammy. He had to speak to Mr. Pratt. As he got back to his desk, Peter Prick Percy was just hanging up the phone. He had a smarmy smile on his face as he tapped a packet of cigarettes; one flew out and landed in his mouth.

"Charlie boy," he said, nodding as he walked off. Charlie had a sinking feeling that he'd been done over, again.

"Hi, is that Stacy?"

"Hi Charlie, I'll put you through."

"Mr. Pratt."

"Hi, Mr. Pratt. It's Charlie. How was Mr. Mamboosa?"

"Hi, Charlie. Well, he's certainly an excellent candidate."

"Sure he is. He said he loved the company and would start on Monday."

"That's good to know."

"So, is that a yes?"

"A yes?"

"Yes, to start on Monday?"

"Hold your horses, Charlie. I just had a C.V. from another agent. Looks as if he's a bit more experienced. So, I'll get an answer to you by four."

"You bastard," he thought about saying. How had Peter Prick Percy found a candidate in just twenty minutes? He was sneakier that the Artful Dodger himself. Rumour had it that Percy often watched Fagan and his devious lads pickpocket over and over again. He'd do anything, oh, just anything to make a few quid.

"Charlie, are you there?"

"Okay Mr. Pratt, I'll call you at four."

Charlie had to be smart and stall the other candidate. He stood up, checking the coast was clear. Charlie walked around, peering down at Percy's desk to see if there were any clues of names. Nothing, his desk was always spotless. It was time to call on Patrick, from Spring IT.

Patrick and Charlie had a lot in common. They were

both 'sales' people, both tried to get leads out of people, both had a similar way of doing things, and both wore the same pants. You see, Patrick, Irish born, was actually Charlie's twin brother. Okay, it was just Charlie, but with an Irish accent.

Charlie had been trained to practice his second accent for difficult moments when he might need to extract further information from people. Percy had a scouse accent, which he did pretty well because his uncle was from Liverpool.

So, Patrick picked up the phone with his shaking hand and called Mr. Pratt's office. If he got caught, he'd lose the whole deal.

"Mr. Pratt's office," answered Stacey, "How can I help you?"

"Why hello there, top of the morning to ya," said Patrick in his best, or worst, Irish accent. "You may not know who I am now, but I'm calling from Computer Jobbers, we had some people down for an interview with you yesterday and today."

"That's right, yesterday, but not today."

"Oh, you see my sales guy told me we had a candidate today."

"From Computer Jobbers?"

"That's what he told me."

"Well, we have someone from CP Institution."

"Oh right," said Patrick, recognizing the fake name that Percy normally used. "That was our old name. Great, so could I just confirm that Harvey Gold will be attending the interview?"

"Harvey Gold? No, I have a John Dilbert at three."

"Okay grand, must have got my wires crossed. Thanks a million."

Patrick hung up and quickly typed John Dilbert into the system. There he was, called by Percy and sent on an interview to an unknown place at three.

Within ten minutes, Patrick had called John and set up a new interview for a highly lucrative position on the other side of London, with a made-up company, just to stall him making a decision.

"Everything all right, mate?" asked Shane. Charlie realised he'd bitten off most of his nails and had spat them all over his keyboard.

"Yeah, fine. I'm taking an early lunch," he said, heading for the door.

Charlie wandered the streets of London: up Regent's Street, along Oxford Street, and back down through Soho. As he walked all he could think about was that prick, Peter Percy. How the hell had he known about his client? He must have rang Mr. Mamboosa by chance and got the information from him. He hated his job and how it made him feel: silly, foolish, and naive. He had to get this deal to motivate himself to stay on, or at least get some cash for all the hours he'd put in.

"Oi, Charlie," said Tony, as Charlie came back. "Any news on that deal?"

"Four o'clock, Boss."

"Better be. Get back on that blower."

"Sure."

Charlie was too nervous to concentrate and ended up just calling the speaking clock until four. He was losing the will to phone. When four o'clock came around, Charlie called Mr. Pratt.

"Hello, Mr...."

"Hi Stacy, it's me, can I have a chat with Mr. Pratt please."

"Sure, he's just come off the phone."

"Great."

"Hi, Charlie. So, I guess you're hoping for an answer."

"You could say that; Mr. Mamboosa is very keen to start…"

"I'm sure he is, but…" there it was, the 'but' he'd heard so many times, the 'but' which normally ended in disaster. "You see, this other guy I've just seen was pretty good too, plus he's a bit more, how can I put this, normal."

"Normal? But what's wrong with Mr. Mamboosa?"

"Let's just say he was a little socially inept."

"Why do you say that?"

"Well, firstly he was dressed in shorts and sandals, carried a brown leather briefcase, and had this strange habit of scratching his, well, scratching himself. Not the ideal candidate."

"Oh, for fuck sake," said Charlie.

"Sorry?"

"I said 'for fuck sake'. You heard. I'm sick of this. Always getting beaten, always losing my deals."

"I am sorry, Charlie, but I don't think that's any way to speak to a client."

"No, it's not, but I couldn't give a flying fuck. And I'll tell you another thing; John Tilbert was sent to you by someone from here; Computer Jobbers." If he was going to go out, he'd do it in style.

"I don't understand."

"It's simple. This is what we do here: we rob and cheat each other. We rob clients, steal job seekers, make up names, put on funny accents, all for money. You see, Mr. Pratt, that guy who sent you John Tilbert, what was his name?"

"Paul."

"From where?"

"CP Institution."

"Well, that's his fake name. He's actually Peter Prick Percy from Computer Fucking Jobbers."

"Why is that important? All I want in an Oracle database specialist who doesn't scratch his balls."

"Well you've got one now, and I hope you live happily ever fucking after."

Charlie slammed down the phone and shouted out 'BASTARD,' which everyone in the office heard; just as they'd heard his entire conversation.

"I think I need a word, Charlie," said Tony.

Charlie gazed around the office. Everyone was staring at him; most with their mouths open in shock. He was half expecting them to start laying into him for giving away the truth, but it was quite the opposite.

Shane began to clap. Then others followed until finally the whole office was stood up, clapping and cheering, apart from Peter Prick Percy who was sat slumped in his chair.

"Good on ya," said one guy as Charlie walked towards Tony's office.

"You told him," said another.

"Peter Prick Percy, love it, mate."

"You've got some bollocks," said another.

Charlie began to feel elated. He walked into the office and stood in front of Tony.

"What. The. Fuck. Was. That?"

"What?"

"You do realise the whole office heard that?"

"I do now, sounds like they enjoyed it too." He didn't care anymore; he just didn't give a damn about his stupid job. He just wanted to become a guitarist.

"So, what now? I guess you've ballsed up any chances with that company."

"I think you'll find it was Peter. If he had left my client alone, then none of this would have happened."

"Why is he your client?"

"Because I took the call."

"But is it on the system?"

"No, it's not on the bloody system."

"Why?"

"'Cos everyone in the office is a thieving bastard, apart from Shane, and I wanted to finally get a deal with honesty."

"Well, you've certainly been honest today."

"Too right."

There was a pause and silence as Charlie began to smile. He could feel the pressure of the last month rising from his shoulders. Soon he'd be performing, doing what he knew best.

"I can't technically sack you for what you just did. But I'm not sure it's a good idea that you continue here."

"You don't say. It's fine. I quit."

There, he'd said it, finally, those two words that would hopefully change his life.

"Well, it's been a pleasure," said Tony. "I have to say, in all my years here, no one has had the balls to do that, especially to Peter Prick Percy." He laughed as he shook his hand. "What are you going to do then?"

"Dunno, I've got a performance tonight, so maybe I'll get snapped up and become a famous guitarist; anything but work in a sales office."

"Best of luck, now you better clear your desk before you get mobbed."

"Mobbed for an autograph?"

"I wouldn't push your luck."

As Charlie came out the office, the whole sales floor was on the phone again, apart from Peter Prick Percy, who was still slumped in his chair, speechless. Charlie gazed around for one final time; he wouldn't miss the thieving atmosphere. Not the pressure, targets, meetings, or tricks, there was absolutely nothing he would miss, apart from Shane.

"I'm off."

"Off?" asked Shane.

"Yeah, I quit. I'll be in touch."

"Shit, okay, take it easy. Well done mate; that was a classic."

"Cheers."

Charlie shook hands with his team, and they wished him good luck. He grabbed his guitar, keen to get playing. There was just one thing he had to do before leaving the office though. He ran up to the deal bell, grabbed it, and shook it hard.

"GOODBYE COMPUTER BLOW JOBBERS," he shouted as he made for the door, sticking a middle finger up at Percy.

As Charlie passed through the ticket barriers at Piccadilly, in slightly less of a crowd than usual, he began to focus on the next task ahead; to win Bandoff and play well enough to conquer Cass.

"Shit," he said loudly, startling a group of Chinese girls huddled around a tube map. His plan of winning over Cass by having enough money to move out of home had taken a severe setback.

"Damn it," he muttered as he hit his thigh in anger while on the Piccadilly line heading up to King's Cross. In a moment of madness, he'd lost the bonus he'd been praying for. What had he been thinking? Probably that he'd had it with the world of sales and was utterly cheesed off with getting done over.

He had to keep it bottled up from Cass and Joe - his best mate - until he found a solution. They wouldn't ask him anyway; the band competition was far too important. They'd been dreaming of winning something ever since they started back at university.

The band had been his and Joe's idea. They had been best mates ever since infant school when they were sent to the book corner after ganging up on Samantha and pushing her down the slide backward.

They had both dived for the same book- Little Red Riding Hood- and sat reading it together, taking turns to make the deep nasty voice of the wolf, and laughing in unison when the innocent granny got gobbled up.

They went to the same primary and secondary school, and even to Bournemouth University to study music.

"Shall we start a band then?" asked Joe one night as they sat in the uni bar watching a very average band getting booed off the stage.

"Might as well," said Charlie, "can't be much worse than that bunch of wasters."

"Great, we just need some more band members."

"Mission set."

The next morning, while waiting for their lecturer to turn up, they met Cass, sweet Cass. Charlie and Joe were sitting at the back discussing what they would call their band, when in she walked. Her long, wavy auburn hair sprang up and down on her shoulders as she bounced into the lecture hall.

It was the first time that Charlie had ever felt a weird

mushy feeling in his stomach. The desire he felt to speak to her was so strong that when she smiled and headed towards him, he turned into a complete dickhead.

"This seat taken?" she asked, in her soft voice.

"No, it's still there," Charlie said. She winced as if his cruddy joke had punched her in the gut.

"So, can I sit in it then?"

"As long as you don't have AIDS." Why had he said that? He still cringed at the thought.

"Well, last time I checked I was fine, but don't worry, we won't be sharing any bodily fluids anyway, so you'll be all right."

"That's a relief," he said, wiping his brow and blowing softly.

"I'm Cass."

"Charlie. This is my mate, Joe."

"All right, apologies for my mate," said Joe. "He's a bit of a twat."

"I'd already got that."

Charlie nodded and grinned in agreement.

After the lecture, Charlie asked whether or not she wanted to join their band without even knowing if she played an instrument, and luckily, it turned out she was a pretty decent singer.

Charlie soon fell in love with Cass. Not a crush, or a feeling of fondness, but pure, mushy, gooey love. He worshipped the ground she walked on. He loved the way she sang, moved, and even sneezed. It made her look so vulnerable and needy, and he wanted to help wipe her nose.

Everyone knew he fancied her, even Cass, but Charlie was too wussy (half wimp, half pussy) to do anything about it.

They'd kissed once while playing 'pass the ice-cube' at a party.

"Blimey," said Cass, the next day.

"Yeah," said Charlie, about to say that he'd really enjoyed it.

"Imagine if our tongues had actually touched."

"But they did," Charlie wanted to say. He was sure he'd felt it; soft, squishy, and perfect. But instead, he just nodded, not wanting to seem like an idiot.

So, he spent his whole university life in love with Cass and never grew enough balls to open his heart. But that was going to change tonight. He was sure she liked him now. She'd split up with her boyfriend 'Jules the Rapist' (a nickname Charlie had given), and made a tape for his twenty-fifth birthday, which started with *I Wanna Be Adored*, by the Stone Roses. He took it as a massive hint. They'd been hanging out more too, going for a beer just the two of them, and Cass had admitted how she found guitarists sexy. She'd even started calling him Charlie-sweets.

There was just one annoying person who might get in his way though; Hans. The only thing that Joe and Charlie had ever disagreed about was Hans, their second guitarist.

Joe had met him at a music convention. He wouldn't have, had Charlie not come down with a severe case of man Flu, but Joe went alone and struck up a relationship with, of all people, a German.

Charlie hated Hans. Not because he was German, although he wasn't too keen on the German type, purely based on footballing tragedies- nothing to do with the War. He respected Hans as a guitarist but despised him as a person. He hated the smug look on his face when he played, the way his biceps always bulged through whatever he was wearing, and the way he did everything so mechanically and perfectly.

Plus, the fact that he fancied Cass. He'd been slowly trying to smuggle his way in with her, but Charlie had him sussed out, and there was no way he was going to lose her, especially to a German.

As he got off at Camden Town those guitarist flames ignited through his body. He was bursting to show his skills to the crowd and judges at The World's End. He felt excited about lifting the trophy and sharing the night's celebrations with Cass.

As Charlie entered, he was surprised by the lack of people. Hardly any of the bands were there yet. Joe was at the back of the bar, crouching in front of a fruity.

"All right, mate." Charlie tapped him on the shoulder.

"Who the..." said Joe, almost falling backward. "Blimey, you're early." Joe stood up, flicked his fringe out of his eyes, and hit roll.

"Yeah, the boss let me out, you know, after getting that deal." *What are you saying, you Muppet? Keep it quiet.*

"Oh wow, congrats mate, that's excellent. What the..." Joe was far too engrossed in his battle with the fruity.

"Cheers, pint?"

"Just a half, save the pints for after."

As Charlie headed for the bar he regretted lying, but there was no other option; he wanted no negative energy flying about; a positive state of mind was the way forward.

"Here you go, mate," said Charlie, handing him over half a Carling. "Any luck?"

"Nah, just lost a tenner, didn't I? Fucking fruity. So, tell me about this deal then."

"Oh, it was nothing; my guy got the job that was it."

"You must be really happy; you can finally get some

cash, move out, and change your dull and boring life."

"Yeah," he said, trying to sound upbeat.

"What's up?" said Joe. "Thought you'd be a bit chirpier."

"Oh nothing, guess just a bit of stage nerves kicking in. Where is everyone?"

"They'll be here soon. Oh look, there they come now."

Charlie glanced towards the door, and his heart began to race as if someone had injected him with speed (not that he'd ever taken speed). There was Cass, with her long auburn hair blowing behind her. She looked gorgeous. She was wearing a tight white shirt open at the top. She was smiling too; in fact, she looked like she was laughing.

Strange, thought Charlie, taking a swig. Then when she turned around to hold the door open, Charlie almost spat out his beer.

Walking in behind, laughing, smiling, and wearing a skin tight white vest top to show his perfect bloody bulging biceps was Hans. Had they come together? The dirty, bloody German was getting his nasty paws on her.

"All right Charlie boy," said Cass, planting a soft kiss on his cheek. What happened to Charlie-sweets?

"Charlie, how is you?" asked Hans, shaking his hand.

"All right. That's a coincidence, you two turning up at the same time."

"Not really," said Cass, "we caught the tube together; he only lives up the road now."

"Yes, I just moved into a new flat, on my own."

Bastard

"That's lucky," said Charlie, biting his lower lip.

"Yeah, just got promoted at my job to head of the team."

"Nice one," said Joe. Charlie told himself to keep calm and not headbutt anyone.

"So?" said Cass.

"So what?" said Charlie, defensively.

"The deal, did you get it?"

"Oh, the deal, yeah, sorted, fine, yeah."

"Oh, that's great news, mate, you must be over the moon." Why was she calling him 'mate' all of a sudden? Something was up.

"Well, guess it hasn't sunk in yet, but yeah, it's a weight off my shoulders that's for sure."

"Drink?" said Hans. "Is time for a celebration!" Charlie and Joe held up their halves and shook their heads.

"Hang on, I'll give you a hand," said Cass, following behind.

His heart dropped when he saw Cass leaning on Han's muscular shoulder. Hans was one of those lucky gits, in the same league as Prick Percy; the body builder, the head of his team, the one who could afford to move in on his own, in London, and get a different woman back to his pad every night.

He was also the one hitting it off better than ever with Cass. Of all nights, he had to choose this one. The tosser, the two-faced tosser was moving in on his woman. Trust him to get a place around the corner from her, just as he'd lost his job and would be stuck at home for god knows how long.

Cass and Hans returned with drinks, and they all stood around the high circular table. The venue began to fill up with bands, and the atmosphere was starting to liven up. Soon they would be on stage performing. Charlie had to get a grip; he was letting his emotions take over.

"I've got a new guitar for tonight," said Hans.

"New guitar?" asked Charlie.

"Well, it's not technically new," said Hans.

"Yeah, it's my brother's," said Cass. Jealousy was burning up through Charlie's body.

"Wouldn't it have been better to have practised before though?" said Charlie.

"Oh, he did," said Cass.

"Right," said Charlie, wanting to ask how and when.

"Yeah, last weekend, round hers with her brother, great jamming session," Hans said, winking. Charlie had asked about going around, but she'd never invited him. She was slowly slipping away, just as his deal had, but he wasn't going to go down without a fight.

"We'd better move into the main hall," said Joe. "It'll be starting in a bit."

In the main hall, about three hundred people were gathered waiting for Bandoff to start. It was mostly groups of four or five, some Gothics, some mods; a total mixed bag.

"Okay, guys and girls can I have your attention please?" asked the host as he stood on the stage in a shiny mauve top.

"Tonight is Camden's annual Band off. We have bands from all over the country and three judges to decide on the winners, who will walk away tonight with two grand, and a deal with Erupto Studios. So, let's get kicked off with the Greasy Monkeys."

As Charlie watched the first five bands, he was confident they could play miles better. He was getting distracted though. Cass and Hans had spent the last thirty minutes bopping up and down together. Maybe she was making Charlie jealous to push him into making a move. Well, if that's what she wanted, then so be it.

"We're up next," said Joe, heading back stage. The time had come to show Camden and the judges they were worthy of first prize.

"Okay guys and girls, and now time for our next band; The Moonraders."

"Let's do it," said Joe, leading the way.

"Yeah, yeah," said Hans. Charlie wanted to trip him up but refrained. He had to keep his cool.

As they stood on the stage in front of three hundred people, Charlie faced them and smiled. He was confident of his skills. He believed in himself.

"One, two, one, two, three, four," said Joe. And they were off. Cass bopped about at the front, singing their song. Hans and Charlie stood behind, strumming in sync as Joe played on the drums.

Charlie could feel the euphoria they were making together. The crowd was jumping up and down, waving their hands in the air. He kept one eye on Cass, hoping she would notice he was playing better than Hans, but couldn't work out why she kept wiggling her hips. Maybe it was for the crowd and judges; to be sexier, but when she turned and winked at Hans, something snapped in Charlie's brain.

He could feel himself burning inside with rage. He glanced over at Hans, who was moving side by side, grinning and flexing his muscles. What a cock!

Then she did it again. She turned her back to the crowd and bent down to flash Hans her cleavage. She even looked up and licked her lips. The whore!

Charlie suddenly felt lighter, his hands free. He watched as his guitar (and connecting cables) spun through the air, making its way towards Han's head.

The crowd stopped jumping.

Joe stopped playing.

Hans crashed to the floor, knocked down by Charlie's

flying guitar.

The judges froze.

"What are you doing, you dickhead?" shouted Cass, bending down to help Hans, lying on the floor.

Joe and Cass huddled beside Hans, blood was dripping down his face. Charlie looked at the crowd, half laughing, half in shock. One bloke even mouthed *'What the fuck?'* while shrugging his shoulders.

Charlie glanced over at the judges, who were busy scribbling in their black notepads; no doubt crossing them off the list. The worst thing about it was that Charlie still felt jealous, even more now that Cass was lying beside Hans, flashing her bare skin at him. Hans sat up and held his head.

"Am I in the Motherland?" he said, confused.

"No, you're not. You're here in Camden playing, or you were playing," said Cass, sneering at Charlie.

"What the fuck was that, mate?" said Joe, waving his hands about. Charlie had never seen Joe so pissed off. He felt a pang of guilt.

"Err, excuse me," said the presenter, "will you be continuing?"

They all looked at Hans, who was sitting with his head and hands covered in blood.

"I don't think so," said Joe. "Can someone call an ambulance?"

Charlie grabbed his guitar and followed behind as a couple of people carried Hans off stage and sat him down on a chair.

"What the hell were you thinking?" said Cass, as they stood around him.

He wanted to be honest and tell her the truth. He'd had a flash of jealousy, was upset she had given Hans her brother's guitar and had stopped calling him Charlie-sweets. He wanted to cry out that he was in love with her. Instead, he did what he'd been trained to do, to lie.

"I was trying to spin my guitar round, and it flew out my hands."

"What absolute bollocks!" said Joe.

"It's true. I've seen it done loads of times on MTV," said Charlie.

They ignored him. Within ten minutes the ambulance arrived, and Cass jumped in the back with Hans.

"Send me a message," said Charlie, "let me know how he gets on."

Cass threw him a disgusted look as the doors closed.

"What now?" Charlie said to Joe.

"I dunno, mate. What's all that bullshit about spinning your guitar?"

"I just got angry, that's all."

"About what?"

"About Hans, the way he was moving, and the way Cass wasn't concentrating."

"What are you on about? You have to get sorted, you've been strange ever since you turned up tonight. I think you'd better just go home."

"What you gonna do?"

"Go back in and watch our prize get given to someone else," he said, turning around. "I'll give you a bell."

"All right, sorry, mate."

"Yeah, whatever."

And just like that, he was alone, standing outside The World's End on a Thursday night, while people dodged around him. What a bloody day, he thought to himself as he walked, unsure where he was going.

It was still only ten at night, so there was no way he was going home, even if the only person who could console him was his Mum. He couldn't face sitting down to a plate of chips, peas, and faggots either.

So, he continued, cursing himself for being such a plank. How had everything he'd been working for just ended like that so quickly? He had nothing left: no job, no band, and no potential girlfriend.

By the time he'd walked most of Camden High Street, he was at a loss of where to go. In the distance, he noticed a queue of people waiting outside a bar with flashing red lights. The last time he came out of a bar with flashing red lights his mind had been corrupted, but this one looked less sordid. He shuffled closer, squinting at the sign outside.

Live Flamenco Show

Free Entry

Charlie knew of flamenco music, of Paco de Lucia and Cameron de la Isla, but had never seen it live. Once inside, Charlie could feel the presence of Spain. Soft flamenco guitar music played in the background. Photos of expressive flamenco dancers and singers hung up on the deep blood red walls. They seemed so different, foreign, and passionate.

He sat down at the back and waited. On the small stage at the front were two red chairs in front of a black curtain. Out popped a tall, dark haired man with a perfectly trimmed goatee.

"Ladies and gentlemen, *señoras y señores*. Welcome to tonight's flamenco performance. Our dancers and guitarists are all original flamenco experts, from the south of Spain, where flamenco was born, Sevilla."

Charlie admired the way the guy had said Sevilla with

such pride, as if it was the centre of the universe. Surely it was a less stressful place than London.

"So, here are our first *artistas Manuel y Isabel.*"

The crowd clapped as Manuel came out, holding his guitar high in the air. He was dressed in all black, a suave Spanish man with long dark hair and a designer stubble beard. The way he did a small circle on the stage before taking his chair and spinning his guitar onto his knee made him look so stylish and sophisticated.

As Manuel played, Charlie relaxed for the first time that day. The nightmares drifted away as Charlie was transported to a Spanish land. The soft way that Manuel played was soothing; such a lovely, romantic sound. His quick and nimble finger work was inspiring to Charlie. He wanted to play like that. He knew he could. He was able to pick up most guitar styles. He studied Manuel's hands; how they moved along the strings and began to copy on his forearm. Why had he never considered playing flamenco before?

Then, as if he wasn't already completely absorbed in the performance, out came Isabel. She appeared from the corner, walking slowly from behind the black curtains with her head held high. She oozed confidence and style. Her black hair was tied up in a bun with a pink rose in the back. Her red and white spotted dress fit snugly against her voluptuous figure.

Charlie had seen Spanish women before, he'd always been slightly partial to the foreign look, but never before had he been struck by such beauty. Isabel waltzed across the stage, moving her hips up and down in a hypnotizing way, gazing powerfully into the crowd.

She clonked her feet on the floor as Manuel played. They looked so proud of their flamenco, their art. Charlie imagined playing the flamenco guitar, growing his hair long like a sexy Spanish man, maybe even some stubble, and finding his own *señorita*. Surely life in Spain had to be better than London; no tube, no office, no stress, and certainly no faggots.

Watching Isabel filled his heart with mush—a type of soppy mush that you never admitted to your mates. He'd never experienced instant passion. He'd felt attraction to dancers before: the time in the school nativity play when he had a small crush on Kate, the Christmas tree, and another time when he'd gone to see Disney on Ice and fallen in love with Cinderella, but this was different. The exotic, foreign look captured his curiosity. Was it time to get out of London to search for a different life?

The thought of leaving his country, his safety, and his family filled him with dread; would he have a chance of becoming a professional guitarist out there? How would he learn the language? What if Spaniards just laughed at him for trying to play flamenco?

His life couldn't get any worse though. He thought back over his disastrous day: getting screwed over again at work, losing out to Peter Prick Percy and Mr. Muscle Hans. He wondered how many stitches he'd had and whether Cass was still flashing herself at him.

Spanish women were a lot classier, sexier, and honest. None of this *Charlie-sweets* one minute and *mate* the next.

When Isabel finished with a stamp on the floor, the whole crowd stood and applauded. Charlie shot up clapping. He had fallen for flamenco. If Isabel had come up with a contract to join their flamenco group right then, he would have written his name down quicker than you can say, 'th, th, th, th, th, Chris Waddle.'

Charlie considered hanging about backstage and trying

to speak with Isabel, but he figured Manuel would try to break his legs, and he'd had enough trouble for one day, so he went home.

If he wasn't already convinced that it was time to leave London, his trip back home on the tube hit that final nail in the guitar case. He sat on the tube, watching a group of drunk thugs throwing beer at each other and pissing on the seats. He wanted to call them a bunch of Muppets, but what was the use? He wondered what word Muppets was in Spanish.

"So?" asked his Mum as Charlie poked his head round the lounge door, smiling. His Mum and Dad were sat on the sofa with Corrie paused on TV.

"So what?" he said, trying not to seem so joyful.

"Someone's happy," said his Dad. "How did it go? Did you get that deal? Win the competition and win the heart of Cass?"

"Nope."

"What, none of it?" asked his Mum.

"Nah."

"Then why are you so happy?" asked his Dad.

"Because I've found my new vocation in life."

"What?" asked his Mum.

"I'm going to become a flamenco guitarist."

His Mum and Dad gazed at each other for a second and then burst out laughing.

"Sure, sure," said his Mum. "Ole ole," she added, clapping her hands in the air.

"Yeah, I know Spanish. What it is? *Dos cervezas, por favor*," said his Dad.

Charlie fumed inside; why wouldn't they take him seriously? He'd show them.

"What made you think of that then?" asked his Mum.

"Long story, I'll tell you tomorrow."

"Sure, okay, well, chuck Corrie back on, Luv," said his Mum, facing her husband. "And don't forget…"

But Charlie was already halfway up the stairs, about to search on his laptop for flights to Seville.

Chapter 2 SICK OF MUMMY'S BOYS

Seville, a couple of months earlier

Mercedes glared deep into Javier's twitching left eye. He was about to let her down, again.

"What do you mean 'I, I, I have to tell you something'?" she asked, mocking his blabbering stutter. They were in Javier's shiny, black, air-conditioned Porsche under a blossoming orange tree in Plaza de Santa Cruz; the square where Mercedes lived with her parents.

"Well, I, I, something has come up."

His true side was coming out. He was such a rubbish boyfriend. She'd fallen for his cute smile, toned body, and larger than average nose. She'd hoped he would be well hung, but, in Javier's case what they say about men with overly large hooters was a myth.

"Go on then, why can't you make it to the most important flamenco night of my life? The night which I've reminded you about every day for the last week." She flicked her hand towards him, just missing his conker.

"*Es mi Madre.*"

"*Tu Madre*? Well, that's a surprise."

Paco's face flashed in her mind. Gorgeous Paco with his olive skin, dark hair, and perfect abs. She missed his body, but not his mind. Paco Calvo, a successful bullfighter in Seville, was one of Mercedes' ex-boyfriends. They'd dated for a few months, and she'd gradually fallen completely in love with him, his body, and their sex life. There was something thrilling about making love to a guy who was risking his life to dance about with terrifying bulls. But Paco was a soft touch, at least to his *Madre*, who had insisted on ruining their relationship.

She even knew when they were at it. Whether they were having a quickie in the morning before work, or a planned romantic evening at the weekend; she always seemed to pop up and spoil the moment.

Once she tracked them down while they were out celebrating their six-month anniversary. She turned up, ordered a glass of white wine, and forced Paco to scribble down some instructions on how to work her DVD.

The last straw was when she appeared in the queue at the cinema as they were about to see 50 Shades of Grey. Inside, she wangled her way between them and snatched the bag of popcorn.

Mercedes decided to end their relationship once she'd heard his mother's orgasmic gasping noises during the raunchy sex scenes.

"A surprise?" said Javier.

"You are a complete loser," said Mercedes, grabbing the car door handle, but Javier pulled her shoulder.

"No, Mercedes, please, let me explain."

"Explain what? That you were never really interested in supporting me through one of the biggest nights of my life? Or that you were only going out with me so you could get your mouth around these?" she said, thrusting her boobs in the air. She was sick of her perfect breasts. Sometimes she wished she could get a reduction so the leeches wouldn't stare.

"Of course not," said Javier. But she knew he was lying. When they made love, he buried his face in her breasts and hummed. If he loved them so much, why didn't he just get his own pair, for God's sake? *"Mi Madre* needs me tonight."

She'd heard that phrase before from Pepe, the doctor she'd been seeing. Pepe was shorter, weaker, and only average in bed compared to Paco, but he was a sweet, kind, and considerate man, at least to his *Madre*.

Mercedes had met him at the local hospital after she fell and twisted her ankle while dancing one evening. They'd gone out on a few dates, but Mercedes soon realised he was dominated by his mother; a complete hypochondriac. Mercedes was convinced his mother had pushed him in to becoming a doctor, so she had her own one.

She would call him complaining about her weak hip, swollen ankles, or a strange lump in her throat. No matter where they were, Pepe would always whizz off to give his full attention.

Their last date had been a joke. Mercedes had booked a double room and dinner at Seville's most prestigious hotel - Alfonso XIII. Pepe had promised not to bring his mobile, but there was no stopping the witch hunting them down.

Just as the waiter was pouring out a €20 bottle of Rioja, the owner of the restaurant came over with a phone.

"*Tu Madre,*" he said, smiling sympathetically at Mercedes.

"*Si, si, si, si, si,*" said Pepe as Mercedes knocked back a glass. "*Mi Madre* needs me. She's pulled her neck and needs a massage."

Mercedes wanted to cry out and ask why she couldn't massage her own fucking neck, but Pepe was already out the door.

"Oh really, why is that then?" said Mercedes, looking deep into Javier's eyes. "Come on, I'm intrigued, why does she need you so much?"

Javier sighed. He knew Mercedes was about to blow.

"Well, there's a special offer at Mercadona on her favourite tinned tuna. It ends tonight, and I promised I'd drive her; you know how frail she is."

"Frail? She did a ten-kilometre jog about three months ago. She's about as frail as Cristiano bloody Ronaldo."

"But you know she lives out of town."

Their idea of 'out of town' was a ten-minute bus ride away from the town hall.

"What about a taxi?"

"It's an emergency."

"An emergency? You are blowing me out on my first night dancing flamenco in front of a live audience for a special offer on tinned fucking tuna?"

"They are the double packed ones. An offer like this only comes along once a year."

Mercedes took ten seconds to breathe deeply; like her mother had told her to do many times when aggression overtook her body. She thought of her three favourite smells: lemon scented candles, spring orange blossom, and Narciso Rodriguez perfume. As she inhaled, she smelt the three things in turn. Slowly she began to relax, but then rage built up as her nostrils filled with the stench of tinned tuna.

"We're finished. I can't believe that you're putting your mother's low budget fish addiction in front of my dancing career."

"I'm sorry, *cariño*." Javier reached out to grab Mercedes' hand.

"Don't you *cariño* me, you coward. You know your problem, Javier?"

"No, but I'm sure you're going to tell me."

"You're just not man enough to stick up to your own mother. She walks all over you, smothers you, and makes your decisions. You're almost twenty-five, and it's as if you're still stuck on her nipple."

"That's ridiculous. I love my mother; like any good son,

but she doesn't own me."

"Oh really, so where are you living?"

"With *mi Madre*."

"And who pays for your car and petrol?"

"*Mi Madre.*"

"Is your *Madre* on your Facebook?"

"You know she is."

"Who still reads you bedtime stories?"

"They are not bedtime stories."

"What are they then?"

"Her diary entries."

"You are a pathetic man, Javier. I'm just glad I realised now before it gets too late." As she said those last words 'too late' she accidentally spat at him, and saliva landed in his eye. "*Adios, guilipollas.*" She pushed the door open and slammed as she got out.

The intense smell of spring orange blossom hit her in the face as she stormed across the square towards her flat.

"Tinned tuna? Is that all I'm worth?" she muttered. "Useless mummy's boys. Why are all the men I meet so lame?"

It had to stop. No more boyfriends with over-controlling mothers. She was sick of them. She needed a real man.

She stormed into her flat, whizzed past her mother in the kitchen, and grabbed some chocolate from the fridge.

"*Hola Hija,*" said Rosa.

"*Hola Mama.*"

"What's the problem?" Rosa held Mercedes' shoulders and faced her. Mercedes gazed into her mother's deep brown caring eyes and immediately calmed.

"Men, why are they all so pathetic?"

"Not all of them; don't forget your father and Raul."

She was right about her brother, but her father could

easily fall in the 'pathetic' category. "What's happened anyway?"

"It's that *imbecil* Javier. We are over."

"But why, I thought you liked him?"

"I did, but he's not coming tonight."

"Is that a reason to break up?"

"It is when their mother's involved."

"Oh." Rosa gazed at her daughter and smiled apologetically. There was no need to ask any follow-up questions.

"I just want to meet a man who doesn't put his mother before me all the time."

"Well, you might have trouble finding one. Your father is always running around after your grandmother."

"Yeah, but she's in a wheelchair. Where is he anyway?"

"He took her to Mercadona. Apparently, there's a special offer on her favourite tuna." Mercedes laughed; it was either that or cry. "What's so funny?"

"Nothing. I need to get ready."

"Of course, your big night. Are you sure you don't want us to come?"

"No, it's fine," she said, knowing full well that her mother was just trying to be civilised. There was no way her father would set foot in a flamenco *tablao*. "Besides, Lola will be there."

"At least you won't be on your own then. If you change your mind...."

"*Gracias Mama*," she said, kissing her mother on the forehead. "I'll be fine."

She loved her mother. She'd always been there to give sound advice. Not the preaching type that she had to take from her father: a pure traditional man who wanted Mercedes to get married as soon as possible and stay at home with the kids. She was glad he was out; she couldn't take any more men today.

Within thirty minutes, Mercedes had showered, done her makeup and got ready.

"I'm going," she said to her mother as she made for the door.

"Wait a second, *Hija*." Rosa stood up from her armchair. "I want you to have this." She handed over a silver pendant. Mercedes opened it and smiled as she saw her grandfather. He had his arm around her as she wore her first ever flamenco dress, back when she was six.

"*Gracias, Mama*," she said, almost welling up. "It's beautiful."

"Wear it close to your heart. I hope it brings you luck."

"I'm sure it will."

As they hugged, Mercedes wished that her grandfather could have been there to watch her. He'd been a huge influence on her; a real man who had loved his mother. He had been an independent man and controlled his own world. If only she could meet someone like him.

"Okay, I need to go."

"Best of luck. It's a shame your father isn't back. I know he wanted to wish you well."

"Sure, sure. There must have been an enormous queue at Mercadona."

As she darted out the door, late, as usual, she thought about the importance of the night ahead. Mercedes had been dancing flamenco since she was six; right after her grandfather took her to see a live flamenco performance. She'd been in various dance academies, studied the top dancers, seen hundreds of shows, and performed in plenty of dancing competitions. Tonight was her first live performance at *Las Almas*; the most famous *tablao* in the heart of flamenco, Triana.

As she made her way through the back-streets of Seville, hopping in and out of the crowds of tourists and locals enjoying a cool beer in the early spring evening, nerves pulsated through her entire body. She was so glad Lola would be by her side.

Lola had been Mercedes' best friend since they were six when they'd joined the same flamenco class. Now they were both just under 6ft tall, had a similar slim, curvy build, and the same shade of black hair. The only real physical difference was their eye colour: Lola's were sea green while Mercedes were opaque. In fact, a lot of people thought they were sisters, and they might as well have been.

"Any later and I was about to go in without you," said Lola, stamping her feet on the floor. They kissed each other on the cheek.

"Sorry, I had a bit of a row with Javier."

"Where is he?"

"Probably being breast fed."

"Not another one."

"Yep, come on, we need to be on stage in a few minutes."

As they walked through the door, Jaime, the suave owner of *Las Almas*, was waiting just inside.

"*Señoritas,*" he said, glancing at his Rolex. "I was beginning to worry."

"Worry?" said Lola, "The only thing you need to worry about is how popular this place will be after word gets around about us."

"*Si,*" said Mercedes, shyly from behind. Lola was the professional at getting what she wanted.

"Well, get a move on please; the guitarist and singer are

out there waiting."

"Don't rush us, Jaime; flamenco should never be rushed. Go sit down, find yourself a cold beer, and get ready for the show of your life."

Jaime mumbled something about 'typical flamenco women' as he turned his back and marched off. The two ladies laughed and made their way to the dressing rooms.

As they both slipped into their same coloured scarlet flamenco dresses, Mercedes' throat became dry and clenched up. She knew this was it; her first chance to impress real flamenco fans with her talent. She'd been dreaming of this moment for years. Anguish inside her belly made her queasy, doubting her ability to go out on stage, but the fire in her soul was yearning to explode.

"What's up?" asked Lola.

"Nothing, just a bit nervous."

"Well, don't be. You'll be amazing." They both turned, looked in the mirror together, and smiled. Mercedes felt proud of their beauty and how they'd become women.

"I hope so."

"Of course, you will. Never doubt yourself. Come on, we'd better go."

As she pushed a red rose tighter to steady her black bun, her grandfather's face flashed through her mind. She wished he could be there, but Lola was the next best person to have by her side. She looked down her top to check the pendant was still there.

"You can do this," Lola said, kissing her on the cheek. "Just remember what I told you; don't let anyone in the audience put you off. There can be some grotesque men out there, so just ignore the slimy bastards. Never look at the men in the front row. They are perverts and will try to distract you."

Mercedes began to feel panicky, but as long as Lola was by her side, she felt strong enough to perform.

Jaime was backstage and introduced the guitarist and singer quickly. There was no time to get to know each other, just a quick kiss on the cheek and a brief mention of names. Mercedes was too nervous to even notice what they were called, all she could think about was that she was going to be on stage soon.

"Get a move on then," said Jaime.

As they came through the black curtains, the tightly packed crowd hushed and fell silent. Once they'd occupied their stools, the guitarist began to play.

Mercedes sat with her back straight and kept her head down; not wanting to look up and see the audience. She waited patiently for the signs to begin dancing. As the guitarist picked up the tempo, gliding his fingers graciously over the strings, the singer let out a low soft wail which ricocheted through the room.

Mercedes could feel the passion from his powerful voice; the strength behind his soul. She copied Lola as she raised her hands up to her midriff and began to clap slow, firm *palmadas*, finding the *compás*.

"*Guapas*," shouted several people. Mercedes knew they were pretty, but that wasn't why she wanted to turn heads: it was her dancing which made her thrive.

The singer deepened his chant and let out a stream of sound that resonated through the bodies and hearts of the audience. Mercedes could feel the emotion building from within, which was enhanced as the guitarist began to play faster and stronger.

They began to tap their feet. Slowly at first, firm short taps, alternating from one foot to the other, setting the rhythm. The *compàs* began to control their bodies, as if in a hypnotic trance.

Lola sprang into action. Standing up and smashing her heels on the floor. Mercedes followed slightly behind. She blew air up on her own face to try to cool down, but it was no use. Her whole body was on fire. Sweat was dripping from her brow. She kept her eyes down, concentrating as she moved her arms above her head, rotating her wrists while raising her head up to face the crowd. The impact of the numerous eyes staring almost distracted her, but she battled on.

They sped up. Moving their feet faster. Spinning round and letting their dresses follow. Mercedes felt euphoric. Adrenaline was pumping through her body as she showed the world her talent.

Then she did exactly what Lola had warned her not to do. She looked at two men in the front row. They were both leering at her. One licked his lips, and the other poked his tongue out in a creepy way.

"Come on, darling," shouted one. "Why don't you show us a bit more chest?" he added, nudging his colleague on the arm as they both laughed.

The comment completely interrupted her concentration, and she lost her way. Her left foot buckled underneath her and she stumbled and fell. The crowd gasped. The singer and guitarist stopped and dashed over. She winced, distraught that she'd lost concentration. She could feel her face going red.

"See, she's not a real dancer," said the man. "Perhaps she'd be better in a strip bar." Several men began to laugh.

She looked up and saw them pointing and laughing. She was furious. She could feel the tears building.

"That's right *guapa*; this isn't your type of dance," said the man again.

"*Imbeciles,*" shouted Lola, stomping over and slapping one. "You are scum, no better than the pigs that you probably eat; you fat, greasy arseholes."

But they just laughed louder.

"Is your ankle okay?" asked Lola, turning back to her best friend.

"Sure, I'm fine," said Mercedes.

"Come on then," said Lola, grabbing Mercedes by the arm and helping her off stage.

"Bastards," said Mercedes as they reached the dressing room. "Why is the world full of such bastards?"

"Good question," said Lola, obviously raging, but for a second Mercedes thought she was angry at her. "I was worried this was going to happen. You shouldn't have looked down at them. I warned you. There are some vulgar men in the flamenco world, and you've just experienced it first-hand."

Mercedes had known Lola for years, but she'd never lost her temper with her like that. She was unsure how to react. She felt guilty.

"I know, I just lost concentration for a second. I wasn't expecting that sort of comment."

"Well, you know now," she said, snapping.

"It's not my fault; you saw what they were like."

"Yes, but this is flamenco. It's a cruel world. Trust me; I know from my mother. She danced for years, and each time she went on stage she got teased and laughed at. She never broke down though, and she never, ever fell."

Lola's eyes were raging.

"I'm sorry," said Mercedes, remembering that she was weaker than her best friend. "You know what I'm like; I'm not used to such comments."

"Rubbish, how many times while you're out do men try

to get in your knickers and say they want to eat you up?"

"Once or twice."

"A day." Mercedes smiled. Lola was right, as usual. She was unaware, but she had already built up enough confidence to battle with these worthless cretins. "So what's the problem with a few more comments? Get back out there. Show the world who you are; the beauty that you have, the passion for flamenco, *joder.*"

Lola was welling up. The occasion had got to her. They hugged.

"What's going on here?" said Jaime, bursting through the door. "You two better get back out there and finish that performance, or you will never dance in Seville again."

"You better watch your mouth, or you'll lose two of the most upcoming dancers in Seville," snapped Mercedes. Her own comments shocked her. Lola grinned.

"Yeah, can't you see this woman has been abused? Tell the audience if they want to see real flamenco, then they can wait five more minutes."

Jaime went to speak again, but both women gave him a stern look. He nodded and left the room.

Mercedes was buzzing with adrenaline, desperate to get back out there and show the audience what she was really made of. There was no way she was going to let a couple of fools ruin her career. She knew they would be waiting for her; eyes like daggers, stripping her naked, but she would show she was better than them and prove they were just scum of the earth.

"Let's get back out there, *guapa,*" said Lola, squeezing her hand as they stood backstage; waiting for the guitarist and singer to stop.

"*Gracias,*" said Mercedes.

"For what?"

"For being an inspiration."

"Shut up. If anyone is the inspiration, it's you for putting Jaime in his place like that." Lola blurted out a laugh to stop her crying and wrapped her arms around Mercedes.

"Ready?" said Mercedes. Lola nodded as they flew through the curtains. A low, surprised murmur spread through the crowd. All eyes fell on the women as they took their seats. Mercedes glanced over to the guitarist and singer, who both winked.

The guitarist began to play slowly, and the singer clapped as he let out a soft wail. The crowd fell silent.

"Venga, guapa," said the cretin from before. Mercedes ignored him.

"This one you do alone," whispered Lola. Mercedes nodded; she had to get through this test of courage. She clapped lightly at first, finding the rhythm of the singer and prepared herself for the performance of her life.

She could feel the passion and anger rising from within. She thought of her grandfather and knew he would be smiling now, proud of the way she was showing her courage and talent.

She stomped hard on the ground as she lifted her arms and tapped her feet, slowly at first, but gradually becoming faster. The singer sang louder and followed her moves.

Mercedes kept her mind focused and her head down. She refused to look at the idiots in the front row. She wouldn't give them the satisfaction. She thought of Javier, loading his car full of tinned tuna, and felt even more enraged. Adrenaline and energy ran through her body, guiding her moves, feeling the emotion build up inside her.

Soon she was in full swing; rotating her body in quick

short bursts as she twisted round, all the while smashing her heels on the floor as fast as she could while she took over the stage, engrossing the audience in her moves.

She felt the muscles in her body tense, and become stronger. It was time. The climax was coming.

"*Ole, ole,*" shouted people from the crowd.

"*Guapa, guapa.*"

The guitarist played faster, and the singer bellowed with all his might as they guided her towards the finale.

Then, as if some strange telepathic message vibrated through the three performers, Mercedes jumped a little just as she threw her arms down and stamped on the floor stopping dead alongside the music. The crowd went wild with applause.

Mercedes looked up, face serious. She held her head high. Lola came up and yanked Mercedes' arms in the air. The singer and guitarist moved towards them, holding their hands high in appreciation.

Mercedes had seen many live flamenco performances. She'd always admired the great dancers in Andalusia; the capital of flamenco, and that's why she felt so proud to be standing there on stage in front of Triana, showing them the talent she had, and not having given up after those crude comments. She looked down at the fools, who sat quietly as a couple of guilty teenagers after getting caught smoking in the bike sheds, and winked.

"What a night," said Lola, chinking glasses of white wine with Mercedes as they sat in a bar around the corner.

It wasn't bad, was it?" said Mercedes, beaming, on the outside.

"Not bad, we were brilliant. I loved watching the faces of those idiots while you danced. You really showed them."

"You were amazing too, dancing like that after me. The crowd loved you."

"Thanks. It was great for Jaime to offer us more work too."

"A perfect night," said Mercedes, suddenly feeling down.

She wished her family had been there to witness it though. She knew her mother would have been proud, and her father may have changed his tune of the world of flamenco. She wished he'd been to see her more often, then maybe he wouldn't have such a twisted opinion of her art.

She also thought of Javier, and, even though he was a ridiculous mummy's boy, she couldn't help feeling disappointed that he hadn't seen her dance.

"What's up?" asked Lola.

"Oh, nothing."

"Don't lie to me. I know you. What is it, Javier?"

"I don't know. I just wish I'd had a man by my side to support me."

"But you had me, what more do you need?"

"I know," said Mercedes, trying to force a smile. "You know what I mean, though."

"Yeah, you're right. I wish Miguel had been there tonight too."

"Why wasn't he?"

"I told him not to come; in case he cramped my style. He's always so loving in public, and I just couldn't deal with that tonight."

"I'm sure you'll deal with it when you get home though," Mercedes winked.

"Oh, of course. He'll be waiting up, and even if he isn't, I'll find my way of bringing him round."

They both laughed, but Mercedes felt empty. She wanted her own place to go back to with her boyfriend; not to her parents' place where her father would be snoring in the armchair waiting to make sure she got back in one piece, or have a go at her.

"So, what are you going to do about it?" asked Lola.

"About what?"

"All these mummy's boys that keep ruining your life."

"I don't know. I've run out of ideas."

"Have you thought about looking further afield?"

"What, like in Barcelona?"

"No, not dirty Catalan men; they are the worst. A foreign man is always more exotic, and there are plenty of them in Seville."

"But wouldn't getting attached to a foreign guy be dangerous. What if he wanted to leave?"

"All men want to leave; it's just how to make them stay."

"I suppose you're right. I have always had a soft spot for English guys."

"English? Yeah, why is that?"

"They are gentlemen, like that actor, what's his name in Four Weddings and a Funeral?

"Hugh Grant?"

"Yeah, aren't all English guys like that? Polite, caring, not obsessed with their mothers."

"But you also get those drunken English guys who come over here to ruin our beaches and lose their virginity."

"Yeah, that's true."

"But there's no harm in looking, is there?"

"I guess not. I suppose these things you can never plan."

"Exactly, another glass?"

On the way back to her house, Mercedes thought more

about seeing an English guy, and the idea grew on her. She'd always enjoyed English at school and loved a lot of English music. She could imagine getting married to a cute blond English guy and having a couple of blond kids with him. They seemed so much more exotic than Sevillanos.

As she crept in the door, trying not to make too much noise, a tall shadow scared the hell out of her.

"*Papa,*" she said, placing her hand on her chest to calm her beating heart.

"*Hija*, what time do you call this?" he asked, looking at his watch. His tired face was stern.

"Sorry, I went for a drink."

"What, with those gypsy flamenco louts?"

"No, with Lola. We got talking."

She really didn't have the energy to fight with her father, but she could sense something else was coming.

"What's this I hear about Javier?"

"It's over, *Papa*."

"But why? He was a good Sevillano, an honest, proud man."

"He was an idiot; he wouldn't even come to see me tonight." She knew her father would hate that comment.

"What's that supposed to mean?"

"That I want a man who will support and understand me." Not like you, she wanted to add.

"But Javier is a good man. He called me to say he was upset and he had to take his mother somewhere; surely you can understand his position."

She wanted to say she didn't care what he thought, and ask what sort of father would not support his own daughter's real passion in life anyway, just because he wasn't a fan of a certain type of people. She wanted to tell him that she didn't like Sevillano men anymore. She was sick of them, and that her next project was to find a gentle English man. But, as usual, she didn't.

"*Si, Papa.*"

"So, will you try to get back with him?"

"No, Papa. Look, I'm going to bed. Good night." She kissed him on the cheek and turned to go to her bedroom.

"You're making a big mistake," he said.

"Sure," she said, not turning around. She just didn't have it in her. She'd had enough of men for one day.

Once she'd showered and was tucked up in bed, she said her prayers. She wished for all her family to be healthy and gave thanks for the courage she'd found in her soul. For the first time ever, she asked for a real, honest, and reliable man to be dropped in her path.

Chapter 3 LOVE AT FIRST FLAMENCO

Mid-August, in a local Wetherspoon's pub in Northwood Hills

"What the hell have you done to your hair?" asked Joe as he stood at the bar with two pints of Carling. "Or should I say, what haven't you done, are you trying to become a Jesus Christ Superstar?" He let out a cackle as he shook Charlie's hand for the first time since that dreaded night at Bandoff. Charlie ran his hand through the back of his mane, which was starting to look longer.

"I'm growing it actually. Nice to see you too, mate," said Charlie, suddenly feeling guilty for not being in contact with his best mate for so long. He'd been too focused on his new life though; hiding away from anything British so he could concentrate on becoming a flamenco guitarist. "See you still have that creative fringe." Joe brushed his fringe to one side and smirked.

"It's an emo look."

"Gay look more like."

"Whatever you say, mate. So, you still going to sunny España?"

"You bet. Two days and I'm off for Seville."

"Bit of a drastic move, don't you think?"

"Drastic? You're joking. I've thought about this long and hard. It's the perfect time to go. I need to get away man; London has been getting me down, after all that madness at Bandoff…"

"Yeah, what the hell was that all about anyway?"

"Oh nothing, just stage nerves," he said. There was no way he was going to admit he'd been jealous of Hans, and in love with Cass. Had been. He was no longer, though.

How could he be in love with such a tart anyway? His new love in life was flamenco.

"Sure, sure. Saw Cass the other day." The mention of Cass made Charlie jumpy, and jittery.

"Oh yeah. She all right?"

"Not too bad."

"Still with Mr. Muscle?"

"No, some other bloke. Why, does it matter?" Silence followed as Charlie went for his pint. Did it matter? Nope. He didn't give a damn anymore.

"Not at all. What makes you say that?"

"Oh nothing, just the way you used to talk about her, drool over her, throw evils at Hans, and pretty much try to kill him."

"Was it that obvious?"

"As plain as the testicles on my face."

"But you don't have testicles on your face."

"That's not the point. Of course, it was bloody obvious. Why else would you launch your guitar at him?"

"I guess you're right," he said, suddenly feeling relieved. "I should have mentioned something before, but I wanted to keep it hush until I was sure."

"Is that why it's still hush then?"

"Yeah, I guess so. I suppose I did go a bit mental, but that's the funny thing about women, isn't it?"

"What's that?"

"They change you, manipulate you, and turn you into a fool."

"Yeah, I guess they do."

"Well, that's not going to happen to me again. I'm going away to learn the flamenco guitar, and I don't want any woman to get in my way."

"Sure, pint says next time I see you, you'll have a

señorita by your side."

"Deal."

They spat on their hands and shook them. As they stood in silence, sipping on their pints, Charlie began to relax as the beer hit his bloodstream and he felt the tension ooze away. He'd been worried about seeing his mate again, after ruining such an important night, but it seemed Joe could see the funny side already. That's what mates were for.

"Why Spain, anyway?" said Joe. "I didn't realise you could speak Spanish."

"I can't, well, couldn't, but I've been learning. See..." Charlie pulled out a Spanish phrasebook, a Spanish-English dictionary, and a photo of Paco Lucia.

"Who's that?" Joe said, laughing.

"He's one of the greatest flamenco guitarists of all time: Paco Lucia."

"Paco? Typical, I bet most Spanish blokes are called Paco, or Manuel. Like that waiter in Fawlty Towers. *Que?*" Joe looked up at the ceiling in a lost sort of way.

"Very funny."

"Can't believe you're leaving, mate."

"I know, feels weird to think soon I'll be in sunny Seville. My plan is to find a decent flamenco teacher, learn well enough, and then maybe come back here and set up my own flamenco school."

"You've got high hopes. How the hell are you going to do that?"

"By learning how to play like this legend," he said, holding up the picture.

"Have you been practising then?"

"Just a bit, yeah; a few hours a day."

"A day? What about Computer Jobbers?"

"I sort of quit."

"When?"

"A while back now." Charlie thought back to that day when he put Peter Prick Percy to shame and smiled.

"But why suddenly flamenco?" asked Joe, finishing his pint. "Two more pints, please," he said to the barman.

"I passed by a flamenco joint, just as I left Bandoff actually, and as I went in it just felt right, I felt at peace. Watching a couple perform flamenco on stage was exotic, different, and…"

"Was the dancer fit?"

"Yeah, she was actually. But that's not the point. I just want to try something different, mate. London is the same, so samey, same, same but the fucking same. I need some more excitement in my life, and I think flamenco can help."

"But won't you have to live with a bunch of gypsies?"

"Nah, I've found a flat online, opposite the river, right in the heart of Seville where flamenco first started, a region called Triana."

"Look at you, getting all cultured."

"Well, if I wanna make a go of this, then I need to be in the know."

"You're serious about this flamenco lark, aren't you?"

"Bloody right. Fancy a listen?"

"Go on then."

Charlie pulled out his flamenco guitar from its case and threw it up on his knee.

"What do you want me to play?"

"How should I know, flamenco, whatever, just make it snappy before someone comes over and beats you up for attempting to busk with that ridiculous haircut."

As Charlie whizzed through an array of rasguedos that

he'd learned over the last month, Joe watched in awe, impressed by how much his friend knew already.

"What do you think?"

"Not bad mate, enough to pull a couple of señoritas."

"Nah, I told you; that's not why I'm going."

"Ah, come on, Spanish women are gorgeous."

"Yeah, I know, but I don't need any distractions, not after…"

"Cass?"

"Yeah. The whore." They both laughed.

"Bit harsh."

"But fair. I'm not going to let a woman get in the way of my life anymore."

"Sure, that's what we all say. But in the end, it happens to the best of us," said Joe.

Charlie was convinced though. He wanted to remain single, go to Seville, and learn the flamenco guitar. Certainly no time for women.

Soon Charlie was saying *adios* to his parents. He was stood in the hall, with his rucksack and guitar resting against the giant, almost full, coca cola piggy bank.

"Don't forget, when that's full we'll take you out for a meal," said his Dad, trying not to get all emotional, unlike his mum.

"We're gonna miss you Charlikins," she said, giving him a hug.

"I'll miss you too, Mum." Charlie's throat seized up a little as he saw his mum was about to ball.

"You got everything; passport, boarding pass, the frozen faggots?" she asked, wiping her eyes.

"I can't take faggots to Spain, Mum."

"Why, are they illegal?"

"They should be," said his Dad, moving back in case she swung out and hit him.

"You've never complained about them before." She patted his belly.

"Get off," he said, pulling his t-shirt over his bulge.

"So when will you be back, Charlikins?" asked his Mum.

"Not sure, maybe at Christmas; not booked my flight yet."

"And you have a place to stay?"

"Yeah, the address is on the fridge. It's got a landline too in case you need me."

"But you'll have your mobile."

"'Course Mum."

"I just worry, that's all. Ah, my little boy running off to Spain, who would have thought it?"

"Not me," said his Dad, "could at least have chosen a country with a decent national football team."

"They've just won the World Cup and two Euros in a row."

"It was a fluke."

"Not bloody football again. Our son is going away, and all you can talk about is bloody football."

"He's only popping up the road; it's not as if he's going to Ausbloodystralia, which is just as well because the only people who play football out there are kangabloodyroos."

"Just be careful, don't do anything stupid, don't get drunk, and don't come back married to a Spanish woman."

"No chance of the last one happening," said Charlie, laughing. "Flamenco, flamenco, flamenco, that's me now. Ole," he said, stamping his feet and lifting his arms in the air. His parents frowned, worried about their son.

"Right, let's get you to that airport," said his Dad,

leading the way out the door.

"Okay, bye Mum." Charlie gave his Mum a stronger hug than normal, one that brought a tear to her eye. He even felt a bit choked up himself.

"Bye son, just enjoy yourself, and be good," she said, sobbing slightly with a tissue scrunched up in her hand.

"Sure," he said, wondering what 'being good' was in his mother's mind. Obviously, a lot different from his.

On the journey to the airport, Charlie and his Dad spoke mostly about football, nothing about missing home, looking after himself, struggling to communicate with local people in a different language, running out of money, or, especially, falling in love with a señorita.

But they didn't need to because they both knew deep down that it was all going to happen anyway. They were men and that shit normally happened. Women were always in the picture somewhere; whether they liked it or not.

"Right, son," said his Dad, giving him a hug at the drop off zone at Gatwick. "Be good, but if you can't be good, then don't let your guard down and never pay for sex."

"Thanks, Dad, good advice."

"Well, not directly, but if you get them a drink, or shout them a meal, then that's fine. That's how your mother and..."

"Great Dad, better go. See you when I see you."

"Not if I see you first." His dad winked and pointed his index finger at him. Charlie would miss him. As he got to the check-in desk, he realised he was alone, on his way to live in another country, with nothing but a guitar to keep him company.

When Charlie got off the empty airport bus by some

modern trams, he scrunched his eyes at the blast of August heat. He'd wanted a bit of sun, but this was ridiculous. It was absolutely scorching.

"Must be siesta time," he muttered to himself as he wiped his brow, leaving his wrist hairs smudged with sweat. He found some shade in a park opposite and checked his map to see if he was heading for Triana, where his new home awaited.

As Charlie made his way towards the River Guadalquivir, he felt excited that he was finally in mainland Spain. It was nothing like he'd expected: hardly any people, no wild bulls running around, and he was the only one with a guitar, but he could sense he'd arrived at a tranquil time. Wandering around Seville at four in the afternoon in August, on a crazily hot day, didn't give a true reflection of the city's full potential.

Once he'd got to the river, the beauty of the view surprised him. He hadn't imagined it to be so pretty, so quaint, like some made up city in a fairy tale. He stood in the middle of a bridge and gazed upstream. Towards the right was the mighty Giralda tower, sticking out over the city. In the distance, far away from the river was the countryside and a hill of light brown grass, obviously dying in the blistering summer heat. Little did he know, he was standing in a spot that would become extremely important to him throughout the next few years.

He gazed up to the flats overlooking the river and hoped his would be there; with a perfect view over the city where he could learn flamenco. He made his way over and soon found the block of flats. Within a few minutes standing in the blistering heat, a tall, lanky man pulled up in a car and got out.

"You are Carlos?" he asked, holding out a sweaty hand,

which Charlie shook.

"*Si, Carlos,* but most people call me Charlie."

"Okay, okay, Charlie. I am Manuel."

"*Que?*" said Charlie, stupidly mimicking Manuel from Fawlty Towers.

"Manuel," said Manuel, frowning. Typical, thought Charlie, thinking back to what Joe had said. He hoped Basil Fawlty's series had not made Spanish soil.

"We go up?"

Charlie followed Manuel into the stuffy building and up a dark staircase. He was worried whether he'd chosen the right place because of the depressing lack of light, but as soon as he entered the flat, he knew he'd hit the jackpot.

"Nice one," he said, scanning the one bed flat.

"You like? Good. Here, this is the kitchen, is clean, the bedroom in there, and you have sofa and TV, what more you need?"

"A cold beer would be nice."

"Sure, sure, you have time to get *cervezita,* no problem. Look, this is the best part of the flat." Manuel pulled up the rattling blinds to reveal the glorious view.

"Jesus," muttered Charlie as he gazed out over the river with the whole of Seville spread in front of him. The small balcony was just right for learning how to play flamenco. "This is perfect, just perfect."

"Of course it is. This is Sevilla's best location for any *guiri,* right above Calle Betis, and near to the river, you can take the sun outside all you want."

"What's a *guiri?*"

"A foreign person. Normally with a camera and wearing sandals with socks, but is anyone here from a different country."

"I see," said Charlie, wondering whether it was the same

as kraut or frog, but he presumed it was less insulting.

"So, why are you here anyway? An Erasmus?"

"What's that?"

"A foreign student, here to 'study Spanish' in our university."

"No, no, I'm here to become a flamenco guitarist."

"Youuuuu?" said Manuel, in a screeching high pitch as he laughed out loud. "Flamenco, that is funny. Okay, so why you really here?"

"No, honestly. I'm here to play," he said, flicking his guitar round.

"Okay, well, maybe I'll see you play at the Maestranza one day."

"What's that?"

"You don't know much about Seville, do you?"

"No, that's why I'm here."

"It's the best theatre here, look, you can see it over there," he said, pointing towards what looked like an indoor arena. Charlie wondered what it would be like to play there; probably less chaotic than The World's End in Camden. "Maybe I see you there one day, watching a show or something," he added, laughing.

Charlie was beginning to get irritated by Manuel; the half-wit who wouldn't take him seriously, but then again, why would he; he'd obviously never met a guitar genius.

"So, I need two months deposit, and you can have your keys. The contract is for one year, here," said Manuel, placing the Spanish written contract on the table. "You are going to stay for one year?"

"Sure, sure," said Charlie, not having thought much past the next week, but hey, it was just a piece of paper, and one that he didn't understand. His name was correct, as was the address, but that was about all he understood. He didn't care though, he handed over 1000€ and signed.

"*Fantástico,* so, here are your keys. Now, a few rules. Pay me to the account number on the contract here on the 1st of each month. Don't break nothing, and no crazy flamenco sex parties."

"Sure, sure," said Charlie, wondering what a crazy flamenco sex party would be like in the flat, probably pretty cramped.

"But if you have to break one rule, then, of course, I'd like to be invited." Manuel winked and shook Charlie's hand, showing himself out. "*Adios, guiri guitarist.*"

Charlie hoped not everyone in Seville would be as disbelieving of his guitar qualities, but he'd shut them up if need be. He was itching to play, so he dumped his bags, whipped out his guitar and opened the balcony window.

"Blimey," he said, closing it again to shelter himself from the heat. It was far too hot to play on the balcony. He wanted to be outside though, in the Spanish air, with his Spanish guitar, playing his Spanish music.

"Sod it," he said as he headed for the door, "surely, I can find a place under an orange tree or something."

Charlie crossed back over the river and made his way towards the heart of the city, following *la Giralda*. The air was so hot, though, as if a nuclear bomb had been dropped and blasted the citizens away, leaving nothing but the buildings and the horrible intense heat. No wonder the streets were deserted. He was glad though as he wasn't really up for playing in front of people just yet, especially after Manuel's comments.

By the time he got to *Plaza Virgen de los Reyes* round the back of the cathedral, he was gasping for cover. He walked past a line of horses parked up under the shade while their snoring owners kipped in the carriages, and sat down on a concrete bench under a withered orange tree.

As he sipped on some warm water, six dongs sounded above. He held up his right hand to shade the sun and gazed towards the top of the impressive Muslim tower.

He unzipped his guitar case and felt self-conscious, perhaps because he was a *guiri*, where no one would expect him to play well. He was slightly mad to be sitting on a bench at such an immensely hot stage of the day. Surely if a group of Spanish people walked past they would laugh at him.

He had to be brave though. He pulled out his deep brown cypress guitar, rested it on his knee and twisted the wooden pegs as he plucked his thumb along the steel strings. Once he'd tuned his guitar, he began to play slowly; striking his little finger on the lower string, then his ring finger, middle, and finally index. As he strummed over and over again, he felt at peace, glad to finally be in Seville, away from the stress and sameness of London. He was doing something new, exciting, and real.

As he played his favourite song; *Entre dos Aguas*, he closed his eyes and concentrated on his finger movements as the tune filled the empty square. The heat was suffocating, though, and his sweaty fingers slipped on the strings. He was struggling to find a rhythm, which wasn't helped when his foot was hit with something soft and squishy.

"What the…" he said, opening his eyes to see that his sandals and feet were covered in horse shit. The nasty stench shot up his nostrils.

"*Oiga*," shouted a butch horseman standing a few feet away, just in front of his horse and carriage. The muscle bound man wiped his hand on his grey trousers and pointed towards Charlie. "*Tonto guiri.*"

"Stupid foreigner? What's your problem?" Charlie said, kicking the dung off his sandals while rising to his feet.

"*Vete,*" said the horseman, ordering Charlie to leave as he turned and high-fived his colleagues. They all roared with laughter.

Charlie glared at the three men and wondered whether he could take them all out. He thought back to a fight he'd had at school; him against two tough bullies. During break, one had started on him because of his cheap Dunlops (his mother had refused to buy him Nike).

"Oi, cheapskate, your Mum get those from Tescos?" asked one.

"Yeah, where you get your best clothes." asked the other. Rage had built up in his body as he threw himself across the room, grabbing both by the collar and smashing their heads together. The rest of the class stood in awe as Charlie jabbed several punches to their ribs and threw one out the doorway and the other into a corner, smashing over a pile of violins.

If he had done it before, he could do it again.

"Nice shoes," shouted another horseman. The others laughed as they moved their hands in front of their noses and took deep whiffs.

Those painful memories rushed through Charlie's mind, making him tense. He placed his guitar back in its case and stormed over. The faces of the horsemen changed as they saw the angry *guiri* scouring towards them.

"What's your problem?" said Charlie, squaring up to the first man.

"Relax," said one.

Fight, fight, fight, echoed in his head, familiar chants to when he was back at school.

"Why did you throw that shit at me?" he said to the guy with traces of manure on his trouser pockets.

The three men looked at each other, completely unaware of what Charlie had said.

"*Porque?* – Why?" said Charlie, shrugging his shoulders as he moved closer.

Then he took a step back as the taller one lunged forwards.

"*Porque eres un guiri, no es tu sitio.*" Charlie had no idea that the guy had said it was because he was a foreigner, and this wasn't his place. He guessed he'd cussed him though, especially by the way he looked him up and down.

Charlie imagined grabbing the guy's arm and wrapping it around his back, smashing his head onto the horse cart, and kicking the other two in the nuts. But he knew himself, and although he was quite fit, there was no way he was going to take out three butch blokes, who, now that he was closer, did probably eat a lot of beef.

"You no can play the guitar, not like a Spanish," said one.

"Go, go," said the taller one.

"That might be a good idea," said a deep, thick accented voice from behind him. Charlie turned to see a tall, middle aged Spanish man with long, silver hair.

"Who are you?" asked Charlie, surprised, but relieved by the guy's interruption.

"That doesn't matter right now, but it's time to go; these men are not so, how shall we say, reasonable."

Charlie felt as if he'd been ordered by a knight to withdraw his weapon, so he backed away, immediately feeling protected as he followed the guy over to where he'd been sitting.

"*Adios,*" shouted the three men. Charlie went to turn round, but the man kept him moving forwards.

"Just leave it; they are not worth it."

"Sure, you're right. Thanks," said Charlie as they got to the bench. The guy just shrugged as if he'd done it a thousand times. "What's your name?"

"I'm Ramón." He held out his muscular, but slender hand.

"Charlie, *mucho gusto,*" he said, shaking hands.

"Ah, you speak Spanish?"

"Just a bit. Your English is good."

"Thanks. I've visited a few countries; mainly on business."

"What do you do?"

"I am a teacher, of flamenco." The way Ramón said 'flamenco' made Charlie's neck shiver, such passion and power. He wanted to say that he was looking for a teacher, but something was holding him back; could he really trust this bloke? Why was he out wandering the streets on his own?

"A flamenco teacher, eh?"

"Yes, and listening to you, you may need one." *The cheek,* thought Charlie.

"What do you mean? You haven't even heard me play."

"I was watching from over there," he said, pointing to the corner of the square. Charlie felt intimidated by the smooth, charismatic guy. No one had ever criticised the way he played. "Listen, why don't we find somewhere else, away from those *imbeciles.*"

"Sounds good to me."

Despite feeling unsure about Ramón, Charlie packed up his guitar and followed him as he paced towards *Barrio Santa Cruz* - the old Jewish quarter. They walked in silence across a wide patio scattered with parched orange trees, through a small tunnel and ended up in the delightful *Plaza Doña Elvira;* a tiny hidden square where thick trees and three floored buildings provided a cool shade. Empty tables and chairs from several restaurants lined the outside of the square.

"Over here," said Ramón, pointing towards a ceramic stone bench in front of a trickling fountain. "Let's hear you play."

Charlie felt nervous. Since learning the flamenco guitar, he'd only played in front of his parents and Joe. Now he had to play for a flamenco expert.

"Sure," he said, beginning to strum. As he played, he closed his eyes and searched for his rhythm. He thought back to all the videos he'd watched on Youtube and chose a *rasguedo* that he *thought* he'd perfected.

Ramón watched with a serious face, smiling now and then, and nodding with approval.

"You play well for a *guiri,*" he said once Charlie had stopped and rested the guitar on his lap.

"A *guiri*? That word again."

Ramón laughed.

"So, you know what it means?"

"I've been here about three hours, and that's the third time I've been called it."

"Well, get used to it, *guiri* guitarist, because that's what people will call you whether you like it or not."

"Great." Charlie tried to control his disappointment, but he couldn't help feel as if he was being judged already, just because he wasn't Spanish.

"Don't take offence; it really isn't as bad as everyone makes out."

"Sure," said Charlie, but he sensed there was some sort

of negative feeling about the word.

"Listen, like I said you play well, but you are no *flamenco*."

Charlie felt a blow to his confidence. Ramón was probably right, after all, he'd only been playing a month, but he was more used to positive comments about his guitar skills. The truth hurt.

"Have you had classes?"

"Not officially."

"It shows." There it was again, Ramón's condescending tone made Charlie feel like an amateur. "Why do you want to play flamenco, anyway?" Charlie wanted to close up and not answer. Ramón was annoying him. But he felt obliged to speak.

"I just do, I like it. It's so exotic, exciting, and passionate."

"I see, and why are you in Seville?"

"I've heard it's the best place to learn. I want to improve my level, maybe play in front of an audience, and then go home and teach flamenco."

"You have a lot of dreams," said Ramón, the way he smiled in a friendly manner made Charlie begin to open towards him. "Where is home, anyway?"

"London."

"A great city, great women, and great beer; even if it is warm."

"You've been to London?" Charlie sat forward, eager to hear his response.

"Many times. I used to play there when I was younger."

"Did you like it?"

"I loved London, the buzz, the bridges and the blonds. I conquered many of your women, so much easier than the señoritas here."

"Sure," said Charlie, taking his word for it. He had to keep his focus, no women, only flamenco. "Do you still play?"

"Real *flamencos* never stop playing."

Again there was a silence, but a comfortable one. Charlie was beginning to trust him. He seemed like a reasonable guy after all.

"I'm actually looking for a teacher," he said, feeling like a young, inexperienced lad.

"Well, you certainly need one," said Ramón in a lighter tone.

"Why do you keep speaking about my playing like that?" asked Charlie, tensing up again.

"Please," said Ramon as he held out his left hand and eyed his guitar. "Let me show you." Charlie handed it over. Ramon flipped the guitar round, held it in place, and tapped the side.

"*Ole*," he said, beginning to pluck faster and more accurate than Charlie had ever seen. He gazed in awe, amazed at the speed Ramon switched through various styles. Charlie was out of his league, but he was determined to play like him, one day.

"Blimey," said Charlie, once Ramón had stopped.

"Thanks. Listen, you may want to play well, but there are many secrets to flamenco."

"I'm sure," he said, collecting his guitar, "like what?"

"You are keen, I like that, but I can't tell you. You have to see and feel it."

"How?"

"I will help, but you have to listen to me. A *guiri* can never be a real *flamenco*." Ramon grabbed Charlie's hands and scraped his fingers along the inside. Charlie pulled back.

"That hurt."

"It's supposed to; flamenco is about pain. If you want a flamenco adventure, then you must be prepared to feel everything, to put your mind, body, and soul into this."

"I'm ready."

"You think you are, but you are not. Listen, tonight we can meet. I will take you to see a real flamenco *tablao*." Charlie was totally drawn in.

"Great, what time?"

"Here at nine."

"*Gracias* Ramón."

They shook hands.

"Oh, and one last thing," said Ramón.

"What's that?"

"Have a shower, you stink of *mierda*."

"Yeah, I guess I do," said Charlie, laughing for the first time since the horsemen had picked on him.

As Ramon walked away chuckling to himself, Charlie packed up his guitar and made his way back to his flat, completely bewildered by what had just happened; could he really trust Ramon? Was it too good to be true that he'd just stumbled across a real flamenco teacher?

Mercedes was late again. She'd got into an argument with her father about not drying the sides of the shower blinds. Damn him, she muttered as she darted through the park by her flat, almost tripping on the uneven cobbled path. Such a pointless row. She was convinced he always tried to make her late so she would lose her job and give in to his traditional ways. But she wouldn't stand for it. She was not the woman he wanted her to be. She refused to become just another housewife. He was so dated; plenty of women in Seville were hardworking and career minded.

As she reached the river, the intense heat hit her in the face, and she pleaded for autumn to arrive soon. She hated such grotesque temperatures, especially when she was about to dance in a stuffy *tablao*.

Even though she was more confident after three months dancing in public, she was still unsure of what to expect from the men in the audience each night. Some nights were fine, and no one would make any comments, but other times she would have to put up with rude and vulgar remarks from the filthy men, normally in the front row. She hated the way some men ogled her, trying to catch a glimpse of her chest as she danced. How many times had she been put off by men licking their lips or blowing dirty kisses at her? Not to mention the times she'd been groped in the bar after. But she wouldn't give in; dancing and flamenco were her soul, her passion, her dream.

Once at the *tablao*, Mercedes darted through the crowd in the first room, past the pianist warming the audience, weaved in and out of drinkers at the bar, and rushed around the back into her dressing room.

"I was beginning to think you'd finally found a decent lover and was having a steamy sex session."

"I wish."

"Oh well, maybe tonight will be your lucky night," she said, pulling up her dress to make her cleavage fuller.

"Mine, or yours?"

"I don't need another man, I have a real one at home."

"How is Miguel?"

"Just fine. It's a shame you can't find a man like him: real macho and great in the bedroom like a bull on fire."

"No thanks, he's not my type."

"I don't think you know your type, *cariño*."

"True."

Silence followed as they both got ready. Mercedes wondered if she was right. Did she have a type? Or even know what her type was? She'd been thinking about what she had said about finding a foreign guy, one who wasn't such a mummy's boy or as macho as the guys here. She'd seen a few cute looking ones out and about, but they normally had a girlfriend within hugging distance. She'd have to just hope for the best.

Mercedes clipped a white rose on the side of her bun and dried the sweat by the sides of her eyes with a handkerchief. As she put on her black high heels, there was a knock at the door.

"*Venga*," shouted Jaime. "They are waiting."

"Well, let them wait, *joder*, we are worth it," said Lola, flicking her head back and sticking a middle finger up at the door.

Shortly, they left the dressing room, holding hands as always and wishing each other luck. As Mercedes followed Lola through the doorway onto the stage, the stuffy air hit the back of her throat. She glanced at the audience. A hundred heads and two hundred pairs of eyes were staring. She ignored them and focused on the task ahead.

"*Ole*," shouted one man, as she clonked on the wooden stage and sat on a steel stool next to the others.

"*Guapa*," shouted another.

"*Te lo voy a comer*," shouted a third. Mercedes cringed at his vulgar comment that he would eat her up. She had to concentrate. The guitarist began to strum slowly. The singer clapped softly. Silence fell.

Charlie was stood next to Ramón at the back of the

tablao, wondering just how the hell he'd been so lucky. He'd barely been in Seville five hours and had already settled in his flat, found a motivated, passionate flamenco teacher, and was now about to witness his first live flamenco performance in Spain.

He scanned the stage where the four flamenco artists sat: a guitarist, a singer, and two dancers. The guitarist and singer were darkly tanned, tall men with long black hair hanging over their black shirts. The dancers were exactly how he'd imagined flamenco dancers to be: black haired, attractive, wearing colourful dresses, and proud looking women.

Charlie noticed how one seemed much more confident, scanning the audience as if looking for her lover, whereas the other just stared at her feet.

"Focus on the guitarist," said Ramón, sharply in Charlie's ear.

"*Si, si,*" said Charlie, nodding, surprised at Ramón's tone. "Watch how he moves his hands, arms, body, and face. If you want to be *un flamenco*, then this is what you need to do."

Charlie followed the guitarist's moves and began to realise that maybe he was out of his league after all. The guitarist was so cool and natural and the way he captured the audience was impressive. He was broken out of his gaze by the singer wailing. At first, it sounded as if he was in some sort of pain, the way he scrunched his face as he belted out his flamenco words, but soon Charlie began to feel the emotion igniting the audience and became absorbed in the show.

Despite the genius guitar player and magically powerful singer, Charlie's eyes kept wandering over to the dancers. They were still sat next to each other, clapping more furiously now. The more confident one was making expressive facial moves, suggesting she was angry about something. He felt her passion. Then, as the other one sprang up, Charlie's heart moved.

It was as if some miraculous force dragged his eyes towards the dancer. He stared at her face, desperate to catch a glimpse of her eyes. He'd never felt such power and curiosity about someone he'd never met before. He was petrified.

As she patrolled along the stage, moving her body in quick fiery motions, Charlie felt inspired, blown away by her performance and beauty. The way she stomped on the floor, keeping her head down in the process, made Charlie eager to see her eyes properly. Suddenly Cass's face flashed in his mind. He'd fallen for her firstly because of her eyes, and look what mess that had gotten him into. He had to control his emotions. He was there to become a guitarist; a woman would only get in his way and ruin any chances of success.

But he couldn't take his eyes off her. He was desperate to catch a proper glimpse of her face.

Then he started to have weird thoughts. Instead of imagining her naked, like most guys do when they meet someone attractive, he was picturing her walking with him along the river laughing at his jokes. He also imagined how she would look in the morning as she opened her eyes and smiled at him. He was convinced she would look fine, with no need to put on makeup; a sign of real beauty. Surely, she'd look great walking around his flat in only one of his shirts, showing her cute behind.

"Focus, *joder*," snapped Ramón. Charlie jumped, completely woken from his daze. But after a couple more minutes watching the guitarist, his eyes fixed on her again, impressed by how she was dancing passionately and winning the hearts of the crowd.

Then he witnessed her full beauty. She came to a halt by stomping her feet on the ground and raising her hands. As she lifted her head and eyes, she stared straight at him. Her brilliant opaque eyes caught him. Her look of innocence and pain struck his heart as if she was crying out for someone. He smiled. A pathetic smile that his parents, and Joe, would have laughed at. One of those smiles that take control of your face when you watch a romantic film and realise that the two main characters are, after all, actually in love.

Mercedes' body had frozen. It was as if she was on the beach, staring out to sea, with a tsunami heading straight for her. She couldn't move. Fear had taken over. She was in shock. A guy had never looked at her like that before. His deep blue piercing eyes met hers and sent a wave of emotion straight to her pulsating heart. Where was he from? Not from Seville.

She had never felt such power from a gaze before, such a strong feeling of admiration. Normally men stared at her in a sex obsessed way, but his look was soft and sensual. For the first time ever, she smiled on stage after a flamenco performance. He smiled back, and her heart jolted.

She inhaled in short, sharp bursts as her eyes fixed in a trance, oblivious to the cheers and applause from the crowd as his smile hypnotized her. She felt as if she had just fallen from an orange tree and was drifting through the air in slow motion, waiting for him to catch her and tell her that everything was going to be all right. Who was he? And why did she suddenly feel a burning desire to run through the crowd and kiss him?

"What's up with you?" whispered Lola, nudging her in the back.

"Nothing, nothing," she said, remembering she was on stage.

Lola held Mercedes' arm in the air. The guitarist and singer got to their feet, lifting their hands and signalling for the audience to stand.

"*Guapa, guapa,*" shouted the crowd, but Mercedes panicked as she lost sight of the man. The crowd was blocking her view. She raised herself on her tiptoes to try to see him, but it was no use, by the time the audience had taken their seats again, he was gone. Panic filled her stomach as she worried she would continue falling and falling from the tree, and never be caught.

Sadness clouded her emotions. She felt scared and alone; as though she'd just said goodbye to her one and only love as he set off to fight a war.

"What's going on?" said Lola, as they got to the dressing room.

"Nothing, why?"

"I've never seen you like that, your face looked so happy for a few seconds, then your expression changed as if someone had told you they didn't want to marry you after all."

What if it was true? What if he was the one and she would never get that chance again. She told herself to buckle up and stop being so sensitive and silly. If he was the one, then he would have stuck around.

"Oh it was nothing, just happy that I danced so well, what did you think?"

"I think the audience told you everything; tonight, my dear, you were better than me."

"*Anda,*" she said, flicking her hand up at her colleague

and belittling her comment.

"Trust me, you were fantastic tonight, you have been growing as a dancer the last few months, but tonight you had a different energy. It was as if you knew that someone in the audience would be watching you, someone who could change your life."

"Who knows, maybe there was," she said, jokingly, but secretly hopeful it was true.

"I'm going for a drink with Miguel, do you want to come?"

"No thanks; I'd better get home."

"Fine, I need to go, you know how he gets if I'm late; turns into a bloody psychopath. I'll call you, well done again." Lola kissed her on the cheek.

As usual, she left on her own but sneaked in through the bar just to see if he was there, but there was no luck. As she made her way home, her mind felt clouded. What had just happened? She felt as if it had been a dream. Where had he gone? Where was he from? With those blue eyes and blond hair she guessed from England or America, or maybe Scandinavia. Would she ever get to see him on top of her? She blushed at her own imagination. She had fantasized about many men, but this one was different.

She imagined him next to her in bed, flicking his hands through her hair and smiling at her, making her laugh, making her feel special. She couldn't even imagine what he looked like naked, didn't need to, it was the person within that she was curious about. He seemed gentle and kind. She wondered if he was a mummy's boy. Obviously not if he was in a foreign country on his own. No man she'd met in the past would have the balls to travel to another country alone.

To think she would never see him again filled her heart

with sadness. Maybe he would return the following night. She prayed that he would.

As Charlie walked alongside Ramon, clonking along the cobbled streets lit up by the dimmed lights, he felt an aching pain in his gut. It wasn't the effect of the several beers mixed with the spicy kebab they'd just eaten, but the influence of the dancer. He felt as if he'd just come across a five hundred euro note on the floor, and someone whipped it out of his hands before he had the chance to enjoy it. He'd witnessed real class and beauty, and had unwillingly been torn away from any hope of showing his appreciation.

"Now we go to meet a friend of mine," said Ramón, patting Charlie on the back.

"Sure," he said, trying to hide his lack of enthusiasm. He wanted to run back to the *tablao* and test whether the emotions he felt were real.

"What's wrong? This next *tablao* is *impressionate*. I thought you wanted to know about the world of flamenco?"

"I do, I do," said Charlie, nodding his head and smiling. But it was a false smile; the kind of smile he used to throw at his grandmother when she plonked her famous lemon meringue pie on the table, usually full of surprise nose hairs.

"So?"

"Nothing, it's just I liked that *tablao*; the flamenco was amazing."

"The flamenco or the dancers?"

Charlie turned to Ramón, trying to hide the smirk appearing at the corner of his mouth. "What do you mean?"

"What did you think of the guitarist?"

"He was brilliant."

"Really, why?" said Ramón. He stopped and grabbed Charlie's shoulders. "What made him so brilliant?"

Charlie felt startled. He didn't want to mess up with his teacher.

"He had style, the way his fingers moved quickly showed his skill. But…"

"But what?"

"He was no touch on you."

"No touch?"

"Not as good as you, and, I think I can play better too."

Ramón laughed.

"Well, you are right that he is not as good as me, but whether or not you can play better is another question. I'm not sure you have what it takes."

"Why not?" said Charlie, suddenly feeling threatened.

"Because you were more interested in the *tetas* of the dancers."

"I was not." How could he think such a thing? It was perhaps the only time he hadn't noticed the perfectly formed breasts of a woman - or maybe he had, subconsciously.

"Do you know how many *guiris* I've taught?"

"Not many."

"None. They don't have what it takes to become *un flamenco*. I thought you might, but maybe I'm mistaken. Flamenco is all about showing the world our emotions, but you have demonstrated that you are just another *guiri*, only interested in coming here to drink our cheap beer and try to bed our women."

"That's not true Ramón, look, I'm sorry. It was my first live performance; I just got a little distracted."

"Look," said Ramon, sharply. "I want to believe in you, but you have to promise me you can't get involved with these women. Concentrate on your talent, you have a gift, but that gift needs wrapping before you can give it to the world."

Charlie remembered why he was there; to learn flamenco. He thought of Cass, of Hans lying on the floor in a pool of blood, and felt foolish for getting caught by the dancer's beauty so quickly. As if she would be interested in him anyway.

"I suppose you're right," he said. "Let's start again."

"Fine," said Ramón, "in the next place I want full details on the guitarist, not fantasies about the dancers, or they'll be trouble."

"Deal," he said, holding out a hand. As he shook hands he promised himself he'd try his best to maintain his focus, but his devious side was telling him to keep his options open.

Chapter 4 THE TRUTH OF FLAMENCO

Two weeks later

Mercedes' pulse shot up. Was that him? She extended her back so she could see over her mother's head as they sat having breakfast. She peered at the guy with long blond wavy hair waiting in the queue for *churros*.

"Mercedes," snapped her mother.

"*Como*?" she said, shaking herself out of her gaze.

"The coffee," said Rosa, eyeing towards Mercedes' cup.

"Yes?"

"What do you mean 'yes'? You've spilt it again."

Mercedes hadn't realised she'd knocked into the table causing the coffee to spill over the side of the cup into the saucer. She hated it when that happened. She reached out and grabbed a wad of serviettes from the small tin dispenser, lifted her cup, and began to dab away.

As she raised her head and glanced towards the *churros* stand, she saw him walking towards her, but, yet again, for what seemed like the thousandth time in the last two weeks, her soul misted over as she realised it wasn't him. Not unless he'd aged ten years and his nose had grown a further three centimetres.

Mercedes had been driving herself crazy. She probably could have avoided getting herself in such a state had she tried to forget about the blue-eyed *guiri*, but she just couldn't let him go. Whether she was nipping out to buy bread in the morning, having a coffee with Lola before work, or on stage dancing, she was on the constant hunt for him.

She tried to make it easier on herself and just except there was no way she would ever see him again, but when she got crude comments from builders asking her what time her legs opened, or when a sleaze tried to grab her behind after a flamenco performance, she kept her fingers crossed that he would appear again.

She was most hopeful of spotting him when she danced. Each time she came out on stage, she held her head high to scan the crowd. When he didn't appear, her heart felt a pang of sadness and left her empty, as if she'd lost someone close.

"If your father was here now, you know what he'd say," said her mother in a stern voice, yet again snapping her out of her daydream.

"Yes, *Mama*," she said, raising her eyebrows. "But he's not, so let's not worry about him." She sighed as she took a sip of coffee and felt relieved her father had gone to see a client. God forbid he'd seen her spill her coffee; what a disastrous start to the day it could have been.

"So," said her mother, in an inquisitive tone as she flicked her straight black hair over her shoulder. "Who is he?"

Mercedes tensed up.

"He?" she asked, mirroring her mother's action with the same flick. They were like twins at times, apart from the twenty-five year age gap, a few wrinkles, and slightly flabbier body parts.

"Don't play with me, *Hija*," she said in a soft tone. "You are my blood." Mercedes blushed. "You have been acting different recently, perhaps the last two weeks or so. At times there's a spring in your step; you seem happy, content, but other moments you are in your own world and sadness fills your eyes. Those are sure signs of being in love, so who is he?"

"I don't know what you're talking about."

But as soon as she denied it, she regretted not telling the truth. Maybe this was the chance to pour out her emotions. It made her feel silly though; she had fallen for a foreigner who she'd not even spoken to.

"You are a terrible liar Mercedes; from the age of four I've always known when you lie; you fiddle with your hair."

Mercedes looked down and saw that she'd weaved plaits around her fingers. She glanced up at her mother, whose warm smile seemed trusting.

"Let's walk," said Mercedes, sipping the last of the coffee.

As they made their way towards the park entrance, a slight chill blew through the air, rippling the conifer trees. Mercedes decided that she would let her mum in on her secret, but not give away too many details as she knew what a state she could get in.

"So, tell me about this new boyfriend. What's he like?"

"I don't have a boyfriend."

"Okay, maybe it's early days, but someone has entered your heart." Mercedes was amazed her mother knew her so well. She thought she'd covered up any signs of falling for him.

"It happened a couple of weeks ago, while I was dancing."

"I knew it." Rosa clapped her hands and grinned like an excited adolescent.

"Calm down, *Mama*."

"Was it Jaime, the owner? He's a good man, strong, rich, and a true Sevillano."

"No, *Mama*. He's my boss; that would just be wrong." Maybe this was a bad idea, how was she going to say she'd grown attached to a *guiri*?

"So, who is it then?"

"You don't know him." I don't even know him, she thought.

"Oh, someone new. Well, that's fine, as long as he looks after you."

"I'm sure he would," she said.

"So, what's his name? How many times have you been out with him? Why haven't you said anything before? When can we…"

"*Mama*, stop. Listen, he was a guy I saw in the audience."

"Well, that's good, isn't it? At least he knows you're a fantastic dancer. Did he come up to you after?"

"No, *Mama*."

"Wow, you made the first move. That's brave of you dear, but you should really let the man come to you, after all…"

"I didn't make a move."

"So who did?"

"No one, yet."

"Oh. So, let me get this right. You have fallen for a man, but you haven't spoken to him." Rosa looked deep into Mercedes' eyes.

"Yes." She was feeling stupid now.

"Okay. And he was in the audience."

"Yes."

"Right, so how can you have fallen for him without speaking to him?" Exactly.

"I don't know; that's the problem."

"Do you know where he lives? Where he works?"

"No."

"His name?"

"No."

"Then, what do you know about him?"

"That he seems like a kind, charming man."

A split second of silence followed as Rosa tried to work Mercedes out. Meanwhile Mercedes looked away, hoping that this conversation would just end.

"How do you know he's a charming man?"

"Because he didn't stare at my chest like most of the other men."

"Well, that's a start I guess. What else?"

"That he looked straight into my eyes as if he'd just fallen in love with me."

"Go on." Rosa smiled at her daughter.

"And that he is unlike the usual men from here." As soon as he said the word 'here' her mother frowned.

"What do you mean 'here'? What, is he an alien or something?"

"Of course not, but he isn't your typical Sevillano, with drool hanging from his mouth as he watches me dance."

"Don't be ridiculous. Why do you have such a jaded opinion of the men here?"

"You're not the one on stage four times a week."

"Where is he from then?"

There it was; the key question that she had been dreading.

"Guessing from his blond hair and blue eyes, I'd say not from Spain."

"Not from Spain?" said Rosa, laughing nervously. "Well, that just won't do. We have not brought you up to get married to some Egyptian."

"He's hardly going to be from Egypt with blond hair. Maybe he's English or American."

"Oh my, so far. America is on the other side of the world, and how would we ever communicate with him?"

"You both know a little English."

"Well, your father does…" Rosa suddenly jolted as if she'd realised something awful. She had. "What in the name of God will your father say?"

"It doesn't matter."

"Doesn't matter? Your father? But listen to yourself child. You have just told me you have fallen for an American you haven't even spoken to, what has got into you?"

There it was. Reality hit home. Maybe she was daft, but even so, it would have been a relief to know she had her mother's support. By the sounds of it, that wasn't going to happen. At least Lola would stick by her.

"Let's just leave it; you obviously think I'm a silly young girl. Anyway, I need to get to work."

"I'm sorry. I know you need to go, but I'm just concerned. I want to see you happy, and the last two weeks you haven't been yourself."

"I know, but there was something about him. I've never felt such a connection before."

"I see," said her mother, sounding worried, "but he's a *guiri*. How do you know he's the one?"

She remained silent. She looked ahead towards the end of the gardens. She felt young and foolish. She knew it was a long shot, but she had faith that there was something special about him. She wanted her mother to be happy for her, to trust her, but it seemed she was already against the idea, and she was scared of her own husband.

"I just know, *Mama*." A tear trickled from her eye.

"Come on, *Hija*." Her mother pulled her closer and wrapped her arms around. "You've always had a soft spot for blond men." Mercedes felt slight relief. "Perhaps that's why you haven't met the right man yet."

It was useless. She would never understand. They hugged and kissed each other on the cheek and Mercedes headed towards the flamenco studio; partially relieved that she'd been able to let her feelings out, but also upset that maybe her mother was right, was she hoping for the impossible?

Charlie's mind had also clouded over with a similar desire. Each day, as he played his guitar, he thought back to that night when she'd smiled at him. He imagined her walking slowly in front, tapping her shoes on the floor and bending her head slightly to flash a deep sexy smile, one of love and devotion. He'd never been captured by such beauty before.

The feeling of attraction and curiosity scared the hell out of him though. He didn't want his emotions to get the better of him; not like they had with Cass, the cow.

"Carlito," Ramón shouted. "What the hell are you playing at?"

Charlie gazed up as Ramón stood in front of him, arms folded, with a scouring face. They were on the terrace in his studio. Scattered around were red roses in wide blue pots and *La Giralda* towered over Ramón's shoulder in the background.

"Sorry, I was just warming up."

"Warming up? This is flamenco, not Guns and Roses."

"Guns and Roses?"

"Yes, you started playing *Live and Let Die*."

"Oops, sorry about that," he said, looking down at the position of his fingers. How had that happened?

"Come on, we are here for a reason." Ramón spun on the spot, clapped his hands, and paced over to Charlie. His thick heeled black shoes clonked on the panelled floor, denoting his aggression. Once Ramón was next to him, he turned, pulled at the groin of his beige trousers, sat down, smoothed down the crisp white shirt over his chest, and breathed in deeply.

"Listen, Carlito," he said, calmly. "You are a gifted guitarist, but you have to take these classes more seriously."

"But…"

"No buts. Come on, play with style, like I showed you, like *un flamenco*."

Charlie tried to concentrate as he played, but his imagination wondered. She appeared again; turning in slow circles, teasing him with her voluptuous moves. He craved to see her, to get close and feel her energy. The problem was he didn't have the guts to go and see her.

"Not bad," said Ramón as Charlie finished. "You are improving."

"*Gracias*."

"But you are not *un flamenco*."

Charlie felt a pang of resentment. Ramón was a great mentor, but his direct ways were destroying at times.

"But how can I be *un flamenco* after only a couple of weeks in Seville?"

"Good point, but by now I was hoping to see some more style, more *arte*. Let's see, something is not quite right."

Ramón stood up and stared. As he paced back and forwards, stroking his stubbly face, Charlie noticed the style with which he moved. He was like a matador; every twist and turn was forceful, important, and dominating. He wondered what Ramón had been like back in his prime; surely a popular man, and a world class guitarist.

"It's not just the playing," said Ramón, walking up close. "Stand up."

Charlie did so. Ramón grabbed his guitar and rested it on a stand.

"That's the problem," he said, smiling, "your clothes." Charlie looked down at his sandals and shorts, then at the rolled up sleeves on his tatty crumpled shirt. "You cannot be *un flamenco* dressed like that. Even the poorest of gypsies have more taste."

"What do you mean?" said Charlie; no one had ever said anything about his dress sense before. "What's wrong?"

"Wrong? What's right? Everything is wrong, the colours, style, you need to start dressing like *un flamenco* if you are to become one."

"But why is that important?"

Ramón let out a deep laugh.

"Because flamenco is about the show, dressing right, and making an impression. Think back to all the performances you've seen so far, do the guitarists ever wear shorts and old sandals? Is the dancer in nothing but the most immaculate dress?"

Charlie thought of the woman and how perfectly her dress fit to her slender figure.

"Okay, you've got a point."

"Of course I have. I should have told you the first time I met you, back in the plaza when your sandals were covered in horse shit. Anyway, tonight you must wear a white shirt and black trousers – it's important."

"Why, what's happening?"

"If you want to be the best, you must learn from the best. A friend of mine is singing tonight with a gypsy guitarist; he's astonishing."

"Great," said Charlie, feeling excited. "Where are we going?"

"You remember that place I first took you? *Las Almas*."

Charlie's nerves blasted out of his heart through his veins and hit his stomach with a punch. "Meet me over the road in the bar at nine."

"Sure," said Charlie, suddenly edgy.

"What is it? A *problema*?"

"No, not at all; everything is fine."

"Hmm," said Ramón, "there's another thing."

"What's that?" Charlie dreaded that Ramón would confront him about the woman.

"You need to practice more, much more. Until your fingers mould to the guitar. How many hours are you playing?"

"About three or four a day."

"Pah," Ramón said, flipping around and stamping on the floor. "Only? That is nothing. Do you know how many hours Paco Lucia plays for?"

"Quite a few I guess."

"Quite a few I guess," Ramón mocked in a perfect English accent. "Eight or nine," he added, almost shouting as he switched back into his strong Andalusian accent. "That's how much I practised to start with, now you should do the same. You need to play until your hands and your guitar become one; like a painter and his brush, a writer and his pen, a flamenco dancer and her castanets."

Now his energy was motivating, why couldn't he always be like that? Charlie grinned as he held out his hand. Ramón smiled back and shook it firmly.

"Thanks, Ramón."

"Don't thank me just yet; you still have a long way to go."

He was thankful though, not only because of his inspiration to play even more but because hopefully, he was going to lead him to her again.

As Charlie left the studio, the sun was shining, and there was a slight breeze in the air. He was glad the intense summer heat had disappeared, and autumn was on its way. It just wasn't comfortable wading through desert temperatures in Europe.

As he made his way home, whistling along past the cathedral and up towards the river, his eyes kept looking out for her. Every time he saw a woman with long black hair his heart beat faster, hoping it was her. But it never was. The curious urge to see whether the feelings he had for her were true were doing his head in. He felt ashamed for not having the courage to go back to the *tablao* and see her dance again, but he just couldn't bring himself to do it.

He'd tried lying to himself, pretending that she was probably a mad, psychopathic woman who would overpower him, demand to get married, and have five snotty babies, but he knew in his heart that she was more likely a gentle, funny, and loving person, who may only want one or two kids, which he could probably cope with.

What was happening to him? Why was he having these bizarre thoughts? Usually, his images about potential girlfriends were about how they would look naked, or whether their bum would be lean. Even though he had imagined these things, of course (and he was convinced her bum would be lean), the curiousness of finding out her personality and passions were stronger.

He tried to switch off his feelings as he'd promised himself not to get involved with anyone; flamenco, flamenco, flamenco, but the thought of seeing her again filled him with a new, strange desire. He'd felt attracted to other women before, but this was different; it was more than lust, something pure and real.

He was anxious about the night. What if she wasn't

there? If she had moved on and he'd lost his chance. He'd only have himself to blame, sometimes he was such a fool. If she was there, he'd have to make a move.

"See you tonight then," said Mercedes as she kissed Lola twice on the cheeks as they locked up the dance school and began walking towards the centre.

"Unless something interesting happens to me," said Lola.

"What do you mean?"

"I don't know. I'm just a bit tired of *Las Almas*, we've been there for ages now, and I need a new adventure."

"At least there's that new singer and guitarist tonight."

"Yeah true, but we don't know anything about them."

"You can only hope for the best," said Mercedes, thinking of him.

"What's up with you?" asked Lola, smirking. She stopped walking and tugged Mercedes' hand.

"What do you mean?" asked Mercedes, feeling tense like she had with her mother.

"No need to get touchy. I was just asking. You don't seem yourself, like you are in a different world or something, deep in thought. Have you met a sexy man and not told me about him?

"Of course not," she lied, feeling guilty. She wanted to tell Lola that she was losing her mind, but she had to rush home.

"I hope you're not lying to me."

Mercedes couldn't help but grin.

"You know I'd tell you if I was sure. Look, I need to go."

"Sure? So there is someone, you dirty little cow." Lola tried to grab her arm, but Mercedes pulled away.

"See you later," she said, running off laughing.

She hated this part of the day. The hour she had between leaving the dance school, going home to get ready, grabbing something to eat, and getting to *Las Almas* on time was the most stressful moment of her week, especially if her father was home.

She loved her *Papa* like any daughter, but he could be a pain at times. The way he went on at her each evening about being more punctual, not eating in a rush, and pestering her about getting a more 'respectable job' was starting to push her.

She could cope with the moaning about being late, which was quite normal; she'd tried to be more punctual, but it was as if no matter how hard she tried she just couldn't arrive on time. The constant nagging about getting a 'respectable job' that really made her furious though. His comments would ring in her mind as she danced. *'You'll never become a real flamenco dancer, why don't you just give up now and become a good secretary while you find yourself a rich Sevillano.'*

It was the way he stressed the words 'rich' and 'Sevillano' as if all men from Seville were rich, and that was the most important aspect of finding a man. Nothing to do with his looks, his gentleness, and if he would make a good father.

All she wanted was for him to support her in what she was doing; let her follow her dreams, and choose the man of her future. But she knew he would give her hell for dating a *guiri*, whether he was a gentleman, or not. He would never be macho enough, rich enough, and, not to mention, Catholic enough.

She hoped her mother hadn't said anything. She was tense as it was without worrying about a huge argument. She planned to go in quickly, have a chat, and leave for *Las*

Almas.

"Late as usual," said her father in his solemn voice as she flew into the lounge. Francisco sat up straight in his armchair reading the paper, his long back as straight as the wall behind him. He was always dressed immaculately; today in a crisp light blue shirt and dark blue trousers. Mercedes could have sworn he'd cut his hair again, only two weeks since the last time. He placed the paper on a table and turned around. When Mercedes saw how serious his face was, her heart jumped. For a second she was convinced her mother had said something.

"Hola Papa," she said as she kissed him on the cheek, trying to sound cheery, while not acknowledging how annoyed he looked. "How was your day?"

"Could have been better," he said. His tone was torn.

"Oh why, something happened?" Mercedes gulped and waited for the onslaught.

"Just some idiot clients; nothing you need to worry about. Aren't you late, again?"

"Not really, same as usual," she said, letting out a sigh, such relief.

"There is something I want to talk to you about, but when you have more time." She was intrigued; now she'd be thinking about it all night.

"Can't you just tell me quickly?"

"Not really. I don't want to be responsible for you losing your job. If you can call it that?"

Snap.

"What's that supposed to mean? You know how much I love dancing."

"I also know how much you get paid. Come on Mercedes, isn't it about time you got a job in the real world?"

Crackle. Could he not just leave it for one day?

"Why are you doing this now? You know I need to leave soon."

"That's why I wanted to talk to you about the job offer."

"What job offer?"

"It's a fine, honest job. One to give you security. I know someone who is about to retire as a civil worker, and I can get you straight in, no exams, nothing."

And pop. Did he never listen to her?

"What utter nonsense!" said Mercedes, fuming. There was no way she was going to get a normal job, especially with government workers.

"I know flamenco is important to you. That's why I thought about this job, so you would still have the afternoons and evenings free for your precious dancing."

The way he said 'precious' with such sarcasm and ridicule filled her with anger. He just wanted to get her in with more civilised people so she could meet *his* perfect man. She was tired of not having a voice in her own home.

"I need to go, I'm late," she said, turning her back on him.

"Mercedes," he said, "promise me that you'll think about this. Maybe you'll finally get on in life, and see the importance of punctuality, not like these gypsies."

"Go to hell," she said, storming off.

"How dare you. To me, your father, after all I have done for you. How can you disrespect me like that? You are an outrage, here I am, trying to help you out and all you can do is tell me to go to hell. I'll show you. You will regret ever speaking to your father like that."

The last phrase she heard from a distance, as she slammed her door. She just wanted to dance, couldn't her father see that? Was it so difficult to really understand his daughter after all these years? How was she ever going to become a real woman with such a macho pig of a father? At times he could be such a moron. Usually, she kissed her father on the cheek before she left, but not that night.

As Charlie clonked his way through the back streets, he began to realise the importance of image in Seville. The difference a pair of smart black trousers and an ironed white shirt made was astonishing. Suddenly people were looking at him as if he was some sort of famous rock star. It wasn't as if he'd never dressed up before, those days back at Computer Jobbers had shown him a thing or two about being smart, but in London, no one looked round at him, he was just another suit trying to make a bob or two.

Heads turned as he bounced his way up to meet Ramón, who was standing with two cold beers outside the Columnas bar just up from the cathedral.

"I can't believe it," said Ramón, almost spitting out a stream of beer. "Camerón has risen from the dead," he added, letting out a deep chuckle.

"What do you mean? It's just a shirt."

"Oh, but it is so much more; a white shirt does wonders for a man. You even look like *un flamenco*. Now all you need to do is play like one." He winked.

"Cheers," said Charlie, feeling slightly revived.

After they'd downed a couple of beers, they weaved in and out of the back-streets towards *Las Almas*. Charlie was in a calm mood, and not as chatty as usual as he was nervous about what to expect in the *tablao*.

"You seem a bit quiet tonight," asked Ramón, "are you all right?"

"Sure," said Charlie. "Just excited to see a new guitarist."

"This guitarist is amazing, one of the best in Seville. And the *cantante*- the singer, too. He's a friend of mine. Well, an associate, you'll have to excuse his behaviour."

"Why is that?"

"You'll see. He's just a bit *loco*."

"Crazy?"

"Absolutely crazy. Okay, here we are, just around this corner."

Charlie felt his stomach tighten and heart race faster as they turned round the corner to see a queue formed along the street. Once inside they squeezed through the crowd to get to the main room which was packed out and stuffy. Eager, well-dressed spectators chatted loudly while lining up on the benches waiting for the show to start. Some were Spanish, others *guiris*. Ramón nodded to several people and shook hands with others.

"Do you know everyone in here?"

"Not everyone, but a few; I've been in this business for years now. Flamenco is my life."

Charlie kept his eye out, scanning the Spanish women in the *tablao*. They all looked similar; dark haired, tanned, and pretty, but none were a touch on the one he was looking for.

"Come on *Carlito*," said Ramón, sliding past the first line of people sat down on a bench. "My friend has saved us a space." Charlie felt a jolt of fear in his stomach; he would be even closer to the stage. "There he is."

"Ramón," shouted a short, chubby bearded man as he stood up and bear hugged Ramón. "Great to see you, *maricón*." Charlie was surprised at the vulgar way he'd called such a respected member of flamenco gay, but Ramón just laughed it off.

"Jesús, this is Carlito; a new star of flamenco."

"Don't fuck with me," said Jesús, letting out a howling cackle of a laugh, "this skinny blond *guiri*, a guitar player?" Charlie felt angry, how could he judge him so quickly?

"Don't listen to him," said Ramón. "He's just jealous because you are more handsome than he is."

"He might be, but he'll never have the women that I have," said Jesús. "But if Ramón says you have something, then it must be true. Nice to meet you, *rubio guiri*," he added, holding out a hand. Charlie squeezed tight; trying to denote his manliness, but Jesús left his hand crushed.

"What are you two drinking?" said Jesús.

"I'll have a *manzanilla*," said Ramón.

"Good choice, and you *guiri*?"

"Yeah, me too," he said, not sure what he was asking for. Jesús disappeared to get the drinks and Ramón placed a hand on Charlie's shoulder to sit down. Charlie's knee was bouncing up and down. He hadn't been this nervous for ages.

"Listen to me," said Ramón, sternly. "Focus on the guitarist. He is one of the best in Seville, and you need to learn from the best. Don't get carried away, or distracted."

"Sure, that's why I'm here," said Charlie, "one hundred percent, devotion for the guitar." Just then a pretty Spanish woman squeezed past them, and Charlie looked up to see if it was her.

"I can see past you *guiri*. I know you Englishmen better than you think."

"What?" said Charlie, trying not to smirk.

"We'll see."

"Here you go, *maricones*," said Jesús, holding out two glasses of sweet sherry. "Enjoy, right, catch up with you on the break." Jesús bowled across the stage, clapping as he went through the back stage doors, humming a low wail.

Mercedes arrived with only ten minutes to spare as usual, but this time she was in even more of a state than normal after the bust up with her father. She hated fighting with him and was tired of the constant battle. Lola could tell straight away.

"What's up with you?" she asked as Mercedes burst in the dressing room door.

"Nothing, just in a rush that's all."

"Then why is your bottom lip quivering? I know you well enough now, *Hija*. Don't lie to me. We can't go out there and make our usual excellent performance unless you tell me what's wrong."

"It's not important; I just had a row with my father, that's all." Mercedes felt instant relief, knowing she could share her feelings with Lola.

"Not again; does that control freak never leave you in peace?"

"I guess not."

"What's he been going on about this time? Problem with your makeup? Showing too much flesh? Or did you spill some water on the floor again?"

"If you must know, he's trying to find me a job."

"What the hell for? He knows you're working for me. Who does he think he is?"

"My father." As Mercedes said the words, she realised the power he had over her.

"Some father, mine stopped telling me what to do when I was fourteen."

"Yeah, but that was because you called social security after he tried to make you do the washing up."

"True." They laughed together, and Mercedes could feel

the tension ooze away.

"Look, don't worry about your father. He'll always be on your case. One day when you are a true flamenco star, he'll realise that the best thing he ever did was to let you become a dancer."

"I don't think so. Maybe he'll calm down when he sees me dance again."

"Yeah, it's been a while now."

"Yeah, too long." All she really needed was to have recognition from her father about her dancing. He used to come and watch her when she was a kid but had stopped when she started to take it more seriously. If only he would come and see her again.

"Listen, we're on in five minutes. I'm just going to pop out and see Miguel. We haven't seen each other for a couple of hours."

"Poor you."

"Is that all the thanks I get for calming you down? You cow. Get ready. I'll be back soon."

As the door closed, Mercedes stood in front of the mirror and breathed deeply. She made some slight adjustments to her dress, making sure her chest was covered enough. She moved the white rose in her hair and pouted her lips to do her lipstick. There was a knock on the door.

"One second," Mercedes said, but the door opened.

"*Hola guapa,*" said Jesús, poking his head round the door.

"Who are you?"

"Your new lover." He stormed in and shut the door behind him. Mercedes pulse began to race and fear entered her stomach.

"Get out. Who are you? I'll call for someone if you don't leave right now."

"Come on *guapa*, I've just come to introduce myself."

"Why should I be interested in knowing who you are?"

"Because you'll be on stage with me in a few moments. Jaime sent me. I'm singing tonight." Jesús looked her up and down in that sleazy way that she hated. She cringed inside, how was she going to dance for this cretin of a man? She had to though, or she'd lose her job.

"Fine, *mucho gusto*," she said.

"What, no kiss on the cheek?" Jesús moved closer. Mercedes sighed, and leaned forward and kissed him on the cheek. His stubbly beard and the stench of alcohol and body odour made her feel sick.

"So, are you going to dance for me in private after the show?" he slid his hand round her waist and pulled her towards him.

"Get off me," she said, pushing him hard in the chest. He jolted back. "How dare you come in here and touch me like that."

Jesús laughed.

"Oh, don't cry baby, come on, we need to get to know each other," he said, holding out a hand. Mercedes slapped it away.

"Get out," She was raging inside now.

The door burst open.

"What are you doing you son of a bitch?" shouted Lola as she flew across the room and elbowed Jesús in the back.

"Ah, you whore," said Jesús. As he turned, Lola slapped him round the face.

"Do you not know who we are? You filthy pig. Who the hell are you?"

"Your worst nightmare, woman. I'm Jesús, the new flamenco singer," he said, holding his jaw.

Mercedes stared at the porky leech hoping this was all a

bad dream. Surely Jaime had better taste than this. How were they going to dance with such a vile man?

"Well, there's no way we are going out on stage with you. How dare you grope my friend like that? What sort of man are you?"

"A real man; one who can take any woman to paradise."

"The only paradise you'll be going to is one full of mud and shit; you sleazy pig. Now get out of here before I kick you in the balls."

"You wish," he said, grabbing himself and thrusting his groin towards Lola.

"Get out," shouted Lola, pushing Jesús in the back. Just as she did the door opened.

"What's going on here?" said Jaime.

"This man is disgusting," said Lola.

"Yeah," said Mercedes.

A look of anger spread across Jaime's face.

"I want you all out on stage in the next two minutes, or you'll have to wait until pay day. Is that clear?"

"But..." said Lola. Mercedes pulled back her arm; there was no way she was going to risk her wages because of this idiot. They'd just have to put up with him.

As Jesús left, he poked his tongue out and slammed the door behind.

"He's such a cretin," said Lola, storming up to the mirror to check her makeup. "That won't be the end of this."

"It will for tonight," said Mercedes, suddenly feeling braver than normal. "I can't risk going home without my wages; I can't give any more ammunition to my father."

"Will you just forget about your father for a minute? Now let's get out there, try to remain focused."

"I am focused," she said, firmly, but inside she knew

there was too much going on for her to concentrate on performing. She prayed that her grandfather would be watching, and if not, then the next best person.

Charlie was sipping on his Manzanilla when the clapping started. He shot his eyes over to the door and saw the guitarist walking towards the stage.
"Focus on him," whispered Ramón. Charlie nodded but sat up straight as he searched for the dancer. He saw Jesús, bowling on stage and waving his arms in the air. He looked more like a football player greeting his fans than a serious *cantante*.

Charlie's heart beat faster, and the nerves in his stomach became unbearable, leaving him feeling slightly sick in anticipation. When he saw her glide through the crowd and raise her head just as she got to the stage, he felt sad as the look on her face seemed solemn and in need of help.

"The guitarist," whispered Ramón, "stay focused."

"Sure, sure." Charlie hadn't even noticed the guitarist was playing. He switched his feelings off and tried to study his moves.

He could immediately see the *arte*. The way he held the guitar and darted his hand up and down, and the speed his fingers moved was inspiring. Charlie became wrapped up in his playing, imagining that it was him on stage, playing in front of an audience. He knew he could become just as phenomenal.

When Jesús clapped his hands together and startled Charlie out of his gaze, he began to focus on other things. Why wasn't she dancing? Charlie thought, as the other dancer shot up and began to perform. He felt pity again as she remained seated and kept her eyes fixed on the ground. Jesús and the guitarist were staring too, no doubt getting impatient as the other dancer started to get in full swing.

Charlie felt sorry for her, something was up. What could he do? He wanted to help her. He felt the air of Ramón's breath on his neck.

"What are you listening for?"

"*Compás*," said Charlie, as if in a trance.

Mercedes glared at the wooden floor and tried to battle with the anger inside her. She was in shock and remained still, searching for the will to perform. She was aware the guitarist kept looking over, and could sense the crowd was getting restless, but all she wanted to do was slap Jesús round his dirty, bearded face. Why did she always get lumbered with such scummy people?

She thought of her father's reaction if she lost her job, the satisfaction in his voice would be too much to take. Life would become unbearable. She had to get in gear.

"*Venga guapa*," shouted someone from the corner of the stage. Mercedes noted the strange accent, almost foreign like. Was it him? Another cry of '*guapa*' came from a different side, and then again from the back.

This is my show, she thought as she began to tap her feet, keeping her head down, curious as to who had shouted. She glanced towards the back, but couldn't see him.

The guitarist began to play faster, and Jesús clapped and stamped his feet. Mercedes listened for the *compás* and began to feel the rhythm.

As Jesús started to sing, she tapped her feet on the floor and began to grow in confidence, searching for the flamenco deep in her soul. She was the one who was going to control the performance and choose her fate.

"*Ole,*" shouted Lola as she stopped dead and turned to Mercedes. Aware that all eyes were on her, she shot up and smashing her heels hard on the floor. She wanted to let out all her frustrations. She raised her head slowly, turned her torso, and snapped her head to the left.

He was there. His warm, comforting eyes met hers, and she felt a glow inside at seeing his smile. Had he been the one to encourage her?

She turned back to the front, building in confidence knowing he had come back to see her. As she continued, moving from left to right in a circle, lifting her skirt slightly, teasing the crowd, the anger began to fade away and became replaced by joy. The fact that he was there made her feel full of life, energy, and a reason to impress.

Mercedes had drowned out the singing from Jesús and was focused on the guitar. She began to get in full stride, tapping her feet on the floor, faster and faster with more force each time. All the anger and passion inside was coming out. She felt euphoric, on a new level; one that she'd been trying to achieve for some time.

As she came to a climax, she stamped on the floor and held her hands high.

"*Ole.*"

"*Venga guapa.*"

"*Eso es.*"

The crowd were on their feet and cheering. She glanced over at him; he was standing up, clapping and smiling, which filled her with a strange mushy feeling. She wanted to get to know him and find out whether he felt the same.

"*Impresonante,*" said Lola as they stood in front of the cheering audience.

"*Gracias,*" she said, winking.

Just before she left the stage, Mercedes glanced back at

the blond guy. He smiled and looked as though he was about to say something, but Lola pulled her away. She wanted to spin round and run over to him, but the more sensible part told her to keep walking. If he wanted to, he could come and ask to see her.

"*Hombre*, that was great singing," said Ramón as Jesús came over and threw an arm around his shoulders.

"*Gracias*, what did you think of the guitarist?" Jesús asked Charlie. For a moment Charlie had to shake himself round, he'd been so transfixed by the dancer again that he'd completely ignored the guitarist.

"Impressive," he said.

"He's not the best student," said Ramón, "he likes to take in all the atmosphere when he's in a *tablao*, isn't that right, Carlito?" He'd been spotted.

"Sure, sure," he replied, trying to play it cool.

"Manzanilla?" asked Jesús, slapping his hands on both their shoulders and turning them towards the bar.

Charlie followed behind as Ramón and Jesús chatted about the performance. The way in which Jesús was shrugging his shoulders and throwing his arms about suggested that he was angry about something, but with the loud chatting, Charlie couldn't quite catch everything.

He was uninterested though, relieved that he'd seen her again. He felt an immense satisfaction inside after helping her to perform. He didn't know what had gotten into him, shouting out like that in Spanish, but her reaction had been amazing. To watch her spring to life and dance the way she did with such emotion and passion was uplifting.

Even though he was torn inside about becoming attached to someone, he wanted to get to know her. He had this overwhelming feeling of attraction for her as well, especially because of the sexy way she moved her slender body and the way she'd looked at him with her longing eyes.

Jesús turned and handed Charlie another cool glass of manzanilla.

"*Gracias.*" They clinked glasses. "So why aren't you out the back with the others?" Charlie asked.

"I like to be here, with the flamenco fans."

"Male, or female fans?" said Ramón. Jesús made a sleazy grin. "Just you wait; they'll be flocking round in a minute." Charlie noticed a couple of ladies already glancing over.

"What about the guitarist? Is he coming out? I'd like him to meet Carlito."

"He's a damn good guitarist," said Jesús, "but he normally goes to meet his folk, those gypsies often stick together."

Charlie was bursting to ask whether he knew much about the dancer and whether she was going to come out for a drink. He didn't want to give Ramón any more ammunition though; he already felt guilty about not really watching the guitarist, again.

"I doubt those dancers will come out though," said Jesús. Charlie's blood began to boil with the tone of his voice. "One of them must be one of the most frigid dancers I've ever met, the whore." Charlie took a sip to disguise his anger. "She's a damn good dancer and has a fine body, but she's not the usual type; likes to keep her knickers on."

"Sure," said Ramón, clearing his throat.

"I need to speak with Jaime about something, and who knows, maybe I'll pass by their room again." He downed his glass, whacked it on the table and darted round the back.

Again? What did he mean, again?

"Calm down," said Ramón, placing a hand on his shoulder. Charlie was fuming inside.

"I can't believe a man of your status knows someone like that. The way he spoke about the dancer, in such a filthy way."

"I know, I know. But that's the world of flamenco, not everyone is well spoken, like you English people."

"I have my moments." Charlie flashed back to those images of his guitar flying through the air at Hans. Was he getting jealous again? He had to keep control. "It was embarrassing, that's all."

"Sure, listen, it's not your place to say anything. Don't get involved. Besides, you didn't keep to your side of the deal. Did you even notice the guitarist?"

"I did at first, but it's true; I got distracted."

"I know. Look, just leave her, she's a proper Sevillana. She won't be interested in a *guiri*."

"But how do you know?"

"Trust an old man, I know people, people speak. I know her family, and honestly, you don't want to go there."

"But…"

"No buts," said Ramón, raising his voice. "You are here to become a guitarist. If you go after her, you will only get hurt and risk not becoming *un flamenco*."

They stood in silence, sipping on the drinks. Charlie respected Ramón, but there was no way he was going to give in so easily. Sure, he desperately wanted to become a flamenco guitarist, but he was so curious about the dancer.

"Here are a couple of ladies I just met," said Jesús, standing next to Charlie with two brunettes. "Carlito, this is Ana and Anabel, old friends of mine." He winked.

Charlie could feel the blood rushing to his face as the two pretty Spanish ladies kissed him softly on the cheeks.

"Carlito is a guitarist too," said Jesús.

"*Ah si,*" said one, rubbing her hand over his shoulder. Charlie gulped.

Lola and Mercedes were getting changed, they hadn't spoken since arriving back in the dressing room.

"What the hell got into you back then?" said Lola as she pulled on her jeans.

"What do you mean?" said Mercedes, trying to conceal her excitement.

"At the start, you were sitting there like a useless bags of potatoes. I was about to give up on you when you sprang into action after a comment flew through the air by that *guiri*." The tone with which she said '*guiri*' bothered Mercedes. Not her as well, she thought.

"What *guiri*?" she said in defence; still not ready to talk about him.

"Don't try to get one over me," said Lola. "I saw him staring at you and smiling as if he was about to get down on one knee. The wuss."

"He's not a wuss..." but as soon as she opened her mouth, Mercedes knew that she'd played right into Lola's trap.

"I knew it, who is he?" she said, smiling. "Do you know him?"

"Not as such, just a guy I've seen before."

"Where?"

"A couple of weeks back, he was watching me."

"Stripping you with his eyes more like, you dirty whore. Look at that smile on your face. I bet you've wet your knickers."

"Stop it," she said, feeling her cheeks flush hot. Sometimes Lola didn't know when she'd passed the line.

"Well, anything is better than that horrid Jesús. Oh god, did you see the way he went on stage, like one of the Chippendale's, but with a much flabbier belly and probably a smaller cock. God, he makes me feel sick."

"I know what you mean. Luckily you didn't see him stick his tongue out at me. That's why I was so furious and couldn't move at the start."

"You're joking. God, if only I'd known, I would have slapped him."

Just then Jaime knocked on the door and came in.

"Well done on tonight's performance, that was brilliant, in the end. I hope you two can get on better with Jesús though; he'll be here for a while."

"He's a pig," said Lola. "He's tried it on with Mercedes twice already."

"Look, I know he's not exactly in touch with his feminine side, and can be a bit creepy, but he's a great singer, and the crowd loves him."

Mercedes could feel Lola about to fly across the room, so she grabbed her hand.

"Sure, we'll try to get on with him."

"Great, okay then, a few of us are having a drink afterwards tonight in the bar; do you fancy it?"

"Sure we do," said Lola, "I could do with one after tonight. We'll be right out, won't we?" Lola turned to Mercedes and flashed her falsest smile.

As they changed, Mercedes began to get those jittery nerves in her stomach. She hoped he would be there and could speak to him somehow. She was curious to find out where he was from and why he was into flamenco.

"You ready?" Mercedes asked.

"Why, eager to meet someone? You haven't even told me anything about him yet."

"I've told you all I know."

"What? Haven't you even spoken to him?"

Another comment which made her feel like a fool. How had she become so absorbed in this guy even though she hadn't even had a chat with him? Sometimes her feelings could be too overpowering.

"Not with words, but we have with our eyes."

"Oh, *por favor*," said Lola, sticking two fingers down her throat. "Could you get any cheesier? Please, let's hope he's out there so I can find out if he's suitable."

"You wouldn't dare?"

"Why not?"

"Let's just see what happens first, he might not even be there."

"Fine, let's go; I'm gasping for a beer."

As they walked in the packed bar, Mercedes looked around casually, not trying to appear desperate. After all, it would be much better if he came up to her. Jaime was waiting at the bar.

"These are on me," he said, smirking.

"Are you feeling all right?" asked Lola.

"Sure, you both know you are my angels."

Lola giggled, but Mercedes had already stopped listening as she'd spotted him. He was on the other side of the bar, looking as cute as ever, with a permanent smile on his face. He was with an older guy she recognised. She was sure he was a guitar teacher, which might explain why he was in Seville: another *guiri* come to learn the guitar. Surely he wasn't any good though.

"Is that him then?" said Lola, nudging her shoulder.

"Might be."

"*Joder*, it is. Well, he's not that bad."

"That bad?"

"Yeah, for a *guiri*. Come on, let's go over and talk to him."

"No," she said, pulling her back.

"Why not? Come on, you can't spend your life like this: waiting for things to change, the perfect job to land in your lap, a prince *guiri* to come and sweep you off your feet. You have to seize the day; Carpe Diem!"

"I know, but I'm not sure what to say."

"Leave it to me."

"Oh God!"

As they went to go over Mercedes felt apprehensive, what if he didn't like her? What if she'd made a silly mistake? What if he was another mummy's boy?

Just as they got close, Jesús turned up and handed the *guiri* a drink. Mercedes couldn't believe they knew each other. A friend of that horrid man was surely problematic. Why were they drinking together?

"Hang on," said Mercedes, putting her arm around Lola's shoulders and pulling her round.

"What are you doing? Don't pull out now."

"But look."

Lola glimpsed ahead and immediately spun around, looking as if she was about to be sick.

"There must be some mistake. Surely Jesús is trying to get some money from him or something. Maybe he knows those women."

"What women?" asked Mercedes, whipping her head round to get a quick look. Two cheap looking brunettes were on either side of him; one with her arm draping over his shoulder. Mercedes felt like such a fool, why had she even bothered wasting her time thinking he could be different? She was ashamed of herself.

"They look like a couple of prostitutes. Why are they

with your lover boy?"

"Another mystery of the world of flamenco."

"Come on, let's find out."

But Mercedes couldn't bring herself to do it. After all this time thinking about him, she couldn't just let it all go in an instant and find out that he was actually a cretin too. She wanted to hold on to her dream, even if it never came true. Besides, she knew exactly the type of women over there: dangerous and mouthy with a knack of making her feel small, weak, and useless.

"Come on," said Lola, twisting around.

"I'm not going over," she said. "If he's really interested in me, then he'll come my way. I'm not making a fool of myself."

"But sometimes you have to make a fool of yourself, how do you think I won Miguel? By waiting for him to get the balls to speak to me?"

"We all know what happened," she said, smiling, thinking back to the reaction on his face when she turned up part naked in front of his parents.

"Come on, live a little."

But she couldn't bring herself to do it.

"Just give me a moment."

"Fine, but don't come crying to me if you never see him again."

Over the next ten minutes, Mercedes went through a roller coaster of emotions. She became angry when she saw how much fun he was having with Jesús and felt rage every time they laughed together. She felt sick with jealousy too when one of the tarts leaned over and rubbed his shoulder or laughed at whatever he said. She wanted to listen to his voice and hear his accent but feared going over.

But for a split second, she also felt pure joy when he peered over and caught her eye. The look of surprise and optimism in his eyes made her feel alive, chuffed and hopeful. She was sure he felt the same as her, but why didn't he come over? He looked several times, but never made the move, until it was too late.

When Jesús brought over a tray of tequilas, it was game over. Within seconds of knocking back a shot the look on the guiri's face became a glaze, his eyes began to squint, and he even started to stumble.

"Looks like one of those typical English men to me," said Lola. "One who comes to Spain to drink their body weight in alcohol because it's so much cheaper; he belongs down the Costa Del Sol."

"*Vamos*," said Mercedes. As she walked home, she felt sickened. She had been convinced he was the man for her; a decent, responsible, and loving guy. But it seemed as though she'd been wrong, yet again.

"What the hell has got into you?" said Ramón, pulling Charlie away from the bar.

"*Que pasa?* Can't a guy get a drink around here?" said Charlie, almost pushing Ramón away. Ramón wasn't having any of it. He twisted Charlie round, pulled his arm behind his back, and marched him straight out of the *tablao*.

"Oi," said Charlie, as he almost stumbled to the floor. "What do you think you're doing?"

"Listen to me, young man. If you want me to represent you, then you have to be on constant performance. You're not even in the flamenco world yet, and already you are making a show of yourself."

"I was just having some fun," said Charlie, feeling angry

for having to be on show at all.

"Fun? That is not fun. Look at yourself, you are drunk. I know I introduced you to Jesus, but there is no need to turn into some pathetic, drunk, foreign hooligan."

"What is it with you people, always going on about being a foreigner, a *guiri*? Just get over it, for Christ sake."

Ramón's face turned to rage, one Charlie found quite daunting, and one he hoped he would never have to see again.

"Never take the Lord's name in vain," said Ramón, and walked off, leaving Charlie swaying to and fro in the street.

"Wait, Ramón, I'm sorry."

But it was too late, Ramón had already disappeared through the back streets, leaving Charlie to find his way home.

The next morning Charlie woke up in a pool of sweat and guilt. Why had he suddenly become 'friends' with such a vile man like Jesús, and been an idiot to Ramón? Why had he not made his move with the dancer before she left? What an idiot! The alcohol was to blame.

He'd desperately wanted to go over and chat with her, but couldn't raise the courage. He either had to grow some balls or just forget about her completely. He was sure she felt the same as him though, so he had to make a go of it.

He was starting to learn more about the world of flamenco: how proud Sevillanos were of their tradition, and how difficult it would be for a *guiri* to make a real impression on the flamenco world. The fact that people would always see him as a novice spurred him on even more though.

There was only one thing for it, continue playing and

improving the way he played, and then go back to the tablao, alone, and face her. First, he had to apologise to Ramón, though.

Chapter 5 ALL OR NOTHING

Early October

Charlie was fighting with his mind as he stood at the back of *Las Almas*. His head was ready to explode into a cloud of strawberry sherbet. Over the previous three weeks, he'd done nothing but play the *palos* that Ramón had taught him to push himself to become *un flamenco* and build up his courage to see her again.

He'd reached a new level playing flamenco, one that Ramón had become proud of, which was lucky after how Charlie had behaved after the tequila shots. Ramón had taken Charlie's apology, but on the condition he would practice for eight hours a day until he was ready to perform.

The ends of Charlie's fingers had formed hard crusts as if someone had dipped them in super glue, his wrists had become suppler than a ballerina's ankle, and his forearms had developed new muscles that only flamenco guitarists, and maybe javelin throwers, knew existed.

As *un flamenco*, he was approaching new heights, but his heart was dented. Ever since Mercedes had whizzed past him that evening, he'd regretted not saying something to her.

Even though there was something inside his brain warning him of going back to the *tablao*, mainly the fear of rejection, he knew he had to give it a shot, or he'd always be wondering 'what if…,' especially when he found himself back in Northwood Hills going out with a local barmaid.

He was unsure how he had such strong feelings for her. Why couldn't he block out the images of her dancing beside him whenever he played? Why was her face the first thing he thought about as he went to sleep at night and woke up in the morning? He had to see her dance again, and then ask her out on a date.

He awoke from a daze as the gypsy guitarist, who Ramón had so much respect for, came out and walked across the stage in style. He cringed when Jesús prowled behind like a sweaty bear though. Charlie despised everything about him: the way he swaggered about as if the *tablao* was his, the way he spoke about women, treating them like pieces of meat and flesh, and especially the way he stared at them; obviously stripping them with his dirty mind.

When Lola came from behind the curtains and waltzed her voluptuous body on stage, flaunting herself to the audience with her head held high, he knew she was close.

As soon as she glided through the crowd, he confirmed his feelings. He was scared of the power and energy which ran through his body. He felt a strong urge to run over and ask her questions: what was her favourite palo? Why did she hardly look up? Would she like to be the first thing he saw every morning?

He had to control his foolishness, play it calm, take it easy, but he couldn't help the electricity running through his veins. He'd never felt such emotion and attraction before. He waited, eager to see Mercedes spurt into action.

The guitarist started with a *palo* that Charlie had been trying to perfect. He listened closely to see whether he was anywhere near his level. Surprisingly, he was, at least in his eyes.

He was reminded of the dark side as Jesús started to sing. Charlie noticed he looked in a bit of a state; he was sweatier than normal and swayed a bit on his stool. Even though the heavily accented Andalusian accent was still a mystery to Charlie, he could tell Jesús was out of tone and wailing like a two-year old who had just lost his dummy. Was he drunk?

It didn't seem to affect Mercedes though as she sprang into life, her colleague watching her proudly. She sat clapping her hands and tapping her feet, sending vibrations through the crowd. Charlie felt his pulse get faster, knowing she was so near to him. He had to make his move and find a way of chatting to her. He couldn't put it off any longer, or he'd more than likely turn into a quivering mess for the foreseeable future.

As Mercedes rose from her stool and whacked her heels on the wooden stage, she felt overwhelmed with emotion. Lola stared at her, smiling sympathetically as only she knew her true feelings. She'd almost called in to say she wasn't able to dance, how could she on such a sad day? Two years had gone since her idol had passed away. She'd spent most of the afternoon with her mother, reminiscing about the great times they'd had together, talking about how much he'd inspired her to become a dancer.

"He will always be with you, *Hija*," her mother had said as she left the house. And he was. She imagined him there at the back of the room, watching with his soft warming eyes, smiling and winking to let her know that she had done well as she showed off her dancing to him, her *abuelo*.

Mercedes was unaware she was putting on one of her best performances ever; the audience was mesmerised by the emotion she emitted through her powerful, quick, and dramatic moves. The sadness came out of her system as she strutted on stage, not looking up, her body releasing all the tension that had been building up since he'd passed away. She was still deeply upset he was no longer there to watch and motivate her. She felt alone.

She opened up her eyes and looked towards the back of the room, hoping to see her grandfather standing, watching her, which was why her heart fluttered when she saw *him* again. In such an emotional moment of her life, the fact that he appeared was enough to bring out her true feelings for him.

Then she remembered she was supposed to be angry at him, for acting like such a typical foreign drunk. But the elation that came from seeing him pushed her anger aside.

She'd almost given up hope, but there he was, when she most needed support, smiling at her. She smiled back. She wanted to wave and shout for him to come over and speak to her, but she carried on dancing.

Foolishly, she turned round and looked at Jesús, who slid his tongue out slowly as he looked her up and down, winked, and pretended to kiss her. Fury ran through her veins. He was such a cretin. She had this uncontrollable urge to kick him right in the balls. All she wanted was to shut that despicable man up forever. She spun around on the spot and planted her feet firmly on the ground as she stood in front of him.

He was in mid-sentence when he stopped and frowned at her. For a split second, she wondered if she was going to overstep the mark, but she didn't care anymore. She raised her hand above her head, held it out straight and brought her arm down as fast as she could as it struck Jesús clean across his cheek. The *tablao* went silent as the wall echoed the crack of the slap.

"*Eres un cerdo* – you're a pig," she said as she kicked him in the shin, knocking him onto the floor. She spun round to face the crowd. "*Lo siento* – I'm sorry. But I cannot dance with this pig of a man."

Lola jumped up and kicked Jesús in the back while he was down, making sure her heel dug right into his shoulder blades. Then she spat in his hair. No one was going to mess with her best friend.

They stomped across the stage, fuming. Jaime stormed behind.

"What do you think you are doing?" he shouted as they went backstage.

"Ask your pig of a friend; he's a disgusting man, I will never dance with him again," shouted Mercedes.

"Then you will never dance here again."

Normally a comment like that would have filled Mercedes with fear, what would she do without her job? But she didn't give a flying fuck anymore, especially not with Lola by her side.

"We don't need you anymore," said Lola, sticking her face in his, almost head-butting him. "You need us more than we need you. This place is finished without us; like a bull ring without those poncy handkerchiefs, Sevilla without Semana Santa, and a man without his *pene*."

"You can stick your job up your arse," said Mercedes, feeling her confidence rise. She turned into her dressing room.

"Don't even think about coming back here," Jaime shouted as she slammed the door.

She wanted to burst into tears. The emotion of the day had got to her. She had to run out, so she never had to see that cretin again.

"What an absolute *cabrón*," said Lola, throwing her shoes at the door. But Mercedes couldn't respond. She was too choked up. She'd never hit anyone like that before, never lost her cool in front of a crowd. What had come over her? The emotion was too much. She knew her *abuelo* would not have been proud of her losing patience like that, but she was changing, becoming a more self-sufficient woman.

What must *he* have thought? More importantly, how would he ever find her again if she wasn't coming back to *Las Almas*?

"Mercedes, are you okay?" asked Lola, leaning on her shoulder, wiping away a tear. "Don't cry, he's not worth it." She wanted to tell her she wasn't crying about Jesús, Jaime, or even her *abuelo*, but the blond *guiri*; he'd actually turned up to see her again. "Come on, say something."

"It's just my *abuelo*," she said, wiping her eyes, unable to tell the truth. "I think I'll go now. I'm sorry."

"Don't be silly. We are both walking out of here together. Come on, grab your things."

"But we've both lost our jobs now."

"Nonsense, everything happens for a reason. Besides, I was thinking of quitting anyway, opening up some new classes, maybe you can work more for me?"

"Really?" Mercedes was almost blubbering again. She was so lucky to have a friend like that by her side.

"That's what friends are for; to be there for each other. Anyway, we can find another place to dance if we need to, but with the numerous clients now we should be fine. Now let's get out of here."

"With pleasure," she said. She forgot someone, though. She wanted to go back to the bar and see if he was still there, but she couldn't chance running into Jesús again, so she dragged herself away out through the back doors.

As she made her way home, alone, Mercedes felt a wave of sadness. She was upset to have to leave the place where she'd learned to become a flamenco dancer and grown in confidence, but, most importantly, fallen in love. She just hoped he would be able to track her down.

The full impact of the cracking slap around Jesús's face hit Mercedes the next morning as she was having breakfast with her parents. There was no way she was ready to tell them about last night yet, so she was quite glad they were arguing about the food shopping and could drift into a daze.

Deep down she was fuming. Why did they have to lose their jobs because of such a pig? It was unjust, typical in such a macho world. She'd miss dancing at *Las Almas*, but maybe it was time for a change. Her heart filled with sadness when she thought of him though. She couldn't believe she'd spotted him the moment she wished her *abuelo* was by her side. It must have been a sign.

"*Hija*, what's wrong?" asked her mother. "You seem sad today, what's up?"

"She's probably just thinking up some dance moves," said her father. "Or maybe she met another handsome gypsy last night and has fallen in love again."

"Again? How would you know whether I've been in love?"

"Surely you have."

"Really?" she said, trying not to bite. Her initial reaction was to splurge that she didn't work there anymore, but she wouldn't give him more ammunition, especially after the last row they'd had about her becoming a civil servant.

"Yes, really. I also know that you think you'll be a famous flamenco dancer one day and that the world will love you. But you'll never be happy until you are married to a Sevillano. Have you thought any more of that job?"

"Not at all."

"Come on, you two, stop bickering. What's up with you, Mercedes?"

Mercedes was trying to keep the lid on a very hot and full pressure cooker about to explode through her nose, ears, and any other possible orifice. What did he know about her anyway? Why couldn't he just leave her in peace and let her do what she wanted? Did he not realise he was driving her away? She wanted to open up to her mum and tell her exactly what had happened. But there was no way she was going to tell her while her father was around. She took the easy way out.

"I think my period is coming."

"Well, there's no need for that," he said, burying his head in his newspaper. She smirked.

Silence followed as they sipped on their usual coffee and munched on their *tostadas*. Mercedes felt a bit guilty, lying like that to deliberately hurt her father, and she was about to apologise when he said,

"Right I'm off. Someone has to earn a living around here." He kissed both on the head and walked off through the park.

Rosa's lips were pursed, and one eyebrow was raised.

"What?" asked Mercedes.

"That's no way to talk to your father; you know you'll never get around him that way."

"He started it, besides, I don't need to get around him."

"Maybe not at the moment, but you never know when you might. So, what's really up? I know you had your period last week, anyway."

"Sure you do."

"Is it that guy?"

"Which guy?"

"I know you too well."

"No, actually *Mama*. If you must know, I left *Las Almas* last night," said Mercedes, harshly.

"I'm sure you did *Hija*, or you'd still be there."

"No, I mean left; for good."

Rosa moved forward as if she'd heard incorrectly.

"Eh? But why? You've been there so long, I thought you loved it there."

"I did until that despicable man started singing there." It was all his fault, that cretin.

"What happened?" Rosa leaned across the table and grabbed Mercedes' hands to calm her down.

"He stuck his tongue out at me again."

"Is that all?" asked Rosa, frowning.

"That all? You didn't see the way he was looking at me; he repels me."

"But if you want to be a flamenco dancer, you know you'll always have men after you."

"I know, but not like that. Anyway, it's time for a change. Lola said she'll give me a few more classes until we find somewhere else to dance."

"Let's hope it works out then." But her mother's tone didn't sound too optimistic. "We are always on your side, you know that," said Rosa, leaning over to kiss her on the head.

"If only," said Mercedes, knowing her father would never rest until he saw her walking out the cathedral dressed in white, with a strapping overly tanned Sevillano by her side. She wasn't going to give in; she knew in her heart who she really wanted. She prayed their paths would cross again.

Charlie hadn't slept for two nights. He was angry at that pig Jesús for upsetting Mercedes, anxious because he might not ever see Mercedes again, and frustrated for not going back stage to find her. His abilities to play the guitar had disappeared as well.

"What the hell is wrong with you?" said Ramón, offering him an olive from the small clay bowl as they sat in a bar opposite the studio after a lesson.

"A mix of things," he said as he took one, popped it in his mouth and pulled off a serviette to wipe the juice away from his fingers.

"Is it home? You never tell me about your country." Charlie thought of his parents and sister. He should have called them more often, and he still hadn't been in touch with Joe.

"No, not really. I don't know. I've been practicing a lot, the other day I played that *palo* so well, but today I just don't have the energy. Maybe I need a break."

"A break? Do you want to become *un flamenco*?" Ramón's abrupt tone caught Charlie off guard.

"Of course I do, but it's just…"

"It's just what? Honestly, you have a gift, but you need to work on it. What about Camerón, do you think he had many breaks? The only time he rested from flamenco was when he died." Ramón crossed himself before taking a swig of beer. Charlie was taken aback by his aggressive manner.

"Sorry, I know you're right. Maybe I'm just having a bad day."

"A bad day, huh?" Ramón snapped. "I know someone else who is having a bad day." Ramón gazed deep into Charlie's eyes. He felt as though he was being told off by his old headmaster.

"What do you mean?"

"A friend of mine came by earlier today. He was irate;

desperate for help."

"Go on." Guilt rose up through Charlie's lungs.

"He asked if I knew a couple of flamenco dancers who were free to start immediately."

"Oh really."

"Yeah, his normal dancers left apparently, after a small incident on stage, with Jesús, who is also out of action after one of them stamped on his back."

Charlie couldn't help but laugh. Good on her, he thought.

"What's funny?"

"Nothing, I guess he just got what was coming to him."

"Why do you say that?"

"Karma."

"I see."

There was a momentary silence as they both sipped on their beers. Why was Ramón angry at him though? He couldn't work out the connection.

"So why are you really having a bad day then?" said Ramón. "Something to do with a woman?" Charlie raised his eyebrows and leaned back. "Come on, Carlito. I know you were there."

"Where?"

"At *Las Almas*. Jaime told me he saw you. He said you were standing there waiting for Mercedes like a sad puppy who had lost its owner."

"He did?"

"Uh-huh. So, what's it to be: flamenco, or Mercedes?"

Maybe it was time to pour everything out, tell Ramón how he felt about Mercedes, how he was ashamed of not having the confidence to speak with her. Maybe he knew where to find her.

"Why not both? Surely she could teach me a thing or

two."

"I'm sure she could, but trust me, that's not how it works here." Ramón faced him, mildly calmer. "I know you feel something for this dancer, but you need to keep focused on your playing. She will only be a distraction at the end of the day, and you'll end up miserable once you realise that you can never be with her."

"But why can't I?"

"So you do feel something."

"Maybe." Charlie felt his defences lower.

"I know her family; her father is extremely traditional, a pure Sevillano through and through. You would have no chance with her; it's simple. So stop killing yourself and take my advice, let her go. There are plenty of pretty women in Sevilla."

Charlie was annoyed that he'd opened up. What was the point? Ramón was never going to see his side; he just wanted him to concentrate on his flamenco.

"Fine," he said.

"I know you don't agree with me, but I just want you to succeed; women are dangerous, especially in the flamenco world."

"We'll see."

"It's your decision. Anyway, I have another lesson now. See you tomorrow. Hopefully, it will be a better day."

"Sure, *adios, amigo*."

As Charlie walked towards his house, he wondered if Ramón was right. He always seemed to talk sense. But his feelings were niggling him. Why should he give up so easily? Ramón was a great man, but maybe love wasn't his thing. If he knew so much about women, then why was he alone? Charlie felt confused but was not willing to just let her go. He had to know if he stood a chance. He had to at least speak with her.

About a week later, as Charlie was tuning his guitar on a stool by the window in his flat, he saw Sevilla in a different light; its beauty had been washed away by drizzling rain, and the view over the river was clouded by the misty sky. For the first time since Charlie had been in Seville, the skies opened up and poured with thick heavy rain. Charlie stood looking out the steamy lounge window and felt sad and nostalgic. After such a long time in the sun, he'd forgotten what it was like to wake up with a grey sky looming and rain splattering on the window. It reminded him of home and was probably the first day that he actually missed his family, mates, and country. Flamenco had taken control of his mind and soul.

He began to play and thought of Mercedes dancing on his balcony in the rain. Her dress was soaked through, tight against her perfect body as she stomped about. She splashed in the puddles while breathing hard and fast as the water covered her hair and face. He imagined himself beside her, playing his guitar in the rain, following her moves, her *compás*.

He had to be more proactive about finding her, and not mope about like some silly schoolboy who'd just found out his first love had run off with his maths teacher.

Since his last chat with Ramón, he'd been practicing more. His hands felt looser and suppler. He was eager to show his teacher just how committed he was.

Later that day in the studio, when he'd finished playing, Ramón stood and applauded.

"You have made this miserable day into one of your greatest here," he said, slapping Charlie on the back.

"*Gracias*," said Charlie, standing to hug his teacher.

"Maybe you are ready now."

"Ready for what?"

"For an audience." Ramón opened his eyes wider and raised his eyebrows as he said so. Charlie had not considered playing in public. How could he? A *guiri* playing flamenco in Sevilla was unheard of.

"I don't want to be in front of an audience yet." He thought back to his last public event. Hans' bloody face flashed in his mind.

"Flamenco is all about the show: playing for your audience, filling them with passion, transmitting your feelings, creating an adrenaline rush through everyone in the room, so they feel *duende*. *Duende* is felt in the *tablaos*, not in the studio."

Charlie felt like an innocent, naive fool. Ramón was right, as usual. Playing in front of people, especially local Sevillanos, filled him with dread, but he knew a crowd would sharpen his playing and build his experience.

"Okay," said Charlie, "let's do it."

"Great, leave it with me. I'll find your first performance. You need to start small and work your way up. That way your dreams will come true."

He thought of Mercedes; the dream of seeing her again and having that chance to speak with her would be enough. What was happening to him? Was he falling in love?

The door slammed open and in barged a women with a screaming young girl.

"Ramón," said the woman, storming up to him. He rolled his eyes and sighed.

"*Hermanita*," he said, kissing his sister on both cheeks. The girl began to hit her mother on the leg. "María," said Ramón sternly, "don't hit your *Mama* like that." The girl screamed louder, and her face turned red as she kept swinging her arms about.

"I need a favour," said the woman.

"Sure."

"Can you take care of your niece for a while?"

"But I'm busy. I have another lesson now," he said, picking up María so she could only wriggle about.

"I know, I know," said the woman, "but a friend of mine has had a nasty fall, and I need to go. María can't miss her class. It's not for another hour, please; you're my only chance."

"Which school is she at again?"

"Los Gallos."

"Ah, okay, Los Gallos, sure, sure, don't worry; I'll make sure she gets there."

"Thanks, Ramón, you've saved my life," said his sister, kissing Ramón on the cheek and sprinting out the door.

"Are you going to be a good *chica*?" said Ramón as he looked at his niece.

"*Si, tito Ramón*. Can I watch you play?"

"Not me, I have a class now, but Carlito here will keep you entertained in one of the other rooms."

"*Si?*" said Charlie, nervous about looking after a ten-year old girl. In some ways she reminded him of his own niece; surely all kids were the same, no matter what nationality.

"Take one of the other studios and just play for her, she can show you what a real flamenco dancer is like. It will be good practice. Come back in half an hour."

"This should be fun," said Charlie. He grabbed his guitar and followed María into the next studio. She flicked on the light, ran into the corner, and put on her flamenco shoes. Charlie pulled a stool from the side, sat down, and began to play.

Watching María dance was inspiring. She was so tiny and moved so fast, so elegantly, and with such style. He imagined Mercedes had started that small and delicate.

After half an hour or so, Ramón came in.

"So?"

"She's an amazing dancer."

"Of course she is; she's in my family. Listen, Carlito. Can you do me a favour?" He knew what was coming.

"Well, I'm not in a rush so yeah, I suppose I could."

"Excellent, don't worry, María knows how to get there. I owe you one. Come back after and let me know you dropped her in okay." Charlie winked in agreement.

Luckily the rain had stopped, and the sun was shining again. María grabbed Charlie's hand and led him up *Mateos Gago* and round through the back streets.

"Do you speak English?" asked Charlie.

"A little," replied María, smiling. "*Hablas español?*"

"A little. *Eres como mi sobrina* – you are like my niece," he said.

"*Es guapa?*"

"Pretty? *Si.*"

"*Gracias.* You play good the guitar."

"*Gracias.* You're an excellent dancer."

"Thank you. I have good teacher; she is pretty." María smiled. Charlie laughed. He missed his niece.

As María had been leading the way, Charlie was unsure where he was.

"Where are we?" he asked.

"In *La Alameda*, my school is on *Calle Amor de Dios*." Charlie smiled and nodded. "*Alli,*" she said, pointing towards the end of the street. A few young girls were gathered together up ahead.

"You want to see my teacher?"

"Okay," said Charlie as he led her closer. As they arrived, the teacher stepped out of the doorway. Charlie froze. She was there; smiling at the girls as they skipped towards her.

"Mercedes," said María, running up and giving her a hug. *Mercedes, what a lovely name,* thought Charlie, astonished by who was in front of him.

"Hola María," she said, bending down to kiss her on the cheek.

"*Mi amigo,*" said María, pointing towards Charlie. As Mercedes looked up at Charlie, she smiled and blushed. His heart filled with relief. He'd found her. He was drawn to her eyes.

"*Hola,*" said Charlie. He stood with his mouth open. He couldn't believe his luck.

"*Hola,*" said Mercedes. "Everything okay?"

"Yeah sure," said Charlie, surprised she spoke in English. María stood in the doorway, grinning as the two stared into each other's eyes.

"María is an excellent dancer," said Charlie.

"Oh, you see her?" Mercedes leaned closer. Charlie could smell her sweet perfume.

"Yes, just now. She's very good."

"Is true, one of my best." She was actually in front of him. He had to do something, quick, think.

"So, you're a flamenco teacher?"

"Yes, flamenco is my passion." Mercedes grinned to show her full set of brilliantly white teeth. Charlie wondered how she kept them so clean. Focus, damn it.

"I've seen. You speak English well."

"I try, I make mistakes, but I enjoy. And you?"

"I speak English, yes."

Mercedes laughed and held her hand to her mouth.

"Where are you from?" she asked.

"*Inglaterra.*"

Mercedes' eyes lit up.

"*Inglaterra?* Really, that is lovely." Charlie's pulse was racing. Finally, he knew where to find her. "Are you okay?" said Mercedes.

"*Si, si.*"

They stood, staring at each other. Ask her out, thought Charlie. Just ask her. But two girls came running up and tugged on Mercedes' arm.

"Sorry," she said. "But I must go."

"*Si, si.* Sure," said Charlie, fidgeting with his hands.

"*Soy* Mercedes." As she leaned to kiss him, he was unsure where to move, and turned his cheek in the wrong direction, receiving a kiss almost full on his lips.

"Oh, sorry," he said, pulling away.

"Is nothing," said Mercedes, blushing slightly. "And you?"

"Me? Oh, right, yeah I'm Charlie," he said. Mercedes laughed and smiled.

"*Mucho gusto,*" she said.

"The pleasure is mine," he said, cringing at himself.

"I go teach now," said Mercedes, backing away. As she walked off, she hit her heel on the step and almost fell back. Charlie reached out and grabbed her arm, stopping her from falling.

"Are you all right?"

"Yes, yes, no problem," said Mercedes, steadying herself. Her tanned cheeks flushed red.

"Watch the step," he said pointing down. She smiled, embarrassed. "See you then." And she was gone, again.

"Idiot," he muttered as he stood peering through the

window into the studio. "Watch the bloody step?" What a fool.

María waved at him as she did her stretches. Charlie waved back, glad that she had led him to Mercedes. He felt like such a tool for not taking his chance, but there was time, at least he knew where to find her now. A new hope had filled his misty clouds.

When Mercedes appeared, he watched as she took her stance in front of the ten girls, hoping that she would look towards the window at him. As she began to dance, the girls followed her moves. He admired what she was doing, helping young girls fulfill their dreams. He was sure something special could happen with her; he'd just have to be patient.

As he made his way back to see Ramón, his heart filled with joy as he relived the moment in his head when she'd noticed him standing there. The smile she'd made convinced him that she felt something too. He could tell by her eyes that she was also pleased he'd found her.

The way she spoke English was cute, but he felt embarrassed about his level of Spanish; he could barely string a sentence together. He'd have to start learning the language better. He would return to ask her out, as soon as he'd learned a bit more.

As he got near Ramón's, he had to conceal his excitement, he was grinning far too much. He couldn't let on that he knew where Mercedes was.

"So, did you find it okay?" asked Ramón as he opened up the door to his studio.

"Sure, took her right to the door."

"Thanks. She's a lovely girl, eh?"

"Indeed." But Charlie was thinking about Mercedes; lovely was the perfect word. "María was an amazing dancer for such a young girl."

"She has flamenco in her blood, in her family, it is easy for her. She will be a great dancer. Anyway, I owe you one."

"Don't mention it," said Charlie

"No, honestly, you saved me then. If there's anything I can do, which doesn't involve flamenco, then just ask."

Charlie's mind started ticking. Spanish classes, he had to improve his Spanish if he was going to stand a chance with Mercedes.

"Actually," said Charlie, "there is something…"

"Anything, *mi amigo*, anything."

"I want to improve my Spanish, you know, to help me with flamenco, understanding the lyrics and everything."

"But you are living in Spain. Learning Spanish is easy my friend. How do you think I have such good English? I lived in your country for five years and picked up everything I could."

"Yeah, exactly, but my life at the moment is guitar, guitar, guitar."

"That's true. You need to speak with people. If you want we can start chatting in Spanish?"

"No, not with you, you are the only person I know who speaks English well."

"Then make some friends; go and speak to the locals, we are friendly people, we don't bite."

"But it's not that easy…"

"Of course it's easy, easier than it was for me in England; you people can be difficult to talk to sometimes, always so busy, rushing around. I learned most of my English in my first year while I was working in a bar." Ramón stopped speaking suddenly and patted Charlie on the back.

"What?"

"That's it. I know how you can learn; get a job in a bar, it's the best way, you can speak to the other workers and also the customers."

"Sounds good; I could do with the cash too."

"Then leave it with me, I know a few people. I can find you a job. Just promise me one thing; don't let it interfere with your playing."

"*Si, señor!*" he said, saluting.

Mercedes' heart had been on fire for the whole class. Her concentration constantly swayed as she thought back to the moment when she'd seen Charlie. She'd felt such intense emotion when her eyes met his and was sure he felt the same.

She'd been desperately hoping Charlie would pick up María so she could find out more about him, so when María's mother turned up, disappointment ate into her stomach. The fear of losing him again was too much to take. She had to find out what she could.

"Excuse me," she said to María's mother.

"Yes, is everything okay?"

"Oh yes, perfect, María is a natural flamenco dancer and one of the best in the class."

"Thank you. She loves coming here; you do a fantastic job."

"Thanks. It's just I have a question."

"Sure."

"The man who brought María today, who was he?"

"My brother."

"Oh I see," she said, confused; she didn't look English in the slightest.

"No Mama, Ramón didn't bring me, it was Carlito."

"Carlito?" said the mother.

"Yes, he's from England, he plays the flamenco guitar."

As María said those words Mercedes' heart filled with joy. He was a guitarist? That must be why he was in Sevilla.

"I see," said the mother. "Well, I don't know him, but if he's a friend of Ramón then sure he's a good man."

"Of course," said Mercedes. "Okay, that's all. Thanks."

"See you soon," said María, smiling as they walked off.

As Mercedes turned to go back in, Lola was waiting for her.

"So?" she asked, smirking.

"So what?" Mercedes grinned to herself.

"Did you find out about him?"

"About who?"

"Do you think I am blind as well as gorgeous? I saw him chatting with you. I could have sworn he was dribbling."

"He was not," said Mercedes, laughing.

"So?"

"Oh, he's so cute; the way he speaks Spanish in that funny accent. He's a guitar player too."

"Really? What does he play?"

"Flamenco."

There was a little pause as the words that left Mercedes' mouth registered with her brain. A flamenco guitarist? From England?

"What, is he a beginner or something?"

"I don't know, but it explains why he's here."

"Yeah, and it explains why he'll probably go home again; once he realises he can never be a guitarist here. Don't forget how he behaved that night with Jesús."

"I know, but I'm sure that must have been a mistake. Anyway, can't you just let me be in a good mood? He came to find me."

"It was a coincidence, anyway, you'll just have to wait and see if he comes back."

"Yeah, I guess I will."

"Come on, let's go out for a quick drink to celebrate."

"I can't. I said I'd get back tonight, sorry, tomorrow."

"Fine, I'll just have to make do with my man."

"Sure you'll survive."

"I hope not," she said, winking. Mercedes tutted and laughed.

As Mercedes walked home, she realised that fate did exist. It was sweet that he'd come all this way to learn the guitar. She wondered if he was any good though, surely not.

She loved his cute Spanish accent, but what got her most was his smile; such innocence and honesty. Also, he was unlike so many of the sleazy men she knew. He hadn't even looked down her top, although, in this case, she wouldn't have minded if he had.

When she got in, she tried to hide her excitement.

"Hola Mama, Papa," she said, kissing both on the cheek as they sat in the lounge watching the T.V.

"Hola Hija, how was your day?" said Rosa.

"Fine, same as always; the girls are coming on well."

"That's good," said her father. For once he didn't have a go.

"I'm going to have a shower. Then I'll help with dinner."

"Sure," said Rosa, turning to watch the news.

Mercedes strolled past and went to her room. When she closed the door, an excited feeling entered her stomach. He'd found her. She threw her hands in the air, spun around in her room, and faced the mirror. She felt happier and more alive than she had for a long time. She smiled as she pictured him standing beside her, and thanked God for bringing him to her. She wanted to tell someone and share her feelings.

There was a knock at the door.

"Who is it?" she shouted.

"The boogie man."

Mercedes smiled, perfect timing. She knew she could trust her brother. She opened the door and pulled him in.

"Why, who were you expecting, your boyfriend?" She wished. Raul plonked down on her bed and leaned back on the heavy cushions. "Why do you have so many pillows on your bed?"

"I like them, what's it to you anyway?" Then she remembered she wanted Raul to be on her side; no arguing today. Mercedes was surprised how much he'd grown up recently, physically anyway, he was turning into an athletic, young man.

"Just asking."

"Sure, sorry, what do you mean by boyfriend?"

"Well, you are female, that's what they normally have; boyfriends." He held his hands up. "You don't need to get so defensive."

"I'm not."

"You are; I know you too well. So, who is he?" Mercedes raised her right eyebrow and stared at her brother. She thought about telling him, he knew lots of her secrets, like the time he caught her reading father's diary, and when she wet herself on her fifteenth birthday because she couldn't find her keys in her bag to get in. As far as she knew, he'd never told a soul.

"If I tell you, then you must promise not to tell *Papa*."

Raul sat up straight and grinned.

"Great, I love a bit of gossip."

"This is not gossip; it's about me. You'd better keep your mouth shut." Raul pressed his index finger closer to his thumb and pulled them along his mouth like a zip. He mumbled to show that he couldn't speak.

"Stop being silly," she said, smiling. Raul nodded, keeping his mouth closed. "Fine, about two months ago I met someone, well, more like saw someone."

"Uh-huh."

"I was feeling a bit down, trying to find the confidence to start dancing, when someone inspired me from the audience. You know what I'm like."

"Of course, shy."

"When I finally look up, guess who's staring at me?"

"Paco Lucia."

"You can be a real idiot sometimes, do you know that?"

"Yes, that's what brothers are for. So who was he?

"A blond man."

"A blond man?" Raul leaned forward and frowned. "What do you mean by blond?"

"Blond, you know, that light colour."

Raul grabbed hold of his sister's hands and pulled them into his stomach. He looked her deep in her eyes and swallowed.

"Are you trying to say that you've fallen in love with a *guiri*?" Raul scrunched his eyes and tightened his mouth. "Do you realise what will happen if Papa finds out?"

"I don't care what he thinks anymore. He wants me to become a civil worker and get married to some rich pompous Sevillano."

"But isn't that what every woman wants here?" Mercedes could tell Raul was getting a bit annoyed.

"Not me. I'm not letting him control my life."

"So what do you want to do? Get married to some hot

shot Hollywood American man?"

"English actually."

"Are you serious?" A silence followed as they looked into each other's eyes. Raul sat back and brushed his hand over his mouth and chin. She knew he'd support their father, but she needed him on her side this time. She bit her lip.

"I need your support Raul, please; tell me I can count on you."

Raul squeezed her hands more.

"You're crazy, you know that? You're playing with fire. If Papa finds out, then he'll completely lose it. I hope you know what you're doing." Raul grinned to show his appreciation. "Well I never, my sister with an Englishman."

"Thanks, Raul," she said, hugging him. "I can't wait for you to meet him."

"Meet him?"

"Yeah, you'll have to meet him one day."

"I suppose so. How many times have you been out with him anyway?" Mercedes went quiet.

"None yet."

"None?" Raul jumped back. "What? So where does he live?"

"Not sure."

"Name?"

"Charlie."

"Does he have big ears?"

"Don't be mean," said Mercedes as she laughed.

"Job?"

"No idea, but he plays the guitar."

"Everyone plays the guitar. So what do you know about him?" Mercedes took a breath, she didn't know much, but enough to feel something.

"That he's a gentle man, but not a mummy's boy. He encouraged me to dance once when I was stuck. He fidgets when he's nervous and is terrible at Spanish. His eyes are a deep blue, and I can see myself waking up with him every day."

"You've lost it," Raul said. Mercedes hunched back. "Look, I'm on your side; you're my sister, but I don't want to see you get hurt. You're falling in love with an English guy, and you don't know where he lives or what he does. You don't even know if he'll be in Spain for long. Please tell me he's Catholic." Raul said, crossing himself. Mercedes hesitated.

"He could be..."

"You don't know?" He crossed himself again. "Look, before you get carried away, promise that you'll find out more about him. Don't tell *Mama* yet, she'll only worry."

"I sort of have already."

"What?"

"It was a while ago, but she doesn't know as much as you."

"Best to keep it that way for a while, you know Papa can always figure out if something is wrong."

"That's true. Thanks, Raul."

"No problem, that's what brothers are for, just be careful." Mercedes sighed, she was scared, but something inside was telling her she was right.

Chapter 6 SPOTTED AT LAST

Mid November

"I have to find a new job in a *tablao*," Mercedes said tensely one dark evening in November as she walked arm in arm with her mother through the *Jardines de Murillo*. The air smelt fresh and wet. It was the first evening it hadn't chucked it down for almost two weeks.

"What for? I thought you were happier away from that world."

Mercedes looked deep into her mother's eyes and knew she was right. What was she thinking? Going back to being stared at by perverts was the last thing she wanted, and what if she bumped into Jesús while performing? She was unsure how she'd respond to seeing that vile man again.

But returning to the *tablaos* seemed like the only way she could bring him to her. She was still waiting for him to come by and speak with her again.

"I just think it will help me," was all she said, unsure about completely opening up.

"Help you what?"

"Keep busy, alive, and get rid of all this energy and emotion that is flying through my body." Mercedes had never felt so worked up. The sadness was eating into her heart; chewing away and nibbling into her soul, making her feel paranoid and worried about her future. Why hadn't he come by? Had he gone home? Tears began to trickle down her cheek.

"Mercedes, are you okay? I've never seen you like this. Are you crying, *Hija*?"

"No, *Mama*, I'm fine. I'm just a bit stressed, that's all. I miss dancing for an audience."

"Then speak to some people. There are plenty of *tablaos* around here." She loved her mother; she always knew how to say the right thing at the right time. "Is that it though, are you sure there isn't something else?" Her mother placed her cool hands on Mercedes' cheeks and smiled.

"*Si, Mama,* that's all."

"Nothing to do with that man?"

Mercedes felt scared, but she wanted to be honest; she couldn't hide any more secrets from her mother.

"Fine," she said, "you're right; it's him."

"What, did he hurt you?"

"Not directly."

"You saw him with another woman, didn't you?"

"Not technically. I wish I had, though. Then at least I'd know whether he was still in Sevilla."

"What do you mean, *Hija*?"

"The last time I saw him was a couple of weeks ago. He passed by my school because he dropped off one of my students. We spoke. He is English and has a terribly cute Spanish accent."

Rosa was smiling as her daughter spoke with such passion, suddenly she seemed alive again.

"Did you speak English?"

"Yes, I did. It felt great. He's a guitarist too. I think that's why he came to Sevilla."

"So why are you so upset?"

"Because he hasn't been back since, for almost two weeks. What if I never see him again? I just want to know whether he's still here."

"But you know Seville, the flamenco world is small. What have you done to find him?"

"Nothing."

"Why?"

"I don't know where to start."

"Were you just hoping he would come by?"

"Maybe."

"Listen, *Hija*, I'll give you some advice that my mother, God bless her soul, told me when I was interested in your father."

"You and *Papa*?"

"Of course, your father was a hit with the girls; they were all after him at school. He could have had any woman he wanted, but I got him."

"What did you do?"

"He was going out with another girl in the group. I knew he wasn't keen on her, so I started to date a lad in the group, just to make him jealous, and it worked, since then he's been mine."

"So what are you trying to say?"

"That the world is out there for you to take hold of. Be your own destiny. If you really think this guy is for you, then you have to fight for him. Think of where he could be. Try the flamenco guitar schools."

"Why the change in tune?" she asked.

"Well, I've been thinking and watching you. You remind me of myself when I was your age, not sure which man to go with, but obviously in love. I want to see you happy, even if it does mean upsetting your father. I'm not saying it's going to be easy. You know how traditional he is, but he does have a sensitive side too. He wants you to be happy."

"Even if that means being with a foreign man? Someone who isn't Catholic?"

"Love is love, my child, and sometimes you just have to accept things for the way they are."

"I know, but that's you. Try saying that to *Papa*. He's so

obsessed with me getting a job working for the government. He won't rest until he sees me walking down Avenida Constitucíon with a huge pram and Sevillano by my side. If he had his way, he would organise an arranged marriage."

Rosa chuckled as she placed an arm around her daughter.

"I think you might be exaggerating slightly. But you do have a point. First, find out more about this guy. Make sure he is still in Sevilla. Let me handle your father."

"Really?"

"I'll try." As her mother kissed her on the head, she felt less alone. Even though her mother had a good heart, she was still afraid of her father's dark side. Would he really tolerate an English guy? "Why don't you go out with your brother tomorrow night? Chat with him, he always cheers you up. He can take you to that restaurant you love in Plaza Doña Elvira."

"*Gracias Mama*, what a perfect idea." They hugged. Mercedes was glad she'd opened up. When they got back to the flat, they went into the kitchen, and Rosa called for Raul.

"*Si Mama.*"

"*Hijo*, why don't you take your sister out for dinner tomorrow night to Doña Elvira? She needs brightening up."

"Brightening up about what?" said Francisco, catching them out. He was nearly always in the lounge reading his paper when he was in, but they hadn't seen him.

"Nothing darling," said Rosa, smiling at her husband.

"What's up? Having second thoughts about flamenco yet?"

Mercedes respond, for once a look from Rosa shut

Francisco up. "Very well, if you need cheering up then why don't we all go out to eat tomorrow? It's been ages."

"Oh darling, let them go out on their own for once, just as brother and sister," said Rosa. But her look was soon cut short as Francisco raised his voice.

"Nonsense; they can go out after. We shall eat together as a family."

As the silence followed, Mercedes felt a wave of fear. Her mother may have calmed him down for a second, but he'd always have the last word. The power and control he had over them was frightening.

On the other side of Seville, waiting on a ceramic bench in Dona Elvira square, Charlie felt nervous as he made sure his tie was on straight. Who would have thought it? From a sales job in London to a waiter in Sevilla. It was his first time in smart clothes for work since Computer Jobbers. He hoped Peter Percy wasn't lurking about in the kitchen, ready to steal his orders.

Luckily, Ramòn had sorted him out with a job in a tapas bar with a couple of his colleagues. Charlie's main aim was to pick up enough Spanish so he could approach Mercedes and defend himself in a half decent conversation.

The square seemed like something out of a Spanish Fairy Tale; a romantic place where lovers came to listen to the water trickling out of the fountain as they kissed. Charlie imagined walking arm in arm with Mercedes around the square, chatting in Spanish and making her laugh.

Charlie gazed over towards the restaurant where he was due to start work and watched the two waiters laughing and joking as they lay the tables. One was a tall, athletic man with long hair and a neatly trimmed moustache. The other was a short stubby bald guy with a thick black beard and giant beer belly.

"*Hola*," said Charlie, walking up as they smoked cigarettes in the doorway.

"*Si señor*, you want table?" asked the tall one in a smooth tone.

"A table for one?" asked the short one, holding up one finger and laughing. Charlie couldn't see what was funny.

"Juan? Or one?" said the tall guy, patting his sidekick on the back.

"*No gracias*," said Charlie, smirking at their silly joke. "*Esta aqui Pedro?*"

"Pedro? You are looking for the Pedro?" said the short one. "Jorge, do you know the Pedro?"

"The Pedro? Let me see," said the tall one, rubbing his beard. "*Si*, yes, I know him, I think he works here, he is a little fatty, and stupid."

"Eh? Less of the stupid, you mudafucka," said the short one, elbowing Jorge in the ribs. "Who are you, anyway?"

"Charlie, Ramón sent me here to work for Pedro."

"Ah," they both said, suddenly holding themselves upright and appearing apologetic.

"*Lo siento*, I am the Pedro," said the short one, holding out his hand. "You can never be sure who is trying to find you. Yes, Ramón, tell me about the *guiri* who want to work. Welcome, welcome, a friend of Ramón is a friend of us."

"That's great," said Charlie, almost getting his arm pulled out of the socket by the force of Pedro's handshake.

"Now come," said Pedro, putting on a stern face. "If you come to work, then you work, please, follow me." Jorge winked and smiled at Charlie as he went inside.

Pedro tapped his fingers along the smooth, shiny wooden bar, dusted along the tops of the barstools and stopped next to the kitchen.

"So," said Pedro, "you can speak the English."

"I am English," said Charlie, smirking.

"Listen, I do the jokes here. How is your Spanish?"

"It's okay, that's one of the reasons why I want to work for you; to practice my Spanish."

"I'm sorry, you want to work here to practice your Spanish?" said Pedro, scrunching his right eye. "Did I hear *correctemente*?" Charlie could sense he was getting off to a bad start, and that his chances of practicing Spanish with these guys was going to be slim.

"Well, that and to work, I like working…"

"Come on, no joke with me; no one likes working, especially in *España* and even more so in Andalucia. If you want to learn Spanish, you can go to Spanish school. Here we serve tapas, we clean, and maybe we have beer when the night finish. Sometimes we have joke, but principally to work. Not to learn the Spanish." As he finished, he let out a long chesty cough.

"Sure, sure," said Charlie.

"Come," said Pedro, walking through the bar into the sticky, greasy smelling kitchen. Once Pedro had shown him the toilets, cloak room, and seating area upstairs looking out over the plaza, he grabbed one of the menus on the table.

"Now, read this menu," said Pedro, almost flinging it at him.

"Okay," said Charlie, holding the leather cover and reading it over. After a few seconds, Pedro interrupted.

"No in head, read, read. I want see how you speak the Spanish."

"Ah, I see. Okay, here goes." He cleared his throat. *"Primera plato,"* he said, slowly. "Ensaaalaaadaaaa." Pedro grabbed the menu and whacked Charlie on the arm with it.

"Look, *guiri*, you have to speak fast, this is a tapas bar, not a home for the old persons."

"Right, of course." He gazed at the menu but felt conscious about his pronunciation.

"Ensalada de polo, ensaladila de gambas."

"Poiyyyooo, ensaladiyyyyya de gambas. The double 'l' is like a 'y' sound. How long you are in Sevilla?"

"Almost three months?"

"And you not know this. Maybe you do need Spanish classes. What have you been doing if you don't know the Spanish?"

"Learning the flamenco guitar." Pedro frowned.

"*Como?* What?"

"The guitar, I've been learning the flamenco guitar."

Pedro began to chuckle. "I sorry, you learn *la guitarra flamenca*?"

"Yep."

"You? A guiri? This is funny, please, where is the camera?" Pedro leaned out a window and shouted down. "Jorge, come, listen, our friend has a funny joke to say." Within seconds Jorge was sprinting up the stairs.

"Yes, what is the joke?"

"Say him, come on, say, say," said Pedro.

"I play the flamenco guitar," said Charlie, beginning to get annoyed.

"He what?" said Jorge.

"Play the flamenco guitar, like my *abuela*, my granny," said Pedro, slapping hands with Jorge as they both cracked up.

"Are you serious?" said Jorge, spluttering.

"Well, how do you think I know Ramón?" said Charlie,

in a serious tone. How dare they insult him? He was about to forget about the whole thing, especially as he wasn't going to practice his Spanish much anyway.

"Is true, is true," said Pedro. "But Ramón teach a *guiri* our secrets?"

"All of them," said Charlie, holding up his hand to show his nails. Pedro grabbed it and felt the hard tips of his fingers.

"Is possible. Then, if is true, tomorrow you can bring guitar, okay?"

"Sure," said Charlie, beginning to relax a little.

"Now, let's look again at the menu. Repeat after me: ensalada de poiyyyo..."

After a quick pronunciation lesson on the menu and a tour of the downstairs area, Charlie was left to get on with it. There wasn't any formal training or group bonding sessions like there had been at Computer Jobbers. This was all about learning on the job, and he didn't get off to an ideal start.

His first night was a disaster. He was jittery and shaky most of the time. He knocked over a couple of glasses of beer and wine, and even messed up orders because he didn't understand the Spanish accent. Pedro and Jorge had to translate most of the time. At the end of the night, he was expecting Pedro to sack him.

"Good work Carlito, see you tomorrow," said Pedro.

"But I had a terrible night. All that beer and wine I spilled on customers, and I didn't understand them most of the time."

"Don't worry, be happy. For a strange reason, there were many clients from the Barcelona, they are dirty Catalanas and speak funny. Silly *accento*. Is no problem if you drop wine on them. Tomorrow we see you, and no forget guitar."

"Great, okay, thanks," said Charlie as he shook his hands, surprised to still have a job.

Mercedes felt better the following morning having a plan to go out that evening, even if she wasn't that keen on dining with her father. She felt tense and didn't want him to find out anything about her feelings. She was looking forward to going out with Raul, though.

The evening was cold, so she wore her favourite blue dress with thick tights, her best blue blazer, a green scarf that her mother had given her last Christmas, and black knee high boots.

"*Que guapa,*" said Francisco when Mercedes came along the corridor, "off anywhere special?"

"Only out with my lovely family," she replied, kissing her father on the cheek, trying to ease the tension.

"That's how I like to see my *princesa*, elegant like her mother."

Rosa appeared in the doorway in a long white dress and a blue jacket. She'd curled her hair, so it bounced on her shoulders.

"Wow *Mama*, you look great."

"You both make me proud," said Francisco, "my pretty wife and daughter."

"They are not that bad," said Raul, coming out the kitchen dressed in his beige trousers and blue and red striped shirt with a burgundy jumper traipsed over his shoulders.

"Typical Sevillano," said Mercedes, giggling.

"What?" he said, looking in the mirror.

"You're the poshest of the posh," said Rosa.

"He looks good," said his father. "Come on, the table is

booked for nine."

As usual, Mercedes walked arm in arm with her mother while the men led the way.

"So?" said Rosa.

"So, what?" said Mercedes.

"Was today a good day?" she said, smiling and winking.

"No, *Mama*, it wasn't, but it's fine. I just want to concentrate on tonight anyway. Let's enjoy ourselves."

"Okay, *Hija*, as you wish."

As they passed Mercedes' favourite fountain, hidden in the back-street of the *Barrio de Santa Cruz,* she remembered how many of her wishes had come true there.

"Wait," she shouted.

"What is it?" said her father, turning angrily. "I don't want to be late."

"But we aren't even meeting anyone, besides, I want to make a wish."

"Aren't you a little too old to make wishes?" asked Raul.

"You are never too old for wishes," said Rosa. "You should always have dreams my son; they are what keep the world moving."

"Whatever," said Raul, "come on; I'm hungry."

"Papa, can you give me a coin?" Francisco fished about in the loose change in his pocket, pulled out a euro coin, and flipped it at his daughter. Mercedes caught it and stood on a step so she could peer over the railings and glance down at her reflection. Was that really her? She had grown into a woman, one she had always wanted to be, a dancer and a teacher, and all she needed now was a man, but not just any man, she wanted Charlie. She wished that their paths would meet again soon. She flipped the coin, and it landed with a splash. For a second she thought she saw her grandfather smiling and nodding at her in the reflection, but he vanished. She missed him.

"What did you wish for?" asked Raul.

"You know she can't tell you, son," said Rosa. "Come, let's go."

As Mercedes walked down the side street towards Doña Elvira, she promised herself that if she didn't see him within a week, then she'd get on with her life. But she trusted her fountain and felt optimistic about her dream coming true.

Even though Pedro had praised Charlie for managing the Catalans, he was still unsure of himself. Speaking in Spanish under pressure was a lot harder than he'd imagined. He seemed to turn into a different person; someone much less confident and more serious. For his second night, he was apprehensive about dealing with tricky customers again.

He'd practised his guitar in the morning to shake off the feeling and gather his strength and confidence, but it was no use; the more he thought about the evening, the further he sank into his shell. He hadn't felt this vulnerable for ages, perhaps since he was at school and had to perform as one of the wise men in the nativity play. He'd been so nervous that he'd dropped the gift of gold on baby Jesus. The laughter from the audience haunted him throughout his school days.

The walk to work was insufferable. His throat was dry, and the guitar case handle became wet with sweat. He kept going over the pronunciation of the menu in his head and muttering to himself as he made his way through the centre. He tried to distract himself by thinking about Mercedes, but even that had the opposite effect and just dented his confidence.

As soon as he saw the welcoming smile from Pedro, he felt nerves ooze away slightly.

"*Hombre...*" said Pedro, reaching out to shake his hand. "The *guiri* guitarist has returned."

"*Buenas noches,*" said Charlie, trying to insist on speaking Spanish.

"*Impressonante*, you have bringed your guitar. Can I see?"

"*Si,*" said Charlie, handing over the heavy case.

"Come," said Pedro, leading him inside.

It was still a bit early for customers, so they sat down, and Pedro placed the case on the table. As he clicked it open and raised the lid, his eyes widened.

"Jorge, come, you *imbecil*, come and see this masterpiece." Jorge ran from out the back and almost slipped on the floor beside the table.

"*Que?*" said Jorge, but he had already fixed his eyes on the guitar. "Is really?"

"Of course it is real," said Pedro, holding it up to the light. "Where you get this?"

"I bought it," said Charlie.

"Ah, okay, Carlito. So, now you can play?" asked Pedro.

"Now?" said Charlie. Pedro gave him the guitar and began to clap, as did Jorge.

"*Ole, Carlito,* come on, show us the flamenco," said Pedro.

Charlie held the guitar and ran his fingers along the strings softly.

"*Ole,*" said Jorge, clapping enthusiastically. Charlie laughed at their keenness as he began to play more.

Soon he was in his own world, playing the *palos* that Ramón had taught him as if he'd played them a thousand times already. His confidence began to grow. Pedro and

Jorge were both in silence now, watching in awe.

He imagined her in the bar now, dancing alongside him, moving gracefully up and down and tormenting the crowd that had formed. He so wished to play for her.

"*Buenas noches,*" said a man from the door.

"*Buenas noches caballero,*" said Pedro, shooting up straight. Jorge followed quickly as if royalty had just entered.

Charlie stopped playing and turned around. A tall, dark man in a navy suit was in the doorway, chatting with Pedro. He'd not known Pedro long, but could see he was more polite than usual.

"Important client," whispered Jorge. "You play later," he added, winking.

Charlie packed his guitar away and left it out the back. By the time he'd returned, Jorge and Pedro were busy rushing about the restaurant making sure all the tables were ready. Charlie could immediately feel the urgency with which they were working, much more than the previous night.

"Carlito, come," said Pedro, waving him over towards the bar. Charlie leaned in as he whispered. "There is important client outside with family. Take his order, be nice; he can be difficult."

"Is he Catalan?"

"Catalan?" Pedro said, laughing. "He is more *andaluz* than the *gazpacho*. Go, don't leave him wait."

Charlie was curious to ask why Pedro wanted him to serve them, but he just got on with it. He felt nervous as he walked outside towards the table in the corner where the family of four sat. Charlie looked straight at the father and smiled as he approached.

"*Si señor?*" said Charlie, standing with his notebook and

pen. The man looked Charlie up and down and smirked.

"*Es un guiri?*" he said, openly across the table. Charlie could tell by the tone that the man was trying to be funny, but he let it go. Charlie scanned the rest of the family, the mother smiled, as did the son, but the daughter had her head buried in the menu.

"*Mira,*" said the man, "*dos cervezas, un botella de vino tinto, Rioja, y un botella de agua.*"

"*Y acietunas,*" said the woman.

"Olives? Very good, I mean, *muy bien,*" said Charlie, flipping his notebook shut as he walked off.

He wondered why the man had spoken with such a sarcastic tone. Was it a problem being foreign in Sevilla? Ramón had said that being a *guiri* flamenco guitarist would be tricky; people wouldn't accept him, but this was the first hostile treatment he'd felt in Sevilla - apart horse shit incident. He tried not to let it bother his mood though.

Once Charlie had the drinks on his tray, he went back out. There were more customers outside, and the place was filling up. On his way over to the table, he looked straight at the daughter, who was laughing at something the brother had said. He almost froze.

Mercedes.

He'd never seen her smile like that before. She'd always been so serious when dancing and had smirked when they met that time, but never laughed to show the full happiness inside her. He couldn't help but smile, her energy was contagious and distracting.

"*Tu vino,*" he said, looking at the father before turning to smile at Mercedes. Charlie's heart fluttered, and adrenaline rushed through his veins as she smiled back, but suddenly sadness crept upon him when she shook her head slightly as if telling him not let on that they knew each other.

Then her jaw dropped slightly as she stood to reach towards him, but it was too late. Charlie woke from his gaze as the bottle smashed on the table.

"*Que idiota,*" shouted Francisco, rising to his feet. He continued to rant at Charlie.

"*Lo siento, lo siento,*" said Charlie, in shock. He gazed down at the red stain on the woman's dress; Mercedes' mother's dress.

"*No hay problema,*" said the mother, wiping herself down with serviettes. The father was still shouting and waving his arms in the air.

"*Buenas noches,*" said Pedro, jumping in to save the day. As Pedro tried to calm Francisco, Charlie glanced at Mercedes. He could tell she felt sorry for him by the way she cowered away, but she also seemed embarrassed about her father's reaction. He wanted to say something to her, but instead just winked and shrugged his shoulders. She smirked back, but only briefly.

"Can you please apologise to the family again," said Pedro.

"Sure, *lo siento,*" he said, facing the table.

"Go get another *botella de vino,*" he said. "I take the order."

Charlie whizzed inside, severely shaken up after making such an error. Was there hope for him and Mercedes with such an aggressive father who had something against *guiris*?

Just as Charlie was about to take out the wine, Pedro entered.

"Look, Carlito, it is better that Jorge serve that family," he said, placing a hand on his shoulder. "That is Francisco Nieto, one of our exclusive clients. He is a difficult man; a bit of a *guilipollas*, how do you say, arsehole, so don't worry."

"Sure," said Charlie, wondering why he was so important. It was probably best to keep a distance anyway. At least he could keep an eye on Mercedes from afar.

"There is a *guiri* family over there on table five, serve them." Pedro took the bottle of wine and whizzed away.

The rest of the night was reasonably uneventful. Charlie managed to keep all the bottles of wine on his tray, and even served a couple of Spanish families without a breakdown in communication. It was a lot easier when they weren't chatting in Catalan.

Occasionally, he glimpsed over to Mercedes, but most of the time she had her attention on her family. Now and then she would glance over at him. She never smiled or winked, but Charlie could tell by her deep stare that she was dying to speak to him as much as he was to her. His pulse raced the whole night, wondering whether he should make a move and approach the table. He had to communicate with her. He couldn't just let her go without saying anything. Then he had an idea.

"Pedro," he said, catching him inside.

"Yes, Carlito, please tell me you not drop more wine."

"No, it's just, I still feel bad about the woman's dress. Can I go over and take the bill?"

"You are sure? Señor Nieto can be aggressive," he whispered.

"I can see that. I have to say something."

"Okay, but be careful."

For a second he'd regretted asking, what was he going to say? He wanted to speak to Mercedes, but that was impossible with her crazy father there. What if he jumped at him again? He had to try something though.

As he walked over, he fixed his eyes on Mercedes and

waited to see her reaction. When she glanced up, he winked and poked his tongue out slightly. She smirked.

"*Señores,*" said Charlie, as he placed the silver tray with the bill on the table, "*por favor, lo siento mucho por el vino,*" he added, apologizing again for the wine.

"*Que?*" said Francisco, rising from his seat quickly. "*Imbecil, imbecil,*" he added as he pointed to the stain on his wife's dress. Why had he bothered? He tried to apologise, but the words wouldn't come out. He looked at Mercedes, who held her hand over her eyes, not wanting to look. Francisco was ranting, but Charlie was oblivious to the stream of words as he stared at Mercedes, waiting to see her look at him.

"*Okay, okay, no problema,*" said Rosa, standing up and placing her hands on Francisco's shoulders. He went to say something else, but Rosa gave him a deep look, as if to say enough was enough.

Francisco sat down, pulled out his wallet and threw notes onto the tray.

"*Gracias, y buenas noches,*" said Charlie as he picked up the money. He peaked at Mercedes. She had a look of pity on her face. He winked. She blushed and smiled. That was all he wanted; a reaction to show she felt something. He didn't care about upsetting her father; it was worth the risk just to see her smile again. The next day, he would go to see her.

"You like the lady, no?" asked Pedro, snapping him out of his gaze.

"What, me? No…" he said, taken aback.

"I am no silly. I see you, looking at her all the night. That is why you want to take the bill."

"Not at all, I was just worried about the father."

"*Si si,*" said Pedro. "You worry about father, if you want

to be with his daughter, then be careful; he is difficult man. Come, people are waiting. Don't forget you play soon, one more hour!"

As the night went on, Charlie felt more comfortable serving and speaking in Spanish. Anything was a doddle after serving Mercedes' father. He was upbeat and glad that he'd taken the risk to see how Mercedes would react but concerned about what Pedro had said about her father.

Once everyone had left, and the restaurant was cleared, Pedro poured three beers and plonked them down on a table outside.

"It's time to watch our *guiri* play," said Pedro.

"Okay, let's do it," said Charlie, undoing his case and getting comfortable on a bar stool which Pedro had brought from inside.

The moon light mixed with the orange glow from the street light came down on Charlie as he sat tuning his guitar. Pedro and Jorge were in front, both clapping softly as he began to play.

Charlie closed his eyes as he let the flamenco take control of his hands. He thought of Ramón, standing beside him as he played for the first time in front of Sevillanos. This was his first real audience.

He thought of Mercedes and felt pity for her, stuck with such an aggressive father. She looked so sweet and innocent sitting there, cowering away as her father let rip. She was such a different woman to the one he'd seen dancing. He imagined her dancing next to him, dressed in the same red dress she wore the first time he saw her, tapping away with her feet. He could feel her presence and passion as she danced for him, slamming her heels and moving her body in rhythm.

He craved to play for her.

When he finished, he looked up, and Pedro and Jorge were both standing, applauding their new friend.

"I no know how you play like that, but you're *impressionante*," said Pedro, slapping him on his back.

"*Fantástico, Fantástico,*" said Jorge.

"You can play more?" said Pedro.

"Sure, sure," said Charlie, plucking away again. He felt great; on such a high after the intense day. He couldn't wait to tell Ramón that he'd played in front of his first audience. The next day he would finally ask Mercedes out.

He was unaware that from a corner of the plaza, in a trance as she hid with her brother, was Mercedes.

About an hour later, while Charlie was making his way home after sharing his talents with Pedro and Jorge, Mercedes was dancing with her brother in a packed salsa bar. It had been ages since they'd been out together dancing. They had grown up with music, always dancing with each other at parties and weddings. Mercedes always wondered whether Raul could have made it as a flamenco dancer, but he was more into his studies.

Raul spun her about the room as they danced in front of the live band, but Mercedes could only think about Charlie playing the guitar. She had been blown away by his skill and talent. She'd never seen a foreigner play so well before and was eager to know how he'd learned. Her feelings for him were all confirmed in those brief moments while she was watching him. She yearned to dance and be close to him while he played, and show him more about the art of flamenco.

"What's up with you tonight?" said Raul as they sat down on some sofas in a quieter area upstairs. Other couples were dotted about the place, chatting contently.

"Don't tell me, you can't get that guy out of your head."

Mercedes smiled.

"You're right, I can't. Did you see how he played?"

"Yes I saw, that's all you asked me during the ten-minute walk here. Listen," he said, grabbing her hand. Mercedes knew what was coming by his serious tone and expression, dread filled her heart. "I know you have feelings for this guy, and he does seem decent, but, it's just…"

"I know, I know, it's *Papa*." She'd seen him lose his temper on several occasions, but she'd never seen him get so irate in public like that before. He was normally more controlled.

"Did you see his face tonight?" asked Raul. "I honestly thought he was going to smack the guy. I felt sorry for him."

"Me too, I wanted to get up and push *Papa* away."

"You wouldn't have dared?"

"Of course not, but he went too far. I've never seen him get so angry before. What does he have against *guiris* so much?"

There was a silence while Raul chose his words.

"It's a bit more complicated than you think. You know what he's like: a real traditional man, he believes in his country, his people. Grandfather was in the war, you know."

"But that was years ago, the world is changing now."

"Not in his eyes. He sees *guiris* as a threat, taking jobs of Spanish people, especially in this recession. In part I agree with him, why he has to work in a restaurant is beyond me."

"But he's just doing a job, working and providing a service for us."

"Yeah, great service, knocking a bottle of wine on Mama's dress. Do you know how much it cost?"

"Too much."

"True. Anyway, the point is that if *Papa* reacted like that after he poured a bottle of wine over, how do you think he will react if you turn up at home with him asking if you can go to live in England?"

"I don't want to live in England, I want to be here."

"Yes, but with someone who wants to live here, a Sevillano, or at least a Spanish man."

"You are just the same as *Papa*, why are you so narrow-minded?"

"Narrow-minded? Me? You're a Spanish woman; this man will only hurt you."

"How do you know that?"

"How do you know he won't?"

"Because I just do, the way he looks at me, the way he smiles. He fills me with joy."

"He will also fill you with sadness. I know you think most Sevillanos are pigs and liars, but how can you be sure he is any different?"

"I just do."

"*Hermanita*, you are playing with fire."

"Look, I need your support in this. You saw how he played; he has a special talent. I have to speak with him, dance for him."

"Dance for him? Are you crazy?"

"Maybe, but that's how I feel. I can't hide my feelings anymore."

"Look, I'll stick by you, but the one you have to convince is *Papa*."

"Sure," said Mercedes. She knew he was right; her father wouldn't approve, but she had to follow her heart.

The following morning, Mercedes heard shouting and banging as she made her way towards the kitchen and realised the full extent of the fight she was going to have on her hands.

"But I still think I should go back and tell them how it ought to be," shouted her father.

"Will you just calm down," said her mother. "The waiter came back and apologised, everyone makes mistakes, well, almost everyone."

"What is that supposed to mean?" said Francisco, throwing his hands in the air. "The point is he should never have even been serving us in the first place. How dare they give a job to a *guiri* over a Spaniard! There are good, hard working men out there with no jobs, it's just not right."

Mercedes stood outside, waiting to hear her mother's response. She wanted to barge in and ask what difference it made if he was English or Spanish? Europe was a free continent, and people could come and go as they pleased. She wanted to remind her father how much tourism brought business into Spain. The world was changing, and he had to accept it.

"What's going on?" said Mercedes as she stuck her head round the door.

"Nothing, *Hija*," said her mother, "are you coming for breakfast?"

"Of course she is," blurted her father. Sometimes he could be such a *machista*. Did Mercedes not have her own voice?

"What's with all the shouting?"

"Nothing, it's between your mother and me."

"If it's between you two, then why can I hear?"

Mercedes felt naughty but satisfied. She wasn't going to shut up anymore.

"Well, maybe you shouldn't be listening in on our conversation."

"It's a bit hard not to with all that shouting."

Francisco stared into his daughter's eyes and seemed to control himself from blowing his top. Mercedes could tell by his look that she had annoyed him, part of her was afraid, but the other stronger side of her, which was starting to flourish, was sick of not being able to express her views in her own house.

"I'll pretend I didn't hear that," said Francisco.

"Come on dear, grab your coat," said Rosa. "It's late, and they might run out of *churros*."

Mercedes nodded, walked towards the hallway and grabbed her coat. She could feel her parents communicating in some way. Sure her mother was telling her father to calm down, it wasn't the first time he'd lost it at her.

They walked over to their usual spot in silence. Mercedes could tell that her father was still annoyed by the way he was huffing and tutting to himself. Once they were sat down around a table in the sun, he darted off inside.

"Was that him?" said Rosa.

"*Mama*," said Mercedes, shocked by her mother's sixth sense. "How do you know?"

"How do I know? Well, for one, you didn't stop looking over at him all night, and two, you smiled every time he came close, and three, your eyes have never looked so in love."

Mercedes blushed, was she really in love?

"Okay, yes it was. What do you think?" Mercedes felt joy. Finally, she could open to her mother.

"Oh, he's lovely, clumsy, but lovely, just the type of guy who you used to talk about when you were younger." Mercedes could tell by the tone that something else was coming.

"But?"

"Did you not see your father's reaction?"

"You said you could handle him and that everything would be all right."

"I know, but his aggressive ways are worrying me. I think he's too stressed out at work. Shush, he's coming."

Francisco came over and slumped in his chair.

"It's just not right," he said, slamming his fist on the table.

"Francisco," said Rosa, in a firm voice. "Leave it, we have had this out. If you feel that strongly about it, then go back and speak to the owners, but as far as I'm concerned this conversation is over."

"I will. I'll go back after breakfast and tell the owners, remind them of their duties as Spanish people to employ their own, not to consider employing clumsy *guiris* who can't even speak our language."

"*Papa*," said Mercedes, but she realised that what she wanted to say was not going to go down well.

"Yes, *Hija*?" said Francisco, biting his lip.

Mercedes imagined telling him that she knew the waiter and that he was a finer man than any she had met; he'd even learned how to play flamenco. She imagined saying that she was seeing him and there was nothing he could do to stop it. But, instead, she said.

"Try to calm down, it won't do you any good being angry, there are plenty more important things to worry about." The tone she used calmed him surprisingly, and he seemed to listen. He let out his frustration in a long sigh.

"I am calm," he said. With that, the waiter brought over their coffee and churros and the topic changed as they spoke about Mercedes' night out with Raul.

By the time they had finished breakfast, her father seemed to have forgotten about going to the restaurant. He went off to work, and she walked with her mother.

"You have to be careful, Mercedes."

"I am careful; I still don't know if he will even come and see me."

"I'm sure he will. I saw him smiling and winking at you."

"You don't miss a thing, do you?"

"That's why I'm your mother. Look, I know you have feelings for him and everything, but you need to consider the impact it will have on your father. I know I said I can handle him, and I can, but if you are to be with this man, then you really need to find out his intentions. Look, I need to rush. I'm meeting a friend."

"Fine, I'll see you tonight," said Mercedes, kissing her mother on the cheek. "*Adios.*"

As Mercedes walked to work, she wondered whether she was playing with fire. She knew that she had some control over her father; she had calmed him down at least, but to imagine turning up one evening with Charlie would probably be suicidal. She knew her father's traditions were important to him: his religion, his church, Semana Santa and his country. He was a patriot, but sometimes he took it too far. Why was he so wrapped up in his own people?

Maybe she was being foolish though. She still didn't know much about Charlie, and to upset her father would cause a massive rift in her family. They were the most important thing in her life, as well as flamenco, so risking it all for a guy that she knew little about could prove fatal.

He hadn't come to see her either, after almost two weeks of knowing where she was. She could tell he was trying to communicate with her the previous night, but maybe it was too late, how long was he going to take?

Feelings were feelings though, and not so easy to control.

She'd never felt so confused in her life.

Charlie was walking along the river towards the centre on his way to see Mercedes. He felt like a complete idiot about the accident. How could he have been such a fool and dropped wine on her mother? He had to apologise again, or at least use it as an excuse to speak to her. He was sure she felt something and was optimistic about not getting knocked back. He was also on a high after the support from his new mates about his guitar playing. He'd always been sure about his talent for playing and wanted to make something of himself. Now that he'd got a taste for it, he wanted to take it to the next level.

As he got closer to the flamenco school, he began to feel edgy, though. What would he say? Should he mention the father? It was probably best not to bring it up.

Once at the end of the road where she worked, he caught sight of her chatting to a group of mothers. He tensed up as he realised that he was finally going to make his move. Hopefully, the Spanish that he'd been practising would pay off.

As soon as he saw the last woman leave, he made his way over to the door. He rang the bell and stood outside, smiling, but jittery.

The door opened, and she peered round, the sweet smell of her perfume filled his nostrils.

"*Hola*," she said, in a surprised tone.

"*Hola*," he said, waving. Not cool, he thought.

"How are you?" she said, pulling the door open, but keeping back.

"Fine, good, and you?" he asked, forgetting about his Spanish straight away.

"Fine, now, yes," she said, smiling. "This is surprise," she added, but the tone was not as welcoming as he'd hoped. He could sense something was up; she wasn't as warming as before.

"Sure, it's just I wanted to say *lo siento*, that I'm sorry."

"For what?"

"*El vino*," he said, imitating when he knocked the wine over. She laughed.

"Is no problem. You say sorry last night, is fine."

"Right, that's good. It's just, your father seemed so angry and…" he stopped, not wanting to put his foot in it.

"Yes, it was an accident."

"*Si*," he said, thinking that he was making one right now. She was still back in the doorway. He had expected her to be much more smiley, or even laughing like she had with her brother, but she was defensive and cold. Had he misread the situation?

"Is anything more?" she asked.

"Anything more?"

"Yes, is just, I need go now."

"Oh, I see, well, no…" Charlie immediately regretted saying no. *Say something you idiot, ask her out for a drink*, said his inner voice.

"No?" she said, raising her eyebrows. "Only you come to say sorry?"

"Yes," said Charlie, "I mean no, well, it's just; I thought that maybe…"

"*Si?*"

"Well, I like the way you dance."

"*Gracias*."

"And, I thought if you dance in a new *tablao* now, where I can see you again?"

"No, no more. I only dance here, with my students."

"Oh I see," said Charlie, losing his confidence straight away. She was practically saying she wasn't interested in him at all, and why would she be? "Okay then, well, I'll see you around."

"Okay," said Mercedes, cowering away, she seemed like she wanted to say something, but didn't. "Bye bye," she said, waving.

"See you."

As Charlie made his way back home, with his tails between his legs, he was angry at himself for getting his wires crossed. How had he been such a fool to think she would be interested in him? She must have thought he was a complete idiot knocking the wine on his mother, and he hadn't even spoken in Spanish.

He felt like he'd just ended a four-year relationship, as if he'd asked someone to marry him and she'd said no, or worse, had been waiting at the church only to be told that his future wife had run off with his best man.

There was only one thing for it. Once he got home, he dived straight into his room and pulled out his guitar, however, for the first time ever, he couldn't play. He stared at his hands, but they refused to move. He tried to force himself to start plucking, but his wrists were weak.

His heart ached deep inside, he'd never felt this way before. He honestly thought there could be something between them. Before she'd seemed so encouraging and positive; her body language showed that she felt something for him. But just then she was a different woman, keeping her body away. He felt like a fool, within twenty-four hours he'd ruined his chances with her.

He went out on the balcony with his guitar and held it tightly as he looked over Sevilla. Was this his place? Why was he really here? He was unsure.

Chapter 7 A TRUE PERFORMANCE

Early December

Lola and Mercedes were standing together outside the dance school. Lola was shuffling about in her suitcase, splayed openly on the floor.

"Now, are you sure you're up to this?" asked Lola, as she delved in for the fifth time in the same number of minutes.

"Of course I am, what's up anyway, why are you so jittery? That's not like you."

"I know, I'm just a bit nervous. I have a feeling Miguel is going to propose to me."

Mercedes let out a scream of joy and hugged her best friend.

"What, really?"

"Yes, and I'm sure I put in my extra sexy lingerie, but I can't seem to find it." Lola scrambled in her bag again.

"I'm sure you won't really need it much though, will you?"

"Dirty cow, you have a point though," she said, looking up.

"How do you know he's going to propose, anyway?"

"Men are obvious. He was playing with my ring the other day, doing some silly game on my fingers to see if this ring fit on all my other fingers. Honestly, does he think I was born yesterday? He also said we are going away for a weekend with another couple. But I know full well that the other lady is working, so he must be about to ask me to marry him."

"Sounds like it, yes. Oh, that's great news." If only someone was going to propose to her, but she was a long way off from that moment.

"So, are you going to be all right?" asked Lola, placing both hands on Mercedes' shoulders. "All you have to do is teach these next couple of classes and then lock up. I've cancelled all my private classes. We'll be back on Sunday night, so I'll see you on Monday."

Just as she said that, Miguel pulled up and tooted his horn.

"You're late," said Lola.

"Sorry, I was cleaning the car."

"Useless. Come on, let's go. We don't want to let your friends down now, do we?" Lola turned and winked to Mercedes, who smiled back. Lola leaned over and kissed Mercedes on the cheek.

"Have fun," said Mercedes, waving as they pulled away. She turned around and looked at the dance school. "So it's just you and me now," she muttered, suddenly feeling the responsibility of looking after Lola's school on her own. It was only really for one morning, but still, if anything went wrong, it would be on her shoulders.

The first class went reasonably well. Mercedes taught the girls a few routines and stretches, and everyone left as happy as ever. It was the second class that caught her off guard. While the girls were practising their steps, Mercedes went into a day dream as an image of Charlie appeared at the back playing his guitar.

He was wearing a smart white shirt and black trousers, his hair hanging down over his face as he played. She was fascinated to know how he'd become such a great flamenco guitarist and was aching to see him play, and dance for him. Why hadn't she spoken up when he came and told him her true feelings?

Then one of the girls fell to the floor with a thump.

Mercedes could have sworn she'd been pushed.

"Carlota," shouted Mercedes, "what are you doing, pushing Carmen on the floor like that? Come here, stand in the corner." Mercedes rushed over.

"She pushed me first, and kicked me," said Carlota as she cowered towards Mercedes.

"Did not," said Carmen, weeping as she got up off the floor.

"I will not have this behaviour in my class," said Mercedes, wagging her finger at Carlota. "If you continue like this, then you'll be out."

"But she…"

"That is the end of the matter. Now go and get changed, both of you."

As Mercedes watched Carlotta storm into the changing rooms, she immediately felt guilty. She'd never lost her temper like that in class before. What if Carmen had actually kicked her? She began to panic about the reaction of Carlota's parents too. Maybe she had overstepped the mark. What the hell was Lola going to say?

When the parents turned up to collect their children, Carlota ran out of the studio crying. Mercedes followed and tried to catch the mother as they got into their car, but she just gave her an evil look and drove away. *Great, just what I needed*, she thought as she cleared up the studio.

She considered phoning Lola straight away before the mother did, but she didn't want to ruin her romantic trip. She needed to chat with her mother.

After dinner that evening, Francisco and Raul popped out for a beer and Mercedes helped her mother in the kitchen.

"What's wrong, *Hija*? You are very quiet tonight." Mercedes was stacking the clean plates away.

"Nothing, well, it's just I feel a bit upset." Mercedes turned to face her mother, slightly teary.

"Why, what's happened?" Her mother pulled up a chair and motioned for her to sit down.

"Well, I made a mistake at work. I saw a girl fall on the floor and I thought one of the other girls had pushed her."

"But did she?"

"I don't know."

"Didn't you see?"

"No. I'd lost concentration." She felt so guilty.

"What about the parents?"

"Well, at the end of class the girl ran off crying to her mother. I tried to explain, but she drove off. I'm worried she'll phone Lola. She'll go mad."

"Honestly, *Hija*, you haven't been yourself recently. Why weren't you concentrating anyway? Was it him again?"

"Him?"

"You know who I'm talking about? That English guy, have you seen him?"

"I wish."

"Then you are still thinking about him?"

"Every second of the day." There, she'd admitted it; he had completely taken over her mind. She'd been such a fool before, being so distant with him like that.

"Listen *Hija*," said her mother, taking her hand. "This must stop, you know that. You will only end up being heartbroken when he goes back to England, or when your father finds out and does something drastic. I've been thinking, and after your father's reaction the other day it's obvious he won't be happy about this."

"What about what you said last month about fighting for what I believed in; having passion. You did the same for Papa."

"I know, but that was different," she said in a harsher tone.

"Why?"

"Because we are both Spanish and from the same background. This guy will only leave you in the end. Do you not think he has a family?"

"You never know, there must be a reason why he is here. He's an excellent guitarist, maybe he's decided to devote his life to it and stay."

"Maybe," said Rosa, in a dismissive way, "or maybe not. Look at the mess you've got into at work. I'm sure Lola will understand, but that's not the point. You're playing with fire. Just let him go. I know it's hard, but it will be better in the long run."

"What's the point?" Mercedes suddenly felt angry, was there no one she could confide in anymore?

"In what?"

"In talking with any of you; no one understands me."

"I do understand you, *Hija*, but I'm just trying to save you the pain that you'll feel in the future."

"Whatever," said Mercedes, annoyed that her mother had changed her tune so much.

They finished cleaning up in silence and Mercedes excused herself to her room. She lit a lemon scented candle and lay on her bed, trying to remember how she'd gotten into this mess. She wasn't going to give up though, no way. She had to fight for what she believed in.

Charlie was deep in concentration, moving his hands swiftly up and down the guitar neck. He was on fire as his emotion flowed through his body and poured out of his system. His mind was clouded over. He couldn't get over the fact that he'd made such a fool of himself in front of Mercedes. He felt a mix of emotion, sadness, anger, frustration, and it was all coming out now, in front of Ramón.

He stopped playing and opened his eyes. Ramón had never looked so in awe.

"I think you have become *un flamenco*," he said, chuckling to himself as he walked over and hugged Charlie. He could feel the positive energy seeping through his idol as he embraced him. "That was pure talent, *amigo*."

"*Gracias*, yeah, it did feel good."

"It should have done; it was perfect. I think you might be ready."

"Ready? For what?"

"The next phase. Come on Monday for a free lesson, my treat, and I'll show you where your future lies."

"Can't you tell me now?" asked Charlie, excited and curious to know what Ramón meant.

"I can't. This is something you have to see with your eyes, feel with your soul; real flamenco."

Charlie wondered what he was talking about, a new guitar, an expert guitarist friend to show him some more moves. For the first time in a couple of weeks, he felt excited about something, not down and saddened after making such a fool of himself. He was on a high and eager to see what surprise lay ahead for him on Monday.

When Mercedes left her house on Monday morning, her hands were shaking. She'd tried several times over the weekend to get hold of Lola to try to explain what had happened, but she couldn't get through. As soon as she walked in the door, she knew something was up.

"Hey Lola," she said, kissing her on the cheek.

"Hey," she replied in an off-tone.
"Good weekend?"
"Depends how you look at it."
"Oh, why, what's up?"
"Well, my useless fart of a boyfriend hadn't planned an engagement. It was a surprise football party for one of his mates, and supposed couples, but I was the only gullible idiot female to turn up. All the other men had given their other halves the option."

"Oh dear." Mercedes was dreading telling her about the student.

"Yeah, I learned just how immature Miguel can really be. Honestly, he turns into a sixteen-year-old when he's with his mates: farting, swearing, and drinking far too much. It was like being on one of those vial 18-30 holidays for desperate men."

"You must have had some fun."

"Fun? If you call watching your partner and his mates doing the can-can round some bars with their trousers and pants by their ankles, then I guess you could call it fun. At least I had a laugh though at some of the penises, and I know Miguel is above average."

"Something positive, I guess." Mercedes could see Lola wasn't all that annoyed; she did have a slight smirk on her face.

"Yeah, but there was something else."

"Oh…"

"Yeah, I had a phone call this morning." Her voice dropped, and she became serious.

"I can explain."

"From a very angry mother."

"I know it probably sounds bad."

"Bad? You shouted at her daughter after another girl

kicked her several times during class. Were you not watching?"

"No, I just…"

"You just what? Mercedes, this is a very angry mother and could cause a lot of problems for the school. What if she starts telling the other mothers? You know what some are like; soon they will be pulling their daughters out of the school, and we will be left with nothing."

"I know. I'm sorry. It was a mistake."

"It's just not on Mercedes. Anyway, I'm worried about you."

"Me? Why?"

"Because you're just not the same person you were a couple of weeks back. The spring in your step has gone. And now this. Are you going to tell me what's up? Or do I have to go find him myself." Lola's tone had become less angry. She seemed genuinely concerned.

"Find who?"

"Come on, stop playing with me. Don't you think it's time you found out for sure? Either you're with him, or not."

Mercedes wanted to weep through relief because she had such an understanding friend.

"I know. You're right. I'm sorry, it's just he's been on my mind so much. I'm sure he's the one for me, but if that's the case then why hasn't he come back?"

"Men are weird, and idiots. If it's meant to be, then it's meant to be. What's more important is your health, and my clients," she said, joking now.

"Yeah. What did the mother say, anyway?"

"She'll be back. Her daughter is a pain in the arse anyway. I never liked her anyway." They both laughed. "Now promise me that you won't let this guy affect you anymore. Give it a little while, then if he doesn't show, we'll go find him."

"Okay, and thanks, Lola."

"No problem, now let's go get a coffee."

Mercedes felt free of stress and resentment finally. Lola was right. If it was meant to be, then it would happen.

Monday morning for Charlie was upbeat.

"So, are you ready?" said Ramón as Charlie sat on a high stool waiting in the studio.

"Sure, can't wait for this," he said.

"Okay, today's lesson is about another aspect of flamenco; one that is possibly the most important for the guitarist, any ideas?"

"Have you bought me a new guitar?"

"I think the one you have is fine enough."

"Another guitarist to show me how to play?"

"I'm the finest teacher you can get," said Ramón, laughing. "No, not a guitarist, but someone who can show you a trick or two, and will take your playing to the next level; really give you a reason to play."

He thought of Mercedes gliding through the door. Wouldn't it be funny if Ramón actually knew her and the whole thing had been some silly joke? He could forgive him, and Mercedes, anything to have a chance with her.

"No idea."

"I thought not," he said, smiling. *"Venga, Angela, pasa."* The door opened.

Angela glided through the door with her head held high, and clonked along the wooden floor, making her presence felt. Charlie felt intimidated straight away by the powerful woman, a real *bailaora*.

"This is Angela," said Ramón, holding his hand out to

introduce her after giving her two kisses.

"*Hola, encantada,*" she said, leaning to kiss Charlie on both cheeks. Her skin was soft, but firm, she wore a lot of makeup and far too much perfume.

"*Hola,*" said Charlie, gulping. He'd seen plenty of women like Angela strutting her stuff in Sevilla. She was an attractive woman, and her tight fitting low cut scarlet top and tiny black mini-skirt left little to the imagination.

"Angela is one of the finest *bailaoras* in Sevilla," said Ramón. "Now it's time for your first lesson with a dancer. Angela, *por favor.*" He motioned for her to take position as he picked up his guitar and sat down on a stool next to Charlie.

"Watch and learn," said Ramón as he began to pluck.

Angela stood proud, taking her stance. Charlie watched as she began to move her arms around her waist and up above her head. She tapped her heels on the floor, finding the rhythm with Ramón. Charlie switched his eyes between the quick and nimble fingers of Ramón and the dynamic performance of Angela.

He was impressed with the way she moved with such force and speed. He felt the passion she was emitting from her quick moves. He was in awe, watching the two complimenting each other. This was the real flamenco that he had been searching for.

"*Ole,*" said Charlie, as they both stopped dead.

"What do you think?" asked Ramón.

"Not bad."

"Not bad? You English are all the same; will you ever show your emotion?"

"It was fantastic, Ramón, just fantastic," he said, flipping two thumbs up.

"Think you could do it?" asked Ramón.

"What, dance like that? I don't think so."

"Dance? Ha! No, play for her."

Charlie was unsure, he still felt intimidated by Angela's presence. She was such a powerful, dominant woman, and danced with such force.

"I can try," he said, smiling.

"Excellent. Angela," he said, signalling for her to dance again.

"You have to let her show you the moves. In flamenco, the woman is the boss."

"Just like in the real world then."

"Yeah, you could say that."

He began to play, slowly at first so he could watch and wait for Angela to show him the pace. She stood in front of Charlie, facing away. Charlie looked down at her long legs, so supple in her thin black tights. She looked so sexy moving her hips.

"*Concentrate,*" said Ramón, spotting that Charlie was being distracted. He closed his eyes and listened to her heels banging against the wooden floor to catch her rhythm. She sped up. He opened his eyes and stared at her feet, astounded by the velocity they were moving. He kept up though. All those hours practicing had done him good. He was in sync with her, strumming fast enough, so the two were alive together. Charlie's body was full of flamenco, of *duende*.

"Excellent, excellent," said Ramón, clapping as they stopped dead. He leaned over and hugged Charlie. "I knew you had it in you, all you needed was the right guidance. You are still a way off, but you make a good team. *Que piensas Angela?*" he said, asking Angela what she thought.

"*Excelente, para un guiri es fantástico.*"

"*Gracias,*" said Charlie, receiving his first compliment from a female in the world of flamenco.

"So that's settled then."

"What?" asked Charlie.

"I think you're ready for your first live performance, what do you think?" Charlie frowned, was he serious?

"A live performance, in front of Sevillanos?"

"Sure, why not? They're flamenco fans, and you are a flamenco guitarist, so what does it matter?"

"Sure, I mean, really?"

"Is this not what you want Carlito, to show the world your talent?"

"I guess so, yeah." Charlie couldn't take it in, maybe because deep down his dream had been to play for someone else.

"You guess so? Sometimes I worry about you. Why are you really learning the guitar?"

"Lots of reasons."

Charlie wasn't sure anymore. Originally it had been to get away from home, to try something new, to really push himself, but so much had changed. He was curious to experience the sensation of playing in front of an audience with a great dancer, but perhaps not Angela.

"There's a flamenco event happening down by the river in a flamenco dance school. I know the guy organizing it. Does the name Amaya Ramos mean anything to you?"

"Nope, should it?"

"I guess not for a *guiri*. She'll be performing after you guys. She's a famous flamenco dancer, so it's likely to be packed. If you guys want, there's a free place before."

"Really? Me with Angela?"

Angela nodded after Ramón translated what was going

on; her level of English wasn't a touch on her dancing.

"Why not?"

He thought about it for a second. The image of Mercedes popped into his mind, he would give anything to change Angela for her, but it just wasn't going to happen.

"Sure, let's do it."

"Great, so you have to practice together a lot more, you can use this studio. The concert is after Christmas Day, on the 26th, can you make that?"

"Sure," he said, ruling out the option of popping back for Christmas.

"Excellent, Angela has already told me she is free and willing, so that's settled. Your first live flamenco performance. You'd better get practising."

"Thanks, Ramón, honestly, this is too good to be true."

Charlie was apprehensive about performing in front of a live audience but glad to have the opportunity, especially with someone as talented as Angela. He was so excited though he had to tell someone.

That evening, when he turned up for work, Jorge was waiting outside smoking a cigarette.

"*Buenas tardes,*" Charlie said.

"*Buenas tardes,* Carlito. What is the *problema* with your face?"

"My face?" he said, frowning.

"Yes, you have a big smile today." Jorge put on his widest grin, which made him look like a strange jester.

"Is that a problem?"

"No, only that in Spain we smile when we finish the work, not when start."

"I see, actually, I had some good news today."

"Really?" said Jorge, turning inside and shouting out for

Pedro.

"*Que?*" said Pedro as he bundled out the door.

"It's our Carlito, he have a good news. So? Tell us."

"I have a concert during Christmas."

"Great, who are you going to see?" asked Jorge.

"Not see, play."

They both stared at Charlie for a moment before bursting out laughing.

"That is British humour, yes, very good. A *guiri* playing the guitar in a concert here," said Jorge.

"Is funny," said Pedro. They both laughed and whacked each other on the back.

"I'm not sure 'funny' is the right word, but it's a great opportunity. Maybe you can both come?" They stopped laughing and stared at Charlie. He grinned and nodded his head.

"Is a joke, no?" asked Jorge.

"Why would I joke about something like this?"

"But how you get in concert?"

"Ramón organised it. I'm performing with Angela."

"Sexy Angela?" said Pedro.

"I guess she is quite sexy, yes," said Charlie.

"*Por Dios,*" said Pedro, walking up and shaking Charlie by the hand. "Is great, we come, no problem."

"But wait," said Jorge, "what about the restaurant? Christmas is a busy time. We cannot all go."

"That's true," said Charlie, forgetting that they were the owners. Sometimes they seemed so out of it that he wondered how they managed it.

"Don't worry," said Jorge, "I find people, we have time. Congratulation Carlito, sure you will be the best."

"*Si*, and we can watch the Angela!" said Pedro, rubbing his hands together.

"That's great news. Having you two there will be excellent."

"No problem, Carlito, for that reason we are the friends," said Jorge, shaking his hand. "Now come on, we have work to do."

Charlie met up with Angela every day over the following couple of weeks, and his confidence grew quickly. He learned more about flamenco with her than he had over the previous couple of months. The way she moved and showed him the *compás*, how she told him to play faster and slower and watch out for her signs of changing pace all heightened his level.

Most guys would have been besotted dancing with Angela every day. The way she tottered about in her low cut tops and short skirts kept Charlie on his toes. Angela wasn't his type though; he made sure he kept clear of anyone with a 6ft 5 bulky boyfriend. He was still pining for Mercedes though, so when Angela danced, he imagined her instead.

He often thought about going back down to see Mercedes, but after the last setback, he just didn't have it in him.

Noche Buena - Christmas Eve - came round quickly for Mercedes. It was her favourite time of year, and she decided to put her bitter feelings towards her father to one side for the festive period and try to enjoy her time. It was mainly thanks to Lola. After her little episode at work, she was more focused on life. She began dancing better and had even visited a couple of *tablaos* about dancing again in the New Year. Charlie still filled her alone time thoughts, so she'd made up her mind that she would track him down in the New Year.

At about 10pm Mercedes was at the end of the table with her head facing down, and her hands clasped together. Her father was speaking.

"And may the Lord make us truly grateful for what we are about to eat, amen."

"I'd like to say something," said Rosa. Francisco nodded. "I want to say I'm proud of you all: my husband with his business, my son with his studies, and my daughter with her dancing. I know some of us have been up and down over the last couple of months, but I've been praying hard for us to find happiness. I would like us to thank the Lord for what we have this Christmas, and to remember all those who aren't here." She was almost in tears by the end. Mercedes knew that she'd be thinking about her grandparents. She imagined her grandfather sitting at the table with them, smiling and joking.

"*Gracias, Mama,*" said Mercedes, standing up and hugging her mother. "We all love you, you know that, and things will be fine in the future. I have a good feeling."

The table was covered in some of the finest Spanish food: strong cheese, olives, salad, chunky white bread, thick juicy prawns, and the best *serrano jamón*. Francisco cracked open a bottle of their favourite Rioja wine, and they toasted.

Once they'd finished their meal, Rosa brought out a tray of *mantecados*, a sweet powdery cake, and small marzipan sweets. Francisco and Raul had a shot of anis, a sambuca type drink, while Rosa and Mercedes had a glass of champagne.

When the old grandfather clock on the wall struck twelve, they hugged and kissed each other on the cheeks, and Raul slipped a white envelope in Mercedes' hand.

"What's this?" she said, squealing with delight.

"Have a look," said Raul.

"But what is it?"

"Hope you like it," said Raul, grinning.

Mercedes peeled back the corner, stuck in a finger, and ripped it open. Inside were two tickets.

"What are these for?" she asked, flipping them over.

"Someone you've always wanted to see."

They watched as Mercedes read the information on the ticket.

"What, here in Seville? I can't believe I didn't know. Amaya Ramos?" said Mercedes, jumping to hug her brother.

"That's right. It's a treat from all of us," said Rosa. Even her father smiled.

"I can't believe it," she said, holding the ticket. "When is it?"

"Can't you read?" said Raul. "It says there, on the twenty-sixth. And down by the river, where you learned to become a dancer."

"That's just perfect. And in two days?" said Mercedes, feeling a surge of adrenaline. "I'm going to see one of my favourite flamenco dancers, Amaya Ramos, in two days?" Mercedes felt like a little girl again, getting excited at *Noche Buena* like she had years ago.

"But we have to get there early," said Raul. "There are a couple of new artists playing before; it might give you an idea of what lies ahead in the future of flamenco."

Mercedes couldn't wait. To imagine she would be at a concert where she learned how to become a flamenco dancer filled her with such joy and emotion.

When Charlie woke up alone in his flat in Seville on the 25th of December it was as if Christmas had never even existed. Had all those Christmas childhood memories been a dream, made up events by his parents just to fool him into being a 'good' boy all year?

There was no smell of ham and eggs blowing up under his bedroom door, no stocking at the end of his bed, or even a stinking Christmas Day hangover. He walked into the lounge and looked straight at the windowsill.

"Merry bloody Christmas," he muttered to himself as he saw the muffin and carrots still left over. "No Santa for you this year then, must have been a 'bad' boy." Now he knew exactly how Scrooge felt being on his own. He wished three ghosts would appear and take him on a tour of his past, present, and future. At least then he'd know whether he'd ever end up with Mercedes.

He made a coffee and called home.

"Charlie boy," answered his dad. "Long time no speak. How you doing son? Got a hangover as usual I expect. Bet you have a couple of señoritas back there with you right now, ain't you?"

"Afraid not Dad. Quiet night in with the guitar last night. Seems like most of Sevilla were at home with their families anyway. Not like back home."

"Blimey, sounds dull. Well, you're not missing much here. It's just your Mum and me this morning, both walking round in our Christmas undies."

"Sounds lovely, bit too much information though Dad. Thanks for the image."

"Ha, sure yeah. If I had my way, I'd stay like this all day, but you know what your Gran's like; wouldn't stop staring at my snowman carrot. And we wouldn't want her to have a heart attack on such a special day, now. Know what I mean?"

"Yeah I do, Dad." Charlie laughed. He missed his dad.

"How you doing, anyway? Learnt how to play the spanolo guitaro yet?"

"Yeah, I have as it goes. Seems like I've picked up the knack. Got a decent teacher and even have my first concert tomorrow."

"Well I never, that's great news. Do you have to dress up as a bullfighter or something? Wear one of those funny hats like the Beatles did that time?"

"No, I'm just going to keep it simple. White shirt, black trousers. Everyone will be watching the dancer anyway."

"What? You have your own señorita dancer, what's she like? Bet she's gorgeous."

"Yeah, she's quite sexy actually."

"Good lad."

"But there's nothing going on with her."

"I see, well, keep trying son." Charlie could hear his mum in the background asking who it was. "Listen, I've got your mum here hopping up and down like a rabbit on a trampoline; not a pretty sight in her new Rudolf bra, so I'll pass her over before she puts me off my ham and eggs. Have a great day, mate."

"You too."

"Hey Charlikins, Happy Christmas, son."

"Thanks, Mum, yeah you too. How's it going?"

"Oh a bit of a quiet one, just your sister and that coming over with Gran later. Hopefully try to burn the turkey, just how she likes it. What you up to?"

"Oh not much today, probably just practising for the concert tomorrow."

"Oh yeah, that's great. I got your email. Sounds like you're settling there."

"Well, wouldn't say that. But yeah it's pretty good here. The teacher is ace."

Falling for Flamenco

"Maybe me and your Dad could pop over for the next concert, just let us know when it is."

"Okay, sure, that would be great."

"You all right though?"

Charlie wanted to open up, and say he was pretty miserable not being back there on Christmas Day, but why spoil her fun as well.

"Yeah, I'm cool. Going to meet some friends later anyway."

"That's great. Okay Charlikins, well, we'd better push on. Gotta get the grub ready. Have a lovely day. Miss you."

"You too Mum. Have a good one."

"Bye," shouted his parents.

As Charlie hung up the phone, it was the first time that he missed being in England. Not just his family, but his country, tradition, and humour. Spain just wasn't the same at Christmas, especially alone.

He felt nervous about his first concert. At times he felt on the ball about his playing, but realistically how was he supposed to get up to such a level with only a couple of weeks with Angela. Surely the greats were playing for years before they went on stage. Luckily all eyes would be on her anyway. He had to be bold though. There was no going back now.

As Mercedes glided into the lounge, she felt like a queen.

"Are you dancing tonight?" asked her mother, looking at her daughter's stunning long red satin dress.

"Don't be silly, mother. Well, at least not on the outside," said Mercedes as she unhooked her coat from the rail.

"You look wonderful, *Hija*," said her father, kissing her on the cheek. "Look after her, son."

"Of course, *Papa*. Ready?" asked Raul as he held out his arm to lead her. Mercedes felt special; spoilt even, like a princess.

As they entered the taxi, Mercedes was overly excited about the concert. She couldn't believe she was going to see Amaya perform after being such a fan for most of her life. She'd seen her once before, at the Maestranza when she was just twelve years old and had been so influenced by the way she danced. She was anxious to see her again, especially as she was performing in a place close to her heart.

As they made their way along the river, Mercedes thought of her grandfather. She missed him; not a day went by that she didn't wish he was still there, still able to watch her dance. There had been a time when she lived for the moment when she could dance for him. He had been such an inspiration to her, always so gentle and motivating. He always said she could make it on her own, which was exactly what she had done.

She also thought of Charlie and wondered what he was doing. Would he be back in his country, in the snowy land so far away, enjoying the festive period with his family? Or was he still in Sevilla, maybe working in that bar, or sitting on his own somewhere playing the guitar. In a way she felt sad for him; how could he just leave his country and family and come away like that. She admired him but found it difficult to understand how he could make that sort of decision.

She didn't want to get upset though. Tonight was about her, her brother, and seeing one of the best flamenco dancers alive.

Charlie was alone in his dressing room, pumped up and raring to go. He was ready to perform and show the world his talent. In walked Ramón. Charlie stood up.

"Looking good," said Ramón, as he whistled. "Who would have thought it, the scruffy *guiri* who turned up several months ago now looks like *un flamenco*."

"Thanks, Ramón. I couldn't have done it without you."

"Nonsense, I have only found what was inside and brought it to the surface, like a good gardener with his flowers."

"Don't get all sensitive on me now," said Charlie.

"Sensitive, me? Pah. I have to warn you though, the Sevillanos here are a touch above the rest. The tickets are expensive, and they expect to see magic, feel *duende*. There may be some important people here as well, big names in the flamenco world. If you do well today, then who knows where you could go."

"I'm ready," said Charlie, grinning.

"Come on; let me show you where you'll be playing."

As Charlie followed Ramón through the corridors towards the main stage, he began to feel the pressure. He was actually going to perform in front of an audience.

"Have a look in there," said Ramón, pulling back a curtain.

"Blimey," said Charlie when he saw how grand the place was. There were two floors of dark red seats full of flamenco fans. "There must be a hundred chairs in here."

"One hundred and fifty," said Ramon. "You'll be over there," he said, pointing to a black stool in the centre of the wide stage. Charlie's throat dried up. One thing was to play on his balcony in the sun overlooking the river with the cathedral in the background, and another to play in front of one hundred and fifty people.

"Look, here's the line-up," said Ramón, showing Charlie a program.

"Who's Carlito Rubio?" said Charlie.

"You of course; it's a guitarist's name. What was I going to put Charlie Smith? No one would take you seriously."

"And with Blondy after my name they will?"

"Trust me, I know my people, they will love you."

"Are you sure I'm up to this?"

"Look," he said, grabbing Charlie's hands. "These hands have something, they are special. Let them do the work, feel the flamenco in your soul, play like you play with me, just imagine it's just you and me, or someone close to you. It's much better to imagine just one person than the audience. That's what I used to do."

Charlie thought of Mercedes, he'd already planned on imagining her dancing next to him, instead of Angela.

As Charlie followed Ramón back to the dressing room, he told himself that he had to focus. This was his big chance to feel success. He wished his parents could be in the audience, but he'd have to make do with Jorge and Pedro.

Once in the dressing room, there was a knock at the door.

"*Si?*"

"*Soy yo, Angela.*" Ramón opened it and in came Charlie's partner for the evening. They were both speechless. Angela had her hair tied tightly in a bun and just enough makeup to show her strong features. Her dress was more elegant and much less revealing than the ones she'd previously worn. She had transformed into a glamorous bailaora. Charlie was gob-smacked; would he really be on stage performing with such a woman?

"Wow," said Ramón. "*Estas muy guapa.*"

"*Gracias,*" she replied, holding her head high.

It wouldn't be long until they were on stage together. Charlie was ready for one of the most important moments in his life so far.

Mercedes took her seat in the centre at the back and looked again over the program.

"We missed the first one," she whispered to Raul.

"Don't worry; the first support act is never any good anyway. Who's this guy?"

"Pepe de Sosa," she said, giggling. "Sounds like a type of sauce." They both laughed and the woman behind hushed in Mercedes' ear.

"Who's next?" whispered Raul.

"Angela Marques. Oh, she's an excellent dancer."

"From what I remember she has a great personality," Raul smirked.

"Sure, like you'd know anything about her personality. Who's this guy she's with, Carlito Rubio?" As she said the name her voice dropped slightly. How many blond flamenco guitarists did she know? Just one, and there was no way he would be here. She laughed to herself, imagining him at the front of the stage playing.

"Carlito Rubio? Never heard of him," said Raul, "but I'm sure Angela will be in top form."

"You're so immature sometimes," said Mercedes, tutting at her brother's one tracked mind. "Oh good, Pepe has finished," she added as he left the stage.

"*Ahora,*" said the presenter, "we have our second performance. This bailaor has toured around Andalucia, and it's a privilege to have her here this evening. Her guitarist is relatively new here in Sevilla, but I've been assured he's excellent. Ladies and gentleman, please welcome Angela Marques and Carlito Rubio."

When the curtains drew back, Mercedes gasped.

"But..."

"How is..." said Raul, with his mouth open.

Mercedes felt a pang of adrenaline in her stomach. He was here, on stage in front of her. She was in total shock. How had he managed to get on there?

As he began to play, she drifted back to the plaza where she had first seen him. She remembered that feeling of being in awe, impressed by the way a foreigner had learned flamenco so well. Her heart began to open as she listened to his beautiful playing, but when the clapping started, she realised he wasn't alone.

As Angela faced the crowd, Mercedes stared straight at her. She felt a strange wave of anger pass through her body. Confusion clouded her mind. How was he on stage with *her*? Was there something more to their relationship? She felt annoyed at herself for not being more open with Charlie when he came to see her. It should have been her up there, performing alongside him.

Angela jumped to her feet and began to strut along the stage. Mercedes couldn't fight away the jealous feeling eating into her stomach. She felt in shock, almost sickened. She'd never felt anything like it before. Her heart felt as though it was beating a thousand times faster. She was jealous. Jealous of the way Angela could hold herself with such pride and dance so well, jealous of the fact she was dancing with Charlie, the man who was slipping through her fingers.

"Are you okay?" asked Raul.

"Yes," she mumbled.

"Sure? You seem a bit tense, don't you like the way he is

playing?"

"I love it, that's the problem."

The crowd was silent as Charlie kept up with Angela, who was in full swing. He watched her feet, legs, and hips waiting to see where she would go, listening for the change in pace and signals to follow.

He was playing well for his first live performance. He was doing exactly as Ramon had said, blocking out the audience and imagining Mercedes by his side. He wished they were performing together; perhaps he would have his chance with her one day.

He woke from his daze as Angela stepped into another gear, taking the speed of her moves faster. Charlie could feel himself slipping away from her pace as if he was slowly falling back down a well. He concentrated, though, and found extra energy deep in his body and soul; there was no way he was going to mess this up.

The audience began to let out shouts of *'Ole'* as Angela spun on the spot, twisting her whole body round and round. Charlie had to guess where she would move next. She was so sporadic in her movements that he had no way of knowing; two weeks with her just wasn't enough.

The real artists rarely practised precisely anyway, it was more about the spontaneity. Miraculously, he managed to follow her, and they reached a *duende* climax.

The audience rose to its feet and applauded. Charlie stood, holding his guitar with one hand as he raised the other in the direction of Angela, standing proudly in front of the cheering fans. A wave of emotion ran through his body as he scanned the smiling faces. He'd never expected such a good response, some were even in tears, and so, nearly, was he.

He spotted Pedro and Jorge waving from a corner with massive grins on their faces.

"*Venga guiri*, you are the boss," shouted Jorge.

"Yeah man, the king of flamenco," shouted Pedro.

He bowed, thanked the audience, and left the stage with Angela, pumping with adrenaline and emotion.

As Mercedes was watching Charlie leave the stage, she squeezed her brother's hand.

"Do you want a pañuelo to wipe your eyes?" he asked. Mercedes snivelled and let out a muffled laugh.

"Sure," she said, taking his hanky and blowing her nose.

"That was some performance," said Raul.

"I can't believe he's here playing with her; it should have been me. I can dance better than her." She hadn't felt such an empty feeling before, one of despair and fear. How the hell did they know each other? What had happened since the last time she'd seen him? He'd practically asked her out, and now, he was on stage with another dancer.

Raul put his arm around her, but she didn't want sympathy. She was angry at herself and the control that people had over her life. It was time to act and put a stop to everything holding back her happiness. She wasn't going to let him slip away again.

"Where are you going?" asked Raul.

"To speak to someone I should have done ages ago," she said, waltzing down towards backstage.

Charlie was back in the dressing room with Ramón, who had just popped open a bottle of champagne. Charlie felt euphoric and on such a high after being on stage and it all going well.

"You're a legend," said Ramón, patting Charlie on the

back. "You were amazing, for a guiri, of course."

"Thanks to you Ramón, you've helped me so much."

"Don't thank me. It's been great watching you improve. This is just the beginning, you know that, no?"

"Sure, sure."

"So, how do you feel?"

"Good, very good," he said as he grinned.

"Only good? You are too modest; you should be in the clouds."

"I guess I am." Which he was, but he wished his parents had been there to see him, and someone else, of course.

"Yes, but don't let this go to your head. There is still a lot to do, which reminds me, I need to just go out for a second and speak to someone. Don't drink all the champagne."

Within seconds of Ramón leaving, there was a knock at the door.

"That was quick," said Charlie, opening the door. His jaw dropped when he saw who it was.

"Oh, you were expecting me?" said Mercedes, smiling. "Can I come in?" she added, peering round the door.

"Sure," he said, letting her in and closing the door behind. Charlie was bewildered. Mercedes was in his changing room. She must have been at the concert, he thought to himself. He couldn't believe his luck.

"Were you there?" he asked.

"Yes, you play well."

"I have a good teacher."

"And the dancer?" said Mercedes, in a coy tone. Charlie was surprised by her directness, he hadn't expected her to ask about the dancer.

"Oh, she's Angela, a friend of Ramón's. She's a great dancer."

"Yes," said Mercedes, who seemed to want to ask

another question.

"But I know a better one." As soon as the words came out, he felt his face go red.

"*Ah, si?*"

"*Si*, she's much better, more style, more passion, and more attractive." He wasn't going to mess this one up.

"Really? Do I know her?"

Charlie paused as he chose his words carefully. He could feel the attraction between them; a strange electronic force pulling him towards her.

"Definitely." When Mercedes grinned, Charlie felt warm inside. He liked seeing her smile and happy.

"How you learn to play guitar like that?" she asked.

"I've played the guitar since I was young, but more acoustic stuff. I was in a band in London, but things didn't work out. One night I saw a flamenco concert and fell in love with it. So I came to Sevilla, and here I am."

"Wow. You were great, really, especially for a *guiri*."

"So they keep telling me," said Charlie. "Do you want a glass?" he said, holding up the bottle of champagne.

"Okay, *gracias*."

As Charlie handed a glass to her and began to pour, he felt the power between them again. Was it possible to fall in love so quickly? He remembered the times he'd fallen in love before, many times when he was on holiday with his parents. They had all been crushes though, silly holiday romances, but this seemed real and deep.

"You have a gift," said Mercedes. "The audience think you amazing, me too, and my brother."

"Oh, your brother is here," said Charlie, immediately remembering her father.

"Yes, don't worry; he is no like my father."

"That's a relief." They both laughed. Charlie looked into

her eyes and could see himself kissing her. He wanted to move closer to feel her soft lips on his.

"So, this dancer, Angela…"

"Yes?"

"She is a friend of Ramón, no?"

"One hundred percent, don't worry, she's not my type."

"You have a type?"

"Possibly, I'm still trying to decide."

"I see," she said, smirking while playing with her hair. He had to make a move.

"So, Mercedes," he said, turning his body more towards her.

"Yes?"

"Well, I was wondering if maybe you'd like to go out for a drink, and dance sometime. I'm not a good dancer, but maybe you could teach me."

There was a knock at the door.

"Hey, *Paco de Inglaterra*," shouted Pedro. "What are you doing? Making love to your fans?"

Charlie gulped as he looked at Mercedes, who was blushing.

"Sorry, my friends," he said, raising his eyebrows and tutting. He was going to kill Pedro.

"Open the door," said Pedro, banging again.

"Wait a second," he shouted. "Sorry," he added, gazing at Mercedes, who was giggling now.

"*No problema.*"

"So, what do you think?"

"Is good idea, but call me," she said, pulling out her phone and quickly finding her number to show him. "I have no plans for *fin de año*."

"*Fin de año?*" he asked, tapping in her number.

"Yes, end of the year."

"Oh, you mean New Year's. Great, maybe we can do something."

"Sure, but late. I always have dinner with my family and eat the grapes at twelve."

"Sure, late, no problem."

The door knocked again.

"Come on, we want to congratulate our star," shouted Pedro.

"Wait," shouted Charlie. "Fine, so when is a good time to call?"

"Tomorrow morning, or the morning after." Mercedes smiled. "You were grand tonight, you played like a Sevillano."

"I had a lot of inspiration."

Mercedes blushed again. The energy between them was getting unbearable. Charlie wanted to go for the kiss, but Pedro knocked again.

"I go," said Mercedes.

"No, just wait a second," said Charlie. He couldn't just let her go again.

"I must; my brother is waiting, and I want to see Amaya. She is an excellent dancer."

"Sure, okay, I'll call you."

"Excellent," she said, kissing him twice on the cheek, "and well done."

Charlie opened the door.

"*Que coño...*" said Jorge, who stood with his mouth open as Mercedes glided past. Charlie raised his index finger to his mouth and motioned for them to be silent as he dragged them in.

"Adios," she said, turning round to wave at him.

"See you later," said Charlie, waving. "Get in," he added, pulling Pedro and Jorge in.

"How the fuck…" said Pedro once they were inside.

"I don't know, but I have her number," said Charlie, holding his phone in the air as if he'd just won the FA Cup.

"Lucky for you, and that was a great show, amigo," said Pedro.

"*Impresonante,*" said Jorge.

"*Gracias, gracias,*" said Charlie as they both shook his hand and hugged him. "Next time, be a bit more discrete though."

"How we know you have a hot lady in here already?"

"Yeah, I suppose you have a point. It was a bit of a shock for me too."

Just then Ramón came in again.

"Ramón," said Jorge and Pedro, almost running up and hugging him.

"You never guess who was just here?" said Pedro. But luckily Charlie caught his eye and shook his head; if Ramón found out that Mercedes had already been in, he'd surely be in trouble.

"Who?"

"Oh, no one special, just Paco from the churros stand."

"Why is that important?"

"It's not," said Charlie. "You know what these guys are like."

"True, true. Anyway, come on, we have some celebrating to do."

Charlie sighed with relief as they changed the subject and spoke about his performance. But he zoned out, trying to comprehend what had just happened. She'd been there. She'd seen him play. She felt something towards him. This one he was not going to mess up.

Chapter 8 FIRST DANCE

Just before New Year's

As Charlie held his mobile in his hand, staring at the call button next to Mercedes' name, he wondered what she was doing. It was late evening, so he guessed probably dealing with a couple of teenage girls fighting over their favourite flamenco shoe, or wandering the streets getting wolf whistled at by sleazy men, or dancing in her room in nothing but her underwear. Whatever the case, he couldn't put it off any longer; it was time to make his move.

"*¿Digame?*"

"*Hola, Mercedes?*"

"Yes, is me. Hello, Charlie. How are you?"

"Good, good. And you?"

"Fine, thanks."

"So, I was wondering if you'd like to get together?"

"Get together? What's mean?"

"Meet up."

"Up, where is up? Is new bar?"

Charlie realised he was chatting with a Spanish lady, who might not actually have ever been taught phrases like 'get together' and 'meet up.' He had to keep it basic if he didn't want to scare her off.

"Would you still like to meet for a drink on New Year's?"

"Oh yes, that would be good, and some dancing? I was thinking, maybe if you no have plans, we can go out on *fin de año* to dance."

"Yeah, that would be *fantástico*." Charlie cringed at his awful attempt at Spanish. "Do you know any good places?"

"Of course," she said, laughing, but he didn't see the

joke. Was this Spanish humour? "We are going to a salsa bar."

"We?" Charlie was hoping he'd be alone with her for the first date, but, then again, he supposed it was a bit much to ask for New Year's.

"*Si*, with my best friend, and her boyfriend, Lola and Miguel."

That must be the other dancer, he thought. Maybe a double date would be all right.

"Yeah, that's great for me. So, where and when?"

"First I have family dinner, so after, at about one."

"In the afternoon? Great yeah."

"No, silly. In the morning."

"The morning?"

"Yes, yes, oh you are a funny man. I like the English humour." As far as Charlie was concerned he hadn't even told a joke, yet. "That's what we do in Sevilla on *fin de año*, is tradition. So, we meet in Plaza Triunfo, by the statue?"

"Sure, perfect, perfect," he said, lying. He would still be alone until after the New Year's dongs. What the hell was he going to do before then?

"Okay, I need go; my students are waiting."

"Okay, well, see you then."

"Yes, adios *guapo*."

"Adi…" but she was gone.

Guapo, she'd called him handsome. Did she really think so? He knew she was *guapa*, probably every man in the world would say she was *guapa*, but only a few women would say he was *guapo*, including his mum and sister.

Come to think of it, Mercedes was way out of his league. There was no way she would have even used him as a coat hanger if she was British. She wouldn't have cared about his silly Spanish accent or his genius guitar skills.

She was Spanish though. Spanish and *guapa,* and had agreed to go on a date, albeit a double one, on New Year's. Finally, he'd have his chance to impress her.

Mercedes was squashed up on the sofa with her family in the lounge as usual on New Year's Eve. Each had a tin foil cup with twelve grapes ready to pop in their mouths. Mercedes was hopeful of it being a great new year, especially as she was about to go out with Charlie, and even more so because she had on a new red bra; a sign of luck for the year to come. Not that Charlie was going to see the bra, well, only maybe a bit of one of the straps, he'd have to wait for the rest.

Being the superstitious type, the whole year's luck depended on the next couple of minutes.

"Are you all ready?" said her mother, as she held her grapes eagerly in her hands.

"May we all have luck and be healthy," said her father, with his grapes by his side.

"Good luck everyone, don't drop one," said Raul, nudging Mercedes in the arm.

"Don't even think about it," she said, snarling at him. "If you even…"

"What?" he said, innocently holding his free hand in the air.

"*Mama*, tell him to stop; the last time I dropped a grape, I had a terrible year."

"Raul, leave your sister alone. We don't want her having a bad year, or we'll all suffer."

"What's that supposed to mean?"

"Silence," shouted her father reaching for the remote. He turned up the TV so they could hear the crowd cheering in

Puerta Del Sol in Madrid.

"Here we go. Twelve grapes, twelve wishes," said her mother.

They stood up and watched as the countdown began, like all Spanish families at this time of year.

"Go," said Raul, knocking back his first grape as the dong chimed.

I wish that Miguel would propose to Lola, thought Mercedes.

Dong.

I wish that Raul would pass his degree this year.

Dong.

I wish I would get another job in a *tablao*.

Dong.

I wish Jesus would choke on a grape right now.

Dong.

I wish Lola would get more students.

Dong.

I wish Papa would stop being such a pain in the arse.

Dong.

I wish all civil worker jobs would disappear off the face of the earth.

Dong.

I wish Mama would be firmer with Papa.

Dong.

I wish I had more power to stand up to the macho men in the world.

Dong.

I wish tonight's date with Charlie to be a success.

By now Mercedes was feeling the strain of chomping on so many grapes and juice was starting to trickle down her chin.

Dong.

I wish one day I could dance flamenco for Charlie.

Dong.

I wish that Charlie...

But she didn't get a chance to make her last wish as someone jogged her arm, causing her grape to fly out of the foil packet, roll across the floor and under the dusty television cabinet. She swung out and hit her brother.

"Ow," said Raul with a mouthful of grapes.

Then she realised no one could speak as their mouths were full of grapes. She gazed at her brother, who was shaking his head violently, and motioning for her to look at their father. She turned and looked. His face seemed guilty. Maybe Raul was right. Had her father actually jogged her so that she would have a bad year? Did he really have what it took to make her so sad she'd forget about the dream of being a successful flamenco star and become a bloody civil worker? She wasn't having it.

"Papa?" she shouted, hitting him on the arm.

"Sorry, *Hija*, it was an accident. I went for my glass of champagne when you moved in the way."

"I did not. I was still. Anyway, why were you going for the champagne if we were still eating grapes?"

She could feel the rage rising up through her body.

"I'd just finished mine."

"Well, that's bad luck," said Rosa, with anger in her voice. "How could you?" Maybe one of Mercedes' wishes had already come true.

"Oh, it's all nonsense anyway. You make your own luck in my book, eh son?"

"Sure Papa, it's just a superstitious thing to keep women entertained."

Slap.

And there it was, the extra strength Mercedes had

wished for, coming straight across her brother's face. Everyone stood in shock, even Mercedes.

"Sorry," she said, immediately. "I didn't mean that."

"Wow," said Raul, holding his jaw. "That was one slap, what did you just wish for?"

"Wouldn't you like to know?"

"It is actually New Year's, you know," said Rosa. "*Feliz año nuevo,*" she added, kissing her daughter on the cheek.

As the family hugged and kissed each other, Mercedes felt bitter. She was convinced her father had deliberately jogged her. She refused to let him ruin her year, and night, so she just let it go, for now. She'd be out soon anyway.

Once they were sat down sipping champagne and eating marzipan sweets, she texted Lola wishing her a happy new year and asking her to call.

"Si?" said Mercedes.

"*Hola, guapa.* Happy new year, are you ready to come out?"

"He's done what?"

"What are you talking about you silly cow?"

"Miguel's been in an accident."

"Oh I see, trying to escape now, are you? Well, okay, yes he has, he seems to have broken his lower lip as he hasn't kissed me yet and it's gone past twelve already."

"I see, so you want me to come to the hospital with you."

"No, it's fine, we'll just leave the bugger to die. Sure I can pick up a new man tonight anyway, maybe an Englishman."

"I'll be right round," she said as she hung up in a panic.

"What's wrong dear?" said Rosa, standing to console her daughter.

"It's Miguel, he's been in an accident. I need to go out,

sorry."

"Out?" said her father. "Where's a young lady like you going to go now on her own?"

"I'm twenty-seven, *Papa*. I'm not a little girl anymore."

"Could have fooled me, with all those wishes you make."

"Typical response from you, so funny. Well, happy New Year everyone. Don't wait up."

She kissed her brother and mother on the cheek, grabbed her coat, and left, walking towards Plaza Triunfo.

As Charlie sat on some chilly steps below a statue of a virgin in Plaza Triunfo, he was amazed at how quiet Sevilla was at one in the morning on New Year's Day. Hardly anyone was about, even the bars he'd passed on the way were only half full, nothing like back in London.

He hoped his night was finally about to get going. He'd never had such an anti-climax at the end of a year before. He'd been sitting eagerly on his sofa looking out over Sevilla, waiting for the fireworks to explode into the sky above la Giralda or the towers in Plaza España, but all he saw were a few drunk tourists by the river with fizzled out sparklers. His excitement had been a couple of glasses of Lambrusco, a bag of peanuts, and a quick rendezvous with Camerón on DVD. His New Year's celebrations could only get better.

"Hola guapo," said Mercedes as she tapped him on the shoulder. *"Feliz año nuevo."* She bent down and kissed him quickly on both cheeks, hardly touching his face.

"Yes, yes, you too. Happy New Year," he said, standing up, surprised she'd actually come, and even more shocked she'd called him *guapo*, again.

"Hola Carlito," said Lola, kissing him too. *"Soy Lola."*

"*Hola, encantado,*" said Charlie.

"*Feliz año, soy Miguel.*" Charlie shook his hand.

"So, ready for a great night out in Sevilla?" asked Mercedes.

"*Si, si,*" he said, smiling, still in shock that she'd turned up. They were finally together, and he didn't know what to do or say.

"*Vamos,*" said Lola, grabbing Miguel and walking across the square.

"Let's go?" said Mercedes, flashing a smile at Charlie. She looked different when she wasn't dancing, so friendly and happy. A strange magnetic force was pulling him towards her. He felt instant attraction and excitement. He wanted to grab her hand and swing it about as they walked next to each other, but he knew he had to take it easy and not rush things.

"So Charlie, what you do this evening?" asked Mercedes as they strolled behind Lola and Miguel. People were starting to come out now, and it seemed as though the city was livening up.

"Not much, I was practising in my flat, watching Camerón."

"Camerón? Tonight? And what about your family?"

"They don't like Cameron. I don't even think they know he exists."

"No silly," said Mercedes, laughing and brushing Charlie's shoulder. "What you family do tonight?"

"Right now, probably dancing a silly dance we do, called Auld Lang Syne." Charlie pictured his family in the usual circle, prancing about as they tried to sing the lyrics. "They are probably at home with my sister, her husband, and their baby."

"It must be strange, not to see them tonight?"

"Yeah it is a bit, but I'd normally be with my mates now, anyway." Charlie thought of Joe and wondered whether he was out performing with his new band.

"Oh, so you don't eat with your family?"

"Yeah, but normally fish and chips, or a curry, at about six, then we go out with friends."

"I see," said Mercedes. She frowned, looking confused. Charlie didn't want to put her off already, so he pushed the conversation onto a topic they would have in common.

"So, are we going to dance tonight?"

"Of course, do you like salsa?"

"Salsa? Yeah, sometimes on my chips."

"No, silly," she said, laughing, and brushing his arm this time. He wondered whether each time he told a stupid joke, she'd laugh. That wouldn't be a bad thing. "Salsa the music, you will see now."

"Great." Charlie smiled, and she gazed back, grinning as proudly as he was. They walked on slowly, glancing at each other now and then. There was a definite spark in the air and Charlie had an overwhelming desire to kiss her, but he waited.

"So, how do Spanish people spend this evening?" he asked as they got towards the river. More people were coming out now, stopping each other in the street to wish happy New Year.

"Oh, the typical. We have the dinner together, watch the TV, and eat the grapes at twelve. One grape for each bell."

"I see. That's good that you do that."

"Yes, it is normally, but this year is bad luck for me."

"Oh why, what happened?"

"My father, he, how do you say, *chocó*," said Mercedes, elbowing Charlie in the arm.

"He nudged you?"

"Yes, nudged me, and one grape is fall to the floor. Now I have bad luck all the year."

"Oh dear, well, maybe I can help you with that."

"*Ah si?* How?" asked Mercedes, sliding her arm under his and linking up.

"I don't know yet, but if we see more of each other, then I'll think of something."

"I like the idea." There it was again, that flash of a smile, winding him in.

"Yeah, I believe that you make your own luck, anyway. If you vision something enough, then eventually it will happen."

"Oh, is a good attitude."

"Yeah, I think so, sometimes it works, but not all the time."

"And tonight, you see tonight? What happen?"

"We'll have to wait and see," he said, winking. As each second passed, he was falling for her more and more. Soon they were on Calle Betis.

"That's where I live," said Charlie, pointing up to his flat.

"Really? But is very expensive down here."

"It's not too bad. I think I got a good deal, it's only a small place. Maybe you can come up and see it one day?" Charlie raised his eyebrows.

"Maybe," said Mercedes, grinning again.

They got to the salsa bar and joined the queue. Lola and Miguel were stood behind, demonstrating to the world how finely suited their tongues were.

"Are they always like that?" asked Charlie.

"Oh yes, this is nothing, wait until they start dancing together." Charlie laughed, but secretly hoped it would be him and Mercedes by the end of the night. He had such an overwhelming desire to kiss her, the electricity he felt as he was near her was frightening.

"*Buenas noches, Mercedes*," said the bouncer, leaning over to kiss her on the cheek. "You're looking fantastic tonight," he added, looking her up and down.

"Thanks, Juan."

"Yeah, so good in fact, why don't you wait for me just inside the entrance? I'm finishing in five minutes."

"Sure you are, sorry, but I have a date tonight."

"A date?" said the bouncer, laughing, "What, with this guy?" he poked his thumb towards Charlie and coughed out a laugh.

Charlie tensed up, did no one have any shame in this city?

"Of course, with this guy," said Mercedes, planting a kiss on Charlie's cheek. "He's much more of a man that you are. Now, are you going to let us in, or are we going to forget about this club forever."

"Whatever, like I really care if you come back or not."

Mercedes felt someone's hand on her shoulder, moving her to one side.

"*Feliz año*," said Lola, pushing past Mercedes. "Is there a problem Juanito?"

"No, not at all. If Mercedes wants to dance with a *guiri*, then that's up to her…"

Miguel lunged forwards towards the bouncer, knocking Charlie to the side, but Lola pulled him back.

"I'd be careful if you want to come in," said the bouncer, raising his shoulders and pumping out his chest. His colleague appeared from the doorway, also showing his stature by standing tall and wide.

"Fine, fine," said Mercedes, "Let's not spoil the night, can we just come in, like we always do?" The bouncer grimaced as he nodded for them to go inside. Charlie failed to understand why he would even care about who Mercedes was going to dance with, but this was just the beginning.

Inside, they stopped at the cloak room. Mercedes took off her long jacket to reveal her tight fitting short black dress. She looked stunning, and she was with Charlie. How the hell had that happened?

"*Vamos,*" said Mercedes, grabbing Charlie by the hand and leading him through the doors. He felt proud to be walking behind the prettiest woman in the place, but his feeling of elation soon took a dive as he noticed just how many of the men were leering at Mercedes as she glided towards the bar.

Charlie was glad the salsa music was so deafening because he was sure that every guy in the place let out a groan as they spotted her. They were so obvious, indiscreet, and sly. Most had girlfriends too, and a few watched with their mouths open.

"Drink?" she said as they arrived at the packed bar.

"Let me get these, what do you want?"

"Oh, an English gentleman. Can I have a ron, and coca cola please?"

"Ron, you mean rum?"

"I think so, yeah. Santa Teresa is my favourite."

"Okay, I think I'll join you, what about Lola and Miguel?" he said looking round. Mercedes pointed to the dance floor, they were already there, grinding up against each other.

"Don't worry, they get drinks when finish."

"Sure," said Charlie, flicking Mercedes a smile as he turned to the packed crowd.

Ten minutes later, he'd finally got their drinks and was

heading back to Mercedes when his heart took a battering. A tall, muscular guy was chatting to her. Adrenaline fired up through his veins, giving him the confidence to stick up for himself. Or, in his case, make an idiot of himself.

He stormed over and nudged the guy in the back, clearing a space.

"Here's your drink," he said to Mercedes as he blocked the guy out the way.

"*Oh, gracias,*" she said, smiling, but frowning too.

"This is Victor," she said, nudging him back beside her. "His two daughters are my students."

"Oh, I see, well, *mucho gusto,*" said Charlie, holding out a hand while burning up inside. Why was he such a dick? He had to keep these new jealous urges under control, but he'd waited so long for this night that he was afraid of losing her so quickly. He had to keep his cool.

He nodded and laughed as Mercedes spoke about how well Victor's daughters were doing, all the time checking his watch, hinting that his time was disappearing. By the time Victor's wife had realised where he was, and almost yanked him away from Mercedes, Charlie had already finished his rum and coke.

"Another?"

"*No gracias.* That was quick. You want to dance?"

Fear spread through Charlie's body. Dance? With a professional flamenco dancer, who half the bar was engrossed in?

"I'd rather play the guitar," he said, trying to smooth his way out of it.

"Sure, but there's one big problem."

"What's that?"

"I want to dance."

Before he knew it, Mercedes was dragging him by the

hand through the crowd right in the middle of the dance floor. Lola and Miguel welcomed them with big hugs as if they hadn't met up since last New Year's.

"Good luck, amigo," shouted Miguel.

"Thanks, I think I'll need it."

"Just let her move you, she knows how to dance. You want a drink?"

"Rum and coke, please."

And he was gone, as was Lola, to leave just the two of them in the middle of the dance floor.

He gazed at Mercedes, who was already moving her feet back and forwards and swaying her hips to the salsa beat. How was he going to dance with her in front of so many people? He'd make a fool of himself.

"Come on, Charlie. I teach you, just leave your body feel the music."

She spun around, and they ended up face to face. She gazed into his eyes, wishing him to come to her. Charlie nodded as he moved his body towards her, his knee knocked into hers, and he trod on her foot.

"Relax, follow me," she said, guiding his arms so that he was where she wanted him. But he kept getting distracted by the blokes staring. Everywhere he looked another guy was staring at her.

"Watch me, not the people," she said, slanting his cheek so he faced her. She grabbed both his hands and pushed him gently but firmly backward and forwards in rhythm as she moved. He kept looking down at her feet, wondering where she was going to move next.

"Look at me, not my feet," she said. "You need feel *la musica*." She smiled as she danced, controlling Charlie's moves to keep him in sync.

He found himself drifting off into a trance as he watched

her face and eyes. She was beautiful. There was no other way to describe her. The way she smiled when she danced was so uplifting, she was high on life, on music, and it was contagious. He could feel himself falling head over heels for her right there.

This was the moment he had been waiting for since he first saw her in Sevilla. He'd wanted to be alone in front of her, just looking at her. He'd forgotten about the people watching, about his guitar, and about flamenco. All he cared about was her, and whether or not he would be able to see her like this for the rest of his life.

After a couple of songs the rum kicked in, and he began to relax. He was following her moves better and was even leading her now and then.

"You are not bad, for a *guiri*," she said in his ear as she moved her head closer, brushing her hair on his cheek.

"*Gracias*." He winked and pulled her lower back towards him. He wanted to kiss her but remained patient.

"Rum and coke?" said Miguel, jumping up alongside him with Lola.

Charlie grabbed the drink, and they clinked glasses.

They all stayed on the dance floor for the next couple of hours, laughing and joking as a foursome. Soon the place was empty apart from them.

"Okay, we go now?" said Mercedes, covering her mouth as she yawned.

"Sure, I can walk you home if you want?"

"That would be good, yes," she said, smiling.

They said their goodbyes to Lola and Miguel, who were quarrelling about how much Miguel had drunk.

"She always thinks I am drunk," he said, slurring into Charlie's ear.

"He is," said Mercedes as she grabbed Charlie's hand,

pulling him off again.

It was a cold night, but nothing in comparison to nights back in London. As they made their way back to the centre, they walked in silence. Charlie was about to ask more about her dancing when she said, "Tell me about you."

"What do you want to know?"

"Why are you here, in Seville?"

"You know why, to learn the guitar."

"Yes, but what about your family?"

"My family is in England, all of them."

"How do you say *'echar de menos'*?"

"Miss, I think?"

"You miss them?"

Charlie thought for a minute. He did miss his family, but he knew they just wanted him to be happy.

"Of course, but they know I want to play flamenco."

"And why flamenco?"

"Well, I guess all my life I've played the guitar in England, all types of music, songs, and styles. I love music, it's my life, but I wanted something different. There's something more challenging about learning flamenco, living in Sevilla, being away from home."

"Is romantic," said Mercedes, squeezing his hand.

"What?"

"You, coming here to learn the guitar, is beautiful." She flashed a brilliant smile.

"I guess it is a bit, yeah. What about you? Why flamenco?"

"My life is flamenco. From when I was little girl, I dance. My grandfather was big *influencia* to me."

"Sure, so where is he now?"

"He die, two years ago." She looked down. Charlie

could feel her pain.

"I'm sorry. That must have been hard."

"Yes, it was, but every day I speak with him, and I know he is watching me. When I dance, he protect me."

Charlie smiled, thinking she was lucky having faith like that. They walked on through the quiet streets until they got to Plaza Triunfo.

"Okay, I go now, when see you again?" asked Mercedes. Charlie panicked. He didn't want her walking on her own.

"But, do you live here?"

"Is close, when can we see?"

"Whenever you want," he said, pulling her close. He surprised himself with his forcefulness. As they stood looking at each other, Charlie felt a knot in his stomach. He loved the way her eyes glistened in the moonlight. He felt so comfortable with her.

Mercedes pulled him towards her and closed her eyes. He closed his as their lips met. He felt electric energy in his heart, and the passion from her filled his soul. He could feel his stomach whirling round, his mind going crazy as they kissed. He wanted to open his eyes, but at the same time he was scared in case it was a dream, and he was actually back in Northwood snogging a waitress in the Weatherspoon's pub.

"Wow," said Charlie, catching his breath as they stopped.

"*Si*. Wow." Mercedes was also short of breath.

"Do you want to meet tomorrow?"

"Tomorrow?" said Mercedes, biting her lip slightly as she thought. "Is possible, but I have lunch with family. Can be later?"

"I'm easy."

"Easy?"

"I mean, that's fine. Where and when?"

"Here, at five in afternoon?"

"Sounds good," he pulled her close and kissed her again. They stayed locked together. Charlie didn't want to let her go, not after all the effort he'd made to finally be with her. But she moved back, gasping and grinning.

"I enjoy tonight."

"Me too, you're a great dancer."

"And you not so bad."

"Thanks. Are you sure I can't walk you to your door?"

"No, is okay, is close, I run." She smiled as she kissed him for the last time that night and walked off briskly.

Charlie was left standing in the plaza, wondering why she didn't want him to go to her door. Then he remembered her father, how he'd got in a strop that time. He hoped she wasn't going to be in trouble.

On the way home, he whistled his favourite flamenco tune, content with his decision to follow his instincts and discover whether she was for him. From what he could make out so far, she was.

Chapter 9 PROMISES

New Year's Day

As Mercedes lay in bed, snug in her covers, she wanted to stay there forever, thinking of that kiss. She was so happy that she'd gone for it and not waited for him to kiss her, he might have taken another three months to pluck up the courage, but that was why she liked him; he was cute, not so in her face, a true gentlemen.

The way he tried to move his arms and legs in rhythm as he danced was funny. She loved the way he moved his hips and tried to mimic her too, also the way he'd stopped caring about everyone watching and just had fun with her. She knew in her heart he was the sort of guy she'd been waiting to find her whole life, someone more down to earth, not so stuck up and pretentious like most of the guys she'd met, and there was no sign that he'd be running off soon to his mummy.

"Cariño," said her mother, knocking on her door. "Are you going to get up anytime soon?"

"What time is it?"

"Almost lunch time, hurry up and get showered; we are going out to eat."

"*Vale,*" she moaned as she cowered deeper in her bed, imagining his kiss again.

Once she was showered and ready, she glided out into the lounge. Her happiness took a dive when she saw her father.

"You're looking happy with yourself," he said.

"And what? Is it a crime to be happy?"

"Of course not, but I thought you would be slightly more sombre if your best friend's boyfriend had been taken to the hospital."

Mierda, she'd forgotten about her lie.

"But that's exactly why I am happy because he's okay," she said, smiling from ear to ear, hoping he wouldn't catch her out.

"Really, so quickly? What happened anyway?"

"He was in a queue to go into a bar and got caught up in a fight."

"Oh really, must have been a big fight."

"It was, but he was helping a couple get out of a difficult situation more than anything." The lie came so naturally from her mouth.

"I see. I thought you said it was an accident, anyway?"

"It was an accident, a misunderstanding. But he's okay."

"No broken bones?"

"Nope."

"Funny," said her father, smiling to himself.

"What's funny?" said Mercedes, sure that her lies were strong enough to have fooled him.

"Oh nothing, just the fact that they called up just after midnight, so they were probably at home with their families, weren't they?"

Damn, she had to think quickly.

"But Miguel has no family, they all died in a car crash a few years ago."

That came out so wrong, *mierda*.

"Oh really, and Lola? She's always with her family on special occasions; I know how close she is to them." Why was he always pushing her?

"She fancied a night with Miguel, is that a crime too?"

"Of course not, *Hija*. Remind me to send some flowers to Miguel for the loss of his family, won't you?"

"I will," said Mercedes, walking up and kissing her father on the forehead. "That's very sweet of you, thanks."

"Not at all," he said, in his ironic tone.

"Maybe you could send some grapes too," said Mercedes as she walked in the kitchen, not forgetting what he'd done to her the previous night.

Why was he so irritating? She felt agitated about being angry at him, but if only he would be more understanding and listen to her, then maybe they would get on better. Why did she always have to do what he thought was right? She wanted to be a free spirit and live her life.

Mercedes kept quiet as she sat in a taxi with her family on their way to Los Remedios: the area with the most expensive restaurants, highest flats, and most pompous Sevillanos, nearly everyone wore a suit on a Sunday, and the parents dressed their kids in funny coloured tights, and that was including the boys. Francisco had booked a table in the finest restaurant down Asuncion - the street famous for the walk down to the Feria.

As they sat in the restaurant, surrounded by the classiest, wealthiest, and overdressed Sevillanos, Mercedes felt so out of place. It just wasn't her scene, nor her family's. They were below the standard of the people there, at least in terms of money and poshness. Mercedes liked to think they were a more 'normal' and humble family.

She kept herself to herself through the first course of jamón and cheese, she couldn't be bothered to contribute to the conversation about the colour of the walls and curtains, or the sparkling cutlery. Even Raúl was ignoring her, had their father warned him of making her laugh?

Once they were half way through the main course, she remembered what had happened the previous night and decided to wind her father up.

"How's your meat, *Papa*?"

"Exquisite," he said, forcing a smile. "How's your fish?"

"Just divine," she said in her posh, visiting relatives, voice.

"It's lovely here, thanks for bringing us, *Cariño*," said Rosa to Francisco.

"That's okay my wife, only the best for our family," he replied, squeezing her hand.

"Of course," said Mercedes. "Only the best," she added, placing a small piece of fish in her mouth. Once she'd finished chewing, with her mouth closed, naturally, she spoke again. "I mean, honestly, if you can't treat your family now and then to an overpriced, smarmy restaurant with ridiculous portions, and pompous service then life's just not worth living."

Rosa reached out and held her husband's hand while looking at Mercedes and shaking her head quickly while tensing her lips together.

"Exactly," said Francisco, much to everyone's surprise, while smiling at his daughter. But Mercedes wasn't going to stand for such simple tactics. She had to push him more, really make him explode.

"We must be grateful that we can come to such a place at all. It's not as if everyone can afford such luxuries as this in Sevilla. Not everyone has our calibre, just think of all those poor people on the streets, living on nothing, not to mention the gypsy flamenco singers."

"Calm down a bit," said Raul, nudging his sister in the arm.

"But I am calm, the calmest I've been for a while in fact, considering how much of a bad year I have in front of me."

"You just won't let it go, will you?" said her father. "It was an accident, an ac…ci…dent." Their voices were rising now.

"An accident? It was about as much an accident…"

"As it was last night when your friend's lover boy got into a fight."

"He's not her lover boy, he's her long-term boyfriend."

"You'd know a lot about those, wouldn't you?"

"What's that supposed to mean?"

"You know what I mean."

"Well, maybe if you let me breathe a little more, then I might have the chance to meet someone."

"Like a gypsy."

"And what if I do?" Mercedes slammed the end of her knife on the table and stared at her father.

"Let's calm down, please," said Rosa, asserting her firm voice.

"Will you just admit that you knocked me on purpose?" said Mercedes.

"No, because I didn't."

"Liar," said Mercedes. Rage was running through her mind, body, and soul. She wanted to pick up her glass of wine and throw it over her father, make him realise that she had had enough, but instead, she did something that she knew would destroy him. She stood up and scrapped her chair on the floor, causing most people in the restaurant to look round at them. Then she pointed at her father.

"That's what you are, a liar, what sort of father lies to his own daughter."

She stomped her heels on the floor, turned, and walked out the restaurant; ignoring the cries of her name from her mother.

Charlie had been waiting for almost forty minutes on his own in Plaza Triunfo when Mercedes turned up.

"I was worried," he said, kissing her softly on the cheek.

Her eyes looked red, sombre, and sad, as if she'd just had a row or found out some upsetting news.

"Don't worry, be happy," she said, forcing a smile.

"Is everything all right?" he asked, noticing her cheeks slightly damp. "Are you in trouble?"

"What is trouble?"

"Like problems."

"No, no," she said, kissing him on the cheek. "I am fine. Come, let's walk."

As they strolled along arm in arm, Charlie asked her what she'd been doing all day.

"Nothing special, you know, the typical on a day like today, lunch with my family." As she said 'family' her voice dropped, and Charlie could sense something was up, but he didn't want to pry and spoil the day.

"And did anyone knock over a bottle of red wine on your mother?"

Mercedes spluttered a laugh, but Charlie wasn't sure if she was about to cry.

"No, no, the waiter was much better, not distracted like someone I know."

"That was your fault, by the way."

"Me? Why?"

"You distracted me with that beautiful smile and lovely eyes." Charlie felt like a cheesy fool the moment the words came out, but, sad or not, that's how he felt.

"Is cute, okay, maybe a little. Was funny to see your face when my father start shouting."

"Funny? I thought he was going to kill me."

"Maybe, but luckily my mother stopped him."

"Is he always like that?"

"Not so much in public, but he can be angry, yes."

"I see."

They walked in silence for a bit as they strolled under the Christmas lights along Avenida Constitucíon. At the end was a tree of lights as high as the normal trees behind it. People were gathered around, taking photos and smiling. Mercedes reached and held Charlie's hand as they went passed. He had never really done that with someone in a romantic way before. He felt weird, unsure what to do. Did he just hold it, or squeeze it, where should he put his fingers? She squeezed more, clinging on as if she needed comfort, strength.

"Fancy a drink?" asked Charlie.

"Coffee?"

Charlie looked at his watch, it was still only 6 p.m. He had to remember he was in Sevilla.

"I was thinking a beer, but okay, if you want a coffee that's fine with me."

"Come on, I know a place."

Mercedes led Charlie up to one of the side roads coming off the river, and they went into a quiet bar.

"So how was your day?" she asked once they'd sat down in the corner.

"Oh, full of activity and fun. Quite exciting really compared to most other people's days."

"You play guitar?"

"Yeah, exactly. I need to practice for when I play for my next flamenco dancer."

"*Ah si?* And who is?" Mercedes looked at Charlie deep in his eyes, tilted her head slightly, and raised an eyebrow. Was he being seduced? He gulped.

"Depends on who comes along first."

"I see."

Mercedes reached out and pulled Charlie by the arms towards her and kissed him lightly on the lips. He felt strange kissing in the day, not under the influence of a couple of beers. As Mercedes continued, Charlie felt like a teenager again as he struggled to remember how to kiss properly, unsure what to do with his tongue and lips. He was also unsure whether or not to let himself get attached to such an attractive and powerful woman.

Wouldn't she just leave him feeling miserable and sorry for himself when she met a stallion flamenco dancer who looked great in thick high-heels? There was no way he was ever going to wear high heels unless he went to a 70's fancy dress party. Also, if he fell in love, then how would he tell his parents that he wasn't coming back, or would he have to take Mercedes to miserable, cold, England? Surely she'd miss her flamenco too much, and so would he.

"Is everything okay?" said Mercedes as she pulled back, gasping for air.

"Of course, everything is perfect, why?"

"What are you thinking about?"

Charlie considering telling the truth, but he thought maybe it was better to say something sweet.

"About the first time I saw you."

"Ah, so cute. Yes, I remember seeing you and thinking, is *guapo*."

"Guapo? Really? With all those handsome, tall, dark Spanish men and you think I am *guapo*?"

"Of course, is your smile, your eyes. I can see you have a good heart."

"I see, well, I guess I do, yeah."

He leaned forward and kissed her again, this time concentrating on how right it felt, how his insides started to turn and how attracted he felt towards her.

"So, when are we going to get a chance to play together?" he said, pulling back.

"When you want?"

"How about tomorrow?"

"Maybe, I will tell you. I am working, back to classes."

"Already? You don't get much of a break."

"No, Lola is a hard worker, she gives lots of classes to the students."

"So what are you trying to do? Make them into professional flamenco dancers?"

"Some yes, some no, just to teach the young generation the importance of our tradition, our art."

"Sounds like a great job, so pure and satisfying. I'm so glad that I started playing."

"Oh, why is that?"

"Different reasons. I've always loved the way the guitar sounds, and I just found it uplifting." Mercedes nodded while frowning. Charlie realised he had to be careful not to confuse her. "It just makes me feel good inside, you know, when I hear a song and can play it? That's why I love flamenco, it's different and is harder for me to play, but I have a great teacher."

"Who is?"

"Ramón, but if he knew I was with you now, he'd kill me."

"Oh, why?"

"Because…" but he stopped as he saw the look of shock in her eyes. If he told her the truth, that Ramón had told him not to play with women, mix business and pleasure, and that her family wouldn't approve of him, he just might ruin it. "…because I should be practising. He is strict."

"I see," she said, smiling as if she understood.

Mercedes leaned forward and kissed him again. He was getting the hang of it now. But the gooey, mushy feeling he felt inside scared him. Should he take it further? How far would things go before they got complicated? He thought of Ramón shouting at him to find his compás before he found love.

"So, tell me about your family?" asked Mercedes as they pulled away for a second.

"Well, my mum's a nurse, and my dad's a security guard at Watford football club."

"Watford?"

"Yeah, that's my local team. He's worked there for years, part of the furniture."

"No understand?"

"Sure, sorry. He's worked there a long time, maybe 20 years."

"And brothers and sisters?"

"One sister, Gemma, she's just had a baby boy, James. Here, I'll show you some photos."

Charlie whipped out his mobile and went through a few photos to show Mercedes. Charlie began to feel a bit nostalgic, wondering what his family was doing. Would his Mum and Dad be down the pub? Probably. He also wondered what they would think of him dating a Spanish woman, surely his Dad would be proud.

"But you miss them?"

"Yeah, of course, I do, but I know they are all fine and I can go home when I want."

"And you want to go home? To live in England again?"

"Not at the moment," he said. "I quite like it here." He held her hand and winked.

"I see." Mercedes face lit up, which made him feel guilty. He was enjoying the flamenco scene and getting to know her, but he was unsure whether it would be for life. He could tell that she was concerned about getting attached to him and then him leaving, which he supposed was normal, maybe it had happened to her in the past. She must have had loads of boyfriends over the years. Maybe she even had one now.

"So, are you seeing anyone at the moment?"

"Seeing anyone?"

"Yeah, you know, do you have a boyfriend?"

"A boyfriend? Me, ha," she said, laughing.

"Why do you say it like that? Sure you have lots of men asking you out for a drink."

"Yes, every day, about ten times, and they ask for more."

"Sure they do," said Charlie, trying to hide his jealous streak.

"But I don't have luck with the men from here."

"Oh, why's that?"

"I don't know. They are too macho, too rude, or too close to their mother."

There it was, the reason for so much prying. Well, he did love his Mum, but she wouldn't stop him marrying a Spanish woman. His thoughts surprised him.

"I see, well you don't have to worry about that; my Mum is about a thousand kilometres away."

Mercedes laughed. This is easy, he thought as she kissed him again. But this time with more force, as if her worries had just drifted away.

They left the bar and walked by the river. The air was chilly, so he kept her warm by placing his arm around her shoulders and pulling her close. Her frame was so tiny and delicate. He tried to imagine whether she was all skin and bone under her clothes. Hopefully, he would find out one day.

After a couple of hours of mainly kissing on one of the benches overlooking the river, Mercedes said she had to go.

"Shame. I was enjoying that."

"Me too, but I have to work tomorrow."

"Sure, sure, I'll walk you back."

They made their way back to the usual plaza. Night had almost arrived, and there was a strong chilly wind in the air.

"So? Do you want to meet tomorrow?" he asked.

"Sure, send me message, and we meet in the evening?"

"Why don't we meet here again tomorrow? I have a guitar class and finish at nine."

"Okay, so I see you here tomorrow."

"Sure."

They kissed one last time, and within seconds she was gone, leaving him with a lonely, but warm, feeling in his heart.

As Mercedes left Charlie, the reality sunk in. Who was she kidding? How was it ever going to work with a father like she had? She'd been in a bubble for the last five hours with a kind, gentle man who she could see herself being with for the rest of her life, but she knew that if she did choose him, then she might lose her family.

Ever since he'd jogged her at New Year's Eve, making that last grape roll along the floor and destroying her last wish, she knew that he was out to get her. Why couldn't he just accept that she loved flamenco and didn't want to become a housewife?

She felt bad about being so spoilt at lunch, but anger had taken over her mind and soul. Maybe she had gone over the top. She'd never been so rude to her father before. She made up her mind to apologise as soon as she got in, clear the air, and start afresh. After all, if she was going to make a go of it with Charlie, then better to at least try to have her father on her side. When she reached her door, she was dreading going in, but she had to face him.

"I demand to know where you have been, young lady," said her mother as she walked in the lounge.

"Just out, walking, clearing my head. Look, I want to…"

"You have no right to do that to your father," said Rosa, looking towards her husband. Mercedes felt pity as her father sat huddled in his armchair. He looked up with a vicious scowl, his cheeks puffy and eyes watery.

"I know, it's just…"

"I only want what's best for you," he said.

"Then let me breathe, let me live, stop forcing me to behave how you expect me to behave and just let me be as I am."

"How can we let you be if you are making a mistake?" said her mother.

"Mistake?" said Mercedes, wondering what she was referring to. What mistake? Dancing too much? Not becoming a civil worker. Then she realised.

"You didn't?"

"I had to," said her mother, firmly.

"No!"

"He's not for you," said her father.

The rage that she'd felt at lunch multiplied. She wanted to punch someone, hit and scream, mainly her mother, but also her father. How could they judge her like that, and Charlie, without even meeting him? What happened to the trust they had?

"I can't believe you gave away my secret like that, without even speaking to me about how I feel."

Rosa stared at her daughter, and Mercedes could see that perhaps something had happened, she wouldn't have just given up information like that.

"She only wants what's best for you," said her father, standing up and walking over, pulling his wife close to him. "I forbid you to see this Englishman again."

Mercedes laughed. It was the way he'd said 'Englishman' as if he'd been at war with Gibraltar, as if all Englishmen had personally ruined his life somehow.

"You're both pathetic," she said. "I'm ashamed to be your daughter."

And with that she left the room, defying her father's chants to come back and take it back, but there was no way, she was mad, real mad. She was so angry at her father for thinking he could control her like that, but more so at her mother for spilling her secret.

This was the final straw; there was no way she was going to stand for it any longer. She wanted control over her life, to be free and make her own decisions. The problem was, she didn't know where to start.

The next day Charlie had his first lesson of the New Year.

"What has changed?" said Ramón in a harsh tone after Charlie had played a few minutes.

"What do you mean?"

"Something is different, what?"

"What are you talking about?" asked Charlie, feeling defensive. In his mind, he was improving, not getting worse. He had a new energy and reason to play.

"Don't play me like a fool, Carlito, you are playing better," said Ramón, smiling.

"Better?"

"Yes you funny *guiri*, better, how?" He stood up and kissed Charlie on the head.

"No reason, I've just been practising." He wanted to tell

him that he'd met up with Mercedes, that she'd given him a further reason to become *un flamenco*, because he wanted to play for her.

"What do you mean 'no reason'," he said, mimicking his accent yet again. "I am a man, I know when one of my students has improved playing because of love."

"Love? What are you talking about?" Charlie suddenly felt hot, blood rushed to his face and head, causing him to feel dizzy.

"What's up? You think you can lie to me? Now, who is she?"

"She's no one. I swear. I've just been practising. After performing so well at the Maestranza I have more confidence, I have a taste for flamenco now, and I want to go further."

"I don't believe you, but if you say so. Watch yourself, there are a lot of dangerous women out there. Keep your head focused and your *pene* in your pants. If you keep going as you are, you could possibly become the first real *guiri* flamenco. Now, let's play."

As Charlie continued to play, he felt guilty for lying to Ramón, after all he'd done for him, but he was confident that once he saw Mercedes and him playing together, then he would see they had to be together.

After the lesson, Charlie made his way down Mateos Gago towards the statue to meet Mercedes. As he got closer he began to smile, expecting to see her there. When she wasn't, his heart sank. Then he remembered he was in Spain, and that Mercedes wasn't the most punctual lady in Andalucía.

But as the seconds turned into minutes, he began to worry she wasn't coming. Had he said something wrong before? Maybe she could sense that he wasn't convinced about staying in Sevilla forever and she had decided not get involved with a *guiri*.

He checked his phone several times to see if there were any messages, but nothing. Where the hell was she? It was almost half past.

Then he got a message.

Sorry, I no can come today, I am ill. Is nothing serious, just my throat, no can speak. I text you soon xx.

Charlie wanted to call her up, just to check her throat was okay, but he didn't want to mess things up. So he texted back.

Okay, no problem. Hope you get better, maybe it was all that kissing. Ha xxx.

On his way home, he kept his phone in his hand, hoping she would change her mind and come and see him. He made his way through the centre, along the river, and up to his flat. Once in his room, he received a reply.

Is true, maybe. Hopefully, we can kiss again soon xx.

Yes, soon xxx take it easy xxx.

Charlie picked up his guitar, stared out at the Sevilla sky, and began to play, dreaming of playing with Mercedes by his side.

Chapter 10 ESCAPISM

February

Mercedes' heart was racing. She hadn't run away from home since she was ten when her mother told her off after she was about to wet her knickers and had to take a pee in the next door neighbours' bushes. After the row, she'd grabbed what she thought was enough to survive on, and ran away to Lola's. She only lasted a couple of hours though, as Lola's mum managed to persuade her to go back once she realised she wouldn't get by with just her flamenco dresses and high heels.

This time was different though. She was definitely going to live with Lola to sort her head out, and she wasn't coming back in the foreseeable future.

At least that's what she wrote in the note to her parents, who had gone for lunch with her Auntie and wouldn't be back until later. She'd planned her escape to perfection, making sure they were out because there was no way she could face them and say she was leaving home; they'd only stop her doing what she wanted like they had for her entire life. Just like they were trying to stop her seeing Charlie, an Englishman, because he was, well, English, and not some rich Sevillano.

She felt ridiculous for not responding to Charlie's messages or answering his calls for the last week, but she had to clear her head, be sure about moving out and living with Lola. She needed to change her surroundings. As soon as she was at Lola's, she would call Charlie, ask for forgiveness and arrange a time to meet.

She was still an emotional wreck though.

Lola had popped round with Miguel to help with her

stuff.

"Are you sure about this?" asked Lola as Mercedes wiped the tears from her eyes. "I'm all up for you staying at mine, but not if you're going to be a snivelling mess."

"I need to get away, I can't breathe here anymore. I haven't spoken to my father for two weeks, and can't bring myself to even look my mother in the eyes. I have to get out of this hellhole."

"If you're sure. Let's get a move on though because Miguel has to be back at work soon. Come on, are you taking all these dresses?"

"Sure, and those boxes of shoes over there."

"Miguel, make yourself useful." Miguel saluted to his boss and began carrying the boxes to his car.

After about thirty minutes of rushing about, they were all loaded up in the car and ready to go.

"Is that everything?" asked Lola, "sure you don't want to take your father's new 100 inch TV."

"You think we could fit it in?" asked Miguel.

"I doubt it," said Mercedes, "anyway, I couldn't take that, it would be like stealing, especially with Semana Santa coming up soon. That was why he bought it anyway, to watch the festival live from his sofa as if he was right in the crowd."

Just as she said that, she remembered she'd left something upstairs. *"Mierda,"* she muttered.

"What is it?" said Lola, "forgotten another box of shoes?"

"No, my handbag, hang on a second."

She darted inside, went up to her room and grabbed her handbag hanging on the side of her chair. She stood for a moment and scanned her room, so many memories of dancing, so much time alone, and too many minutes moping about after rows with her father. It was time for a change, for the better.

"Are you okay, *Hija*?" Mercedes startled and twisted round.

"*Mama*?"

"*Hola, Hija*, did I catch you at a bad time?" Her mother frowned. Did she suspect anything? Mercedes thought quickly. There was no reason for them to know she was leaving, after all, she'd only taken the stuff from her wardrobes. She had to lie fast, and convincingly. "No, of course not. It's just I have an interview with a *tablao* and was getting my handbag. Why are you back so early?"

"We didn't go for lunch, in the end, just a coffee; your Aunt wasn't feeling too well."

"Shame." She looked in her mother's eyes and could see sorrow, and guilt even. It was too late though, there was no going back now. Everything was packed in the car. Damn; Lola and Miguel, she had to get a move on.

"Anyway, *Mama*, I must go."

"Oh, so soon? I was hoping we could have a little chat."

Mercedes knew her mother was trying to draw her in, but she wasn't having any of it.

"Look, we'll chat later. I need to go, all right?"

"Fine," said her mother in an off tone. "I was only trying to help, to make things easier."

"*Adios Madre*," she said, abruptly as she stormed out, without kissing her on the cheek.

As she left the room, she was fully expecting her father to be waiting in the lounge, but he was nowhere to be seen. "Lucky," she muttered as she left the flat, feeling victorious. But as she looked over towards Miguel's car, her happiness oozed away.

How dare he, she thought. He wasn't going to stop her.

"Oh, hello, *Hija*," said her father as he pulled his head up from the car window. "I was just asking Miguel how he was after the accident."

"Oh, he's much better now," said Mercedes, trying not to shout at him for being such a nosy bastard.

"Yes, yes, I am much better," said Miguel, with uncertainty in his voice.

"What was wrong with you again?" asked Francisco, "my mind keeps playing tricks on me."

"You know it was his arm, *Papa*. Now, we need to make a move."

"I guess you do, what with all that luggage in the back. Is someone going away?"

"You could say that," said Mercedes as she got in the car. "*Adios Papa*."

"*Adios*?" he said, looking at Lola, who shrugged her shoulders as they drove off.

Mercedes shed a tear as she watched her father stare into space and scratch his head in a confused way. She actually felt sorry for him, for a second, because she knew when he found out she had left, his world would shatter.

That second soon passed though.

She was leaving, starting a new life, and adventure. She was free. Soon she would call Charlie, and make up for lost time.

As they sped away, her phone rang. It was her mother. She ignored the call, and the next five until she decided enough was enough.

"Listen, *Mama*," said Mercedes, picking up the phone.

"No, *Hija*, you listen. What is this craziness? Where have you gone? To stay with that *guiri inglés*?"

"I wish. Can't you read? I'm going to Lola's to sort my head out. I need space *Mama*, that's all I ask."

"But why the lies before? What about the interview?"

"I knew you'd try to stop me. I need to sort my life out, *Mama*. I hope you can understand me."

She waited as silence followed.

"Mercedes, this is your father."

"What do you want? Where's *Mama*?"

"Here, crying her heart out. How could you do this to her; leave for a silly crush?"

"It's not a silly crush. When will you both start believing your daughter? I'm going to Lola's. I don't want to be bothered, or hassled, just leave me alone."

As Mercedes said the previous four words, the volume got louder until she was shouting. She watched her phone fly out the car window, over the barrier on the Triana Bridge, and head towards the River Guadalquivir.

"Nice shot," said Miguel.

"Yeah, it was, wasn't it?" said Mercedes, happy with herself, free from her problems at last.

"Yeah, shame all your contact are on there, though, aren't they?" said Lola.

"I don't care. Anything to avoid my parents."

"What about Charlie's number, have you got that?"

"*Joder*."

Why had she acted on such a silly impulse? Now her only means of chatting to Charlie and apologising for being such a pathetic person was twenty metres under water.

"I'll just go and see him."

"Where?"

"In the bar. Tomorrow night."

"About time, I don't know why you haven't before."

"True," said Mercedes, "and I'm not going to wait any longer." Mercedes hated fighting with her parents, but it

Falling for Flamenco

hadn't been her to bring them to such a desperate situation. If only her mother had kept her secret and her father gave her some space. She was convinced she'd made the right decision though. The further she got away from the family home the better she felt. She was sure that once she saw Charlie, she'd be completely clear about her future.

Charlie turned up for work panting and spluttering. He was a few minutes late.

"What is this?" said Pedro, "are you turning into the Spanish now? Being late; this is not the case of the punctuality English."

"Sorry Pedro, I was just finishing some final preparations."

"For what?"

"For tomorrow."

"And what is happening tomorrow?"

"I'm gonna do it."

"Do what man? Tell me, this is more excruciating than watching one of my grandmother's soap operas."

"I'm going to play for Mercedes."

"What, the football team?"

"No, amigo. Mercedes, the dancer."

"Oh, *por favor*," said Pedro, "Are you two not married yet? I thought you went on a hot date and everything was fine."

"It was, but she's been ignoring my messages and calls. The only way for me to win her over is to go and play for her."

Charlie suddenly felt weird, saying those words out loud 'win her over' as if he was in some sort of competition. What if she didn't want to be won over, and wanted to be alone, which was probably the case since she'd been ignoring him.

He was beginning to hate that pessimistic voice in his head though, the one that had been stopping him for so long, making excuses, putting things off for tomorrow. But tomorrow had arrived, well, almost.

He'd spent a week practising with Ramón, perfecting his playing so he could turn up and play for Mercedes. Hopefully, he'd inject some romance into the air, and hypnotize her to dance for him.

"I want you all the success. Now get to work, come on man, people are thirsty and hungry," said Pedro, pushing Charlie into the back room.

As Charlie worked that evening, he was whistling more than usual, content that his master plan was about to come into action, or so he thought.

"*Buenas noches,*" said a man with a deep voice as Charlie was taking someone's order.

"*Momento, por favor,*" said Charlie, turning to smile at the man, until he saw who it was.

"Can we speak?" said Francisco, squeezing Charlie's arm as he pulled him away.

"Oi, what the…" said Charlie feeling the rage build up inside as he was dragged around the side of the restaurant. How dare he rip him away from his job! "What's this about?" he said, fiercely.

"About my daughter," he said. Charlie was surprised he spoke English, even if his pronunciation was a bit pigeon like.

"What about your daughter?"

"Where is she?"

"No idea. I haven't seen her for…" then he stopped, not wanting to commit to a time.

"For what? She is with you, no?"

"With me, ha," said Charlie seeing the funny side. "I wish."

"What you wish?"

"Many things," said Charlie, "world peace, that Watford gets promoted to the premier league so my Dad can watch more quality games, that…"

"Stop talking. You must to not see my daughter. She cannot be with *un inglés*. She is Sevillana, and she will stay here, with us."

What was this guy on? Charlie wasn't going to let him control his future like that, even though he did look as though he was going to lamp him one.

"Have you asked her that?"

"Why you…" Francisco pushed Charlie against the wall, pressing against his chest. "Leave! Get out of Sevilla," he said, pushing his face up against his.

"I don't think so," said Charlie, pushing Francisco back slightly. "I'm going to be here for some time, now get used to it."

"What's mean?" Francisco tensed his lips, seeming furious that he didn't understand.

"That I'm staying in Sevilla, with your daughter, if you like it or not."

Francisco scrunched his fist together and raised his hand. Charlie ducked.

"*Señor, que haces, señor?*" Pedro said, holding Francisco's arm back and pulling him off Charlie. "Stop, stop!"

"Yeah," said Charlie, suddenly feeling stronger with Pedro by his side. Just then Jorge appeared too.

"Is there a problem with the fish?"

"No, no. I have finished here, I hope," said Francisco, brushing down his suit jacket while throwing an evil at

Charlie. He clonked off along the cobbled path and disappeared through the back streets.

"Back to work," said Pedro, "we speak after."

Charlie returned to serving customers. As the night went on, he began to realise what sort of mix up he might be getting into. That was one angry father. How was he ever going to get on his good side? Did he even have a good side? Meeting in-laws was tricky enough without one wanting to kill you.

Maybe this wasn't such a good idea after all. He wondered what his parents would say,

Oh that's lovely you've met a nice Spanish girl, do you get on with her parents?

Well, no actually, her Dad nearly broke my arm.

Perhaps that was why she'd been ignoring his calls. Maybe she'd realised it was never meant to be. The fact that her father had asked him if he'd seen her made him think something was up.

At the end of the night, Jorge and Pedro pulled up a stall, and they sat around having a beer.

"Listen, *amigo*," said Jorge, wrapping his arm around his shoulder. "That was a tense moment tonight."

"Yeah, I know. I thought he was going to break my arm, he kept going on about his daughter and asking where she was."

"And do you know?" asked Pedro.

"No idea."

"The problem is he knows where you are, where you work, and can come back. He crazy, powerful man, you no want to play with him…or his daughter," said Jorge.

"Why? What's up with her?"

"Nothing, nothing, she is good woman, very *guapa*, but her father, as you can see, is a little bit *loco* my friend. Is not better you find other fish?"

"But I don't want another fish?"

"You don't like the fish?" asked Jorge.

"Of course I do, that's not the point. My plan is to go and see her tomorrow."

"Wait, my friend, wait. Have patience."

Charlie looked at them, smiling with their honest faces. He'd grown to respect them over the previous months and knew that they were probably right.

"Why don't you have a break from Sevilla? It is a beautiful place, but sometimes you need to escape. Take a week holiday, go home and see your parents, then you can decide about the beautiful Mercedes."

Charlie thought about it for a second. It wasn't a bad idea; a week at home would do him good, especially after not being back there at Christmas. Mercedes could wait a little longer.

"Would you guys be okay for a week?"

"Sure, sure, we miss you, but yeah, is fine. You need a break, *amigo*," said Pedro.

"Fine, yeah, okay, maybe I will."

That evening Charlie got back to his flat and booked a flight home for the next afternoon. He sent Mercedes one final message saying he was going home and that he hoped to see her when he came back, but she didn't reply.

The next day he called Ramón while he was on his way to the airport.

"You are what?" shouted Ramón.

"Going home, I need to get away for a week. Don't worry, I have my guitar."

"I hope you have, *coño*. Get your arse back here soon, we have practice to do, I may have found you a little job in a *tablao* up the road."

"Really? That's great."
"Yeah, so make sure you don't crash!"
"I'll try not to. See you in a week."

Meanwhile, back in Triana, Lola nipped out to the shops with Miguel, and Mercedes spent four hours cleaning the spare room, or more like the junk room. When she entered, she could barely see the floor, covered with shoes, books, clothes, bags of magazines and dusty teddy bears. She'd managed to get the rubbish organised in boxes and had piled them up in the lounge. Now she was busy scrubbing off the mould from the walls with bleach.

"What the hell are you doing?" asked Lola as she got back.

"Sorting out this disaster of a room."

"But it was fine before."

"Fine for a set of badgers to hibernate in the winter, but if I plan on being able to walk from the bed to the door without tripping up and breaking my ankle then, sorry, but I have to get things in order."

"What, you mean it wasn't clean?"

"Clean? I couldn't tell if it was clean because I couldn't see the floor."

"Why that useless pile of horse shit," said Lola. "Miguel," she shouted.

"Yes darling," he called out from the other room.

"Get your lazy arse in here."

Miguel appeared at once, cowering in the doorway. Mercedes continued scrubbing the walls.

"I thought I told you to tidy up this room."

"I did."

"Then why was there still rubbish on the floor?"

"I wouldn't say it was rubbish, I got rid of the empty

beer bottles, packets of crisps and used…"

"Don't worry," said Mercedes, lifting her head and butting in.

"I'm sorry Mercedes, but you know what a man's level of cleanliness is like," said Lola. "Anyway, I have some great news."

"What's that?"

"I've got us an interview, with a new *tablao* opening up."

"Really?" said Mercedes, squealing with delight as she threw her arms around Lola. "That's great, where, when?"

"Not for a couple of days, it's in *La Alameda*, it looks quite classy."

"That's brilliant. Oh, I can't wait to get back dancing again."

"Me too. Look, let's take you out for some tapas to celebrate."

"Sounds like a great idea. I have to drop in on someone after, though."

"I see," said Lola, winking as she let her finish cleaning.

Once they'd been out for dinner, Mercedes left Lola and Miguel and made her way over towards Plaza Doña Elvira, where she hoped she would find Charlie working.

Mercedes could feel the butterflies as she got to the square. She thought back to the first time she'd seen him playing that evening and sighed, feeling empty inside without him. She hoped he wasn't annoyed with her.

She watched as the two usual waiters ran about, laughing and joking with each other. After ten minutes of not seeing Charlie, she began to worry. She was sure he worked on Thursdays. Maybe he had the night off, or was ill, or had found another dancer. Panic rose up in her body as she thought that she had missed her chance, blown it, all because of her parents. She rushed over.

"*Hola,*" she said to Pedro.

"*Hola, señorita,*" he said, raising his eyebrows. "Table for one? Or two?"

"No it's fine, I'm not here to eat."

"So why are you here, *guapa*?"

Pedro stood with his arms folded, as if being defensive in some way.

"To see Charlie. Is he working tonight?"

"No, not tonight."

"When is he working next? There's something I need to say to him."

"I'm not sure, *guapa*."

"Oh, but does he still work here?"

"I think so."

"Damn it, can you give me a straight answer?" she asked, raising her voice.

"Okay, okay, no need to get angry, lady." Pedro held his hands up and smiled. "Fine, yes, he still works here, but he's gone away for a while."

"Gone away, but where?"

"Back home."

"Home? For how long?"

"He didn't say, he just left. He said he needed to clear his head, get away."

"Get away, but what for?"

"I'm not sure if I'm the one who should be telling you this, but a man came by, very angry, and threatened Charlie. I think he scared him, he scared me."

"What man?"

"That's not for me to say."

"But…"

"Sorry, *guapa*, but I've told you enough as it is. Now if you'd like to sit and have some tapas then do so.

Otherwise, I need to serve my customers."

"Fine. Thanks for your help."

Mercedes turned away and went back over to the benches and sat down. The night was getting colder. She wished that Charlie was by her side to warm her up. Why had he gone home? And who was this man who had come by?

She felt distraught. Why hadn't she acted sooner like Lola had said? She'd have to be patient and hope he came back quickly, if he did at all.

As Charlie rattled his keys in his front door, he heard a scream. He frowned, sure that it was his mother.

"Hi honey," he shouted, "I'm home."

"Bloody hell," said his dad from the lounge. "Charlie, is that you?"

"Yeah, Dad, who else is it going to be?"

"Oh right, well, probably best if you go upstairs for a minute, you see your mother and me…"

"Shut up, George. Charlikins just be a good boy and pop upstairs for a second, will you? We'll be out in a second."

"Ooohhh…kay…" said Charlie, hoping that his parents were watching a horror film or something.

By the state of his mother's hair when he finally came down into the lounge, and the strange, sordid smell in the air, Charlie guessed that they weren't watching any horror films, rather making one.

"Well, this is a nice surprise," said his Mum, planting a big kiss on his cheeks.

"Yeah, maybe you should ring next time son; a bit of notice might do us all a world of good. Give us a hug anyway you silly old Spanish git."

Charlie's Dad gave him a big bear hug, it was great to be

home.

"What brings you back Charlikins?" said his Mum, wandering into the kitchen to put the kettle on. "Everything okay?" They followed after her.

"Yeah fine, fine. I just wanted to pop back and say hello."

"And scare the shit out of us in the meantime," said his Dad.

"That wasn't in the plan actually. But I'll definitely let you know next time, just to avoid any surprises."

"How long are you back for?" asked his Mum.

"Just a few days. I need to get back, I might have a gig."

"Another one? That's great, mate," said his Dad, punching him lightly on the arm. His parents were grinning from ear to ear, proud of their son. Charlie remembered just how much he loved being around his folks. "Let's get out some *vino* then, to celebrate."

"Cheers, Dad."

Once they'd moved into the back room, his mother questioned him about what he'd been eating, whether or not he was keeping his flat clean and tidy, and if he'd found a place which served faggots. Then she moved onto the heart to heart stuff.

"So, what about the girls?"

"Yeah, thought you'd have a few señoritas up your sleeve by now, young lad. They must be crawling all over you."

"Don't pay any attention to him," said his mum. "Have you fallen in love? You look different; happy, but sad."

"But how…"

"I'm your mother." She put on her, 'obviously' face, and leaned forward. Charlie was unsure whether he wanted to reveal anything just yet, until he'd worked it out for himself. "Who is she then?"

"I bet she's got a nice pair of personalities?" asked his dad as he held his hands out in front of his chest and moved them up and down while raising an eyebrow.

"Well…" said Charlie, smirking, but his parents were already ahhing. "It's nothing official yet, but yeah, I have met a girl."

"That's great news," said his mum.

"It is, and it isn't."

"Oh, why, is she a gypsy or something? You haven't been getting involved in that drug world, have you?"

"No, of course not." He considered telling them the truth; that he'd fallen in love with a gorgeous, attractive woman. A perfect dancer. A perfect future wife. But her father was a nutter and had almost chased him out the country because he wanted to kill him.

That would only cause panic though, so he decided to keep the mood light and positive.

"It's just early days, that's all."

"We'll have to come out then, as soon as you get settled in this new job, then we'll see you in action," said his Mum.

"Yeah, but not that sort of action, if you know what I mean," said his Dad, winking.

"I think I'll leave that for you two."

That night Charlie had more fun than he'd had in a while. The world of flamenco and Sevilla had been an adventure, but hard work, and at times draining. He loved being with his parents and chatting without stress or worrying about what he was saying. For the first time since he'd left, he missed home.

The next evening he met up with Joe to fill him in on the gossip and try to work out what to do.

"So, let me get this straight," said Joe after their third pint. "You've fallen in love with a flamenco dancer, who is pretty damn fit, and you've only kissed her a couple of times."

"Yep."

"You haven't really had much time together, and haven't seen her naked."

"Yep."

"And her psycho dad wants to chop your balls off."

"Yep."

"And you're asking me whether I think you should make a go of it with her."

"Er, yep."

Hearing his hour conversation, and six months stint in Sevilla, summarised in three sentences made him feel daft.

"It would be a shame not to at least try to see her naked, especially after all that trouble you've gone through."

"But that's just it."

"What?"

"It's not about sex, or pulling her, or seeing just how fit she is naked."

"Then what, don't tell me you're in love?"

Charlie felt like a bit of a fool, but it was time to open up to someone.

"I think I might be."

"Oh dear Charlie boy, you have got yourself in a pickle, haven't you?"

"I guess I have, yes."

"What's the beer like out there, anyway?" asked Joe.

"Cold, a lot colder than here, and fizzier."

As they sat staring into their pints, Charlie wondered whether he'd sold his story short. It wasn't just about Mercedes, but the fact that he'd become a flamenco guitarist, *un flamenco*. He'd not even mentioned Ramón, or Pedro or Jorge, or the adventure of struggling with the guitar to perfect his moves. So much had happened that it would have been impossible to tell everything.

"So, what you gonna do then? Stick it out and fight off the dad, or come back and get a job in a fish and chip shop?"

"Hello big boy," said a familiar voice. Charlie turned to see Annette, a girl who'd had a crush on him at school, standing behind. She'd obviously attempted to put on an extra bit of lippy for Saturday night because it had smudged all up her cheek.

"Oh, hey Annette, finished early tonight?"

"Got the night off, ain't I? Off on the pull with Trace here, you guys fancy a bit of Watford boozing?" she asked, raising her slightly revealing bosom.

"I'm not sure that we do, sorry Luv," said Charlie, nodding his head and winking. Annette waddled off, pulling her skirt down to hide her chunky arse cheeks.

"I think there's your answer son," said Joe. "Just stay there man, nothing is gonna change here. Might as well make of it what you can."

"Wise words, mate, wise words."

His parents were all for him giving it a go as well, they were happy if he was, unlike some other parents he knew.

On the flight back he was on a high. He couldn't wait to track down Mercedes and declare his undying love for her. He was still cautious, though, and obviously had to play his cards right. She was still ignoring his calls and messages. He'd just have to hope that her father hadn't found her and managed to brainwash her in such a short period of time.

Mercedes and Lola were on their way to the new flamenco *tablao* in the Alameda; the bohemian area of Sevilla. Mercedes had been dying to get dancing again. She had so much energy and passion inside her that she couldn't let out by just teaching. She had to do more, give more, be more creative. She felt grateful that she could teach kids to improve their skills and bring out their talent, but it wasn't enough. She felt as if her gift was being wasted, and no matter how hard she tried, she felt unfulfilled by just teaching.

She missed performing too. The thrill and buzz of being on stage. The unpredictability of the night: what would happen, how would she move, how would the guitarist play.

"So, are you ready to become a flamenco dancer again?" asked Lola as they stepped up to the door.

"Sure am, let's do this."

The interview was over within five minutes, and they were soon on stage, showing José, the boss, what they were made of. As usual, they sat with each other on the wooden stools, listening for the guitarist to get warmed up. When they both sprang into action, dancing with each other the way they always did, with such rhythm, style, and passion, the owner stood clapping and shouting 'ole.'

"That wasn't so hard now, was it?" said Lola as they made their way back to the flat.

"No, it was rather easy."

"That's what happens when you put your heart and soul into things."

"I know."

She was relieved to be getting back into the dancing world but still felt incomplete. Since Charlie had gone back home, she'd done nothing but worry about why he'd left.

She was such a fool for throwing her phone in the river. She needed to hear from him before she could really get on with her life.

Charlie made the mistake of going to see Ramón on his way to see Mercedes.

"Don't ever do that to me again," said Ramón, sitting down after Charlie had scared him by jumping out behind the main entrance.

"What?" said Charlie, laughing at Ramón's reaction.

"Put me in such a moment of tension."

"Tension? Why? What did I do?"

"Going home like that, letting me think that maybe you weren't coming back. That all my hard work was flying back to that dreadfully cold and miserable country."

"Don't forget you had a great time in that cold and miserable country. And besides, I said I'd be back, and here I am."

"I know, but it's just I have something for you. A new gig, and we must leave now."

"Now? But I was…"

"No buts. We're going now to see this guy before he fills the spots."

Charlie had spent all morning gearing himself up for Mercedes, but he couldn't let Ramón down, so he went with him.

Ramón shut up his school and whisked Charlie off to the Alameda. On the way, Charlie thought of his parents. How proud they had been to see him doing well in Sevilla, becoming a flamenco guitarist, against the odds, and was glad that they were going to come over and see him. He had to get this gig, had to be at his best, and had to show the world his talent.

"So, you are telling me that this guy is *un flamenco*?" said José, the owner.

"I wouldn't have spent so much time on him if I didn't think so, come on José, just give him a chance."

"But, he's well, not very Spanish is he?"

"This is the 21st century, come on man. The world is changing, we have to be more open to ideas. If you want a reliable, dependable, and hard-working guitarist, then Charlie is your man."

"Charlie, you say? Or Carlos?" asked José, looking at Charlie.

"I don't mind," said Charlie. "I just want to play."

"Well then, let's have a look at you, Carlito."

Charlie walked up the wooden stairs and sat down on a stool in the middle of the stage.

"Venga, Carlito, show them what you are made of," said Ramón, clenching his fists in the air. Charlie nodded, swung his guitar on his knee, and began to play.

His playing took him on a trip home, seeing his parents smiling at him again as he performed on stage to a full audience. As he played, he thought of them watching him, with Mercedes by his side, beating the odds, battling against all the possible obstacles and fighting for what they both believed in; love.

"*Fantástico*," said José, clapping as Charlie finished.

They arranged to start the following night, straight in with a new singer and two dancers.

By the time Charlie had turned up to Mercedes' dance school, the lights were off and shutters down. He'd catch her first thing in the morning, to tell her the good news. He was ecstatic after the news that he'd gotten his first chance to perform on a regular basis.

Mercedes was happier than she'd been for a long time. Knowing that she'd be back on stage that evening filled her with joy. Luckily she had the morning off to save her energy, so she spent the day strolling up along the river, thinking about her night's performance, and her grandfather. He would have been proud to see her that evening. She knew in her heart that he would be watching her from wherever she was, unlike her parents.

She was still angry at them. At her mother for not keeping her secret, and at her father for being a constant pain in her side. She felt sad that she couldn't share this moment with them, all she wanted was to get their support and approval, to show them how well she danced. Deep down, she wanted her father there, watching her like he used to. But it wasn't to be. Maybe someone else would pop by and see her; if only.

By the time she got back to the flat, it was time for a bite to eat, a quick siesta, and then she got ready.

"Are you coming?" asked Lola, knocking on her door.

"Yeah, won't be long."

As they made their way towards the Alameda, Mercedes felt confident that having Lola by her side would mean they were a success.

"*Gracias*," she said as they were about to arrive.

"For what?"

"For everything. For sticking by me in these difficult times, for letting me stay at your flat, for finding me a new job dancing."

"Don't be silly, woman. This is nothing. I'm sure you'll pay me back by attracting new dancers to our school over the next however many years."

"Hopefully."

"How are you feeling about tonight?"

"Good, good. Let's just hope the crowd is okay, and the singer and guitarist."

"Sure they will be."

When they stepped inside the *tablao* Mercedes could feel the excitement pulsate through her veins. She was back. She had been far too long away from her passion. They walked through the main doors and passed the audience, who were already taking their seats. Mercedes followed Lola as they went into the dressing rooms.

"*Hola José*," said Lola as they knocked on his office door.

"Ah, my new dancers, excellent," said José, opening the door. "That's everyone here now. Come on, let me introduce you to the singer and guitarist. I'm sure you'll be pleasantly surprised."

As she followed, José and Lola were chatting away, she thought she could see a familiar face in front.

"Hey, Ramón," said José, walking up to the tall man. "Allow me to introduce these two: Lola and Mercedes, they'll be dancing tonight."

"I see," said Ramón. He kissed them both on the cheeks. "Well, this is a nice surprise. I've seen you both in action before, at *Las Almas*, no?"

"Yes, that's where we used to dance," said Lola. "Big fan of flamenco, are you?"

"Just a little, yes. I guess you should meet the guitarist for this evening," he said, knocking on the door. "Charlie, look who's here."

Mercedes' heart fluttered as she heard his name.

"Hey," he said, poking his head round the door. As their eyes met Mercedes' heart filled with joy. He was there, in the flesh, standing in front of her.

"*Hola guapo*," said Lola, kissing him on the cheeks. "Long time no see," she added.

"Oh, you guys know each other?" asked José.

"A little," said Charlie, smirking as he winked at Mercedes and kissed her on the cheek. She went to say something, but Charlie shook his head slightly, and then she remembered what he'd said about not letting Ramón know about her.

"What's that my dear, were you going to say something?" said Ramón.

"No, no, just a pleasure to meet you."

"Anyway, I thought that maybe…" said José, but Mercedes stopped listening as she stared at Charlie, who was glaring back with his slightly watery eyes. She felt ecstatic, knowing that she was going to perform with him.

Charlie was in a daze. Fate had brought them together again. Here he was, on stage in a flamenco *tablao*, tuning his guitar, with Mercedes to his side looking out towards the crowd. He knew her well enough to know that she normally kept her head down. He could feel her new confidence and admired her beauty. This was his chance to win her over.

By the way she'd smiled at him before, it seemed as if there must have been a reason for ignoring his calls and messages. Maybe he had been worrying about nothing, as usual.

Just then he noticed Ramón, sitting proudly in the front row, nodding his head for Charlie to get going. He wondered if Ramón had triggered that maybe they knew each other better than he thought. It didn't matter now though; he had to focus on his guitar and impress. For the next twenty minutes, he would put his heart, body, and soul into playing alongside the woman he'd fantasized about for far too long.

It felt so natural to be there next to her, watching her steps, trying to keep up with her. The signals she sent out from her powerful moves told him when to change pace. Now and then she would look behind and smile at him, something he'd never seen her do while dancing. He knew the moment for them had arrived, and it had been totally worth the wait.

Mercedes was on a high knowing she was finally dancing for Charlie, and she couldn't, for the life of her, keep her usual serious flamenco face on as the emotion rose up in her body. She was on stage next to him. Her future love. There, she admitted it to herself, she was in love.

Fate existed, he was playing for her, her own Englishman. She was in a trance and felt euphoric, did it get any better than this? All the emotion she felt, the anger from her parents, the fact she had been fighting for something she believed in, something she loved, came out in her dancing, showing the force and energy she had. It was the first time she danced with her head held high through the whole dance, and the crowd loved it.

A tear formed in her eye as she stood proudly once they'd finished. Charlie moved and grabbed her hand, holding it above her head. His firm hand showed her that he could support and protect her.

"That was a great performance," said Charlie as they stood in a corner alone backstage.

"*Gracias*, you were good too; you played like *un flamenco*," said Mercedes, smiling.

"Really?" said Charlie, moving a bit closer. Mercedes could tell he wanted to kiss her, and she did too, but they'd have to wait.

"Of course. We need to practice more though," she said.

"How about tomorrow?"

"Why not?"

Charlie's smile was catching, and filled her heart with devotion. She wanted to pull him closer and kiss him, but she had to remain professional, after all, other people were lurking about.

"So," said Ramón, creeping up behind. "The two love birds are in their nest, finally."

"I can explain," said Charlie. Mercedes panicked, what would he say now, catching them so close?

"There's no need to explain," said Ramón. "I knew ages ago that you two would end up together, it was only a matter of time."

"But I thought you were against the idea of Mercedes and me together."

Mercedes had a warm feeling inside, knowing that he'd spoken to someone else about them made it seem more real, more certain.

"I was, and still am. I think you need to be careful, especially in this flamenco world, but after seeing you two like that, I can tell you have something special, something pure, more than I've seen in a lot of performances."

As Charlie hugged Ramón, Mercedes was certain she'd found the man for her. She could see in his eyes he was emotional, and was proud that he could show his feelings.

"*Gracias,*" said Mercedes, kissing Ramón on the cheek. "He has a great teacher."

"Yes, but now he has a better one. Come on, it's time for a celebration. Drinks are on me."

Mercedes was full of joy and emotion, everything had gone the way she'd hoped. She wanted to ask him why he had gone home, but that would involve bringing up her parents, and she didn't want to have to think about them. She knew that deep down, the real test of their relationship was still to come, but tonight was about celebration and happiness.

Chapter 11 SEMANA SANTA

March

Mercedes rested herself on her elbows and ran her fingers through the hair on the back of Charlie's head. She loved the way it turned wavier in the morning. It was the third time she'd stayed over in his flat in the last two weeks, and each morning she woke and just watched him. She lifted the sheets and peeked down his back towards his cute behind; so firm and juicy. She hadn't imagined him to have such a pert bottom and found herself grabbing it a lot, maybe too much. She kissed the back of his neck.

"Wake up sleepyhead," she said, mimicking what he'd said to her once.

"Eh? What? Who are you and why are you in my bed?"

"You know who I am, your girlfriend." She adored the way it sounded in English, much cuter than *novia*, the same word used for bride, although perhaps she would like to be called that too when the time was right.

He turned round to face her, opening his eyes slowly and went to kiss her on the mouth.

"No no, I must to clean my teeth."

"I don't care," he said, pulling her closer. She wrapped her legs around him, feeling comfortable in his arms, safe, cozy, and in unison.

In the last two weeks, they had gone from being practical strangers to lovers. They had to hide it at work, of course, it wouldn't be professional to let the boss know they were an item, according to Lola anyway. As soon as they left the tablao each night, they were all over each other, kissing with passion, hands wandering.

The sex had been amazing. The best she'd ever had. Charlie was different; she felt like a woman, not some piece of meat. She had fallen for him, completely, and he with her.

"Have I told you how pretty you look in the morning?" he said, to which she oozed inside and kissed him on the lips.

"I think, one or two yes."

"But you don't understand, it's not easy to find a girl who looks like you in the morning, so sexy, so cute, without needing makeup."

"*Si, si*, you are only saying that, what do you want?"

"Nothing," he said, smiling, pulling her towards him.

"Oh, someone is happy to see me this morning," she said, feeling something hard poking into her belly.

"So?" asked Charlie, raising an eyebrow.

"You know I need to go, I have class in an hour."

"An hour? It won't take that long."

"I can't," she said, deeply wanting to be with him again, but she had to go. "You will see me with more *ganas* next time."

"True," he said.

"Come on. I'm going to have a shower, why don't you make the breakfast."

"*Si señor*, whatever you say," he said, saluting. She laughed, kissed his head, and jumped out of bed.

As she was in the shower, she heard familiar Semana Santa music playing from next door. Holy Week was due to start in just ten days. She listened as the trumpets played and felt the emotion of the week ahead. There was so much of it at this time of year, remembering her religion, her God, and Jesus Christ. She thought of her Virgin, and felt sad that her grandfather wouldn't be there to watch it with her.

Then she thought of her parents. She still hadn't spoken

to them and was starting to feel guilty. She thought that maybe her mother would have passed by at work and said something, but she hadn't. Maybe it was time to see them and set the record straight. She was with Charlie now, whether they liked it or not, although she'd prefer to have their blessing.

"Grubs up," said Charlie, poking his head in the shower.

"Hey," she said, covering her chest with her hands.

"What's up? It's not as if I haven't seen them before."

"Out," she said, laughing.

"Okay, but move your arse, or your coffee will get cold."

She whistled to herself as she got dressed, and thought that maybe it was time to tell Charlie about Semana Santa and make sure he had some time off, so she could show him how important the festival was to her.

As they sat in front of each other, sipping on coffee and eating toast with jamón, she brought it up.

"So, do you know anything about the next week?"

"The next week?"

"Yes, is a big moment in Sevilla."

"Oh, yeah, I think Pedro and Jorge were arguing about it the other day. Jorge said something about some crazy religious festival."

"Crazy?" she asked, wondering if he was talking about the same serious, meaningful festival that she was asking about.

"Yeah," said Charlie, laughing, "he showed me some pictures of guys dressed up in funny pointy hats with their eyes peeking out, like some weird KKK procession."

"I'm sorry?"

"Yeah, there were some figures too, of Jesus and a Virgin, or something like that, lots of different ones; it all looks quite miserable and scary."

"*Pero que coño dices*," she said, raising her voice. She'd never sworn in front of him before, at least not like that, but she'd never had reason to before.

"What the fuck am I saying?"

"*Si, imbecil, ignorante.*"

"Hang on a moment," he said, laughing, which aggravated her even more.

Mercedes could feel the tension taking control of her mind. How dare he insult her festival and religion like that, what did he know anyway?

"You need be careful what you say. Semana Santa is very important to the people of Sevilla, to me, to my family."

She was shouting now, throwing her arms about uncontrollably as she held a knife.

"Okay, okay, calm down. But, wait? You mean you like all that stuff? The men walking about dressed up like some racist gang?"

"They are not racist, is a penitence, to show their faith in God."

Charlie frowned and stared at her for a few seconds as if trying to work out if she was serious, or about to burst out laughing. She started to feel guilty, maybe she had overreacted.

"You're serious, aren't you?"

"Of course, why?"

"Oh, I'm sorry. It's just that Pedro and Jorge were joking about it with each other. Come to think of it, Pedro was quite angry at Jorge. He kept saying he was a *puto ateo*, but I wasn't sure what he meant."

"It means he doesn't believe in God, but in a rude way."

"I see."

Mercedes wanted to ask him whether he believed in

God, but she guessed he didn't. She wasn't really surprised though as she knew that other nationalities were maybe less fanatic about religion. But she sensed this could be a problem between them.

"I'm sorry if I upset you, really," he said, smiling as he grabbed her hand.

"Is okay, sorry for being a little angry."

"A little? I thought you were going to throw that knife at me." She smiled. How did he make her do that so easily? Forget about all the tension in her life.

Even though he'd apologised, she still felt a cloud of doubt over her head. This wasn't just a taste in music they were talking about, but something serious, pure, and essential in her life.

"I have an idea," she said.

"What's that?"

"Well, maybe you can come out with me in Semana Santa and see some of the processions. You will see the true side of Sevilla and its people, maybe you will like?"

"Sure, sure, who knows," he said, half-willingly.

"Look, I have to go now, but we talk about it later. I see you tonight?"

"Okay, sorry about before."

"*No problema.*"

They kissed briefly, and she left. On her way to flamenco class, the enormity of the difference began to sink in, and she worked herself up into a state of panic. With such an important festival coming up she wanted to enjoy it, but would Charlie really take to it? It was a delicate subject, one that wasn't to be joked about. She couldn't just give up on him though, rather try to make him understand her more, especially if her family was ever going to accept him, and they were going to become a real couple.

Charlie was slumped on the floor by the door with his knees wrapped up close to his chest.

"What the hell was all that about?" he muttered to himself. "Religion. God. Catholicism. Scary woman with a knife. What have you gotten yourself into, you silly git?" he said, in the voice of his father.

He glanced across the room, out through the patio doors and straight to la Giralda. Then it suddenly dawned on him the immensity of the cathedral. That major religious place which thousands of Sevillanos, and Españoles, worshipped.

He stood up quickly, went out on his balcony and scanned the city. It seemed as if he had missed something vital, an aspect of the city which he had completely neglected. It was as if the churches had just popped up, right there and then. The influence of religion was all around, staring him in the face.

It wasn't as if he was a complete atheist. After all, he did know the Lord's Prayer off by heart, but how? His mother had taught it to him as a lad, said it with him by his bed each night. His father hadn't though, he was the true atheist in the family.

He also remembered learning about religion at school and singing religious hymns in assembly. But come to think of it, he and his mates had tended to change the lyrics. "He's got the whole world in his pants (not hands)" "Cucumbers my Lord, cucumbers, (instead of Kumbayah).

And then there were the boy scouts. His parents had put him in there to 'keep him off the streets' and make an honest boy out of him. At the start he loved it: making knots, going camping, and playing on the football team. He became captain and even won a medal for the top goal scorer one year. He suddenly remembered going to church on Sunday too, participating in the parades, carrying the flag. The famous flag, he remembered now where the problems had started.

For some unknown reason, he'd put a firecracker in the harness of the flag during Sunday Mass, so when the Priest said 'please be seated' he pushed down and made a banging sound. He'd even grinned as the scout leaders gave him evils.

That was his bad year, when at scout camp he chucked a dead rabbit on the fire; stinking the place out for a week. The last straw was when, while playing some weird water carrying game, he threw the opponent's bucket of water over the Archala. That's when he got chucked out of scouts and had stopped going to church. That's when religion ended for him.

Now and then his granny would bring it up.

"Still saying your prayers Charlie?"

"Sure Nan, every night," he lied.

So it was hardly a surprise that he hadn't noticed just how important religion was in Sevilla. What the hell was he going to do about it though? He'd already fallen in love with Mercedes. There was no way he could fall out of love with her just because she believed in God. There wasn't anything bad about that, was there?

He felt ignorant and stupid for making fun of her beliefs, but the concept did scare him. The idea of one man having power over the world just didn't make sense. If there was a God, then why was there so much war, hunger, and poverty? Couldn't he just sort it out if he had so much power?

He'd keep those thoughts to himself, though, because he was in love, and there was no chance of just turning that feeling off. No, what he needed to do was understand her, get to know about her religion, especially if he was ever going to win over her family. Of course, her family, her father, the guy who had tried to snap his neck off.

He was still dying to ask her why exactly her father had come to his workplace, but whenever he brought up the subject of family she shrugged him off. He could sense that maybe things weren't great at home, which might explain why she'd moved in with Lola, which she'd also ignored when he questioned her about it. Anyway, he guessed he'd meet them eventually, and if he did, then surely they'd ask him about religion, about God, so he had to get clued up.

He remembered how Pedro and Jorge had been arguing about it. It sounded complicated, the divide between believers and non-believers, but if he was to stand a chance with Mercedes, then the least he could do was put some interest into the festival coming up. There was only one thing for it, speak with Pedro and find out about Semana Santa. He'd have to put his flamenco on hold.

"What do you mean, *maybe* you were wrong?" said Lola, as they were closing up the school. It was still light, signifying the start of spring, and the smell of azahar (orange blossom) filled the air.

"Maybe I was, thinking that I could fall in love with a *guiri*, maybe he was right."

"Who? Your father?"

"I don't know."

"You do know. Why the hell have you changed your tune suddenly, after all the hard work you have put in?" Lola was raising her voice now.

"There's no need to get like that?"

"Like that? But can't you see how you have been manipulated your whole life? Get a grip and do what you feel is best. Why have you changed your mind anyway?"

"Because he's not religious. He made fun of Semana Santa, about my beliefs."

"Oh come on *guapa*, there are plenty of Sevillanos who hate and despise Semana Santa, and they are supposed to be Catholic. Take Miguel for instance, why do you think we are going down to the coast again? He hates the festival. So what can you expect from someone who knows nothing about our city? I mean, sure religion is important in Spain, and some of us take things to the extreme, but that's no reason to give up on this guy."

"But how are we going to end up together, get married, in a church? It's useless. I may as well go home, become a civil worker, and find a good Catholic man to settle down with."

Lola laughed and hugged her friend.

"That's a great idea, and while you're at it why don't you break your legs so you can never dance flamenco again. I mean, honestly, pull yourself together woman."

"But…"

"There are no buts. Do you love him?"

"Of course."

"Then remember what you did to get him, don't give this all up for religion."

"I'm not…"

"So?"

"It's just I've been thinking about my family too, what with Semana Santa coming up. Maybe I should start afresh. It must be awful for them me not being there, especially next week."

"But they drove you away."

"I know, but they are my parents. Maybe I can make them see the light."

"Well, if that's the case, then you'll have to start with lover boy, because without him having a vague idea about religion and Semana Santa then there's no way your father will let him through the front door."

"That's what I'm worried about."

"Everything will sort itself out, you'll see. Now, come on, let's get back, Miguel said he was cooking one of his *tortilla de patatas* and I'm famished."

"Thanks."

"Not another word, let's go." They hugged again and began to walk home, but Mercedes spotted someone waiting.

"*Que pasa hermanita?*"

"Raul," she said, running up and hugging him. "Oh, it's so great to see you." She felt so good to be in the arms of family.

"It is?" He pulled back, frowning.

"Yeah, why do you say that?" Mercedes felt bad all of a sudden.

"Why?" said Raul, as if it was obvious. "Well, apart from the fact that you left me alone with Mama and Papa, you also caused one of the biggest arguments in the history of our family."

"Don't be ridiculous."

"I'll catch you at home," said Lola, "*adios* Raul," she added, giving both a kiss on the cheek.

"See you tomorrow, and thanks," Mercedes said to Lola. Then she turned back to her brother. "Why? What's happened?"

"Papa is close to moving down to Cadiz to live with his brother. He said he can't live at home anymore; it's as if you've died."

"Really?" Mercedes laughed at first but soon realised that Raul wasn't messing about.

"Yes, that's why I'm here. *Mama* is going crazy too. She's not the same without you, working herself into the ground. She's hardly at home either. The place is like a ghost house."

"What? And it's all my fault I suppose?"

"Not all of it. I know they went over the top about that English guy."

"Charlie."

"Yeah, what's happening with him by the way?"

"Oh, he's fine. We're still seeing each other."

"So you are living with him?"

"No, I'm with Lola."

"Do you love him?"

"Yes."

"Well, that's it then."

"What?"

"If you feel that strongly about him, you'll just have to bring him over."

"What, to the house?" As Raul smiled, so did she. She knew it was his doing, he'd persuaded their parents that she could bring him round, and give him a chance.

"Yeah, it's all sorted. Look, you come round for lunch on Domingo Ramos, you know how important that day is for us. Clear the air with *Papa*, and then during the week maybe they can meet him."

"You think they will?"

"He's too old for all this stress. He told me. He's realised he just wants to see you happy."

Mercedes couldn't believe her ears. She hugged Raul and tears formed in her eyes. She'd missed him.

"Okay, let's do it."

"Great, how about a beer, we can catch up, and you can tell me all about this guy."

As they sat and had a beer Mercedes told Raul all about Charlie: how they were performing together, how they were falling for each other, and even about the amazing sex. She kept that little issue of religion hidden though, as she was still unsure how to handle it.

"You said what?" asked Pedro as he was sitting up against the bar with Charlie having a beer after work. Charlie had just explained how he'd said Semana Santa was a crazy festival. "Honestly, no listen to that idiot Jorge, he is only interested in the Feria, dancing the stupid Sevillanas dance and getting drunk on rebujito."

"Drunk on what?"

"Don't worry, you will soon learn about la Feria too. What were you thinking? Saying that to a Catholic girl?"

"I know, I just didn't realise the seriousness of it all."

"God help you son."

There it was again, that word, God. Charlie had really started to notice just how much influence there was in Sevilla. He'd counted ten churches on his way to work that evening. He'd also noticed all the images of Jesus outside the churches. It was all getting a bit much, and the festival hadn't even begun.

"I think she was okay when she left, but she hasn't replied to my text."

"What did you say?"

"That I was sorry for being an idiot."

"That should be fine. Women love when a man admits he's an idiot. I have to do it three times in a week just so I can have sex."

"Really?"

"Trust me, after twenty years of marriage, is the only way."

"Blimey." Charlie was sure he was exaggerating, at least he hoped he was.

"Listen, *amigo*. If you really love this woman, and you can see a future with her, then you have to respect her religion."

"But I do."

"Sure, are you Catholic?"

"No, but my mother is."

"How?"

"Well, my father isn't, so they just never got round to baptising me."

"I see. Crazy English. Anyway, it would be a good idea if you know something about her religion, be interested."

"I am, a bit."

"Then why you don't come with me on Domingo Ramos; the first Sunday of Holy Week. I can take you out, show you processions and then when you see her, you'll have an idea of our crazy festival," said Pedro winking.

"Perfect. How can I thank you?"

"Just get me some beers while we're waiting for the processions, be prepared to stand for a long time. Think of it as one good Christian helping another."

As they shook hands, Charlie looked deep into Pedro's eyes. They were becoming solid mates, and he was honoured that he'd been able to find such a decent man to help him out. He couldn't wait for Semana Santa to start.

Domingo Ramos came round a lot quicker than Charlie had expected. He was curious to find out what this religious, uncrazy, festival was all about, and hopefully, discover that it wasn't as daunting as it sounded. He'd try to understand and appreciate it as much as possible, and then he could show Mercedes just how much he loved her.

He had a feeling it wasn't going to be that easy though. When he saw Mercedes during the week, she had been a bit off with him, not as loving as before, and when he asked if she wanted to come back to his, she said she was tired. She also said she was seeing her family on Domingo Ramos, but that she would be free to show him round on Monday.

Rather than ask her about why she was a bit off with him, he figured she was feeling emotional about the week coming up, and it was probably best to give her some space, even though inside he missed her.

This gave him even more reason to find out as much as possible, though, so that when he saw her, he could impress her with his knowledge and prove to her his devotion.

As he left his flat, at about one in the afternoon on Domingo Ramos, he was first hit by the number of people who were out and about, and secondly by how well dressed they were.

Pedro had told him to wear his Sunday best, which was the same as his Monday, Tuesday, or any other day best because all he had was his smart flamenco clothes: white shirt and black trousers, and black shoes. He wished he had a suit jacket though, to blend in with the rest of the men walking about.

The women looked stunning. Surprisingly, for such a religious day, some of the younger ladies wore quite elaborate and flesh showing dresses. He wondered what Mercedes would be wearing, surely something a little more appropriate.

As he made his way over Triana Bridge, which was even more packed than ever with people heading to the centre, he spotted his first KKK follower, or Nazareno as they were actually called. He watched him walk along the bridge, marching on as if about to start a long mission. He noticed people stopped and pointed at the Nazareno, and a few took photos, which he found weird as surely they didn't know who he, or she, was. Did women do the processions too?

"How are you, *compadre*?" said Pedro as Charlie turned up.

"Great, great, amazed at how much the city is buzzing. I can't believe how many people are interested in this."

"Most people are, apart from a few *idiotas* like Jorge. Soon you will see the power of Semana Santa, and how the passion of our religion affects everyone."

Charlie grinned and looked Pedro up and down. He'd never seen him so smart; dressed in a smooth navy suit, with his slick back hair, and closely shaved, he looked a few years younger.

"You're looking good, Pedro."

"Thanks, you never know, I can get lucky today, my wife and children are in the home, so I am free for a few hours."

"Why didn't they want to come out?"

"My wife did, yes, she is just as passionate about this week as I am, but the children are so small, two years, and nine months, so it would be a nightmare, with all the pushing and waiting, also we need to be quick and able to move about and get to the best places."

"Sounds good to me, let's go."

"Of course, but first, a beer my friend. Follow me."

Within a few minutes, Pedro had led Charlie deep into

the heart of Sevilla, to one of his favourite bars, el Rinconcillo. Charlie wasn't a massive fan of packed bars, though, and soon became edgy with the amount of barging and pushing. Luckily Pedro sorted them out quite quickly with a couple of beers and a plate of jamón.

"So, how much you know about Semana Santa?" asked Pedro.

"Not a lot, just from what you told me."

"You have read anymore? Seen a program?"

"A program? Is there a game on?"

"*No tonto*. Here, this is the program for the week," he said, handing over a pamphlet of the order of the processions. Charlie flicked through, oblivious to what he could actually do with it.

"You really know nothing, no?"

"You could say that."

"Well, here, let me explain." He took the book and started flicking through it, explaining how each day had a different run of processions and that each brotherhood had a different route.

"See here," he said, pointing to the map for the day. "This is where we are, and in an hour or so a few of the processions will leave their church. All of them have to pass through the Campana - the central point of Sevilla - and they go down Sierpes street, and make their way to the cathedral. Inside they have to salute the Virgen de los Reyes, and then take their own route back to their church."

"Sounds complicated."

"Yes, it can be, but it is very organised, unless there is the rain."

"What's the actual point of the festival though?"

"It's to remember our religion, our God, and the sacrifice that Jesus Christ made for us. That's why Thursday is such a big day, and night."

"How come?"

"Because that was when Jesus Christ died on the cross, in *la Madrugada*, early morning, which is why that night has some of the most spectacular processions."

"I see," said Charlie, still feeling daunted.

"That is why each person participating in the procession does it, as a penitence, to remember the people they love, to ask for forgiveness, or to become closer to God."

"Sounds deep," he said, remembering how serious Mercedes had become that day. It wasn't a joking matter.

"Yes, it is, but it is still enjoyable for people who do not really know what is going on."

"Like me."

"Yes, for the moment, but after today you will know more. Come, let's make our way to the Alameda, one of my favourite processions will pass there at six."

"But that's still four hours away."

"We have time to chat, and have a beer. Plus the crowds will be big, so let's go."

Meanwhile, an extremely nervous daughter was having a beer with her brother down a street running up from the cathedral.

"Here we are again, *hermanita*," said Raul, hugging his sister and pulling her close as a line of Nazarenos shot past.

"Yes, another year, another Semana Santa. It's hard to believe the year has passed by again and so much has happened." She felt teary, emotional, but mostly scared of seeing her father again. She knew she could trust Raul though, and that if he had said he was going to be fine, then he would, but it was that unknown feeling that filled her heart with anxiety.

"I know, some good, some bad, as usual, but it's time to start from scratch, be a family again, and get rid of this tension. Trust me, *mi hermanita*, just be honest with *Mama* and *Papa*, and they will give you their blessing."

"Well, if you're sure."

"I am. Come on, let's go, Father will be waiting."

As they left the bar, Mercedes thought about Charlie, what he would be up to, whether he'd even noticed what was going on. She hoped he'd get a chance to see something. She wished she could show him around to witness the special moments of Semana Santa, and take away that dreaded opinion he'd picked up. First, she had to hear her parents out though, maybe she would be wasting her time.

She felt weird, standing outside her own home, like a guest waiting to be met. As the door opened, her heart filled with joy as her mother stood smiling.

"Oh, *Hija*," said Rosa, opening her arms out to hug her, as if she'd just got back from a two-year world trip.

"*Hola Mama*, it's good to see you."

"You too, you too. Thanks for coming, you know how important this day is to us, and your father."

"Of course, where is he?"

"Where else?"

Mercedes could feel her legs shaking as she wandered over to the lounge, she could smell her father already, the usual lemon scent he loved to spray on his clothes. He sat in his chair, reading a guide of Semana Santa.

"Decided which processions you are going to see yet?" she asked. As he turned around, her heart dropped. He looked as though he'd aged almost ten years in the last two weeks. He looked pale, and his bottom lip was quivering.

"*Hija,*" he said, standing slowly.

"*Papa.*" As they embraced, Mercedes felt certain that Raul had been right, her father had not hugged her like that since she was a young adolescent girl.

"I'm so glad that you are home, *Hija.*"

The way he said home, made it sound as if she'd come home for good. Mercedes wanted to snap out and say it was only for today, but she found patience.

"Me too," she said. "I couldn't miss today with my family."

"That's great, just great," he said, holding her in front of him and gazing into her eyes. He looked weak, as if he'd just come home from the war and had seen a thousand men die. She hated seeing him like that, even if he had been a nasty father at times. Everyone made mistakes and had to be forgiven at some point.

"Come on *Papa*, don't get all emotional on me now. I'm here, let's enjoy the day."

"Sure, sure," he said, pulling her close to hug her again. As she stood in his arms, she promised herself that she'd try to make peace with her family. She loved Charlie but didn't want to put her father through any more agony.

"Shall we eat?" said Rosa. They both nodded and made their way into the lounge where the usual Domingo Ramos feast was laid out. The table was set out with the best silver plated cutlery, the finest crystal wine glasses, and the thick white cotton napkins. Jamón, prawns, and sliced pork was spread out, ready to be savoured.

Once Rosa had served out the red wine, Francisco clinked his knife on the side of his glass.

"Today is Domingo Ramos, an important day in our history. Let's first remember all those who aren't with us this year, *abuelo* Miguel and Marco. I'm glad to have us all together today, and may we have another special week today witnessing the magic of Semana Santa. God bless."

As they clinked glasses and looked each other in the eyes, the tension in Mercedes' stomach eased slightly.

"Let's eat," said Rosa, "I made the tortilla this morning."

"Looks great *Mama*," said Raul.

"I've missed this," said Mercedes.

"So, what have you been eating the last couple of weeks?" asked Rosa.

"Oh, you know, the usual."

"Which is what?" asked Francisco.

"Just food, you know."

"And how is Lola?" asked Rosa.

"Fine, fine, the business is going well, and we have a lot of students now. We are also dancing at a new *tablao*. I feel as if I've found my old self and I have more confidence."

"Oh, why's that?" asked her father, seeming genuinely interested. Mercedes wanted to say it was because of Charlie, because he'd helped her grow in strength and power, with him by her side she had the courage to face the crowd, and the sly comments and seedy looks no longer affected her. But she thought it was too soon to bring up her new boyfriend.

"I think I'm just a little older, less sensitive, and more agile on my feet."

"That's great, *Hija*," said Rosa.

"And how was it living away?" asked her father. She had to play it carefully now, she could feel him testing her already.

"Oh it was okay, you know how well I get on with Lola, but Miguel can be a bit lazy and dirty sometimes."

"Like most guys," said Raul.

"Yeah," she said, laughing.

"And did you miss home?" asked Rosa.

"Yeah, of course, I thought about you all every day."

"Sure," said her father, smiling now. She couldn't work him out, whether he was being false or not. She was waiting for the question about Charlie to come up.

"So what processions are we going to see today?" asked Raul.

"*La Hinesta* to start, of course," said Francisco. "Then I thought I'd let you guys decide this year."

"I'd like to see *La Estrella*, on the bridge maybe," said Mercedes.

"I thought you would, coming from the gypsy Triana," said Raul, getting in there before his father could say anything.

"Of course, and you, which do you want to see?"

"*El Amor*."

"Naturally, the serious ones as usual."

"They are the most respected ones."

"Both good choices," said Francisco. "I am a fan of them both, so that's what we'll do."

"Sounds great, let's eat up then because we need to get a move on to see *La Hinesta* before the crowds get there," said Rosa.

They sat and ate, chatting about previous Semana Santas, about how they used to spend most of the week in *Las Sillas;* the designated chairs set up for the spectators. That was when they were younger, and it was more difficult to see the processions out and about. They used to spend all week in the same seats, but they loved it because their friends were there.

As they got older though, they preferred to witness the real essence of Semana Santa 'in the street' watching the processions through the city, squeezing through the crowds, smelling the incense, getting caught up in a *bulla* - crowd and waiting at church entrances to see the exit or entries of the Christs and Virgins. That was where the real emotion was. That's where Mercedes had grown to become a fan of the week, following her father around and being by his side. She was glad she was back but was on edge in case they brought up Charlie.

It didn't take long.

Rosa brought out the *torrijas* - bread soaked in honey - and Raul and Francisco had a shot of anis, then began his questioning.

"So, Raul says that you continue to see this English man," said her father.

"His name is Charlie," said Mercedes, smiling politely, automatically feeling defensive.

"Oh Charlie, a true British name," said Francisco.

"Well, he is patriotic." Like others I know, she wanted to add.

"And all is well with him?" asked Rosa.

"Yes *Mama*, he's a kind man, a great guitar player, and he loves me."

"He loves you," said Francisco, smiling. "Well, you have been busy the last couple of weeks. Have you fallen in love?"

She could tell where this was going, and she didn't want to back down, but she didn't want it to kick off either. Raul had said to be honest, so that's what she was.

"It's been coming for a while, *Papa*, but yes, I am in love."

"I see, I see," he said, sipping on his anis. Mercedes looked up at Rosa, who smiled at her and at Raul, who winked. "Then, if that's who you have fallen in love with, I suppose we'll have to meet this Charlie."

"Really?" said Mercedes.

"I told you," said Raul. Mercedes looked at her father, who did actually seem to be pleased with the idea.

"*Gracias, Papa,*" she said, standing up and running over to hug her father.

"I said meet, but that doesn't actually mean I'll like him."

"Oh, but you will *Papa*, you will, he such a kind, loving guy."

"We'll see about that, enough already, let's get a move on, or we'll never get through the crowds."

Mercedes couldn't quite believe the turnaround. What had Raul said to get him on her side? She didn't care though, she just wanted to enjoy this Domingo Ramos.

Charlie was squashed up in his first *bulla*, surrounded by short, stocky men in suits, tubby women in elegant dresses, and a few prams and pushchairs with sleeping kids. He'd been out of his house for about four hours and had still not seen a procession. Pedro had taken him on a tour of the churches through Sevilla, plus several bars so he could soak up the atmosphere, and beer. He was getting a little tired though and was wondering what all the fuss was about.

"Don't worry, my friend, this is normal in Semana Santa," said Pedro as they stood in the tight crowd. "It will be worth the wait, you see, you see."

"I bloody hope so," he muttered.

"What, my friend?"

"I said I hope so."

"*Tranquilo*, relax, now come on, follow me."

"What, you mean we have to get through this crowd?" asked Charlie, standing on his tiptoes over the sea of people.

"Of course, we have to get to the other side; is the best place to see it."

"Christ," he said, but immediately held his hand to his mouth as several people turned and tutted.

After Charlie had squeezed through the crowd, luckily opening up for Pedro as he called out that he had to get through as his grandmother had fainted in a bar opposite, he stood in a reasonably spacious area in the main square and could hear the trumpets playing in the distance.

"Here it comes," said Pedro, pointing to a line of Nazarenos wearing light blue pointy hats coming down through an opening in the crowd. "Here we go my friend, here we go, look, you can see *el Cristo*."

Charlie gazed ahead and could see the figure of Christ hanging from the wooden cross, moving slowly from side to side. "Come, here, you need to watch from the start," said Pedro pulling him into a gap in the crowd.

Charlie felt guilty about pushing past several people to get a decent view, but he didn't want to lose Pedro.

"Look, up there," said Pedro, pushing his head into the opening. As he gazed up, he got a fright. He'd never seen anything like it. At the front of the procession was a man, dressed in a white robe with a light blue hood and cape, carrying a huge wooden cross. On each of his sides were men holding a strange box on a pole with a candle inside. Behind them was a line of about a hundred Nazarenos leading up to the Christ.

"What do you think?" whispered Pedro.

"Err, well, I don't know, I guess it's pretty, err, unique."

"Of course, it's unique. This is Sevilla, the best place in the world to witness Semana Santa. Watch. Watch."

Charlie was impressed with Pedro's enthusiasm, but he

just didn't get it. He had a thousand questions building up in his mind. Who were these people? Had they come from around the world to participate in this procession? How did they know where to walk? How heavy was that cross? And why, just why were they doing this?

He was baffled, miffed, and confused. The only time he'd seen people dressed like this was on television in American films, normally on horses galloping about burning down black people's houses. It was just madness.

Then he thought of Mercedes. She was a fan of this, as were her family. Was she involved in some weird sect? If he wanted to continue with her, would he have to get dressed up like this every year? He began to panic.

"Charlikins, what sort of mess have you got into?" he heard his mother saying this time. Even as a Catholic woman, she would think the whole ordeal was just, well, weird.

The man with the large cross was now in front of Charlie. He noticed the harness around his waist, carrying the load. Had he been extra nasty over the previous year and this was his punishment?

"That is *la cruz de guia*," whispered Pedro. "It signifies the start of the brotherhood."

"But how does he carry it?"

"He is strong, it is an honour to carry the cross. Not just anyone can, you have to be in the brotherhood for many years."

"I see," said Charlie, slightly impressed. He supposed it did have some sort of value, to be able to carry it. It must have weighed over twenty kilos. "And how long does he hold it for?"

"This one, about eleven hours."

"Eleven," said Charlie, raising his voice in surprise. A

few people shushed him. "Eleven hours, what with no break? What if he needs a…"

"Some men go, some hold it in. It depends on how much of a man you are."

Charlie wanted to say Christ again, but he refrained. He stood in the crowd, occasionally getting knocked or pushed out the way so people could get past. He didn't get how, for such a religious and respectful event, so many people were pushing and shoving each other out the way.

The sound of the band was getting closer, he could hear the trumpets leading the way.

"Is coming, is coming," said Pedro, nudging him in the ribs. Charlie looked up and saw the Christ on the wooden cross moving from side to side in rhythm to the music. He had to admit that even if it was a bit weird, a bit KKK, a bit well, old-fashioned, the way the Christ moved about was impressive.

Like most people, he watched, eyes glued to the image of Christ as it made its way towards him. As it got closer the power of the sound of the trumpets and drums filled Charlie with goose bumps. Then it paused and lowered slowly right in front of him. The band stopped.

"This is lucky, you are lucky my friend. For your first time, it has stopped here, in front of you, welcoming you to Semana Santa."

Charlie was right in front of the gold plated wooden box carrying the Christ. He looked down and could see the legs of the men carrying it. There must have been twenty or twenty-five guys underneath.

"Why have they stopped?" he asked Pedro.

"Why?" he whispered back. "Are you crazy? They carry almost forty kilos on their back, they need to rest, for a break, for water, some of them piss on the floor too."

"Bet it smells nice under there."

"Is not so bad."

"You mean you know?"

"I have been a *costallero* before, when I was younger, but is terrible for your neck, a lot of pain for many weeks. These are the strongest men in Sevilla. They train all the year. You can see the *costalleros* when the festival finish, they all have ball on the back of their neck, is very painful."

After a brief pause, a man dressed in a suit shouted to the men underneath.

"*Animo, valiente* – let's go, brave ones." And he smashed down a golden knocker three times. As he did the men shouted together and heaved the wooden box with the Christ, up in the air, making a thud sound as it got into position. The drums and trumpets started again, and off it went.

As it got further away, Charlie concentrated on the members of the band and could appreciate how proud they probably were, playing for an audience for such a length of time. It was impressive, and he was beginning to see what the fuss was about.

"What happens now?" he asked Pedro once the Christ was out of sight.

"Now the Virgen, you will see."

"How long?"

"A few minutes, maybe twenty, thirty, it depends. Is a shame we not on other side, we could get a beer."

Charlie gazed over to the other side of the path and noticed a familiar face in the crowd, one that was crying. His heart took a dent. Why was she so tearful? Next to her was her father and mother, and brother, they all seemed to be in tears. What had happened? He wanted to go over and ask, console her, but he knew she wanted some space.

He suddenly felt scared, and sad, what sort of power did this have over them to be able to cry like that, the whole family. He'd only seen his Dad cry once, when England lost on penalties against Germany in 1990.

He went to ask Pedro, but thought better of it, in case he wanted to go over there.

"We move up, closer to the virgin?" asked Pedro.

Charlie gazed over at Mercedes. She looked so pretty, with her hair done up and extra makeup on. Her smart jacket and white blouse were much classier than some of the women he'd seen. But he knew it was a time for her to be with her family. Plus he was a bit miffed still and wanted to see more before he could have a conversation about it.

"Sure, let's go."

It was hard walking away from her, but it was something he had to do. It wasn't the time or place to interrupt her.

By the end of the evening, Charlie had seen three different processions and was a little less daunted. He loved the music and atmosphere, especially as night fell and the Nazarenos lit their candles. They watched *La Estrella* – the Star, over the bridge in Triana, which was especially spectacular with the moon in the background. Then Pedro made him stay up until two in the morning to watch it go inside the church.

"The *entradas* are the best," Pedro said as the Spanish anthem stopped once the Virgin was safe in her church. "You see the real beauty as she comes back after her route. The emotion is incredible," he said, also with a tear in his eye.

Charlie had wondered how long it took before you felt

such emotion for this. He guessed most people had seen it from when they were kids, with their parents, and had a lot of memories.

Pedro had been a great guide, answering all his silly questions.

"Thanks so much for today. It was a privilege."

"It was nothing. An honour to show you the ways of our city. I hope you enjoy more, but more importantly, you can speak with Mercedes about what you know now," he said, shaking his hand and winking.

"Let's hope so. What are your plans?"

"Tomorrow I am with my family, but maybe later in week we can meet."

"Sounds great, I'll give you a bell."

"Sure, *adios, amigo*."

As Charlie made his way back to his flat, he thought about Mercedes. Why had she cried? He was eager to know. He was still freaked out by the religious aspect, but had some respect for the seriousness of the festival and was now eager to share what he knew with Mercedes.

Chapter 12 PRIDE

The next day
Mercedes was early for once. She was standing anxiously gazing up Triana Bridge, hoping to see him soon. People were already sitting down on the curbs with their little folding chairs to witness the next procession, San Gonzalo. She hoped their musical band would impress Charlie and show him just how wonderful Semana Santa could be. She was still wary about his attitude and hoped that he'd seen something the day before so the impact of the evening wouldn't be so daunting.

She couldn't wait to tell him that he would be meeting her family and was so glad that the tension had gone at home.

Domingo Ramos had been one of their best ever. They had seen all the processions they'd wanted to, which was as emotional as always because memories of loved ones who weren't around came flooding back.

She was so relieved that her father had changed his tune, and glad she'd stood her ground. He'd been wrong after all, with his pompous traditional ways. But she supposed he had just been looking out for his daughter, in his own weird way.

She was also grateful to her brother for persuading him. She still had no idea what he'd actually said, but maybe it was best not to know. All she needed to do now was clue Charlie up by showing him a few processions before meeting everyone.

Just then he appeared through the crowd halfway along the bridge. She waved. He stuck his hand up and waved back, smiling in his cheery way as usual.

"*Hola guapo,*" she said, planting a big kiss on his lips.

They were so full of energy. *"Todo bien?"* she said, looking into his eyes.

"Si, si, I'm great," he said. "A bit tired. I was up till three in the morning watching processions last night."

"Really?" asked Mercedes, feeling honoured that he'd made the effort.

"Yeah. I was with Pedro, he showed me around."

"And did you like it?"

"I did actually, yeah, more than I thought." Mercedes felt a warm happiness inside. "I liked the music, and it's impressive how the men carry around the Christs and Virgins..." his tone wavered off.

"But..."

"I guess I still don't really understand it all, it just seems a bit..."

"Yes?"

"Scary."

Mercedes giggled at his innocence.

"I suppose it is a little, but don't worry, you have time to understand more."

"Sure," he said. "You look different by the way, happier. Are you in a good mood?"

"Of course, I am with you."

"I see." He grinned. "I did miss you yesterday actually."

"You did?"

"Of course," he said, pulling her closer for a kiss. She half wanted to go straight back to his flat and rip his clothes off, make up for the last week, but she had to keep focused on her mission.

"So, maybe you would like to come and meet my family tomorrow, at their house."

"Your family? What even your father?"

"Of course, he wants to meet you now?"

"Now?"

"Yes, he is just a little protective, that is all."

"Sure, yeah that would be great." Charlie smiled, but she could sense he was nervous, and deep down so was she.

"Okay, let's go?" she said, pulling away and leading him over towards Calle Adriano where crowds of people were heading.

"Where're we going anyway?"

"To see some processions."

"Some?"

"Yes, of course, you said you wanted to appreciate my festival."

"I do, I do."

"Well, come on then."

She led him down Calle Adriano, through the crowds, and into a spot right next to a church on the right-hand side. It was a relief to have him by her side; she'd missed him the day before.

"This is a perfect place to see San Gonzalo," she said, squeezing his hand.

"It's certainly a busy spot," said Charlie. He was gazing around at the people and then stood on his tiptoes. "There's the *Cruz de Guia*."

"Wow, Pedro is a good teacher. What more did you learn?"

"Oh, just about the men under the *pasos*, the *costaleros*, and how much they have to carry. About why the locals dress up to hide their faces from the public and what they think about on their penitence. That sort of thing."

"Impressive," said Mercedes. She couldn't believe how much he'd picked up already. "So, not so crazy?"

"I wouldn't say crazy, no, but it's scary, the whole

thought of God, and this control, and the devotion of the fanatics; it's overpowering."

Mercedes just smiled. She wasn't completely sure what he meant but tried to remember what Lola had said about how complicated Semana Santa could be. She had to give him time.

They stood in silence for a while, just watching the Nazarenos go past until the Christ appeared at the end of the road.

"*Alli esta,*" said Mercedes, pointing up ahead. Charlie grinned, looking excited, she was surprised he seemed so energetic about it all, especially for a *guiri*. As she watched the procession come down she thought about her father, how he'd changed in the last month, perhaps there was hope for her and Charlie yet.

As the Christ arrived, she crossed herself and thanked God for her health, peace in her family, and having a loving man by her side. While the *paso* moved around slowly, saluting the *Virgen* inside the church, the whole crowd gazed up in awe; inspired by the band's trumpets. Then it made its way up the road, and the crowd applauded.

"What did you think?" she asked, looking up at Charlie with a tear in her eye.

"*Impressonante,*" he said, smiling back.

"You like?"

"Yeah, yeah, it was pretty good, especially the music. But why did they do that little dance in front of the church?"

Mercedes laughed, she'd never thought of it as a little dance before.

"Is a sign of respect, when a procession passes another church it stops. Is like a greeting."

"Fair enough."

"You want to see more?"

"Sure, why not?"

"That's great," she said, pulling him closer for a kiss. She felt so proud of the way he was interested in her culture.

They walked towards the river, pushing through the crowds, and Mercedes led Charlie down a side street, so it was quieter and less manic.

"Now we are going to see my *Virgen*."

"Yours, why is it yours?"

"It's a way to speak. I mean, is the one I have more connection with, most people in Sevilla have their own *Virgen*."

"But how do you chose it?"

"When you are a child, you feel a connection, and from then on, it's yours."

"So which one is yours then?"

"*El Museo, esta preciosa*."

"I'm sure."

"The only problem is late."

"How late?"

"To see *la entrada*, when it goes in the church, is about two."

"Two? In the morning? Not again."

"I know, but is, how do you say *'vale la pena'*?"

"It's worth it."

"Yes, why don't we go for some tapas now?"

"Good idea."

After a stressful tapas meal in a busy bar in the back streets, they made their way towards Plaza Museo to get a spot for the next procession. As usual, Mercedes found a place right by the huge tree opposite the church entrance and huddled up to Charlie as the night air became chilly.

"So, I saw you yesterday," said Charlie.

"*Si?* Why you didn't say hello?"

"It seemed like a bad moment."

"But when, where?"

"I was watching *la Hiniesta*, with Pedro, and once the Christ had gone past I saw you with your family."

"I see," said Mercedes, thinking back to the emotion occasion.

"Why were you all crying?"

Mercedes was a bit taken aback by the question.

"Is hard to explain. It was a procession of my grandmother, on my father's side. It was her favourite procession because they used to live in the area where the church is. So it has a lot of memories for us, especially my father."

"I see," said Charlie, seeming genuinely interested.

"Yes, that is one problem with Semana Santa. Is a time to remember people you lose too, which is why many people cry when they see some processions."

Charlie nodded and kept quiet. Mercedes was worried he would be even more frightened now, but she hoped he'd understand.

They waited in silence until the *Cruz de Guia* arrived and watched patiently as the *Nazarenos* led the way for the Christ. As each line passed, she became more and excited to see her *Virgen*. She had a lot to thank her for, and a lot to ask for too.

As the *Virgen* came into focus, as usual behind the musical band, Mercedes felt that arrow of energy she always did and her heart filled with joy, emotion and also sadness.

Her grandfather appeared in her mind, as it was normally him stood by her side, and she prayed for him.

She thanked her *Virgen* for the situation she was in, for her father's change in attitude, and bringing Charlie to her. She glanced at him and smiled. He smiled back, and she was sure he was the man for her.

As the *Virgen* came closer, she prayed that all would continue in peace and harmony, and asked for a sign that Charlie was the one for her. When it entered the church, and the doors closed, she turned to Charlie and could feel the tears rolling down her cheeks. He wiped them away.

"*Esta preciosa*," she said, delving into his arms. As he hugged her, she remembered the way her grandfather used to hold her and made her feel safe. She missed him, but she knew he was at peace, watching her. He would have given his blessing over Charlie.

"Are you all right?" asked Charlie.

"*Si, si, perfecto*," she said, hugging him harder. He held her close, protecting her, which was all she wanted.

Once the crowd had gone, he walked her back to Lola's flat.

"You sure you don't want to stay tonight?" he asked.

"No, is fine. Tomorrow maybe. I need some time to think after an emotional evening."

"Okay, no problem, so what time shall we meet tomorrow?"

"About half one."

"Great, see you then."

"Make yourself *guapo*."

"Of course."

As Mercedes went to sleep on her own that night, she thanked God for such a beautiful day with her Charlie and was pleased that he was making an effort to understand her ways. She felt so lucky to find a guy so interested in getting to know the real her. She also prayed that the next day would be a success with him meeting her father, and she was quietly confident that it would.

As Charlie made his way over the bridge to meet Mercedes in Puerta Jerez the next day, he thought back to the previous night. Seeing Mercedes cry like that had shown him how important the festival was to her. He wanted to appreciate it more, but it was so hard to understand the power involved. He'd have to try though, after all, it was only a week, and hopefully, after they'd just get on with their normal flamenco lives again.

He was massively concerned about how to play it with the family. Not only had he dropped a bottle of wine over her mother, but had also been threatened by her nutcase father to leave Sevilla. Maybe he should have brought it up before with Mercedes.

"Oh yeah, by the way, I never did tell you that your psycho father dropped in on me one night and almost tore my balls off," he imagined saying. He figured that surely her father knew exactly who he was anyway.

Also, his Spanish was still nearer the pre-intermediate level rather than the advanced one. Did any of them know any English? What if they started asking him about God as well? He had to find out from Mercedes.

As Charlie reached Puerta Jerez, he smiled as he saw her. She was surprisingly early again, already waiting, looking fine in an elegant, slender navy blue dress.

"Hey sexy," he said, kissing her on the lips.

"*Hola guapo*. Ready to meet my family?"

"Yes, and no."

"Oh, why no?"

"I'm just not sure what to say about this festival. What if they ask me about religion, and God?"

Mercedes laughed.

"Why would they do that?"

"I don't know because I'm English?"

"Don't be silly, and just be honest. My father will know if you are lying, and he hates lying. It's the worst thing for him."

"Sure, sure," he said, but that wasn't enough.

He obviously wasn't going to tell the whole truth and nothing but the truth, but what if he started asking about whether or not he'd slept with his daughter. Was that the normal thing to talk about with possible parents-in-laws in Spain? His Dad would just be cracking jokes the whole time and winding up the future son-in-law, trying to embarrass him, but from what he'd seen from her father, he guessed jokes would not be on the agenda.

"Just be you," said Mercedes. "My father is a serious, strict man. He is formal, traditional, and loves Semana Santa. Tell him is your first time and you are learning about everything. He will be impressed that you are trying."

"Fair enough. What about speaking?"

"You need to speak, yes. Is a good idea."

"No, I mean, English or Spanish?"

"I guess just see, my father can speak English a little. Don't worry, you will be fine." Mercedes gave him a reassuring hug.

"Let's hope so."

As they walked through the *Jardines de Murillo*, Charlie kept glancing at Mercedes. She seemed happier than ever, walking with him by her side. He could sense the tension that she'd spoken about at home had probably drifted away. Maybe it wouldn't be so bad after all.

"So I'm finally going to find out where you live."

"I lived. I am still with Lola, you know."

"Yeah, but aren't you moving back?"

"I don't know yet. I like living away now, but who knows." She pulled him closer and rubbed her nose on his. He took that to mean she wanted to live with him, which wouldn't be such a bad idea, he guessed.

"There, up there," she said, pointing to a flat overlooking the gardens.

"Your parents live up there?"

"Yes, is beautiful, no?"

"Sure is." Charlie was expecting a smaller, normal flat; not one of such a high standard and right in the heart of *Barrio Santa Cruz*. He was impressed with how close it was to one of his favourite parks. The views must be amazing, he thought to himself as the nerves began to electrify through his heart. His hands became hot and sweaty. His pulse raced.

As they stood outside, Mercedes squeezed his hand as she rang the bell. The door opened.

"*Hola Hija,*" said Rosa, leaning out to kiss her daughter on the cheek.

"*Mama, este es Charlie.*"

"*Hola,*" said Charlie, holding out a hand.

"*Hola,*" said Rosa, pulling him in for two kisses on his cheek. "*Encantada.*"

"*Encantado,*" said Charlie, feeling a bit awkward.

"So, how is your Spanish?" she asked. Charlie was relieved she spoke in English.

"*Esta mejorando* – it's improving," he said.

"*Bien, bien,*" said Rosa, smiling.

"Come on Charlie, come and meet my father." As Charlie walked down the corridor, he noticed the photos of Semana Santa processions on the wall. There were several pictures of Jesus on the cross too. It seemed like some sort of shrine. What was he getting himself into?

He followed Mercedes into the spacious lounge, where her father was standing up, facing the door. His serious, stern expression startled him at first, but then he relaxed as he smiled.

"*Hola Hija,*" he said, kissing and hugging Mercedes. Charlie waited patiently, not knowing where to look.

"*Papa, este es Charlie,*" she said, gazing at him in the eyes.

"*Hola Señor, mucho gusto.*"

"*Hola Charlie,* welcome to our home," he said, holding out a hand. Charlie felt instant relief again hearing English.

"*Gracias, es muy bonita, tu casa.*"

"Thank you, thank you."

"Charlie, would you like a drink?" asked Rosa, holding up a small bottle of beer.

"*Por favor.*"

"I get a glass," she said, walking off.

"Please, sit down," said Francisco, nodding towards a sofa. Mercedes and Charlie sat down.

"So, Mercedes told to me you like the flamenco guitar," said Francisco.

"Just a little yeah. She's a wonderful dancer."

"Wonderful?"

"*Maravillosa,*" said Mercedes.

"*Si, si.* She loves flamenco," said Francisco, smiling slightly. "And you like Sevilla?"

"*Si, es muy bonito.*"

"Good, good…"

"*Hola Papa,*" said Raul, coming in and kissing his father on the cheek.

"Hi Charlie," he said, shaking Charlie's hand. "Good to see you again."

"You too."

"No wine today then?"

Charlie laughed at his attempt at breaking the ice.

"No, I think I'll leave that to my colleagues at the bar." Raul laughed back. Charlie looked up at Francisco, but he was just smiling politely.

Just then, Rosa came in with a tray of jamón, small bread-sticks, and beers poured out in glasses. They all picked up a glass and clinked while saying *salut*. Charlie began to relax, maybe it wouldn't be so daunting.

Mercedes, Raul and their father began to chat about Semana Santa in Spanish. Charlie made out that they were talking about the processions on that day and which ones they wanted to see. He could sense that the conversation was going to turn to him as they spoke about the flamenco guitar, but luckily Rosa came in, and they went to sit at the dining table in another room.

Once they were all seated his father stood up.

"I'd like to welcome Charlie to our house. We hope you have good Semana Santa. *Salut*."

They all clinked glasses again and sat down. Then Francisco placed his hands together and began to say a prayer in Spanish. Charlie looked at Mercedes. She eyed towards her hands as she prayed, indicating him to follow. He thought back to his days as a boy scout and placed his hands together, but it felt weird, so much time had passed.

He was oblivious to what Francisco was actually saying, but it was something along the lines of being grateful for the food and being all together on a special occasion and welcoming him again. He smiled throughout but felt daunted, especially when they all crossed themselves. He didn't even attempt it, in case he messed it up.

"Please, eat," said Rosa, handing him a tray of cold

meats. He picked a few slices of salami and took some small pieces of bread.

Then the real test came.

"So," said Francisco. "Mercedes tells me is your first Semana Santa."

"*Si, si.*"

"And what you think?"

All their eyes stared, the pressure was on. He thought back to what Mercedes said about telling the truth, but was he really going to say he found it weird, a bit scary?

"*Es muy interesante,*" was all he could muster up.

"*Interesante*, oh, why?" asked Francisco, smiling. He obviously wanted more.

"Well, the music is impressive."

"*Impresonante,*" said Mercedes, translating. They all nodded and smiled.

"And I like the devotion."

"*Devocíon, si, si,*" said Francisco.

"And, well, it's all quite overwhelming really." He looked at Mercedes to translate, but even she didn't know what it meant.

"What's mean?" she said.

"Well, you know, all those people, the images of Christ and the Virgins. It's all so powerful, and it makes you think."

"Think?" said Francisco.

"Yes, think about religion, and about if God exists, or not..." The smile and look of interest on Francisco's face quickly turned to a frown, but it was too late to trace his steps.

"I see, I see," said Francisco, sipping on his beer. Charlie knew that he'd said the wrong thing. Francisco remained tight lipped. "But you must be sure, no? Especially as you are *católico*?"

"Catholic," said Charlie, laughing nervously. "Me? Why…"

"Of course," said Francisco. "Is not the true?"

"Well, not technically," he said, looking at Mercedes for help as he shrugged, but it was too late. Francisco glared at Raul.

"*Lo sabia*," muttered Francisco, saying he knew it. Then he threw an evil at Mercedes and shook his head.

"I mean my Mum is Catholic, but my father isn't, and well, they never got me baptised."

Mercedes squeezed his hand under the table, telling him to shut up.

"*Pasa algo, Papa?*" she said, asking if something was up.

"*No, no, todo bien, muy bien,*" said Francisco, saying everything was fine.

"More beer?" asked Rosa, stepping in to break the tension by pouring out more beer into their glasses.

"*Gracias,*" said Charlie, feeling extremely awkward. If they weren't sitting having a meal, he would have tried to escape through the window.

"So, you are not, in fact, *católico*?" said Francisco, sitting up straight and opening his shoulders.

"No, no, I'm not. I'm just your average English guy looking to play the flamenco guitar," he smiled as he looked at Mercedes, trying to show him the real reason he'd come to Sevilla and fallen in love with his daughter.

"But you are a *guiri*, how can you know the guitar?"

"*Papa!*" snapped Mercedes.

"It's fine, it's fine," said Charlie. "Maybe you will come and see us one day, then you'll see for yourself."

"What's mean?" he asked. Raul translated.

"Come and watch flamenco? Never. Not while I'm

alive."

"I can help you with that," muttered Mercedes.

"*Basta*," said Rosa. "We have a guest. Now please, eat the food. It is Semana Santa."

The conversation turned to Spanish, so Charlie just nodded and smiled now and then, not wanting to come across as a useless language learner. He got a bit lost at times, but most of the conversation was about processions for the day. What bugged him though, was that no matter how hard he tried to seem interested, Francisco never looked him in the eye again. It was an uncomfortable situation, and he felt unwelcome. How was it ever going to work with such a traditional father?

"So, Charlie, do you want to see some processions?" asked Raul.

"Sure, sure, that would be great."

"Okay, *Papa, vienes*?"

"*No, yo no, voy a quedarme aqui un rato, luego os veo.*" He wasn't going to come, and he'd see them later.

"*Vale,*" said Mercedes, standing up. "I'm just going to the toilet," she said to Charlie, who panicked as he was left with the three. But they all got up straight away and began to clear the table. He helped, taking plates out, but no one said a word.

"Ready?" said Mercedes, kissing Charlie on the cheek.

"Sure."

They walked out into the hall and began to put on their shoes.

"Mercedes," called out her father.

"Just a second," she said, kissing Charlie on the head.

Once Mercedes was inside the lounge, the shouting started. Charlie could pretty much make out what they were saying.

"I never want to see you in this house with that heathen again."

"Fine, I won't bring him. I mean, if you'll never come and watch me dance again, then what's the point of having me as a daughter."

"Good question. If only you had listened to me all those years ago, you would never have got into this mess."

"What mess? Charlie is a great flamenco guitar player, and has even shown an interest in our festival, why judge him because he's not Catholic?"

"Because it's just not right. I won't change my mind."

"Neither, will I."

"Then just go."

"I will, *adios*," said Mercedes as she came storming out, grabbed Charlie by the hand, and left. Charlie followed behind Mercedes as she paced in front.

"*Imbecil, idiota*," she said, waving her hand back towards the flat.

Charlie felt sorry for her as he could see tears forming in her eyes. What sort of father treated his daughter like that? He just didn't get it.

"Mercedes, wait, come on; let's talk."

"Talk? But that is all I do at the moment. I'm tired of talking. I just want to live my life, and love you. Is it that hard?"

Charlie couldn't help but smile, in such a dramatic moment, all he could think of was that she'd said she loved him. "What is funny?" she said, frowning.

"You love me?"

She gazed at him, as if unsure whether she'd said that or not.

"Yes, of course. I only take men to my house if I love them," she said, which was followed by a tut, as if it was

Falling for Flamenco

the most obvious statement in the world.

"Right, well, that's cute."

"Cute? Only cute?"

He kissed her, but mainly to stop her from talking so she could listen.

"I do too," he muttered once they'd finished.

"You do what?"

"Love you."

"*Ah, si?*" she said, smiling as she pulled him in again for another kiss.

"So, where do we go now?" asked Charlie, stopping for breath.

"For a walk."

They walked in silence through the park as people buzzed about dashing to see the next procession. He felt warm inside, knowing that they'd told each other they were in love, but also a bit frightened. There was no going back now, and with the state of affairs with her father, he was unsure it was going to be the easiest romance.

As they walked up along the river, catching each other's eye now and then and smiling, Charlie wondered why there was such a feud between her and her father. It was strange to think that a family didn't get on; he'd just presumed every family did.

As they did a full circle round the river and got nearer the centre again, Charlie could sense Mercedes was a bit calmer: she was squeezing his hand less and was sort of smiling. He wanted to ask her a bunch of questions about her family: why her brother had to lie, why her father was so against non-Catholics, but he didn't want to stir the pot again. Instead, he asked the question that she'd been waiting to hear.

"Fancy a dance?" he said.

"Yes, of course."

That evening they spent it at Charlie's flat, him on the guitar, her dancing, and they shared a bottle of Rioja.

For a night they became one, performing together, forgetting about the world, enjoying their passion, their soul, their bodies, and being in love. When they lay tucked up in bed that night, Charlie knew that he was going to love Mercedes forever, and he'd have to continue fighting for her.

Mercedes woke earlier than Charlie the next morning. She sat in bed, thinking about the fun night they'd had; probably one of the best moments since they'd been together. She had completely fallen for him: the way he was with her, so gentle, so loving, she wanted him so much. But that niggling pain kept digging in her heart, the row and tension with her father were affecting her far too much.

How could he have been so rude to Charlie, treating him like that in his home, asking him straight up like that about religion? He had such a nasty streak at times. She wasn't going to let him destroy the only love she'd ever found. She got up, leaving Charlie snug, and went over to check her phone. Seven missed calls from Raul. She nipped out on the balcony and called him.

"About time, I was worried sick."

"Maybe you should have thought about that before you lied to *Papa*, do you realise what you've done?"

"I know. I'm sorry. I never thought he was actually going to ask him like that. Are you okay?"

"No, I'm not. I've had it with *Papa*. He told me to stay away."

"So you're not coming today?" Mercedes could hear the

disappointment in his tone. It was *Miercoles Santo*, the day both her brother and father did their penitence. She wasn't going to back down.

"No, I'm not."

"Not even to see the procession?"

"No."

"But you've never missed it. You know how important this is to us."

"And you know how important Charlie is to me. I need a break, from Semana Santa, from you all."

"A break?"

"Yes, I'm tired of this. I just want to be alone with Charlie."

"Can't you let me explain?"

"What?"

"Why I lied? You should have seen him, he was in such a vulnerable state. He was a broken man."

"That's not the point, where do we go from here?"

"Leave it to me. See how he is after today. It's his penitence, maybe he will come round."

"But don't you get it? Don't you see? I couldn't give a damn anymore. I couldn't care less."

"Fine. You're obviously not worth speaking to at the moment. Let's talk tomorrow."

"Don't bother, just leave me alone."

And she hung up. Never before had she had a row with him like that. She felt terrible, but it was all his fault.

"Hey sexy," said Charlie sneaking up on her.

"*Joder, que susto.* You scared me," she said, turning round.

"Am I that scary?" he said, ruffling his hair up even more than it was. He looked so sexy in the morning, with his hair everywhere, especially with stubble too. "So, did you enjoy last night?"

"Of course, and you?" she asked, kissing him strongly on the lips.

"It was wonderful. I heard you speaking loudly, is everything okay?"

"Not really. I had a discussion with Raul."

"About what?"

"It's his and my father's penitence today, and I said I'm not going."

"They do that too?"

"Of course, every year. Is their passion. He wanted me to come and watch, but I said no."

"I see."

She could tell by his look of surprise that maybe she was overreacting a bit.

"What?"

"Nothing, nothing, it's just, I guess it's important for them if you are there."

"Of course it is, but I'm not going; not after yesterday. I need a break from Semana Santa. Why can we not stay here all day, and repeat last night?"

"I'm not sure I have the energy, but I could try."

They spent the day in his flat, together, wandering from the balcony, to the kitchen, to the bed, to the balcony, to the kitchen, to the bed. As evening approached, Mercedes began to feel guilty.

"What's up?" asked Charlie as they were out on the balcony sharing a beer together. Charlie was plucking on his guitar.

"Nothing."

"We can still go if you want. I'll come too."

"I don't know, I'm so angry at my father."

"I'm sure, but maybe if they see me, they will appreciate

how serious I am about you."

"Oh, and how serious are you about me?"

"You'll have to wait and see. Come on, let's go before it's too late."

She knew she had to go; she didn't want her father to have even more ammunition against her. Plus she felt guilty about the way she'd spoken to Raul.

It took them an hour to get over the other side of Sevilla through the back streets until they arrived at San Pedro square, just as the *Cruz de Guia* was arriving. The street lights went out, leaving only the *Nazarenos'* candles to light the way, ready for the procession to get back to its church.

"Where will they be?" asked Charlie.

"Just before the Christ. I will tell you."

"How will you know? It's so dark."

"I just will. Is my family."

Mercedes watched in awe as usual as the Christ of *el Cristo de Burgos* came down the square. She prayed that her brother had had a decent penitence, but not for her father. She hoped he was suffering, hurting like she was inside.

"There's my brother," she whispered to Charlie as Raul went past. She crossed herself. She couldn't see her father, and wondered if maybe he hadn't done it after all; he must have been feeling guilty.

As they watched the procession enter the church, Mercedes couldn't help but let out a tear, why was everything so complicated?

"There, finished. Let's go now," she said, trying to be tough, but as they walked up the main road back to Triana, she began to feel the emotion inside get the better of her. As they got to the bridge, she burst into tears; in pain for the heartbreak that was disrupting her family and her soul.

"Hey, hey. It's all right to cry," said Charlie, hugging her close. "What's up?"

"It's just I feel sad for my brother. I know he was only trying to help. He's important to me. I hate fighting with him."

Charlie pulled her close, and she let out the tears inside, bawling while looking out over the Sevilla night sky.

"Don't worry," said Charlie. "Sure you'll be friends again tomorrow."

"I hope so. *Gracias*."

"For what?"

"For coming tonight, for trying to understand my festival, my family. Is complicated, I know, so thank you."

"My pleasure. I'm actually starting to enjoy it. I liked that last one, in the square in the dark, so spooky."

"Then tomorrow you have to see *el Silencio*, is the best of *la Madrugada*."

"So you want to see more again tomorrow?"

"Of course, tomorrow is the best day. If you see Semana Santa, then *la Madrugada* is when you really appreciate the special of our festival."

As they walked back to Charlie's flat, she prayed that all would be resolved, and quickly.

Charlie's head was ready to pop like a bottle of bubbly. He hadn't slept all night. What the hell was going on? Why all this drama all of a sudden? One of the reasons he'd come to Sevilla was to get some peace and live the chilled Spanish way of life, but he'd fallen right into the trap of getting hooked on a Catholic, Spanish lady with a crazy Dad.

He'd tried to get away from the stress at Computer Jobbers and Peter Prick Percy, but Peter had returned in the form of an aggressive over controlling, racist father. How was he going to deal with this? Easy.

He'd finish it.

Right after Semana Santa, when things had blown over, he'd thank Mercedes for her useful insight into the world of flamenco, and do a runner. He had no other choice. In the long run, he'd be doomed. Even if he did manage to learn Spanish to a decent level, and make a living playing the flamenco guitar, he'd still have that lingering shadow of doubt over his head that one day Francisco would turn up at his flat and throw him off his balcony into the River Guadalquivir.

It would be easy.

To turn off his feelings and just go.

Out of sight, out of mind.

But then he remembered why he'd fallen in love as Mercedes came out of the bathroom, hair dripping wet over her slender shoulders, a towel wrapped around her body. She smiled with that longing smile of affection, attraction, and love.

He couldn't do it, not after all they'd been through.

"What are you thinking about?" she asked.

"Just how beautiful you are when you come out the shower."

"Really?" she said, moving close, kissing him softly on the lips.

"Well, you are always beautiful, but today especially more."

She kissed him strongly on the lips.

They lay on the bed for a while, just chilling, listening to each other's breathing and hearts beating. Maybe things would calm down after the festival, thought Charlie. The funny thing was that he was actually beginning to like

Semana Santa: the atmosphere, the music, and especially the learning curve, he felt cultured all of a sudden. He was curious to witness *la Madrugada* too.

"So, are you ready for tonight?" asked Mercedes.

"Sure, sure. Do you still want to go then?"

"Yes, I cannot miss *la Madrugada*. I have never missed it."

"Why's it so special, anyway?"

"Because of the processions, of the symbol of Christ, because it was tonight when Jesus Christ died for us on the cross. Some of the processions are spectacular, *la Macarena, Los Gitanos, el Gran Poder, and el Silencio.*"

"*El Silencio* sounds interesting." Nodding his head.

"It is. If you want, we can go see when it comes out the church, is amazing. The music, the dark, the pasos. We have to get there by twelve."

"In the afternoon?"

"No, in the morning, the procession starts at five past one."

"I guess this is the last night then?"

"Why? You are tired?"

"Depends, for what?" he said, stroking her neck.

"Not today," she said, smiling, but pulling away. "Is respectful day. Come on, let's go out for the day."

"Yes sir," he said, standing up and saluting. She laughed as he walked into the bathroom, muttering that he was 'a silly English.'

They spent the day wandering round together, seeing different processions and keeping clear of anywhere Mercedes thought her family might be. She didn't speak about how she felt about her brother or father, so Charlie just left it, but he could tell she was still upset about everything.

In the evening they went back to his flat to chill out, then left about half past eleven to see *el Silencio*. The streets were packed again. Eager fanatics were walking at a faster pace than before. Everyone knew they had to get a decent spot before the main processions started.

Once over the busy bridge, they headed straight for the centre. Charlie could sense the atmosphere was a lot livelier. It seemed more like a carnival. There were more people gathered in the street. Groups of teenagers were hanging out together, and some were even walking along with beers or plastic bags full of bottles of spirits.

"Let's go, it's up here," said Mercedes, taking a short cut through a back street until they came to the square called 'El Silencio.'

"There's a load of people already," said Charlie. He followed behind Mercedes as she pushed her way through the crowd. "Where are you going?"

"Don't worry, follow me. We must see the door, is where…"

But she just stopped talking, as if remembering she didn't want to talk about something. Charlie immediately thought of her father. He wondered if he was there. More than likely if Mercedes just stopped speaking like that.

He thought about his parents, and what they would say about Mercedes. Obviously, his Dad would give him a pat on the back for finding such a stunner, and his Mum would be happy too, as long as he was. He wondered whether they would come over to visit him and meet her. What the hell would he say when they asked about meeting Mercedes' parents?

Mercedes had led Charlie through the crowd, and they were under one of the orange trees. The smell of azahar was stronger than ever.

"We stay here, look, you can see when the door opens," she said, pointing up to the dark solid door.

Charlie stood on his tiptoes and looked over the crowd. There were police in the middle of the street, making people move over, so there was space for the procession. The atmosphere was electric, he could sense something memorable was about to happen.

"How you feel?" she asked him.

"Good, excited, and you?"

"Happy, to be here with you, to see this. Is spectacular."

"I'm sure," he said, kissing her on the head. As he did, he peered at her and saw, on the other side of the street, two people he'd really prefer to avoid. Raul and his father were there leaning against a wall chatting. He tried not to tense up, but Mercedes could feel it.

"What's wrong?" she said, trying to stand up taller.

"Nothing, nothing, just thought I saw someone I knew from the *tablao*, but I was mistaken."

"Oh, the *tablao*, I miss it. I can't wait to dance again."

"I can't wait to play for you either," he said, pulling her close.

As time went on, the number of people gathered grew and grew. Charlie kept an eye on Raul and his father, making sure they hadn't spotted them. He began to feel tense. What if they came over? What the hell would he say?

"Not long now," he said, glancing at his watch. Just as he said that, the street lights went out. The crowd gasped.

Silence prevailed, and everyone stared at the door.

Knock, knock, knock.

From inside, someone moved a thick metal bar across to open the doors. Flashes from people's mobiles began to light the sky as the *Cruz de Guia* appeared, followed by dark, black, perfectly lined up Nazarenos.

"Watch," whispered Mercedes. "See how they move."

Charlie gazed at the soldier like Nazarenos move out in file, fixed ahead, the same distance apart. These were the serious ones who got the most respect. The crowd was still silent.

Then the oboes began to play a sombre, dark, sad tune, perfect for the occasion. A knock from the paso echoed from inside the church.

"It's coming," said Mercedes as the sound of men grunting and shuffling their feet echoed through the square.

Charlie gazed inside the door, waiting to catch a glimpse of the Christ. Then slowly a shadow appeared on the side of the wall, moving towards the door. Yet again flashes of mobile phones lit up the dark sky as the start of the *paso* crept into sight. First came the candle holders, and then the rest of the silver *paso* with the Christ on top.

Charlie was impressed by the size and height of this Christ. It was enormous, his hands so life-like, and it emitted a more powerful energy than the others, at least in Charlie's eyes.

As it began to turn right into the street, a man appeared from a window behind and started to sing a saeta- a powerful religious song. Charlie listened, trying to work out what he was saying as the style was similar to that of a flamenco singer, but all he could work out was how 'el Silencio' was a symbol of God.

Charlie watched in awe as the Christ bumbled past. He felt the power and energy it emitted, and for the first time, he felt a weird sort of connection. He was overwhelmed by the magical moment. He held Mercedes close as the Christ drifted up the road quicker than he'd seen before.

The crowd kept silent until the Christ disappeared round the corner. As soon as it was out of sight, people began to speak, but others hushed as the *Virgen* was still to come.

"What did you think?" whispered Mercedes.

"Now that was impressive. Whether you're religious or not, you can't help but feel the power."

Mercedes pulled him close and gave him a kiss on the lips. As she did, his eyes wandered again to the other side of the street to the direction of Raul and his father. They were still there.

"After this, we will go to see *el Gran Poder*, is also impressive, some say more."

"Sounds good to me," he said, smiling. He had not only fallen for her but was also becoming part of her culture and existence. He was so happy that he'd been able to witness something so special, even if he didn't still completely understand everything.

"What's that?" said Mercedes, frowning as she turned to the direction where a strange rumbling sound was coming from.

"Maybe a herd of elephants has escaped from one of the churches," said Charlie, laughing to himself. But the rumbling got louder.

His smile soon vanished as he sensed a sort of panic in the air. They were both looking to where the Christ had just gone and could see a commotion. People were trying to cross each other from all directions, which they normally did after a procession, but this was different, people were moving quickly and aggressively. Even the line of Nazarenos was getting knocked about.

"It doesn't look good," said Charlie, on his tiptoes now.

"What's going on?"

"I don't know, people are coming this way, it looks like something has happened."

"BOMBA, BOMBA," shouted someone from behind and suddenly Mercedes and Charlie felt pressure from all angles. Charlie held onto Mercedes, but they were getting pushed about and squashed.

Another shout of *bomba* added tension in the air.

"Quick, come on," he said, pulling Mercedes in front of him as he turned round, but someone shoved him in the back, and he accidentally pushed Mercedes on the floor. He tried to hold his balance and elbow back, but a few people trampled on Mercedes.

"*Oh, mi pierna, mi pierna,*" she screamed. Charlie reached down and yanked her up. She was hobbling as a new wave of pushing started.

"Over there, look," shouted Charlie, pointing to some large bin containers which had been pushed against the wall. "Get on those," he added as he helped her over.

As they got on top of the bins, a sea of people went past, bodies pouring down the road. Some were getting trampled on, others flailing their arms about, all were panicking.

"Are you okay?" he asked.

"No, no, it hurts. What is happening?"

"No idea, but it's bad."

Then Charlie remembered Raul and his father had been on the other side. He looked over, trying to see them. Raul was deep in a crowd of people rushing past, then he fell and disappeared.

"Shit," said Charlie.

"What?"

"Raul, he's just fallen over."

"My brother?"

"Si."
"But where is he?"
"I saw him fall down over there. Wait here, I'll be back."
"No, don't, you will get hurt."
"Hang on, I think I can see your father too."
"Papa?"
"He's just fallen."

Charlie jumped off the bins, ignoring calls from Mercedes, and battled through the crowd. People were pushing into him, but he had to save her father first. Maybe this was his chance to really make an impact on him. He managed to squeeze through the crowd and reach the door of the church, which was now firmly shut. He looked at the wall and saw Francisco squashed against it. He hauled himself along the side of the church until he got to him.

"Francisco, Francisco," he shouted, just as someone else pushed into him, but he managed to knock them away and reached his arm out.

"Charlie?" Francisco's eyes widened, and Charlie could sense the fear, but also relief seeing him. "It's you, *ayuda, ayuda,*" he said as he slid down the wall.

"No, no," said Charlie, battering the rest of the group out the way as he managed to get over towards him, barricade him off the crowd, and lift him to his feet.

"Are you okay?" he said.

"My leg is hurt, but yes. I am okay now, thanks to you." He threw him a smile and wrapped his arms around him. Charlie was unsure how to deal with such emotion from a guy who a day earlier had wanted to punch his lights out, so he just held him up, and thanked God he was alive.

"Just wait here, when the people go we can walk to Mercedes," he said to Francisco.

"Is she okay?"

"Yes, she's there, look." Charlie pointed over to Mercedes, who was still sitting on the top of the bin container, and stuck up his thumb. She waved and wiped her eyes, obviously in tears. He looked at Francisco, who had a tear in his eye, and winked at Charlie. It was a wink that said it all; that he had done well, and was welcome in the family.

Mercedes began to look around. People were scattered all over the place, injured, some cut up, and some lying unconscious. How had this craziness happened? Was it really a bomb?

Once the square was clearer, Charlie helped Francisco limp over towards Mercedes. She wished she could jump down and run over to her father, but the pain in her leg was too great. She prayed that she could dance again.

"*Papa*," she said, welling up as they got closer.

"*Hija*," he said, helping her down from the bin.

"Are you okay?" she said.

"*Si, si,* thanks to him," he added, patting Charlie on the shoulder.

"It was nothing, I saw you go down and ran over."

"Your boyfriend saved me," Francisco said.

"My boyfriend?"

"Of course, any man who can rescue my daughter and save me is welcome in my family." Mercedes hugged her father, tears fell from her eyes. "Yesterday I saw you both as I was walking back to the church, in Plaza San Pedro. I spoke to God and prayed for you. I was asking for a sign when I saw you together. You looked so happy in love, and that's what I want for you; to be happy."

"*Oh Papa*," she said, hugging her father harder than she

had for a long time. She felt so relieved that finally, he'd seen the real Charlie.

"That's great, but what about Raul?" said Charlie.

"Por Dios - Oh my God," said Francisco.

"I'll be back," said Charlie as he rushed off.

Mercedes felt frantic. On one side she was overjoyed that her father had finally given Charlie his blessing, but also petrified that something serious had happened to Raul. She felt so guilty for the day before, speaking to him like that.

"Don't worry Hija, he will be fine. Our Raul is strong."

"What happened though? I just don't get it, why all the madness?"

"I think some idiots were playing a joke, pretending there was a bomb, and causing havoc. The bloody fools should be thrown in prison: a shameless, disgusting act of violence."

"It's so terrible. I hope Raul is okay."

Charlie was looking frantically for Raul. He couldn't believe the number of people on the floor, men and women lying holding parts of their bodies which had been crushed in the madness. Charlie wondered why these sorts of things happened, and again doubted his belief in God. I mean, if he had real power, then why would he let these things happen?

Then he saw Raul lying in a heap on the floor. He ran over.

"Raul, Raul, are you okay?"

He picked up his head and shook it slightly, hoping for a sign, but his eyes remained closed. He held his hand over his mouth and felt for breath, there was something. "Raul, it's me, Charlie, wake up."

He shook him again, slapping him lightly on the face.
Raul opened his eyes.
"*Eh? Que pasa, donde estoy?*"
"It's fine, you're here by *el Silencio*, you are safe. Your father and sister are around the corner. Don't move."
"I don't think I can."
Just then Raul's mobile called, it was Mercedes.

Mercedes' hand was shaking as she called her brother.
"Raul?"
"No, it's me."
"Charlie, is Raul okay?"
"I'm afraid not. He needs an ambulance."
"Oh my god."
"*Que?*" said her father.
"Come quick, we are around the corner."
She called an ambulance to be sent straight away. When she saw Raul lying on the ground, she burst into tears.
"*Raul, Raul, lo siento, lo siento,*" she said, sitting by his side, saying she was sorry.
"*Hermanita,*" he said, smiling. "Don't worry, I'm going to be okay."
"Where does it hurt?" she said.
"My head, chest, and legs. I fell and then got dragged along the ground. Luckily Charlie found me."
"Yes, it was," said Mercedes, looking deep into her man's eyes. He smiled back. His warm smile always made her feel safe.
Several ambulances pulled up, as it wasn't only Raul who needed to be whisked off to hospital. They also took Mercedes and her father, but there was no room for Charlie.
"Where will you be?" he asked as he helped her on.

"In the Virgen de Rocio. Don't worry, I will call you tomorrow. Go home, get some rest, and thank you, thank you really."

"No problem, anyone would have done the same."

"I think not."

"*Señorita*," said the driver.

"I call you later."

They kissed quickly, and the ambulance driver shut the door. Mercedes watched him through the window and waved, so proud of herself for finding such a man. She knew now that he was definitely the one.

As Charlie made his way back to his flat, he missed Mercedes. It was a weird feeling, to miss a woman, but he guessed that was probably what being in love was. He felt torn inside, knowing that she had suffered and he couldn't console her anymore. What had happened to him in such a short space of time? A few months back he hadn't even wanted a girlfriend. He wanted to focus on his flamenco, but now flamenco had taken a back foot. All he cared about was that Mercedes was okay, and so were her family.

Maybe they weren't that bad after all. The look in her father's eyes when he turned up to save him would always be there at the forefront of his mind in the future, hopefully, to help him if things ever got tricky, which he supposed would, especially if he remembered he wasn't Catholic.

Once he got in the flat, he collapsed on his bed. His body was battered, and his mind distraught. His heart was pounding, but also aching as all he wanted was to have Mercedes by his side, forever.

Chapter 13 THE APRIL FAIR

April

Ramón paced up and down his wooden floor, looking at Charlie and Mercedes, who were sat holding hands on stools in front of him after just performing something new they'd been working on.

"*Dios mio,*" he said, scratching his stubbly chin. "I think this is it."

"What?" said Charlie, leaning forward; he knew when Ramón was about to say something inspiring.

"You two, are the magic of Andalucía."

He felt the back of his throat seize up as he tried to thank Ramón, but all he could do was swallow and wink at him.

"What do you mean, the magic of Andalucía?" said Mercedes. She wrapped her arms around Charlie's neck as she spoke.

"That you two are ready, for the performance of your life."

"Why, what's going on?" said Charlie.

"Do you know the Alcázar?"

"Of course," said Charlie, he'd seen it from the outside a few times while walking with Mercedes, but stupidly had never been inside. "It's some sort of palace, isn't it?"

"Some sort of palace, isn't it?" copied Ramón in his perfect British accent. "It's the centre of Sevilla, Andalucía, the world, and in a week's time, there is a flamenco concert there. I want you both to go; you will be the finale."

"*El Baile de Alcázar*, you can get us in there?" asked Mercedes, raising her voice as she leaned on the edge of her stool.

"Are you having a laugh?" said Charlie, who had guessed it was quite a prestigious affair.

"Don't you believe anything I say?" said Ramón, stamping his feet on the floor. His face grimaced as he flew at Charlie.

"Sorry, sorry," said Charlie, holding his hands up and cowering away.

Ramón burst out laughing.

"What was that for?"

"For not believing your professor. Now, are you in, or out?"

Charlie looked at Mercedes, who was nodding and grinning violently, he'd never seen her look so excited.

"Let's do it," said Charlie, turning to kiss Mercedes on the lips. He could feel the happiness in her entire body pass through to his.

"Then it's done. Next Saturday night you will show the best, most respected flamenco fans in Andalucía what you are really made of."

"*Oh my God*," said Mercedes, almost in tears.

"Is it that big?"

"That big? It's enormous: the Champions League final of flamenco. And luckily, for you, the man organizing it is a good friend of mine."

"How do you know all these people?" asked Mercedes.

"I just do, that's not all either. This friend of mine is looking for a new flamenco couple to travel with him on a tour of the best *tablaos* in Andalucía. What could be better than that?"

"Us, travelling around Andalucía playing flamenco?" said Charlie. He turned to Mercedes again, whose jaw was hanging loose. It was a dream come true. He could continue with his new passion, and travel with Mercedes by his side.

"Are you interested, or do you want to go back to your

guiri country?"

"I'm in," he said. Mercedes was nodding ecstatically.

"Great! I have extra tickets too, so let me know how many you want."

Charlie thought of his Mum and Dad but wasn't sure it was the best time to let them meet with his future in-laws. He wanted them to come and see him perform but was still finding his feet with Mercedes' family, even though he'd saved the father and brother from a mauling. Perhaps they could come instead.

They both stood up and hugged Ramón, thanking him for his offer. Charlie was so grateful, but he didn't appreciate the full impact the festival could have on their future career in flamenco, unlike Mercedes.

As they left, Mercedes was quiet, taken aback by the news.

"You okay?" asked Charlie.

"*Si, si,* is wonderful, such a beautiful place to play, with such a beautiful man." She gazed at him and let out her usual comforting smile.

"Do you think your family will come?"

"Mama, and Raul yes, but I don't about *Papa*; he has no seen me dance flamenco in so much time. I don't think is good idea to ask him."

"You have to," said Charlie, passionately. "Sure he will. Let's ask them together. Aren't we going round for lunch this week, during the Feria?"

"Yes, but…"

Charlie looked deep in Mercedes' eyes and could feel her sadness. He was convinced her father's opinion meant more than she let on. Maybe he could persuade him, after all, he did owe him a favour after saving his life.

"I'll ask him if you like."

"Let me think. I am still in shock from what Ramón said. Is fantastic. I would love to travel around Andalucía performing flamenco."

"Me too, it will be a great adventure for us both. All we need to do is impress Ramon's friend, and the deal is ours."

"It will be great," she said.

"We'd better go back to mine then, and practice a little," he said, kissing her neck.

"What kind of practice?"

"A little of everything?" he said, raising his eyebrows as he held her hand and began to pick up the pace.

Mercedes was standing in front of the mirror, trying to get into last year's blue and white Feria dress with the help of her beloved best friend.

"Have you been eating more now that you are getting regular sex?" she asked, struggling to do the top of the zip up. "You're not pregnant already, are you?"

"Don't be crazy," said Mercedes, holding in her stomach and breathing her chest out to try to allow more room inside her dress. "We might be at it like rabbits, but we are always safe. Besides, I think the dress has shrunk in the wash; it's shorter too."

"That will teach you for doing it yourself. How many times have I told you to send it to the dry cleaners?"

"Don't be silly, waste good money that I could use on my trip."

"Of course, the famous travelling flamenco pair. Are you going to travel in a caravan or something? I still can't believe you're leaving me."

"You wouldn't go anyway, leave your school, and Miguel."

"True, but I'd love to see more of our country. I'll definitely be visiting you."

"But we haven't even been asked to do it yet."

"No, but I know you will, you are both so suited; it's weird to think your combination works so well."

"I guess it's destiny."

"Whatever, come on, suck in, we need to get this dress on. Charlie will be here in a minute. Have you decided what you're going to do, anyway?"

"Yes, and no," she said, suddenly feeling the pressure.

The thought of her father letting her down again was too much to take. Knowing how important this event was to her, and for him to not come and acknowledge that her dream had become a reality, would be heart breaking. She preferred to just avoid any unnecessary stress and not even ask him, after all, he'd only disappoint her.

She did have a slight inkling that maybe Charlie could change his mind though. It seemed as though his father had taken to him after the dramatic Semana Santa. She still couldn't get over what had happened. A group of nasty lads had caused chaos throughout the whole city by pretending there was a bomb. The madness had injured plenty of locals, but luckily no one had died.

She thanked God every night that her brother was okay, and that she'd only gotten a slight sprain on her ankle. She was also grateful that her father was more upbeat about Charlie. He was even learning more English; unthinkable a couple of months back.

The doorbell rang.

"There's lover boy. Right, good luck," said Lola, kissing her best friend on the cheek and pushing her out of the room.

As she walked down the stairs to open the door, she

could see his silhouette through the window. She still felt nervous each time they met. It was funny how love stirred her insides so much when she saw him.

"Hey sexy," he said, as she opened the door. He'd never gazed at her so blatantly before.

"*Que?*" she said, moving her hips and twisting her neck slightly to show her best side. "*Guapa?*"

"*Guapa?* You look stunning." As he pulled her towards him, she caught a scent of his soft smelling aftershave.

"Stunning?"

"Gorgeous, fit, an absolute knockout."

"So you like?"

"Like? If I was a woman, then I'd be jealous of you." He planted a big smacker of a kiss on her lips. It was more of a jokey kiss than a romantic one.

"Ready for some lunch, I'm starving?" asked Charlie.

"Starving?"

"You know, when you need to eat so badly that it hurts."

"I see, well, I am not starving. I don't think I will eat much today."

"Why not? It's *la Feria*," said Charlie, doing a silly spin on the spot and clapping his hands. "Everyone must eat at *la Feria*."

"I'm just too nervous, what if he says no?"

"He won't. Come on, let's go."

Charlie took Mercedes by the hand and led her along the pavement, joining the masses on their way to *la Feria*. Mercedes started to feel self-conscious, surrounded by other pretty women dressed in their spotted flamenco dresses. Suddenly she just felt average, not special enough for Charlie.

"We've got to be strong about this," he said as they got

nearer the flat. "I'm sure he'll give in eventually. I mean, have you actually asked him why he won't come to watch you?"

Mercedes sighed, she really didn't want to get into this conversation.

"Not exactly. He watched me when I was little, but never at work. He wants me to marry a rich Sevillano man and have kids."

"Wanted. He's changed. He knows we love each other. Surely he can come and watch us."

"I'm not sure is a good idea that he comes, I don't want any more pressure."

"Don't be silly. We'll be fine, we've practised enough."

"I know, but you never know what will happen on the night."

"Exactly, so there's no point worrying about it."

"I suppose."

Mercedes went silent as they continued their walk. She wished she could have Charlie's confidence and optimism, but it was difficult; he didn't know her father as well as she did. By the time they got to her parents flat, they had stopped talking about it. Mercedes prayed for a civilised lunch.

"*Hija*, it's so good to see you," said her father as they walked into the lounge. She kissed her father on the cheek and gave him a hug. "You are very pretty today."

"Thanks," said Charlie, winking at the father.

"Not you, you funny English. She will be the star of *la Feria*. A drink?" he said, walking off to the kitchen after shaking Charlie's hand.

They stood in silence. Charlie put his arm around Mercedes, giving her a reassuring hug. "It's going to be fine," he whispered in her ear. She hoped so.

"So," said Francisco as he came back in the lounge with two glasses of chilled manzanilla, "what's new with you two?"

"Well…" said Charlie, but Mercedes wasn't going to let him get in there so quickly.

"We are good, playing well together." Mercedes took a sip of the sharp wine, and the warm feeling travelled through her veins, making her head a little dizzy.

"That's good. And how is your ankle?"

"Fine Papa, *gracias*."

"Your brother is doing well, thanks to this man here. Did I ever thank you for saving us?"

"Oh, just once or twice," said Charlie, smirking as he shuffled in his chair.

"Well, I will thank you again, for being so brave. Today you will enjoy. Eat like a king, and later you will see another side of Sevilla, another fantastic tradition of our people. You like to dance?"

"I normally leave that to Mercedes, but yeah, I'll have a go."

"Good, good. Now, where is my wife, are you guys hungry? Rosa, come, bring some *jamón*."

Rosa brought out a tray of *jamón* and bread-sticks, plus more manzanilla. They sat chatting about *la Feria;* old times when they'd been, and even got out the family photo albums. Mercedes was enjoying showing Charlie more about her family, which was why deep down she didn't want Charlie to mention the concert; it just wasn't the time.

"Charlie, come with me, I'll show you my old room."

"Sure, sure," he said.

"Be good up there," said the father, laughing and winking. Mercedes' cheeks filled with blood.

"So, this is where you grew up," said Charlie as they

entered her tiny room. She gazed around, slightly embarrassed at the childish pink wallpaper and teddies still on her shelves.

"Yes, you like?"

Mercedes felt strange in her old room, like a teenager again. She had changed so much the last few months. They sat down on the bed and kissed.

"Aren't you supposed to be showing me your room?" asked Charlie.

"Yes, and no. Listen to me." The tone in which she said it made Charlie look deep into her eyes.

"We can't tell him today."

"But why? We have to; it's only a week until the show. We have to give him some notice. He'll be fine, honestly, look how happy he is to see us together."

"But he can change quickly, trust me."

"But we've been over this. What's the worst that can happen? He says no, and that's it."

"But…"

"No more buts. I'll ask him after lunch when he's eaten, full and jolly."

Mercedes looked into his eyes. She wished she could have his devotion and passion. At least someone did in their relationship. She had to trust him.

"Fine, but do it softly."

"Don't worry. I'm a master at asking people to important flamenco festivals. I do it all the time."

"Silly English."

She pulled him closer, about to kiss him, when someone knocked at the door.

"*Hija?*"

"*Si Mama.*"

"*Vamos a comer?*"

"Let's go to eat?" she said to Charlie.

Throughout the meal Mercedes was tense. She was glad to see them all together, her brother was fine and recovering with his arm free of the cast.

But all the while she was dreading the moment for Charlie to speak up. She just hoped his father said no quietly, and got on with the lunch without an ordeal. She could deal with an awkward silence for a bit, but not an outrageous fit.

"Are you okay, *Hija*?" Francisco asked.

"Fine, fine," she said, smiling.

"This is really great food," said Charlie, "I'm stuffed."

"Stuffed?" said Francisco.

"Yeah, full."

"Oh, I see. Well, I am stuffed too. A stuffed man is a happy man."

"Indeed, indeed. Actually, there was something I was going to ask you all."

Everyone went silent and looked at Charlie.

"Don't worry," he laughed. "We're not getting married, yet."

They all laughed.

"That's lucky," said Raul. "So you're still a free man for a while then."

"Yeah, for a while. Anyway, it's about Mercedes and me."

"Yes?" said Francisco, sternly, as if he was tired of the small talk. Mercedes knew it was going to end in disaster, but there was no going back.

"Well, my teacher, Ramón, has organised for us to dance in quite an important festival, next weekend."

"Oh, very good," said Rosa.

"Yeah, and it's in la..how do you say it again?" he said,

peering at Mercedes.

"*Alcázar.*"

"Yes, that's it."

Mercedes looked at her father; he was motionless with his poker face.

"And we would like you all to come to watch us. It's a big event."

"Of course," said Raul, "that would be great, we'll all be there," he said, standing up to kiss Mercedes and shake hands with Charlie. "*Felicidades.*"

"Thanks," said Charlie. Rosa stood too, making her comfort face.

Francisco hadn't moved, he sat with his solemn face.

"When exactly is this, this show?" he said, his cheery tone had disappeared. Mercedes sighed and leaned back in her chair.

"Next weekend, Saturday night. How's that for you?"

"For me, for me?" he said, picking up his napkin and wiping his mouth. "For me, Charlie, it's not a very good time, so I'm sorry, but no; I won't be coming to the show."

"Oh, that's a shame," he said. "I, we, were hoping that maybe you could…"

"Don't worry," said Mercedes, getting in quick before Charlie made a fool of himself.

"Sure, sure. Well, if you change your mind."

"No, I think I won't," said Francisco, seeming a tad angry.

"Okay." Charlie smiled and looked along the table at Rosa, who smiled and shrugged her shoulders.

After about a minute of silence, everyone began to clear the table, taking the plates, empty glasses, and leftover food into the kitchen. Francisco went into the lounge and put on the TV.

As Mercedes helped clear up, she kept quiet, only replying yes, no, or shrugging her shoulders to her Mum and Raul's questions. She wished that Charlie had listened to her. She should have been stronger.

It was enough to think that her father had sort of welcomed Charlie into her family, but another to come and see them perform. The question Charlie had asked her before had been niggling in her mind, though. She'd never actually asked her father why he stopped coming to see her, but she guessed it was probably best not to know. Some things were better as secrets.

"What's up, baby?" said Charlie as they left the house for the *Feria*, trailing behind the rest.

"Nothing."

"Sure, nothing. Where's my Mercedes gone?"

"I'm here, just a little sad, again."

"I can see. Look, I'm sorry for insisting on asking your father. I should have listened to you, but it's done now. We know the answer, and we know your mum and brother will be there, so let's be happy with that and enjoy the day. La Feria is not far away."

"*Gracias,*" she said, looking into his eyes, and trying not to well up. Why had her father said no, again? Deep down she wanted to know, but dare not ask.

"*De nada.* That's what boyfriends are for, no? To protect and make their girlfriends happy, or at least try to."

She smiled, knowing that she had a warm, kind and considerate man by her side. She cheered up, bit by bit, as they continued. Once she saw *la portada* - the main door - with hundreds of people gathered underneath, and heard her favourite Sevillanas music, she felt upbeat again and began to look forward to enjoying her day, without worrying about her father.

The day's events, cuisine, and especially alcohol, had become a bit much for Charlie. After the knock back at lunch, he'd tried to put on a brave face for Mercedes, and ignore the tension he felt from Francisco, but the copious amounts of *rebujito* – sweet sherry mixed with lemonade - had started to play havoc with his brain.

They had been in Francisco's work *caseta* - a tent full of people dancing Sevillanas music - all afternoon. He'd tried to master the Sevillanas steps with Mercedes, but they both agreed he was better at playing the guitar, and so he spent most of the afternoon at the bar with Raul.

"*Me gustas tu hermana, mucho,*" he slurred to Raul.

"I know you like my sister, I know. You keep telling me. She likes you too."

"*No, gustar no, amor, amor tu hermana,*" he leaned on Raul and patted him on the shoulder.

"You love her? That's good because I think she loves you too."

Charlie hugged Raul, who hugged him back, but looked at him as if he might need a little help.

"Here, drink this," he said, handing him a large glass of water.

Charlie looked at the glass and as he poured it in his mouth felt instant relief. He was far too out of control for his liking. The *rebujito* had completely taken over his body, mind, and soul. Mercedes bounced over.

"Come to dance," she said, pulling his hand.

"But I'm rubbish at Sevillanas," he said, pushing her back a little.

"Okay, okay," she said, frowning.

"Dance with Raul, he's better than me. I need to finish this water, anyway."

Mercedes looked at him in the eyes and slapped his cheek lightly.

"Are you okay? You are speaking funny. How much have you drank?"

"Not so much."

"Enough," said Raul. "Come, leave him here; let's go to dance, and we'll come back in a moment."

"Go, go," said Charlie, a little louder than necessary.

As he propped up at the bar, watching Mercedes become the star of the dance floor, he'd never felt so in love and so happy to have her as a girlfriend. He smiled, in his own merry way, and drank another glass of water, which the barman had taken the liberty to give him.

The day was dragging though. The repetitive droning music, people constantly knocking into him, and having to say hello to people he couldn't care less about was becoming a bore. The dancing was over the top too, not as sexy and powerful as flamenco and it seemed like any old person could do it. The drinking was definitely knocking him out. Perhaps he ought to go home.

Then he spotted Francisco, sitting beside Rosa, with his back to the stage. The stage where his daughter was dancing.

What was his problem, not wanting to watch her? Was he some sort of moron? He couldn't imagine his parents ever being like that to him, not wanted to see him do something he was good at. They had always supported him in everything he did.

So why couldn't Don Francisco do the same? He'd saved his life; surely he could do him a favor in return and for once be a decent father.

It was time to settle this up. He staggered over towards him, towering high, confident, and angry.

"Hey," he said, thumping his glass of water on their table.

"*Hola, Charlie,*" said Francisco, frowning.

"*Estas bien?*" asked Rosa, standing up.

"Me? I'm just perfect, bloody perfect. It's him with the problem." Charlie waved his hand at Francisco and shouted. "You, what's your problem?"

"I'm sorry, Charlie," said Francisco, looking round, obviously embarrassed by Charlie's motions. "What problem?"

"That," he said, pointing to Mercedes, who was now standing next to Raul with her mouth open. "Why can't you just turn round and watch your daughter dance, for once?" He was swaying now.

"I think you have had enough to drink. Let's go," said Francisco, standing up and grabbing Charlie by the shoulder.

"Don't you touch me," he said, pushing his hand away. He was snarling now and raising his voice. "Look, over there, at your daughter. She deserves it. Why can't you just be a decent father for once?"

"Listen," said Francisco, holding him tighter. "If you leave now, then maybe we can have no problems."

"Have no problems? What is that supposed to mean anyway? That's all you are; one big problem."

He pushed Francisco back into a table, and he went crashing to the floor. Rosa dived down beside him. The whole of the *caseta* stopped and looked over. "*Imbecil,*" Charlie shouted, pointing at Francisco, who looked up in horror.

"*Que haces?*" shouted Mercedes, pulling him back to face her.

"Your father is useless, he wasn't even watching you."

"And that is going to make him?"

"Maybe, or maybe…" The anger in his own voice scared him. He looked around, all the women were gaping at him, shaking their heads and muttering to each other. Raul was helping his father to his feet. Rosa was in tears, ashamed of such an act in front of work colleagues, friends and family.

"Why?" said Mercedes, holding his face in her hands. "Why did you do this?"

"Because, because, I wanted him to watch you; it's the least you deserve."

"But not like this, not this way, Charlie."

"I think you better leave, now," said Francisco, coming towards Charlie. "Before we both do something we regret."

He gazed at him and his family. They were like a mini army protecting each other. Mercedes edged closer to her father, who then put his arm around her.

"I was right, I don't think an Englishman like you has a place in our family."

The comment was like a knife in his stomach. The fact that Mercedes wasn't looking him in the eye made it worse, as if someone had shot a silver bullet through his heart, ripping the love he had for her. He felt destroyed.

"Mercedes?" he said, holding out his hand for her. "Come with me, what about the concert? Our love."

She went to speak, but Raul stood in front of her.

"Just go Charlie, before you make more of a scene."

He'd never felt so distanced in all his life. He wanted to be back in England, with his parents, back in his room, playing the guitar that he'd grown up with. He turned away and made his way through the crowd of people, which opened for him, and didn't look back.

Chapter 14 DECISIONS

Later that night

Mercedes sobbed her heart out the whole way back to Triana, with Raul by her side consoling her.

"I don't understand," she said. "He was fine, what the hell got into him?"

"He was okay," said Raul. "He was just telling me how much he loved you."

"He's got a funny way of showing it. He's really fucked things up for us now. I can't believe he actually pushed *Papa* away like that, all because he wasn't watching me."

"But did you want *Papa* to watch you? Why was Charlie saying that?"

Mercedes looked up at her brother. Deep down she did. She'd been on stage the whole night and not once had her father even acknowledged she was there. It had been tearing her apart. All she wanted was for him to glance around, smile at her, or give her a quick thumbs up; that's all she needed.

"He hasn't watched me for ages," she muttered, her chest rising up and down as she tried to calm down.

"But why? Have you not asked him?"

"No, I feel silly. He must have his reasons."

"You know what he's like. He's a proud man."

"Too proud."

"Yeah."

They meandered on in silence. The pain in Mercedes' heart felt as if someone was squeezing the arteries, causing the blood to slow, making her feel faint and queasy. She was so disappointed in Charlie.

Why had he turned into such a cretin and aggressive

man like that? She'd never even seen him drunk before. *Rebujito* had a horrible way of bringing out the worst in people, but the thought of him doing it again filled her stomach with anxiety. She couldn't let it go. Not yet anyway.

What about the show? There was no way she was going to let this opportunity disappear into the mist. She had to perform. But the pain was too strong to even think about being beside Charlie. She had to speak with Lola.

"Here we are," said Raul as they got to the flat. "Are you sure you'll be all right here?"

"Yes, thanks for walking me back."

"No worries, just be careful now."

"Sure, *gracias*."

As she hugged and gave her brother a kiss on the cheek, she wanted to cry again as she watched him walk off. The day couldn't have gone any worse.

"What the hell has happened to you?" said Lola, as Mercedes walked into the lounge. "Oh my god." Lola ran over and started hugging her. Mercedes began to sob again. "What's happened? Was it your father again? Where's lover boy?"

Once she'd calmed down and told Lola the full story, they sat in silence. Mercedes had never seen Lola speechless.

"So, he actually pushed him over?" she was almost smiling.

"It's not funny, Lola. This is serious. How can I be with a man like that? My father will never let him in the family now. It's all ruined: the relationship, the show, the chance to go on tour, everything."

"Come on, don't feel so bad." Lola put on a softer voice and put her arm around Mercedes' shoulders.

"How can I not?"

"Look, just give it a couple of days. Wait for him to sober up and chat with him. Sure he'll be apologetic, and you can just get on with your lives like before."

"But the fact that he embarrassed my father and family like that will always be in the air. He could have just waited until the next day and spoke to him like an adult. I'm not sure I can forgive him so easily."

"Take your time, and if you're not ready to dance for him, then I know plenty of guitarists who can step in."

Mercedes felt surprised, she'd never even considered someone else playing with her; the thought made her feel uneasy. "You deserve this tour, after all, people are coming to see you really."

"I know, it's just…" But she didn't continue, her head was so mixed up. "I'm going to bed."

"Okay, let's chat in the morning," said Lola, giving her a goodnight hug.

Morning came, and there was a huge dark cloud looming over Mercedes' head. She kept checking her phone to see if Charlie had called, but there was not even a message. She was still fuming. The least he could have done was send an apologetic text. Perhaps he was still drunk.

She called home to see how her father was. He was out, but her mother said he wasn't too bad, which she didn't believe. She spent the day on her own, walking around Sevilla, along the river, through *la Alameda*, all the time looking around at all the places where she and Charlie had been.

It felt so weird to be in the city of her life, where she had grown up, and the only really happy memories were with him. Each time she went past a bench where they had sat and had a chat, or a bar where they'd had a coffee, she felt a digging in her heart, one that made her feel reminiscent and eager to return to the past, just to go back a couple of days when they were happy, and Charlie was himself.

By the time the evening came, she felt annoyed that he hadn't got in contact with her. Maybe he'd changed his mind after all and decided he'd had enough with Sevilla, with her family, and her. Maybe he'd wanted to make a scene to use it as an excuse to go home and leave her. That night she didn't remember falling asleep, but she left her pillow wet with tears.

It had taken Charlie a good twenty-four hours to feel barely human again. How much *rebujito* had he actually drank? What had turned him into such an aggressive fool and ruin everything? He'd never felt so awful, both from the hangover, the guilt, and the broken heart.

All he kept seeing in his mind was Mercedes' look of horror when she pulled him back, as if he'd become possessed by some strange monster. What had he been thinking? Going over to her father like that and behaving like such a fool.

He was still angry at her father for not turning and watching his own daughter dance. He knew he'd behaved like a dick, but so had Francisco, on purpose as well, and for a number of years.

Once he'd shaken off his groggy feeling with a run by the river, he told himself he'd have to get round to Mercedes quickly and try to sort out this mess, but it wasn't as easy as he'd hoped.

"*Hola*," she said, opening the door with her arms folded and barely looking him in the eye. He'd never felt her so cold and distant. She'd certainly changed from the cheery, stunning woman he'd seen two days ago.

"*Hola*, can I come in?"

"What for?"

"To speak."

"There is nothing to speak about. Charlie, you have made a big mistake."

"But I was just trying to help…"

"Help? Threatening my father and pushing him over in front of his family and friends is helping?"

"Of course not, but he wasn't watching you."

"So what? Do you not think I know that? You should have listened to me."

Mercedes' lips were quivering slightly. Charlie reached out his hands, trying to hug her, but she crossed her arms tighter and moved back.

"I'm sorry, can't we just go back to normal, like before?"

"I can't right now. I'm still angry."

"What about the show, the dance? We need to practice."

"There is no 'we'. I am dancing. Lola has found another guitarist."

Charlie raised his hands slightly and frowned as he moved backward as if she had just punched him in the gut.

"Another guitarist?"

"*Pues si.*"

"Already?"

"*Si.*"

"But…"

His throat clammed up. All the guilt was flying around his body, smashing into his anger. Guilt and anger mixed together was a combination looking for an explosion. She was actually still annoyed with him for trying to stick up for her. How had she found a replacement so quickly?

What did that say about how much she really loved him?

"But Ramón is my teacher. He's the one who got us a place at the show."

"Yeah, but I am the dancer, and there are many guitarists ready to perform."

Charlie could sense a bit of Lola talking, maybe she had put her up to this.

"Oh come on, Mercedes, can't we work this out?" Mercedes had her lips shut tightly as she shook her head.

"So, are we over?"

"Over? What's mean?"

"Finished? Done? Bye bye."

"I think so, if you can behave like that to my father, then how can I trust you anymore?"

Anger had pushed the guilt to one side. How could she be so cold? What had gotten into her? Suddenly her father was a God. She had been the one to give such a horrible impression of him. He just didn't get it.

"Fine," he said, putting up his defences. It was either that or breakdown in front of her, and he wasn't going to let her do that to him, not here anyway.

"Don't worry about the show. I will speak to Ramón later," she said.

"What about the *tablao*?"

"You can stay there if you want. I'm not going back. Lola is giving me more classes, and hopefully, I'll be on tour soon."

Charlie felt his neck tighten as if his guitar strings were working their way around, squeezing and squeezing his windpipe. He felt suffocated.

How could she be so cruel, so empty, so unwilling to work things out? If they had been on stage performing, he would have thrown his guitar right at her, just like that cow Cass. Were all women really the same?

"Okay, if that's the way you want it, I guess I'll see you around," he said, turning around.

"Maybe, *adios*."

"*Adios*."

And she closed the door.

Was that it? He walked down towards the river. Over in a flash, now you know me, now you don't. All those months of practising, playing together, falling for flamenco, falling in love, and it was over, gone, history.

His initial thoughts were to go and find Ramón and tell him that Mercedes was going to come and ruin everything. But he just didn't have it in him. Right now he wanted nothing to do with flamenco, so he went back to his flat, went on the net, and booked a flight home in three day's time, on the same day he was due to perform in the show.

After seeing Charlie almost breakdown in front of her, and leaving without really pleading or apologizing properly, she started to accept that maybe it was for the best. Lola had been right, surely she could get on with the new guitarist easily enough and continue with her career as a flamenco dancer.

"So, did you tell him?" asked Lola as Mercedes turned up at the dance school.

"Yes, and he just left, no argument. He said I could have the show and he didn't know whether he would be going back to the *tablao*."

"There you go," she said, but Mercedes could sense she looked doubtful, not as confident as she normally was.

"What's up?"

"Nothing, you'll be fine I'm sure. It was always going to be complicated with an English guy anyway, I mean, what if he decided he didn't like Sevilla anymore and you had to go to live in England, with all that cold weather and horrible food. You're better here, in Andalucía, with the people who love you."

"Exactly."

Mercedes could feel herself welling up.

"What? What did I say?"

"Nothing, nothing, I'm fine." But it was that word, love. She knew he loved her, and deep down she loved him, but it just felt so impossible. With time the pain would go away, surely.

That afternoon at work, she cheered up a bit as she taught her students, but she was still emotional. At the end of the classes, Pepe, the new guitarist, turned up and Lola introduced him to Mercedes.

"Perfect," she thought after they'd finished playing together, he's a great player, and ugly, so there was no way of getting attached.

"So, do you want me to come with you to see Ramón?" asked Lola as they were shutting up.

"Yes, that would be great."

As they walked towards the centre, every street corner, bar, and man's face reminded Mercedes of Charlie. He was everywhere. The times they'd walked about holding hands, the shops they had gone to, and the corners they had stopped to kiss.

Was she making the right decision? She had to be strong. She knew Ramón was a tough character. Luckily, Lola was by her side.

They got to his school and rang the bell.

"*Si?*"

"*Soy yo, Mercedes.*"

The door buzzed and in they went.

"*Hola guapas,*" he said, smiling as he kissed them both on the cheek. "What brings you two lovely ladies here? Why aren't you at *la Feria*?"

"It's a long story. Anyway, we've come to talk about the show," said Mercedes.

"Yeah, I can't wait, only two days to go."

"Exactly, so we thought you should know that we have found a new guitarist."

"Sorry?" said Ramón, letting out a nervous laugh.

"A new guitarist," said Lola. "His name is Pepe, Pepe Sosa."

"I know him, yes, he is a very good guitarist, but what about…"

"Charlie has decided not to enter," said Mercedes.

"Charlie has decided?" Ramón looked at them both as if trying to work out if they were serious.

"Yes, we have had a difference of opinion, and now I will be dancing with Pepe."

"Right," he said, rubbing his chin. "But that's not like Charlie, just to give up like that without even talking to me."

"Sure he will be here soon, but I just wanted you to hear it from me first."

"I see."

"So, do we need to do anything?" asked Lola.

Ramón sat in his chair as if he'd just lost the energy in his legs.

"Err, no. I'll take care of everything. Right, so, are you sure?"

"Very," they both said.

Ramón stood up but looked weaker than normal and frail. Mercedes felt a twinge of guilt. She knew he'd worked hard with Charlie, and finding out the news must

Falling for Flamenco

have been a massive blow.

"Are you okay?" asked Mercedes.

"Yes, fine. Probably just too much Feria, you know how it is."

"I do," she said, thinking of Charlie again. Had that been the real him that night? Was he capable of doing it again?

"*Gracias,* Ramón," said Lola, kissing him on the cheek. Mercedes did the same, and they left.

"There, that wasn't so hard, was it?" said Lola as they walked back towards Triana.

"No, no," said Mercedes. But a feeling of doubt began to cloud her head, telling her she was making a mistake and being a fool. How could she just throw it all away like that?

"All we need to do now is get Pepe over this evening and practice a little more."

"Sure, sure," said Mercedes, as she wiped the corner of her eye.

Charlie was staring at his guitar which lay on his balcony floor in the corner. He couldn't pick it up. It hurt too much.

He gazed out over Sevilla and could spot women walking to *la Feria* in their damn spotty dresses. When would the bloody thing be over? In two days, just like his flamenco career.

The more he thought about it, the more he wanted to be rid of the stress of going out with a Sevillana. He loved her, but it was a painful love, full of doubt and questions. The battle against her father had been too strong. They were family after all.

He'd tried his best to get to know her culture, her religion in Semana Santa and had perfected his guitar playing skills, all to show her he loved her. He'd even saved her father and brother from terrible accidents.

Then he made one silly, grave mistake, and now he was thrown out on his ear. Shown the door, without so much as an attempt to get back together and forgive him. Maybe it was best to end it now, before they got really serious and made a longer commitment. It was probably the easiest way to go before things got really complicated.

There was a knock at his door. Charlie immediately thought of Mercedes. What if she'd come to work things out? He ran to the door.

"*Si?*"

"Charlie?"

"Ramón?"

"Open this door, where have you been man?"

He opened the door and stared at Ramón, who smiled sympathetically.

"Come in, come in," said Charlie, downbeat with his shoulders sagging.

"What the fuck is going on, *amigo*?" he said, giving him a hug. The lump in Charlie's throat was coming back again. He swallowed, forcing it away.

"What do you mean?"

"What do I mean? Yesterday I had two hot-blooded flamenco dancers barging into my school telling me some awful news."

"Oh, that."

"Yes, that. What the hell happened?"

"It's a long story."

"I have time. Make me a coffee and let's talk."

Once Charlie had filled Ramón in on his side of the story, the tanned colour in Ramón's face had become a peaky white.

"You did that? For her? You are a braver man than I thought."

"Brave? Or stupid?"

"Maybe both. Other women would have said you were their hero, trying to end a long and vicious feud."

"What do you mean, feud?"

"You said yourself that her father hadn't watched her for ages, since she was a child."

"I know, it breaks my heart to watch them like that. I just don't get it, and Mercedes won't ask him. I wanted to know, for both their sakes."

"There was no way he was ever going to tell you, anyway."

Ramón looked deep into Charlie's eyes. Charlie frowned, unsure exactly what Ramón meant.

"How the hell do you know?"

"I just do."

"But…"

"Look," he said, moving his chair closer and getting serious. "I need to tell you something, just to set the record straight. But you can't tell Mercedes."

"What the…"

"I know exactly why he stopped watching her."

"Why?"

"Because of a woman."

Chapter 15 ADIOS

The next day

Charlie was on his way to see Francisco and set the record straight. After Ramón had told him exactly why Francisco had stopped watching Mercedes, he could sympathise with the guy, a little, but it was totally unfair on Mercedes. He had to try to persuade him to go and see her, if it was the last thing he did in Sevilla.

He begged Ramón to let him go and speak with Francisco, as there were a few things he had to get off his chest before he left for England.

Ramón agreed, but on the condition he didn't tell Mercedes or let on how he'd found out. Ramón even told him where his workplace was, so he could catch him on the way out.

Charlie was standing outside Francisco's office at six in the evening, and as soon as he came marching out his door, Charlie jumped out.

"*Que haces aqui?*" said Francisco, asking what he was doing there as he stormed past.

"*Tenemos que hablar* – we need to speak," he shouted, jogging behind him.

"*No tengo nada para decirte* – I have nothing to say to you."

"I know," said Charlie.

"You know what?" said Francisco, turning round.

"About why you stopped watching Mercedes."

Francisco stopped and turned round.

"*No hablas tonterias* - don't talk rubbish."

"I know about Macarena."

The blood drained from Francisco's face.

"*Macarena?* But..."

"I saved your life, Francisco, you owe me at least one conversation, but don't worry, after this you'll probably never see me again."

Francisco stared at him, angrily, but he knew he had no choice but to listen.

"Fine," he said "*vamos.*" Charlie followed Francisco into a bar around the corner, where they spoke about the secret that Ramón had told him.

It was the night before the show, and Mercedes lay on her bed, staring at the dark ceiling, praying for God to give her just one night's sleep. She had been a bag of nerves since she said *adios* to Charlie. She felt like a different person; one with a short temper, and whose confidence had taken a severe battering.

The pain ached through her heart. Most of the day she felt nostalgic, running through past images of them together in her mind. The feeling of loss built up in her chest and stopped her breathing properly. She'd lost her appetite and felt irritable through lack of sleep, but, most of all, she felt as if a part of her soul had drifted away.

The worst part of the day was when she danced. She'd been impressed with how quickly she had clicked with Pepe. He was a decent guitarist and did the job well.

Her mind was on Charlie though. She missed him. Deep down she knew he had only been trying to help her; everything he'd done since being in Sevilla had been for her: becoming a flamenco guitarist to try to meet her, getting to know her culture in order to become part of her family, and putting up with her ridiculous father.

There was no excusing what Charlie had done that day, but she knew it was mainly down to the drink, which her own father had plied him with.

So who was really to blame?

She only slept for about two hours that night, and when the morning of the show came around, she was exhausted, an emotional wreck from not seeing Charlie and not sleeping. How was she going to perform in the *Baile del Alcázar*? She had to go and find Charlie and make up with him. There was no way she was going to get anywhere without him, ever.

Charlie was holding his guitar in one hand, and his backpack in the other.

"*Adios Sevilla,*" he said to himself as he stood looking out over the balcony. His flight left in five hours. There was a knock at the door. Charlie opened it.

"Hey, Manuel." The landlord was there.

"Hey Charlie, so, you really go?"

"I'm sorry, but yes. It's time to go home," he said, handing over his keys to the landlord.

"And the flamenco guitar?"

"I'm better now, but I guess it's just not for me."

"Of course, you're a *guiri*, after all."

Charlie smiled. Maybe they had all been right; how was a *guiri* supposed to fit in with Sevillanos anyway. It was an impossible task, everyone had shown him, apart from Ramón.

"*Adios,*" he said, after shaking his hand.

As he left the flat in Triana, he felt the emotion building in his heart. It had been a tough roller coaster over the last few months, and it was time to get off and go home. He couldn't wait to see his parents again, go out for a beer with Joe, and just be in a country where he could be himself, and not worry about being a *guiri*.

As he walked over the Triana Bridge, he gazed over the river, where he'd had so many memories, and thought he saw Mercedes on the other side coming towards him. The woman had long black hair and was smiling. She was walking briskly, just like Mercedes did, and was even looking at Charlie. He stopped and squinted to get a better look as she got closer. His heart was pumping hard and fast but soon calmed down as he saw it wasn't her.

What if it had been her running to apologise for slamming the door in his face and wanted to perform in the show together? Would he have stayed? He was unsure.

He continued his walk, through the centre, past the cathedral, and around the back to his favourite plaza where he'd first played the guitar. He had to say a couple of goodbyes.

"*Carlito?*" said Pedro, holding out his arms to hug him. "Where you go? Back on the street for some money? Here, I give you one euro if you play for me."

Charlie laughed.

"No, I'm going home."

"Home? But this is your home now! What about your job here? What are you saying you silly *guiri*?"

"I'm sorry, Pedro, but I need to get away."

Just then Jorge popped out.

"*Dios Mio, el guiri guitarist.* Hello, hello, how are you?" Jorge gave him a hug too. He could feel his emotion getting the better of him.

"Listen, Jorge. This crazy English say he going to the home, but he no know that his home is here, with his heart."

"*Claro,*" said Jorge, throwing out his hands. "Why you say this?"

"I'm done with flamenco, finished. Mercedes and I

broke up."

"Finished? The love birds of the year? But why? This cannot be!"

"I'm afraid it is."

Jorge and Pedro frowned at each other and were silent. They'd both lost their usual smiles and seemed deflated.

"But your flamenco? You are a genius."

"I might be, but it's too complicated."

"Nonsense. You have to fight for love, like I did with my wife. She is a pain in the *culo*, but I love her, and my kids. Is there no hope?"

"I don't think so. Anyway, I may come back one day, to visit."

"But this can't be, you should not be coming to visit, but to live, to play your guitar," said Pedro. "You make a big mistake."

"It might seem that way, but I think I need to go, get some different air. Maybe I'll come back one day."

Pedro tutted and shrugged his shoulders.

"Okay, if you are sure, but is such a shame. It was a pleasure to meet such a great *guiri* guitarist, good luck, *amigo*."

"Yes, yes, good luck," said Jorge.

Once they'd shook hands and hugged, Charlie walked off, not looking back. He still had his final goodbye.

"So, did you tell him?" asked Ramón. He was sitting on his usual stool with his guitar by his side. Charlie couldn't help but feel guilty for leaving in such a way, after everything he'd done for him.

"Yes."

"And?"

"I think he listened."

"Then that's all you have to worry about. You tried your

best, and you can only try your best. It's just a shame I cannot convince you to stay."

"I just wanted to say thanks for everything Ramón. You really made a real effort with me, and I'm sorry for not going through with this, but it just wasn't meant to be."

"Maybe you're right; the look on Mercedes face the other day said it all. Those women are dangerous. But don't worry, you can take your talent to England and do what you came here for; to teach other people flamenco, and now you have a story to tell them too."

"I guess so. Listen, if you ever fancy coming to England, then you have a place to stay."

"Why thanks, you are a true English gentleman."

"I'm not so sure about that."

The image of Francisco sprawled on the floor at *la Feria* flashed in his mind.

"Ah, don't let it get you down. We all do silly things, just learn from it."

"Thanks, Ramón, and good luck with everything."

"You too."

Ramón placed his guitar down and bear hugged Charlie.

"You sure I can't drive you to the airport?"

"No, it's fine. I think I'll just get the bus."

"Okay, good luck my friend, *adios*."

Mercedes had her smile back, she knew she'd been wrong and could work things out again. She just hoped he could forgive her. She was standing outside his flat and knocked on the door.

"*Hola,*" she said, beaming as the door opened.

"*Hola,*" said Manuel. "Who are you?"

"Mercedes, where's Charlie?"

"Charlie, *el guiri?* Well, I think he's gone to the airport."

"No? The airport?" the blood drained from her face, leaving her pale, and nauseous. Her legs almost gave way.

"Are you okay?" said Manuel, reaching out to hold her up.

"But he can't have, I came to…"

"Maybe you can catch him. I think he went to get the bus."

"The bus, right, of course. Thanks."

Mercedes turned, ran down the stairs, and flew out the door towards Triana Bridge.

She couldn't let him get away, she had to tell him she'd made a mistake. She ran all the way through the centre of Sevilla, past the cathedral, through her favourite park - the one where she'd first realised she was in love with him - and ran over to the bus station.

As she got there, she saw an airport bus pulling away. She ran faster, desperate to stop it, but it was no use. She looked up at the windows as it passed, and saw him, resting his head on the window.

"Charlie, Charlie," she shouted. She thought she saw him turn his head slightly, but it wasn't enough. The bus pulled away, went through some traffic lights, round the bend, and out of sight.

Now Mercedes legs really did give way, and she fell to the floor.

Luckily a man behind caught her from hitting her head on the pavement, but even so, she blacked out.

By the time Lola arrived at the hospital, Mercedes had come round and was sitting up in the hospital bed.

"What the hell happened?"

"He's gone."

"Who?"

"Charlie? I saw him getting on the bus, but then it drove away. I fainted. Luckily some guy called an ambulance and got me here, but Charlie has gone."

She began to sob, deep heavy sobs; the pain was too much. Lola handed her a hanky and hugged her.

"Look, you don't know for sure yet."

"But I saw him leave. He almost saw me. All he needed to do was turn his head just a little more, and he would have seen me."

"Listen, you have to get a grip. The show is in four hours."

"I can't do the show, I just can't."

"You have to, this is everything you've ever dreamed of. You have to show the world your talent. It's all you've ever worked for. Make me proud, make your family proud, even Charlie would want you to do it."

"I know, I know, it's just."

"Just what?"

"I wanted to make up with him."

"If it's not meant to be, it's not meant to be. Come on, let's go, Pepe will be waiting."

Luckily the nurses agreed she could go, after a few bossy words from Lola, and they got in Lola's car.

She felt so stupid, so foolish, for not going to him sooner, now it was too late. He'd surely be in the air by now.

She had never not wanted to dance so much in her life. How was she going to perform with Pepe knowing that he should have been Charlie? That the man of her dreams was probably already in England?

They parked and made their way to the *Alcázar*. A queue of people had formed stretching right out over the plaza. The nerves began to take over her body, she felt nauseous. How the hell was she going to do this?

They went in, through the gardens, and out the back where a stage had been set up.

"Wow," said Lola as they saw how beautiful it was with the lights shining. People were gathered in their seats. She scanned the crowd, wondering if her mother and Raul were there yet, there was no sign.

"Let's go round the back and get ready, Pepe will be there."

Mercedes followed in a daze. Lola signed them both into the competition, introduced them to the judges, and found out where their changing rooms were, all the while Mercedes tagged behind like a poor lamb, scared of what was to come.

"I can't go through with this," she said once they were in the changing rooms.

"Come on, how many more times?"

"Can't you dance for me?"

"Don't be ridiculous. I wouldn't be able to take the prize. Anyway, I have a school to run. You are young, free, and single."

As soon as she said the word 'single,' Mercedes welled up again.

"Oh God, sorry, sorry."

There was a knock at the door.

"*Quien es?*"

"Ramón."

Lola opened the door and in came Ramón.

"Are you ready Mercedes? You will be on after the next show. Pepe will be on the stage waiting."

"*Si, si,*" she said, snivelling.

He gave them both a kiss, whispered good luck, and left.

Lola helped Mercedes to put more makeup on, and clean up her pale complexion.

"There, let's go," she said, smiling.

Mercedes grabbed her hand.

"*Gracias*," she said, with a tear about to trickle out again.

"Don't, no more tears until you win this damn competition. Now let's go." They hugged.

There was another knock on the door.

"*Mercedes, lista?*"

"*Si*," she said, opening the door. A woman with a headset walked her down the hall towards the stage. Lola was behind, nudging her in the back to get her moving and motivated.

As the couple came through the curtains back stage and walked past her, she knew this was it. It was time to show the world her talent, alone.

She thought about her grandfather and prayed that he was watching over her. Her legs were shaking, hands sweating.

She had a quick look in the audience, to check how many people were there. Then she saw them, first her mother, then Raul, and then…

But it couldn't be.

Her father.

There.

Ready to watch her dance, finally.

She almost lost the power in her legs again. What had changed his mind?

"Now, ladies and gentlemen," said the presenter. "For tonight's last dance. I'm sure you will have a lovely surprise when you see these two together. Mercedes y Carlito Rubio."

Mercedes eyes began to water as she heard his name. She turned round to look at Lola, who was smiling, with Ramón behind who nodded for her to go on stage.

The curtain drew back, and there, sitting on the stage, was Charlie. He looked up, smiled, and winked.

She spluttered a laugh, held her head high, walked out on stage, and sat by him, unable to take her eyes off him. He was there, sitting next to her, holding his guitar.

She took a deep breath and turned to face the audience, knowing her father was there added pressure to her performance. She kept her eyes down. She had to focus. This was it.

She couldn't believe he was there though, next to her.

She'd seen him get on the bus.

She had to focus.

Charlie began to play, and passed his love for her through his music. His passion filled her body with energy as she sprung into life. Suddenly her cheeks began to feel alive, and inside the pain and anguish was replaced by joy and love.

She focused on his playing, still unable to believe he was there. Then she leaped into action, showing the audience exactly why she was one of the best dancers in Sevilla, and Andalucía. The glowing way she moved on stage shone across the faces of the audience, lighting them up.

She could feel herself dancing better than ever. Tap, tap, tap, tuk, tuk, tuk. She moved quickly, her head facing the crowd.

They performed the best they ever had together. Who would have thought it, all those months ago, that they would finally end up playing in such an important event?

She finished with several twirls and slammed down hard and fast on the stage.

The crowd leaped up in appreciation.

Charlie came over, holding her hands high.

Her family stood proud, applauding their daughter.

Tears streamed down her face as she saw her father was crying too.

She thanked the crowd, and kissed her man.

Charlie felt proud to be walking along the river with his Spanish flamenco dancing girlfriend. He was so relieved that he'd stayed. He had Ramón to thank for most of it. For being such a great teacher, such an inspiration, and providing him with the information he needed to persuade Francisco to go and watch Mercedes.

He still couldn't believe that Francisco had stopped watching his daughter dance because of his own sister's actions. Macarena was Mercedes' aunt and was also a flamenco dancer. Francisco had always been against his sister dancing; it just wasn't something decent women did. He'd tried for years to stop her, but it was no use.

The last straw for Francisco was when Macarena ran off with a gypsy guitarist to Granada, abandoning the family to pursue her dream of being a flamenco dancer. It tore the family apart, and he swore to himself that he'd never watch Mercedes again.

Luckily Francisco had seen the light after Charlie spoke with him.

"It's your only daughter, you don't want to lose her as well as your sister now, do you?" When he'd said those words, Francisco had looked like a broken father, without the energy to have another family feud. It had worked a treat.

The problem was he'd sworn to keep the secret away from Mercedes; if she ever found out the truth, she'd be destroyed.

"Tell me," said Mercedes, smiling eagerly.

"What?" he said, slightly on edge.

"You know what, about the moment when you realised you were making a mistake. It's so sweet."

"Oh, okay, if I have to. Well, there I was, standing in the queue at the airport when I heard some high heels clicking on the floor. I thought of you straight away, of your dancing, and I remembered that first moment I saw you: so pretty, so helpless, and so perfect. I was convinced it was you, running up to me, to ask me to come back. My heart filled with joy and emotion. So when I turned around, beaming a smile, and saw that it was another woman, my heart sank. I thought to myself that I didn't want that to happen every time I heard high heels on the floor, every time I saw a woman's face, every time I played my guitar, and have that regret that I didn't try one last time. So it was then I got back on the bus and headed straight to Ramón's place."

"And then?" said Mercedes, like a little girl waiting for her Daddy to read her favourite bedtime story.

"Then I burst in on Ramón's class and told him if he knew who the guitarist was, and how to get in contact with him. Luckily he did, and within twenty minutes we were on our way to the Alcázar to rearrange the plans for the show."

"And when you saw me, how did you feel?"

"You really like that bit, don't you?"

"Of course."

"I felt whole, complete, as if my other half, the one that I thought I'd lost, the one I love, was finally close to me again. I wanted so much to kiss you at that moment, to hug you and say that I was sorry. It was the most agonizing moment of my life, watching you on stage, dancing so well, and not being able to kiss you."

Mercedes was welling up again. She looked so beautiful,

innocent, and in love.

"Is a beautiful love story," said Mercedes, wrapping her arms around Charlie's neck and pulling him close.

"It's a beautiful start to a love story," he said, wrapping his arms around her neck. "But I have a feeling there's more to come."

If you enjoyed this book, then I'd really appreciate a review on Amazon or Goodreads. As a writer, reviews really help my exposure.

If you send me your review, then I'll put you down for a discounted copy of Falling out over Flamenco, Book 2: Love and Flamenco in Andalusia. I'm on the second draft, so it should be out in 2018.

You can subscribe to my email list via my blog A Novel Spain, or send me an email bazventure@gmail.com.

Thanks so much for reading. It really means a lot to me.

Printed in Great Britain
by Amazon